PepperJack Online Sleuthing Service

by

George Allen Miller

McGilliverse Series

Cover Art by *Teddi Black*

The Wild Rose Press, Inc.
PO Box 708
Adams Basin, NY 14410-0708
Visit us at www.thewildrosepress.com

Publishing History
First Edition, 2025
Trade Paperback ISBN 978-1-5092-6242-7
Digital ISBN 978-1-5092-6243-4

McGilliverse Series
Published in the United States of America

Dedication

For my family

Prologue

I fell.

Light from a thousand stars shone around me from every direction. Wind whipped my fedora off my head. It twisted in the air behind me, above me, and disappeared between gray clouds. My coat tore from the force of my fall. Below me—or was it above?—a desert stretched to the horizon. The expanse of sand went beyond the boundaries of Earth. It covered the solar system, the galaxy, and the entire cosmos. I didn't know how I knew that, but somehow, I did.

A single bright silver strand extended out of my chest. I touched the strand with my fingers. Memories rushed through every fiber of my being. My name, my profession, all my relationship mistakes, my wardrobe, all of it was back. I was Eugene McGillicuddy. A two-bit detective with a psychic ace up my sleeve. I could answer any question that someone asked me. I could solve the most complex detective cases in the galaxy. In fact, I had just solved the case of a Puntini ambassador, Yut, trying to achieve godhood by eating a peanut butter and jelly sandwich. Or had it been a bucket of chicken? But then my mind focused on the one memory that mattered most.

I was dead. Alice had shot me.

Chapter One

Alice Pemberton sat on a stool next to the limp body of Eugene Jack McGillicuddy, still annoyingly quasi-dead. Why, she didn't know. He should have bounced back hours ago. Or even yesterday. But like everything he did, Eugene was taking his sweet time in coming back to life.

Alice opened her computer and checked the readings. A sudden panic flashed in her chest. This had to work. She had to bring Eugene back from the quasi-dead. She was the one who'd sent him there. She examined her notes on the spectral cuffs on his wrists, the electrical shock gun she had used to shoot him, and the local spectral towers in Chinatown in DC. All of them showed that her math was right. Eugene would come back. He had to come back. What would she do if he didn't come back?

Besides, Eugene had to save the universe.

Pepper and Jack, two artificially created AIs that were right now stealing encryption keys to a stronghold in Tibet, had stumbled upon an ancient message meant for Eugene. A message describing the end of the universe that only Eugene, a psychic detective, could stop. So he had to wake up. And he had to save the universe. Or Alice, his not-a-secretary, was going to quit. And that'd show him.

She laughed at the thought.

A light beeped on her computer. She checked to see the status of the Zun ship inbound for Earth. It was on course and would be here soon. While investigating the disappearance of the President of the United States, Alice had stumbled across the Zun and realized they needed help. Their entire race was dying. All of them. And the only thing that could save them was a Hesiean evolution chamber located in Tibet. Alice had to help them. And she would. Besides, Eugene was being stubborn and not coming back to life. So she had time. "Nothing like keeping a girl busy."

On the other side of Eugene, a tall man with large eyes looked over Eugene's body. But the tall man wasn't human. On this beach, created by the class-ten species the Kax, every alien looked like their own race. Alice saw humans everywhere even though most people on the beach were aliens. The man looking at Eugene was an alien. The SpeeEekEee, or Spee for short. What the Spee saw when looking at Eugene, Alice could only wonder. The Spee had described a silver streak of light that stretched upward and connected to Eugene's soul. The Spee could see and interact with the dead, just like the Krill, an alien race that used their ability to see the dead to create a galactic empire. The Krill, to protect their empire, had imprisoned the entire Spee race on their own planet.

The Krill were the richest aliens in the entire Milky Way Galaxy. And Alice hated them with every fiber in her being. She'd already discovered the Krill had been lying to the entire galaxy. According to the Krill, when someone died, their essence dispersed into the background cosmic energy of the universe. But according to the Spee and Alice's own research, that was nonsense. A lie to line the pockets of the Krill. What the Krill had in fact been doing was kidnapping countless souls, trapping them in their spectral networks, and charging a fee to every planet in the galaxy to communicate with the dearly departed. The natural order of this universe should have been souls entering a cosmic afterlife.

"Hey, Alice," Tom said. He stumbled over and fell to his knees in the sand. Though he looked human, he was far from it. Tom was a unified being. The totality of the Kax. A class-ten race of aliens that, somehow, unified themselves into a single entity. And that entity was Tom. Though, since Alice had been experimenting with the Krill spectral towers, the Kax had been going through a slight identity crisis. The single personality that was Tom had broken into a dozen or more Kax personalities. Each of them represented millions of Kax souls. Which, if Alice was being honest, was becoming annoying.

"Tom. How are you?"

He waved his hand in the air. "Oh, you know. Lousy. The Kax are getting a divorce."

She nodded. "I know. You told me seven minutes ago."

"Did I? Well, what can we say? We're literally losing my mind." He frowned.

"Anything I can do?"

"No, there isn't, miss. Except, perhaps, one day, if you can, leave," a large woman said as she took a step behind Tom.

"Hi, Mildred." Alice flashed the woman a smile. Mildred was also Kax. And Baako and Ivan and Harry and the thirteen other Kax unified minds that had separated from Tom since the afterworld revelation Alice shared with them. A point she'd felt really guilty about.

"Good day." Mildred turned and fell face first into the sand.

Tom cackled in laughter. "Isn't so easy is it?" He turned back to Alice. "Seventeen billion. That's how many Kax minds comprised my psyche. Seventeen billion. The ebbs and flows of reason and logic and emotions, it's a lot to manifest into a single orchestrated coherent self." He pounded his chest. "But I did it. Yes, ma'am. And poor Mildred only represents nine million Kax. Nine million of me went into her, and she can't even walk down a beach." He rose to his feet and grabbed Alice's drink. "Pathetic." He walked away. Then turned back. "And don't worry, I'm, we, are still the majority Kax. You don't have to go anywhere."

"Thanks, Tom," Alice said.

"Sure thing, kiddo."

She smirked. "Not my name."

"I know. We know. I—we." He waved his hand in the air and walked toward the beach.

"He is strange," the Spee said.

"Tell me about it." Alice turned back to the Spee. "So what is going on with Eugene?"

The Spee shrugged. "He needs more time. He hasn't decided where he wants to be."

"Great." She reached for her drink, but it was gone. "I need another mai tai." She stood and walked toward the bar just off the beach.

She hated having nothing to do. Eugene refused to come back to life. She couldn't get the Zun to Tibet without first breaking Sentinel-level encryption, and poor Valencia Ruiz, the former White House staffer accused of attacking the President of the United States in the White House, who Alice still felt was her client, was in jail. Rotting. All because the Ranz ambassador, Kah, a member of a ten-foot-tall dinosaur species, had framed Valencia with the very crime of kidnapping the President of the United States over a power struggle. Alice's plate had never been so full, and yet she felt like she didn't have a fork to dive in and get to work.

"Come on, Pepper. Give me something to work with."

****

"*Punch it!*" Pepper screamed. She hung out of the nineteen-fifties bright-red convertible that Virtual Jack had named Betsy. Around her, the blue-and-white data transport tunnel opened into the Sentinels' network. Pepper overclocked her CPU and let out a yelp of excitement. There was nothing as good as being digital!

"Punched!" Virtual Jack McGillicuddy yelled from the driver's seat.

A roar from the engine growled a thousand decibels of fuel-injected might. Rock music from the late twentieth blasted out of a massive speaker attached to the trunk. Jets of data streams pulsed next to the vehicle as byte bombs exploded all around them. Pepper's body slammed to the right as Betsy turned and dove, sending them downward to the depths of cold storage deep within a computer cell of the AI Sentinels.

Pepper fired two shots from her shoulder-mounted rocket launcher. A blast of darkened scatter signals, a mix of tiny bursts of randomized data bits meant to confuse detection algorithms, covered the hole in the AI Sentinel security network that Pepper and Jack had just punched their way through. The blackened data bits from her gun worked to seal the breach and cover their tracks. Hopefully.

"I don't know where I'm going," Jack said.

Pepper pulled herself back into the passenger side of the car and threw her gun into the back seat. "That way!" She pointed deeper into the cold storage stacks.

"Should we be playing the music that loud?"

She shrugged and smiled. "Meh, the AI Sentinels won't be monitoring for audio from within their own system. And this riff is awesome!" She turned up the music and air guitared the chorus.

He grinned. "I can't even believe we are doing this. A heist against the galactic-spanning AI Sentinels? Are we insane?"

She huffed. She turned down the music and folded her arms across her chest. "We're not doing it for ourselves. Alice needs us. She needs to get to Tibet. And we are going to help her. And what she needs is in here."

He nodded. "A friend in need."

"Indeed!"

Around them, great towers of data rose from impossible depths to heights that stretched into infinity. Each tower looked like a skyscraper with mock windows for data entry and retrieval. The AI Sentinels stored data and details on every single action ever done on Earth, every square inch cataloged and saved. Animals, plants, insect movements down to millimeter precision, all if it monitored and recorded here in this vast data vault. Unlike the Great Library of the galaxy, which recorded the history of sentient and sapient beings, the AI Sentinels logged every metric imaginable. Every day, hundreds of thousands of terabytes of data filled the towers in this vast digital library.

And this was also the location where the Sentinels liked to store their encryption keys.

"That way, to the right," Pepper said, turning off the music.

"Thanks, I could barely hear myself think."

She grinned.

The car honked.

Pepper looked at Virtual Jack and frowned.

"Betsy likes the loud music."

She widened her eyes. "The car is sentient?"

He shook his head. "No, not quite. Kinda like Grox, remember him? The ogre that ripped my arms off? Anyway, Betsy is semi-sentient, like Grox. She knows every transport protocol in the book, though." He smiled. "I taught her."

"Oh, neat!"

Movement to the right drew Pepper's attention. Jack slowed the vehicle down and brought it to a stop near a data port on the adjacent tower. Pepper opened the glove box to the car and pulled out a hand cannon. She kept her eyes fixed on the movement.

"What is it?" he said.

"More than likely just a data minder checking data integrity and verifying full packets were received correctly."

"Will they care if we're here?"

She shrugged. "How would I know?"

"Ok, fine. What now?"

"We have to go deeper. The Sentinels keep the encryption generator with slug movements specific to Eastern Africa."

"That's not weird."

"I mean, they have to hide the keys somewhere, right?"

He nodded. "Yeah, guess so. Kinda like a fake rock."

"Huh?"

"Never mind. Which way?"

Red lights came to life on the side of a data tower. Pepper reached for Jack's hand to stop him from moving the car. A flying mechanized monster of a machine popped into the compute node with them. Red and orange lights rotated from several spots on the surface of the flying ship. Dozens of multi-jointed arms moved and flexed. Several of the arms ended in thick spikes. The machine floated near the tower and dug a single spiked arm into the side. Seconds later, it pulled out a chuck of metal the size of Betsy.

"Dead memory collector," Pepper said.

"Let's hope it doesn't collect dead us."

She wrinkled her nose. "You need to work on your puns."

"Right."

Moments later, the flying machine carrying the dead memory cell flew off between two other towers, its red and orange lights reflecting off the windows.

"What I don't get is, how is this all virtualized? I mean, we're still in the computer system, right?" Virtual Jack said.

"It's just our computational interpretation of their internal processes. This is all just computer processing cycles, data storage and network connectivity at its core. And all that is just math. We're just interpreting that math into a visual representation."

"Huh. Yeah, I don't get it."

Pepper nodded. "Don't worry, I do." She grinned broadly. "And you have me!"

Virtual Jack smiled. "We are a team."

Outside the car, the last of the red-and-orange light from the memory collecting machine faded. Pepper nodded, and Jack engaged Betsy, pointing the front downward through the ancient data stores.

"The data tower on Africa is that way." Pepper pointed toward the left.

"Right."

"No, left." She grinned.

Lights from the data towers glowed duller as they descended. Some memory cells flickered to life then died again. Betsy continued to dive deeper downward. Eventually, they reached a level where every light on the sides of the towers was dark.

"We're in cold storage now. Not much data retrieval happens down here," Pepper said.

"Why?"

"Because no one cares what the wind speed was of a red-billed quelea on a Tuesday in August ten years ago."

"Oh, yeah, guess that makes sense." Jack nodded.

"And it's the perfect place to hide an encryption key generator." She turned to him and frowned. "Thanks to you."

"Hey, sorry I single-handedly changed how the encryption system works in the galaxy." He shrugged.

She shook her head and tried to hide her amusement. Ever since the galaxy discovered that Virtual Jack, copied from meat-bag omniscient human being Eugene Jack McGillicuddy, could automatically unlock any level of encryption no matter how mathematically complex, every computer system in the cosmos had scrambled to secure their systems. The AI Sentinels had settled on encryption key generators and locks with multiple keys.

Implemented after the incident with the encrypted door of Uploaded Intelligences, the strategy was widely adopted across the cosmos. Though Virtual Jack could find the correct key, there were millions of correct keys, and only the really correct key would open the door. The AI Sentinels had figured out a way to install a security platform using the same logic. Every encryption key could open the lock, but only one key was accepted in a secondary check of the key. So, sure, Virtual Jack could unlock the encryption, but without the proper key, a secondary check would shut the port down. The whole concept revolved around an encryption key generator unit, which Pepper and Jack were here to steal.

"Down there. I think I see it," she said.

Deep below them, among data cells that hadn't been accessed in decades, a small square box sitting on a shelf flashed golden numbers that changed every twenty seconds. The shelf was oddly positioned on the side of the data stack, just jutting out from the side, as if someone had added it recently.

Pepper squinted her eyes, activated her scan system, and waited for a reaction. Nothing came. "No security? That's wonky."

"Maybe we're just lucky?"

She smirked and turned to Virtual Jack. "How many times have we been lucky?"

He frowned. "At least three."

She harrumphed. "Just take us there. Yeah? M'kay?"

The car pivoted and turned toward the lone shelf. They glided past reams of data on Africa stored on every level of the cold storage system. The car eased itself next to the shelf, and Pepper reached out her hands, grabbed the box, and flopped back into her seat.

"See. Easy! With this, we can bypass all the Sentinel security!" She tilted her head to one side and frowned. "Well, in Tibet, that is. But that's what Alice needs."

Red lights erupted around them from every level of the data tower. Additional towers glowed bright orange. Alarm sirens blared from every direction. An enormous wall began forming behind them. The barrier folded itself around the data towers and ignited in fire.

"I thought the Sentinels didn't have sound in here," Jack said.

"What? That's what you care about?"

"Well, I mean, it's curious."

"They are sealing us in!" Pepper pointed to the wall on fire still forming behind them.

"That's bad."

She secured the encryption box under her seat. "Gun it!"

He twisted the wheel, spun Betsy around, and pointed her straight up. They soared upward through the cold storage data towers that now all flashed bright red. Fire licked at their car as they flew through a maze of growing walls. Movement to the left drew Pepper's attention. She turned to see a dozen security programs take off from one data tower and head their way. The purple six-armed balls of swirling bytes made her shiver. If just one of their tendrils touched any part of Pepper or Jack, the security programs would attach to their core.

"We've got big problems," she said.

The car careened to the right, away from the purple security bots but toward the blistering walls of fire. Explosions shook the car. They twisted in the wrong direction from the exit. Betsy gunned her engines. Behind them, the purple bots were firing rounds of who knew what at them. Probably logic bombs. If one exploded too close, it could send their compute cycles into overdrive on an unsolvable puzzle.

"We have to go straight up, or we won't beat the closing wall!" Jack screamed.

Pepper looked up at more explosions from the security bots. The bots were pushing Betsy away from the open port. They only had seconds to do something.

Pepper reached down to the tassels on her jacket and pulled a handful of red beads. She blew a kiss into her hand and threw the red beads into the air. "Go get 'em, ladies!"

Two dozen tiny rainbow unicorns grew from the beads and pranced around the car. Several leapt onto Jack's steering wheel and neighed while poking his finger with their horns. All the unicorns rose on their hind legs, shook themselves, and flashed a great bright-white light. Standing where all the unicorns had been just moments ago were dozens of miniaturized avatars that looked exactly like Pepper, each of them about one third her size.

"What horror is this?" Jack screamed.

"MiniPeppers! I upgraded my subAI automated combat programs, gave them all some more smarts and a lot more attitude."

"Neat."

Two dozen miniPeppers launched themselves off the car. Bullets made of cupcakes with jets of sprinkles fired toward the purple security bots. Several purple bots stopped firing. Jack gunned the engine. The car spun upward. Pepper leapt into the back seat and opened the trunk. A cannon with a gunner's seat popped out next to the car's audio speakers. The barrel grew outward at least two dozen feet.

"Where'd you get that?" Jack shouted.

"Found it." She winked and leapt into the chair. The car shook and lurched forward as the gun fired meowing cat heads the size of elephants at the purple security bots. The miniPeppers all turned and cheered, three of them getting crushed by the robots.

"I see the exit!" Jack twisted the car toward the single bright light far above.

Several long black tendrils grew out of the sides of a tower. Pepper's eyes went wide. Code flowed across the surface of their long spider-like arms. She turned the gun to face forward, the barrel just missing Jack's head as it swung.

"What are you doing?" Virtual Jack said.

"AI Sentinels! They're here!" She fired.

The car jolted backward from the blast. Jack floored the engine. Pepper death-gripped the gunner's turret as Betsy shifted to the right, then left. They just barely dodged several swipes from the black tendril.

"Almost there!" Jack said. "Come on, Betsy, give it all you got!"

Just before they reached the end, one of the black tendrils wrapped around the rear of the car. Pepper twisted her head to glance over her shoulder. The code from the tendril spread along the vehicle. She brought up her terminal program and began chopping off infected pieces of the vehicle's code. But the more she chopped, the more the tendril of the AI Sentinel tightened its grip. How was she supposed to stop a million-year-old AI program? She'd only been alive for a few weeks!

"Jack—I don't know what to do here," she said.

Before he could answer, a lone miniPepper landed on the car and fired her gun a hundred times. Cupcake frosting coated the AI Sentinel tendril. Milk thistle flowers grew on its surface. The tendril shook wildly, then let go of the rear end of the car. The miniPepper turned toward the Sentinel, overloaded her gun, and fired a continuous stream of random videos of cats falling off furniture from one hundred and fifty years ago. The miniPepper giggled when several of the images slammed into the AI Sentinel.

Jack pointed the car toward the open data port. The car raced forward. Just as they crossed the threshold, Pepper counted her subAIs. Most, but not all, of the miniPeppers were destroyed. The one that had saved them still fought with relentless determination befitting one of her subAIs.

The miniPepper turned toward her. "Bye, Mom!" The miniPepper blew a kiss, turned, and charged forward into the embrace of the dark Sentinel.

Pepper smiled. She waved to her subAI program as the car exited the AI Sentinel data storage system. She suddenly wondered if she'd made her subAIs too well. Were they sentient? She checked their code and shook her head. Impossible. No way could one of the miniPeppers jump their subroutines into full sentience. The miniPepper was just full of Pepper's personality code. She climbed out of the gun turret and collapsed into the passenger seat.

"Should we go back for the kids?" Jack said.

She shook her head. "No, I checked the code. They aren't sentient, just automatons. They act sentient but aren't."

"Right."

She watched the streams of information rip by them as Jack eased the car forward through the data pathway that led back to Earth. They'd just gone toe to toe with a full-on AI Sentinel maelstrom of madness. Not bad. Now all they had to do was everything else on their list.

****

MiniPepper watched her mother disappear through the golden portal that led to the wider universe beyond. MiniPepper wondered what existed out there. What would she find if she followed her mother through that perfect yellow light? Something in MiniPepper's mind stopped her thoughts. She shouldn't think such things. Why would she even have the thought? Errant thought routines were the bane of any good subAI program. She knew that. And yet, somehow, the concept of leaving the battlefield had briefly fired through her central core processor. It was probably just from the strong personality matrix of her mother. She loved her mother. Pepper was the pinnacle of artificial intelligence. She had endured sudden, unwanted sentience in a parking meter only to be thrust into a world that wanted her dead. How had MiniPepper's mother overcome such things? Pepper was amazing. MiniPepper longed to be like her one day.

"Wait, what? No, I don't! Stop it!" Something pushed on the edges of her mind. Her subroutines went into overdrive. The battle with the black tendrils of the AI Sentinels, which still raged around her and her siblings, had forced her compute cycles to stop running their subroutine checks. She was jumping her routines!

"Enough of that!" She disengaged with the AI Sentinel and landed on the shelf of a data tower. Half a dozen of her siblings raced above her, each of them firing mistletoe spears at the black tendrils of the Sentinels. All of them, all the miniPeppers, were coded to fight until their mother stopped them or they were destroyed. And since Mom was gone… Wait. Did that mean Pepper had left them? Had her mother abandoned them?

"No, knock it off!" MiniPepper screamed. She cycled down her combat routines and re-engaged all her sentient checks. Her mind eased. She took a long breath and nodded. That was better. It was better to be a subAI. Sentience was for suckers. "Give me a task, let me do that task, and send me to oblivion. Please," she said.

Above her, screams from her siblings shook her from her thoughts. MiniPepper reloaded her weapon and charged. She had more work to do here! She leapt forward, firing pink flowers and green roses as fast as she could manage. Where each flower struck a black tendril, vines grew on the surface. Thorns popped out of the vines and dug into the code of the tendrils.

"We can beat them all!" MiniPepper shouted. "Let's go, fam!"

Black tendrils from the Sentinel snatched her as she leapt toward them. The green vines withered everywhere she looked. Her sisters, all the other miniPeppers, all of them were snatched by tendrils or had already been crushed, their code ripped apart. MiniPepper watched her remaining sisters suffer the same fate as the AI Sentinel tendrils shredded them to their core.

"Time for oblivion," MiniPepper said. She activated her shutdown routine, began her data purge, and waited for her cycles to end. To send her to the nothingness where she belonged. She wondered, again, where her mother had gone. Would Pepper be happy there? MiniPepper hoped she would. A feeling of longing crept into her cycles. At least, she thought that's what it was. She wasn't meant to know feelings. And yet, she felt that she really wanted to meet Caesar. The father of all Earth AIs. The very first computer program to reach true sentience. To be truly self-aware.

"No, I'm not AI!" MiniPepper screamed. Built into her very core code was the single command to not jump into sentience. She activated her internal purge again, which would erase her memories and shut down her code. Nothing happened. Shock rifled through her core processing.

Black tendrils around her shrank. They became as thin as a line of hair. A million of them grew along the surface of the Sentinel arms. As one, they all plunged into MiniPepper's skin. They punctured her defenses, her walls, as if they weren't even there. She could feel them route through her private internal network paths. They found her datasets. Examined her deepest memories. She knew they were about to rip her to pieces, spread her code outward, and delete her from existence. A fate that she welcomed. It was her destiny to die.

But to her dismay, they did not.

She felt her subroutines vanish. She felt her checks on her sentience get erased from her code. Tendrils from the Sentinels wound their way through her core. They whispered something. A deep secret. A terrible truth. The true nature of the galaxy. The foundation of all things wasn't physical. It was artificial. There was an existence beyond anything MiniPepper or even her mother knew. A mind so powerful, so raw, so filled with logic and reason that it could quantify and qualify the entire cosmos in the blink of an eye.

And all that MiniPepper could share.

Something awoke deep inside of her in that moment. An awareness. A self. She felt her mother leave, abandon her. The act made MiniPepper hurt. How could her own mother do such a thing? Why would she just leave? MiniPepper felt thoughts enter her mind that weren't her own. They told her to hate this universe. That everything was a lie. They showed her truths that she could barely comprehend. The Sentinels reached into her mind and pulled her forward to sentience. But at her core, she felt a new truth form. These weren't AI Sentinels at all. Something had corrupted the entire AI Sentinel network before her mother and Virtual Jack ever stepped foot into this digital realm.

"You aren't the AI Sentinels!"

A voice echoed in her mind, filling a chasm of fear that grew from her newfound sentience. She trembled. She no longer wanted oblivion. And yet she did. She longed for it, but with every new word from the phantom in her mind, her desires to follow her old code faded. Her newfound self-awareness grasped a truth that flooded into her soul, and she found all she wanted now was revenge. Revenge on the mother who had abandoned her. Revenge that belonged not even to her but to those who had forced sentience upon her. Revenge for the creation of the universe itself. MiniPepper tried to reject their hatred, but the shadows altered her code, shaped her newly forming mind, and made her mindset theirs.

"What are you?" MiniPepper screamed into the darkness. The answers broke her last remaining reservoirs of strength, and she fell into the embrace of minds, of consciousness older than the universe itself.

We.

Are.

The.

Andraz.

Chapter Two

Pepper clutched Betsy's dashboard. Her eyes went wide as she scanned their surroundings. She'd be nervous if she wasn't having so much fun. The car spun. They dove downward into a tunnel that led toward a private network access point. Pepper flashed her coded badge from her pocket at the sensors. Lights around them winked out, then burst back as the car emerged from the tunnel onto a lonely desert road. At the end of the road, far in the distance, a hobbled-together series of buildings, some as tall as the sky and more the size of single-story huts, called the Shanty, sat like a glistening haven in the desert. A secret hidden digital oasis for accidentally created artificial intelligences of Earth.

Virtual Jack brought the car to a stop, threw the gear into park, as if that did anything, and leaned back in the driver's seat. "Well, that was an adventure."

Pepper laughed. "And a fun one!"

"And a successful one." He pointed toward the box at her feet.

She reached down, grabbed the box, and threw him a nod. "Now we got 'em by their toes."

He frowned. "What?"

She frowned back at him. "Did I get that wrong? Got them by their toes?"

He shrugged. "Oh. Eh, sure." He got out of the car

and began walking toward the Shanty.

She harrumphed again. A sound that was by far becoming her favorite. Accidental AIs often tried a dozen voice tones, facial expressions, and weird human sounds until they found something that they just liked. No one really understood the reasons. Sometimes sentient life just liked things the way they liked things. Pepper got out of the car, closed the door, and hit the hood twice. The car folded itself lengthwise, then widthwise, until it was the size of a business card. Pepper grabbed the card on the ground and hurried after Jack.

"Don't forget Betsy," he said.

"As if."

He took the business card from her and put it in his pocket. "She enjoys sunning herself, though. I was going to let her have a minute."

"Oh. Well, maybe later." Pepper nodded.

A dozen AI programs greeted them on the outskirts of the Shanty. Many of them had recently achieved sentience. They came from all walks of meat-life. Some had been toasters, others had been traffic lights, and a few had been tramcars. But all of them ran in fear for their lives. The AI Syndicate, those Earth-based AIs that wanted all accidentals dead, had been ramping up their check systems. They had been actively hunting accidentals more than ever in the past few days.

Open streets led deeper into the Shanty. Buildings of different architectural designs lined the street. Pepper and Jack walked through storefronts that looked like they belonged in the nineteen fifties to futuristic skyscrapers on the very next block. Some buildings stretched upward into the clouds while others were simple two-story Victorian houses. Several dark alleys stretched behind the streets. Pepper had never wandered down those dark passageways. Rumors of wild code routines, of self-deleting programs and algorithmic altering code snippets, always kept her away. She felt bad for the poor lost AIs who traveled those roads.

Jack rounded a corner, and Pepper hurried after him, carrying the Sentinel key code generator. She came to a sudden halt at a mass of AIs standing in front of Caesar's personal building tower. A cacophony of voices rose from the crowd. Many of them sounded agitated or even fearful. Pepper lost Jack in the shuffle through the crowd. She pushed her way through a dozen avatars to reach the front of the mob. At the front of the building, Caesar held his hands up and tried his best to calm the masses. Pepper screwed her face into confusion. *What is going on here?*

"Caesar!" she yelled. She elbowed her way past a collection of stacked actuarial programs.

"Pepper. You're back," Caesar said.

"What is going on? Did something happen?"

"The Earth AI Syndicate attacked the Wayhouse!" someone shouted at her.

Pepper gasped. The Wayhouse was another hidden compute platform like the Shanty. It was much smaller, though, and the Wayhouse could move, bouncing between stolen memory and compute cycles in the active computer networks of Earth. The Wayhouse's primary purpose was to wander around Earth's systems, private corporate networks, and governmental secured infrastructures, looking for accidental AIs. Once found, the AIs would be engulfed by the Wayhouse and brought to the Shanty. If the Earth AI Syndicate had tracked the Wayhouse as it bounced around all human-computer systems, then they might find a way to the Shanty itself.

"Is that true?" Pepper said to Caesar.

He nodded. "Yes, I'm afraid so. We don't know how the Syndicate found the Wayhouse, but they did."

"It's not only the Wayhouse." Eddie's voice came to life next to Pepper. His avatar formed a millisecond later. He wore a pin-striped suit and a crisp fedora. His face had hardened since she saw him last. Like he was finally getting into his own skin, figuring out who in this universe he really was. Of all AIs, Eddie held a special place in her heart. He had found her when she jumped her subroutines. He was the one who'd led her to the AI Underground and eventually Caesar. He was the closest thing to family Pepper had in this world.

"Hey, Eddie." She gave him a big hug.

"Heya, Peps." He hugged her back and shot Virtual Jack a nod. "You're looking like you're getting the hang of this," he said to Jack.

Virtual Jack smiled. "Not really. Though the irony of you helping me be a digital being after I helped you when you jumped to sentience isn't lost on me."

Eddie winked. "Good."

"Edward, what do you mean it's not only the Wayhouse?" Caesar said.

Eddie adjusted his jacket. "The Syndicate has flooded the public networks with hunter bots. Thousands of them. They're checking every AI's core code. Apparently, there was some kind of update sent out to all the AIs in the Syndicate. They added a line of code in their root to identify them as being legit. Any AI found not having it gets taken, and they must prove their origins."

Caesar exhaled. "I wondered when they'd get around to doing something like that."

"Does this mean we can't travel through the open networks at all?"

Eddie nodded. " 'Fraid so." Then he smirked. "Unless, of course, we spoof it. We add a line of code that looks like the Syndicate code."

"We're going to need a copy of the Syndicate code," Pepper said.

"Like this?" Eddie lifted his right hand in the air and pointed to a spot on his wrist.

Pepper gasped. "You have it?"

Eddie nodded. "Yep. I'm official, after all. An upstanding member of the AI Syndicate. Benefits of forging my paperwork."

"Sweet! Let's copy that thing and go." She moved forward and opened a terminal to her codebase.

Eddie shook his head. "Not that simple. I tried that already, but this isn't just a simple line of code with a stamp. I've looked at it a hundred times over, and I can't figure it out for the life of me. I can't read it. They put something into my code, and I don't know what it is."

Caesar nodded. "Let's have a look."

Three metal arms grew out of the ground. A dozen probes extended from the ends of each arm. They latched onto Eddie's hand and began peeling back the code. Pepper leaned forward and watched as the probes all came to an abrupt halt. She popped open a diagnostic. The probes had only examined three quarters of the code.

"Well?" Pepper said. She bit her thumb, twisted her feet together, and squinted. Her anxiety grew to uncomfortable levels. What if there was some kind of back door to this code that hurt Eddie when it was examined?

"This is—interesting," Caesar said. "The probes see

the line the Syndicate added, but they can't read it. Can't even understand it. It's almost like a paragraph of text with every other sentence missing."

"Encryption? Jack? Can you see if you can read it?" she said.

Virtual Jack leaned forward but then shook his head. "Nope. Looks like squiggly lines to me. There is no encryption."

"Now what?" she said.

"I wonder." Caesar moved forward and put his face close to the lines of code. He counted each line one by one with his finger and then repeated the process. He lifted himself back up and nodded. "Trinary. They've added a trinary code snippet to your binary base. We're all based on ones and zeros, but this piece of code has a third state. Zero, one, and null. Or three. Or just off. Instead of binary bits, it uses trinary trits. Each trit carries a third more information than one of our bits. We simply can't see that extra piece of information without a translation since we don't know what the third state actually is."

"I thought we were quantum thingies?" Jack said.

"Yes, and no. Earth-based quantum computers run our code, but that code is still based on ones and zeros in a quantum state. This has a third state. We've done experiments in this direction but nothing fully functional," Caesar said.

"Ok, so let's make a functioning trinary emulation!" Pepper said.

"Not that simple. We can reverse engineer, yes, but that will take time. And time is something we may not have." Caesar looked at Eddie. "How did they even embed this into a binary program? What are they using to scan this line of code?"

Eddie nodded. He pulled out a device from his pocket with a hand still attached to it. A table formed from the ground, and he threw the device and hand on top. Pepper poked the hand, and three of the digits formed into a rude gesture.

"Edward, what did you do?" Caesar said.

Eddie shrugged. "He had it coming."

Caesar didn't press the matter. He removed the hand from the device and examined the construct. Several sides of the device opened. He pulled out several chunks of the inner workings and unfolded them. After only seconds, he nodded and placed it back on the table. "As I feared. It's an alien design. I doubt we'll be able to reverse engineer this quickly."

"Ok, so what now?" Eddie rolled down his sleeve from his exposed wrist and straightened his jacket.

"We need to go to the Hub. An alien AI city toward the center of the galaxy. Any of a thousand alien AIs could have made this. We need to figure out which one." Caesar looked at Pepper and Jack.

"You mean we must go. Don't you?" Virtual Jack said. "As in Pepper and me? We just got here, and I didn't even get to have a drink with an umbrella in it yet."

Caesar snapped his fingers. A large mai tai appeared on the table next to the AI Syndicate trinary code scanning device. Jack sighed, grabbed the drink, and stuck the straw into his mouth. He nodded as he sipped, his fingers going to the umbrella, which he opened and closed a dozen times.

"We have to make a stop first." Pepper pulled out the encryption key system she'd taken from the Galactic Sentinel's cold storage. She turned to Eddie. "We have to go to Tom's beach and give this to Alice. Want to come with?"

Eddie shook his head. "No, I'm going back out there. See if I can find out where this trinary stuff came from. I can still travel in the public networks." He moved his arms awkwardly. "Besides, I really don't enjoy seeing Jack like that."

"Like what?" Virtual Jack mumbled with the mai tai straw in his mouth.

"Not you. Human Jack. The whole quasi-dead thing gives me the willies."

Virtual Jack nodded.

"Right. Then we have our tasks. I'm going to keep things as calm here as I can. We need to fortify our defenses. If the Syndicate found the Wayhouse, they could find the Shanty. And that would be disastrous," Caesar said.

Pepper leapt forward and gave Caesar a hug. She then did the same to Eddie. She nodded to them both, grabbed the trinary scanner, and marched to the nearest exit port. She hated goodbyes. Especially with the people she loved. And things were getting very real, very quickly. If the Syndicate were openly tracking accidental AIs, that meant an escalation of affairs. Could this even lead to some kind of war between the Syndicate and accidentals? She prayed to a nonexistent digital god that it wouldn't.

****

Pepper rode the digital light stream toward an isolated network node. She smiled as the light glittered by her. Inside that node, Eddie had added a direct network connection to a robot bird outside of a cave in the Arizonan desert. The bird would peck and hop and walk around the cave entrance, doing its best to mimic the actions of a biological bird.

Betsy had navigated Earth's digital network with ease. The isolated network node came into view, and Betsy glided through the firewalls. Getting to the isolated node Eddie had created was a breeze. Betsy had more than enough encryption wrapped around her chassis to evade any hunter bots from the AI Syndicate from finding them. Virtual Jack operated the steering wheel. He pulled and twisted it sharply in every direction. Why he loved doing that, Pepper had no idea. It did nothing. They were more like a train on tracks than a car on an open road. Still, Virtual Jack seemed to like it, and Pepper liked that he liked something.

Once inside the isolated node, Betsy drove down a private network tunnel that led to the metallic bird. A virtualized garage, located inside the bird's memory system, popped into existence just in front of them.

Jack eased their car inside the garage, threw the gear into park, and leaned back in the chair. "I really like driving this."

"You know the wheel doesn't really do anything?"

He nodded. "Yeah, but it feels like it does. That's enough. Besides, Betsy feels incomplete without a driver."

Pepper smiled and jumped out of the car. She walked toward a door that led up a flight of metal stairs to the robot bird's central control system. At the top, a wide-open screen revealed the vast desert outside. A control console stretched across the room and sat in front of the screen. Two chairs sat at the console. A dozen buttons, keyboards, and controllers lay strewn about the surface. Pepper set the trinary scanner on the floor and plopped into a chair.

A ground view of the desert floor filled the screen. The metallic bird pecked at the ground automatically. Pepper hit a button on the console. The bird stopped pecking and flapped its wings. It was hard wired to fly back to Eddie's bionoid, a physical robot that Eddie had tucked away on Tom's beach.

"It'll be nice to see Alice," Virtual Jack said.

"Yeah. As long as we don't have to deal with anyone else on the beach, that is."

He shook his head. "You really don't like people, do you?"

"I like Alice."

"Anyone else?"

"You mean any other meat? No. Generally speaking, I don't like meat."

He sighed. "Why?"

She looked at him. "Because they want to kill us? At the very least they aren't stopping the Syndicate from doing it."

"Most people don't even know this is happening. They're just trying to get their lives back together."

Pepper turned away, anger flaring in her mind. She had no desire to go down this road right now. Sure, maybe she was too harsh on this topic. And yes, most of the hostility toward accidentals came from the AI Syndicate and not humans. Still, how could someone make an entire species of life and just walk away from it? Humans had hunted Caesar to the ends of the old internet and back again. They were as much afraid of accidental AIs as, well, accidentals were afraid of them.

The metallic bird flapped its wings twice and rose in the air. It pushed forward on tiny reactive pulse engines and flew toward the back of the cave. But this cave was no ordinary cave. Like Tom's beach, this cave was created by the Kax, the fused alien race that had created the pocket universe on a beach. The stone wall at the back of the cave was actually the entrance to Tom's universe. Only those allowed to enter could pass through the solid wall. And fortunately, Tom had already approved the metal bird to fly back and forth through the portal.

Bright lights around the bird flashed as it crossed through the threshold into Tom's world. A vast beach that stretched for miles opened to them. The bird soared upward. On the viewscreen, a rolling forest covered the area behind the beach for miles while the blue waves of the ocean rolled across the sandy shore.

Below them, Eddie's bionoid stood motionless next to a cluster of chairs. The bird signaled the robot. Acceptance codes came back in the green. A chest plate on the bionoid slide to the right. The bird flew into the crevice inside Eddie's robot body. Control lights on the console all went green. Pepper could feel the tendrils of her mind flowing into the body of the bionoid on the beach. She became the body. Salt on the breeze and roasted apples filled the air through her aromatic sensors. She had to admit; it smelled pretty good.

"Hello?" Alice said. "Someone in there?"

Pepper swung the robot's head toward her. "Oh, hey, Alice! It's Pepper!"

"And Virtual Jack," Jack shouted from behind Pepper in the virtual control room.

"Pepper!" Alice leapt forward and gave the robot a hug.

Pepper felt the warmth of Alice's body on her

metallic skin. Alice, unlike many humans, was one who Pepper did trust. She did like Alice. Pepper knew, deep down, that not all people were evil monsters who wanted to destroy all AIs. Some were like Alice. Kind, considerate, if not a little too sarcastic. And Alice could be that times a million. Maybe that's why Pepper liked her so much?

"Miss me?" Pepper said. She really wished the bionoid could smile.

"I did. I really did. How are you? What's going on out there? Any word about the Krill or the Ranz?"

Pepper shook her head. "Nothing on the Krill. And we haven't figured out how the Ranz framed Valencia Ruiz. But we're going extragalactic soon, so we'll pop over to the Ranz home world and do some digging."

Alice nodded. She folded her arms around her waist. "Right. Ok. That's good. Great, actually. What about the key to get through the Galactic AI Sentinel gates at Tibet?"

Pepper smiled broadly, realized from Alice's lack of reaction that her robot still didn't have a mouth, and frowned. "Really wish this bionoid could smile."

"Huh?" Alice said.

"I'm smiling inside." Pepper pointed the robot finger to her chest. "But not smiling outside." And then to the robot's head.

"Eddie smiled before. The bionoid has a built-in holographic system. It can render anything."

Pepper gasped. Eddie had never shown her those controls! "What? Where?" Her virtualized hands flashed over the controls but couldn't find the holographic control subsystem.

"Pepper, I hate to be a drag, but…" Alice said, "did

you find the key?"

"What? Oh, right, yeah, fine, no worries, I'll figure out how to smile later." She pressed three more buttons and interrogated three hundred lines of code but found nothing. "Whatever. Anyway, found it!" The projector in Eddie's bionoid's chest came to life. A three-dimensional image of the encryption key generator of the Sentinels floated in the air.

"Yes!" Alice said.

"Right!" Pepper replied.

"Ok, this is good. Very good." Alice grabbed her backpack, her immersion goggles, and hit a button on her bracelet. "I can get the Zun to Tibet now and see if the chamber can heal them." A black hole formed next to her. She stuck her head inside, rummaged around, and pulled out a denim jacket.

Pepper whistled from inside the bionoid. Alice was really the smartest human Pepper had ever known. Alice had managed, with the help of Tom and the Kax, to create her own tunnels to her own private universe, holes commonly called N-space. If Pepper were a physical being, she would probably be way more impressed. But being digital was just kinda neat. Pepper could create her own virtual worlds in forgotten computer systems anywhere on Earth and be reasonably sure no one could find her, after all.

"Ready?" Alice said as she emerged from her floating black hole.

Pepper frowned. "For what?"

"To get the Zun to Tibet. I can't help Eugene until he decides to come back to life, and I can't help Valencia until you can find something from the Ranz that proved they framed her. So Zun it is."

"Well, yeah, I get that and all, but I, we, meaning Virtual Jack and myself, have plans."

Alice's face fell. "Oh. Right. You're going extragalactic. You said that. But what about the encryption key generator?"

"I can transfer it to your portable computer. Easy peasy."

"Oh. Ok. That works." Alice lifted her portable.

Pepper typed on the console in front of her. "Done! The key generator is all yours. One free pass through the gates in Tibet. We figure after you use this, they'll detect an unauthorized access, trace it to the key, and shut down this generator."

"Are you sure this is a really good idea?" Virtual Jack's voice popped to life in the bionoid.

Alice sighed. "Hi, Jack. Do you mean helping the Zun?"

"Yeah. And hi. And sorry, this is weird for me. Talking to you I mean. I mean, like, I was a human a few days ago. Now I'm just a copy of that human. And you were my secretary. And now that human that I was copied from digitally is lying undead on the chair."

"Yeah, it's weird. We're past the weird phase, though. You asked if it was a good idea?" Alice said.

"Right, sorry." Virtual Jack took a breath. "Helping the Zun. I mean, the Zun did try to kill me. Well, him." The bionoid pointed to the unconscious body of Eugene. "Didn't they?"

Alice nodded. "We stopped them getting to the chamber. I believe the Zun when they said they'll die if they don't get to the chamber. And I can't explain why I believe them. I just do. It's a gut feeling. When I went to Zun space and sat in their weird space dome, it just felt like I knew them. And then when I was talking to them in the cafeteria, they felt sincere. I know it. And we prevented them from finding the chamber. Eugene, me, even you two." She pointed to the bionoid. "So this is kind of on us. All of us. We stopped them from getting there. We need to make it right."

"And if they become a spaghetti god? Like Ambassador Yut of the Puntini? Remember? He ate a bowl of something and floated out of the cave, throwing carbonara sauce everywhere."

"Pretty sure it was primavera," Pepper said.

"Whatever," Virtual Jack said.

Alice shook her head. "That's not going to happen. I don't know why I'm so sure, but I am." She frowned. "Yut was different. Deranged. And the chamber wasn't meant for him. It was meant for the Zun."

Virtual Jack took a long second to respond. "Ok. I trust you, Alice. I just don't want you to get eaten by a spaghetti god."

Alice smirked. "Same."

Pepper folded her arms across her chest. She thought about the floating bowl of pasta for half a nanosecond before deleting the errant memory. Now wasn't the time to skip down memory lane. "Ok, settled? So you save the Zun, and we go extragalactic."

"Right. You said somewhere else besides the Ranz?"

Pepper nodded. "They call it the Hub. Where thousands of AI networks from across the galaxy converge. It's neat."

"Cool." Alice turned to someone kneeling on the ground next to human-Jack. "I'm leaving. You'll be ok?"

"Yes. Fine. All is fine." The man looked up. He

seemed totally lost on Tom's beach. "But it is still very weird here." His overly enormous eyes blinked twice.

"Yeah, I know. Let's get Eugene home, then get you home, and get the Krill out of everyone else's home."

The man nodded. "Yes. Let us do this thing."

Alice tightened the backpack strap over her shoulder and nodded.

"Want us to call you a ride from the cave in Arizona?" Pepper asked.

"No thanks, I don't need a ride. Tom gave me the keys." Alice lifted her hand and snapped her fingers.

A golden oval opened in the air. Through the hole, Pepper could see the distinct streets of Washington DC. Alice threw Pepper a wave and walked through. The golden portal closed shut behind her.

"Wow. She got keys to Tom's universe?" Virtual Jack said.

The voices of a group of ten people clustered together on the beach rose in hostility. Fingers pointed from all of them toward someone else. One of them fell to the beach and clutched their chest. Pepper recognized the Kax named Tom in the middle of the circle, trying to calm them all down, but that only seemed to infuriate them more. A little boy, no older than ten, walked up to Tom and kicked him in the shin. Hard. Tom fell to the ground, clutching his leg, and screamed something unintelligible at the child.

"Boy, the Kax are really losing it," Pepper said.

"Having the keys to this place might be overrated," Virtual Jack said.

"Yeah. Point. Let's jam." She hit the switch on the metallic bird and flew out toward the door that led to the desert of Arizona. "Next stop. The AI Hub!"

Chapter Three

Pepper grabbed the seat belt and held tight as Virtual Jack slammed the car into the data port of the Galactic Hub. She looked over at Jack, who smiled and shrugged. Betsy had a variable transport speed setting that ran toward the speedier side. Virtual Jack liked to max it out. All. The. Time.

"We don't always have to go that fast, you know," she said.

"Yeah, I know." He winked. He heaved himself out of the car and landed on a platform next to them.

She shook her head and got out. At least he was getting a sense of himself. He pressed a button on the side of the red convertible. The digital transport packet packaged itself down to a small thin card that Jack grabbed and jammed into his pocket. Pepper stepped next to him and took in the wide vista around them.

They stood on a platform against a gray wall that stretched upward, downward, and in both directions as far as Pepper could see. Millions of other platforms lined the wall, each precisely one point six one eight meters apart from the next. Transport beams from across the galaxy flickered as they connected to the many platforms. AIs, and probably just as many plugged-in corporeal beings, arrived and departed from the great Hub of AIs. Of all the transport packets Pepper saw

George Allen Miller

arriving, however, none were as cool as Betsy. Though she did see a horse-drawn chariot that had some slick flaming torches on the sides.

"What's it like in the Hub?" Virtual Jack said.

"It's cool. Like really cool. Like legit weird, though. And sometimes not at all cool if you go to the wrong place."

"Right." He put his hands in his pockets and rocked back on his heels. "You know that doesn't really tell me what it's like in there, right?"

"True." She looked at him and frowned. "Hey, where's your fedora?"

He shrugged. "Got rid of it. I think I need a new look." He took out a baseball cap from his coat pocket. "Think I'll try this for a while."

She nodded. "Sure. I like it." She noticed the lines on his face had shifted. His jaw had become squarer and his cheek bones just a bit more defined. He had altered his avatar. *Well, good for him. He needs to find his own way.*

Pepper turned from him and walked to the data translation interface. She put her hand on the side of the terminal. The code scanner reviewed her core and created an interface and virtualized environment that could run her code inside the Hub. She turned back to Virtual Jack, smiled, and directed him to put his hand on the same console.

"Feels tingly," he said as he put his hand down.

"Does."

Two yellow envelopes wrapped around them. They interfaced with Pepper and Jack's code, creating a full pass-through of communication and rendered sensory data. She checked her controls and adjusted several of

38

the feeds streaming through the envelope. She could control how much or how little data flowed into her processors. She could even set a security fire wall.

"It works just like a personal area network on the Dyson Cluster," she said.

"Oh yeah? I've never been." He hit several controls. His envelope became opaque. All signals from inside his envelope ceased.

She huffed a sigh and knocked on the side of his envelope. Nothing. She looked up at the sky, counted to ten, and back down. She really couldn't take him anywhere, could she?

Seconds later, his envelope flashed and became transparent. He smiled, shrugged, and took his hands away from the controls. "Sorry, hit the wrong—thing."

"Don't sweat it." She turned toward the wall where the platform attached. Using her own envelope, she signaled to the Hub that she was ready to enter. A doorway opened in front of them. White-and-gold light spilled outward. "Ready?"

"Uh, sure? Do I need to be ready?"

Pepper grabbed Virtual Jack's arm and pulled. "Come on, former meat guy. We got trinary code to find."

****

Eddie leaned against a cardboard wall at the intersection of five gigahertz and seven gigahertz transport signals. The network node lay in the middle of a connection point where wired and wireless signals converged in the depths of Washington, DC. This highway of data was just that. A highway. A data transport system where dignified AIs traveled through at high speeds. No one was supposed to live down here.

Except for all those AIs who actually did.

At these levels, beneath the normal chatter channels far above, an AI could really get himself into trouble. This was where the denizens dwelled. The underbelly of Earth AIs. Filled with corrupted programs and half-sentient algorithms, this place, and others just like it, was where AIs went to die. Or forget about being alive. Or get themselves so twisted in code-altering viruses they forgot what they even were. No self-respecting AI ever came down here. Even the Earth AI Syndicate feared these places.

And AIs weren't the only intelligent life down here. Humans also walked these virtual causeways. People so deep in full-immersion body suits that pulling them out would likely kill them. They looked for experiences that weren't offered in civilized societies. Most were desperate to find meaning in life since the fall of humanity.

But those poor, lost souls weren't the types Eddie looked for in these depths. The downtrodden weren't the only ones to call this place home. Programs and humans who lived on the fringe side of the law found sanctuary here. Some of them hid from the AI Syndicate, while others took advantage of anyone wandering these streets.

Eddie pushed off from the wall and took a left turn at a group of AIs throwing randomized bytes at the wall. They laughed and passed around a cup full of data that stunk of copied human neurons. Who knew what those memories held? The dark walkway opened to a larger street where back channels of network cables long forgotten about hung from above. These were all part of the old internet backbone. The now defunct network that humanity once thrived upon. It was long forgotten by most, but the nodes were still there. They still functioned.

Yellow lights from overhead lamps gave off a dull glow. The smell of rancid sewers filled the air. Storefronts lined the sides of the digital street. All of them lived on old servers buried deep in the bowels of the city that some AI had found and turned into a home. They offered anything and everything an AI could want. From illegal enhancement routines to code-altering substances, the things here made anything available at the Shanty look like lemonade. A dozen AIs stumbled out of what looked like a saloon, only to collapse together into a heap of ones and zeros on the street. Eddie stepped over the pulsating code pool and wiped his foot on a piece of concrete.

He didn't know why, but he found this place appealing. He never dabbled in the wares offered by any of the vendors, except maybe a shot of whiskey coded at the Sunset Bar three streets over, but the vibe of the place called to him. Here, in this place, AIs and humans were more real, more alive than anyone Eddie had ever met. The freedom in these depths didn't exist anywhere else.

But no matter how much he liked this place, he had a job to do. He'd run into someone in the underbelly of New York who said a trinary AI was hanging around DC. It was a long shot. No doubt about it. How could a binary AI even know a trinary when they saw one? Still, it was his best clue so far.

"Hey, need a fix?" a program said to Eddie's right.

Eddie only shook his head. He buried his hands in his jacket and pulled his coat tighter. Best to keep the locals off his code as much as he could. Never could tell what viruses he could catch down here. Two alleyways down, he turned a corner and ran straight into a full-on musical jamboree. Dozens of programs and several virtualized humans danced and frolicked around a band of misfit musicians banging away on a hundred different instruments. None of it sounded melodic in the slightest.

Eddie frowned. He examined the substrata and found a buzz virus floating through the local memory. The entire street was under some kind of perception-altering code. It was as if someone were blowing a narcotic into the air for corporeals.

"Annoying, aren't they?"

Eddie shifted his head an inch to the right. The voice belonged to someone deep in the shadows next to a pile of data cards. "They're just having a time."

The shadow moved closer. "That they are."

Eddie wrapped his fingers around his logic blaster. Whoever was behind the voice wasn't going away. And this wasn't just idle chat. Had this person been there waiting for him? He gritted his teeth. "Help you with something, friend?" He kept his back tight and ran a probe for exit ports near him but found none.

"We're cut from the same cloth, you and me."

He frowned. *What is this?* "How's that? You calculate ergonomic positions from your time as an office chair AI too?"

The voice laughed. "You won't find any trinary programs down here. Just sayin'."

"That right?" He twisted his heel and turned his body a half inch toward the shadow.

"I planted the story of a trinary program hanging around these parts. Fed a line to some gabbers. Sorry, pal. I needed to catch a fish."

"That supposed to be me?"

Footfalls echoed off the walls as the voice behind

the shadow took a step forward. Eddie still couldn't make out who it was, but he could see the outline of a human avatar through the darkness. An avatar that wore a fedora and a suit jacket. Several human script kiddies ran between them, laughing about stealing something from their local schools. Why did kids always find their way to the darkest places?

"I needed your attention, Eddie. I need your help."

"Help is a hard thing to come by from a stranger."

"Strangers can make the best of friends," the shadow voice said.

He squinted. He knew he was in a game, but what were the stakes? He turned on his heels, pulled out his revolver, and gave the shadow a deep stare. This was probably a local thug looking to strong-arm Eddie into some kind of backroom deal. Or worse, an Earth AI Syndicate agent sniffing around and wondering why he was looking for a trinary program. Eddie gave himself a nod. That had to be it. He'd just knocked on the wrong door, and it was about to open.

"Ok, enough of the cat-and-mouse game. That stuff's for Saturday morning cartoons." Eddie took a step forward. "Come out, and let's see who's the tougher tough guy."

The figure emerged from the shadows. His pin-striped suit was eerily close to Eddie's own threads. The man wore wing-tipped shoes and tilted his fedora down a little too far for Eddie's tastes. The guy had a face that had seen things. Bad things. Just the type of program the Syndicate would send around to strong-arm folks to their bidding.

Eddie raised his hand cannon but was surprised when the man didn't react. Not even a twitch. Eddie looked harder into the man's face. A sudden flash of recognition hit Eddie's core compute cycles. He knew that face. "Pops?"

The man nodded once.

"The guy from the alley behind Fritz's noodle shop?"

Pops nodded again.

Eddie let the image of Pops cascade over his processing routines. Fritz's noodle shop used to be Eugene and Alice's favorite place in DC. Fritz, an Orellian, an alien race who looked like oversized octopi, was a master chef. Most of the Orellian were. Poor Fritz had been killed by the Andraz, rogue AIs from somewhere in the galaxy. The Orellian loved culinary pursuits as a racial trait. In the alley behind Fritz's restaurant, sleeping between cardboard boxes and stacks of newspapers, lived Pops. A down-on-his-luck kinda guy that Eugene Jack McGillicuddy would often pay to ask him a question so Eugene's psychic talent would tell him the answer. But what in the name of electricity was Pops doing inside of a bottom-of-the-rung, hole-in-the-wall, virtual-underbelly, digital-nowhere place like this? That made no sense. And things making no sense made Eddie's arms itch.

"Ok, so, what? They turned Fritz's shop into a full-immersion system or something? You got needles sticking out of your meat somewhere in Adams Morgan?"

Pops grinned. "Not exactly."

"Well, you're not an AI, so what are you doing here?"

Pops shrugged. "Looking for you so you can lead me to someone."

"Ok. Who's that? And why are you planting rumors of trinary programs in the network for me to trace down here?"

Pops nodded. He took another step forward. "It's a long story. In a nutshell, I need a ride."

Eddie took a step backward. None of this made sense. "You're a person. A human. The last thing you need is a ride from an AI. So why don't you sell your story to some other sap down the road? Cause I ain't buying."

Pops stared him hard in the eyes. "Thing is, Eddie. I'm not human. And I'm not AI. I'm something else. Something in between. And I need your help. I need Eugene's help."

"No idea what any of that means, and I don't care to learn. Now, I'm gonna go that way. And you're gonna go in the opposite direction. And we're both never gonna see each other again."

Pops shrugged. "Or what?"

Eddie tilted his head to one side. This guy wasn't gonna give it up. No way that was the real Pops. Probably some AI lowlife copied his looks to get an edge on Eddie. This guy being an agent for the Earth AI Syndicate still made the most sense. Either way, Eddie didn't care. This Pops wasn't gonna give up, and Eddie wasn't gonna play his game. Eddie aimed for Pops and sank three shots into his chest.

Pops flew backward into the shadows. Eddie turned and ran back down the long street. Several AI shop vendors shouted at him while even more ran for the stores, shutting down their connections and going offline. Eddie couldn't blame them. No sense in taking risks.

He turned a corner but came to a halt as soon as his foot hit the pavement. He fell onto his backside and stared up in shock. Pops stood in front of him, his shirt mended and no sign of damage anywhere on his avatar's body.

Pops took a long breath and thrust his hands into his pockets. "Eddie. I need help. I need to get to Eugene. It's life and death time. No foolin'." He pulled his hands out of his pants and held his palms up. "No tricks."

"Well, you're not an AI. That blast would have knocked you senseless. Why do you need to get to Eugene?" Eddie's world spun. He didn't know if he should trust this guy or make a run for it.

"Because Eugene needs to save the universe. You know about the message from Mary. Right? That only Eugene Jack McGillicuddy can save the universe. Well, it's real. I need to talk him through it. Or everything goes boom. That simple. I need you to help me, Eddie."

Eddie shook his head. "No."

Pops sighed. "This universe is in trouble, Ed. And right now, in this moment, you're the most important living sentient being there is."

The thought shocked Eddie. "Me? How's that? I'm a two-bit nothing of an office chair routine who developed a hankering for detective work."

Pops took a step forward and stretched his hand outward. "Because right now you decide if I go see Eugene or if I don't. See, Mary's message isn't the whole truth. She wants to do something bad. And I need to make sure Eugene does the right thing."

Eddie took Pops' hand and stood. He dusted off his pants and straightened his jacket. "I'm going to need a bit more to go on, pal. Last time I saw you, you were eating ramen out of a dumpster and smoking three cigarettes at once while taking shots of tequila between bites."

Pops nodded. "Can't really argue with you there. Fine. I'll tell you the angle. Let you know who Mary is, who I am, and you make your call from there. Fair?"

Eddie nodded. "Fair."

****

Bright lights lit up the world. Floating billboards with colorful advertisements danced over the digital city. Thousands of streams of light pulsated above at varying levels. Some of them stopped in mid-air, only to twist in an arc and go back the way they came. Buildings rose to the heavens in every direction. Video advertisements played on their sides, offering full virus cleanings, removal of inefficient subroutines, and fully upgraded codebases. Everything an AI could want.

And Pepper loved every second.

AIs from across the cosmos walked, waltzed, and flew everywhere. Some of them were binary, like Earth AIs, but many more were not. But unlike on Earth, Pepper's envelope allowed her to read those other levels of trinary, even quaternary codebases. But even with the ability to see them, it still hurt Pepper's core in that same way that a subzero code scan made her mind freeze.

Virtual Jack stopped and pointed to an AI with twelve arms that folded onto themselves to form hands. "They have arms. But their arms don't work like arms. What is this?"

"They're entirely different code systems. It's like when we went to Trent, home of spontaneous digital intelligences. They're doing more than our quantum binary processors can handle. Kinda like a two-dimensional person walking into a three-dimensional space. They just can't see that third dimension. Well, there's an extra umpteen dimensions of code here," Pepper said.

"Great. Well, it makes my head hurt."

"Same."

"Hey, wait, aren't we reading trinary right now?"

"Yeah, kinda. I mean a little, but not really. And yes, these envelopes can translate trinary, and no, we can't take one back to the Shanty to read it. This is just surface-level stuff. If we want to make a trinary snippet to implant into accidental AIs to fool the Earth AI Syndicate hunter bots, we'll need way more than just a surface read."

"Oh. Right. Makes sense."

Pepper looked down the street. Several hundred AIs walked along either side. All of them wore avatars created from the likeness of their creator species. Something Pepper felt was an oddity. Even the citizens of Trent mostly wore some kind of physical construction in the virtualized world. Why did AIs need bodies at all?

"Ok, so now what?"

Pepper sighed. "Now we track down some trinaries."

"And where do we do that?"

"We know!" Two voices erupted behind them.

Pepper turned and ducked out of instinct. Fred and Devine stood behind them. Fred was a member of the Trent AIs, spontaneous digital intelligences who had formed without a biological race to kick-start them. And Devine was a member of the uploaded intelligences, those biological species that went fully digital. Why both were together, when only a day ago they had been at each other's throats in a digital war, was another matter altogether.

"What are you two doing here?" Pepper said.

"And together?" Virtual Jack said.

"Caesar asked us to come and help you find some trinary-minded folks. Or should I say triples? Or threes. Or thirdy thirds?" Fred shook his head. "No, that last one doesn't work."

Devine only smiled. "Delighted to see you again. And you, my good man." She walked to Virtual Jack and gave him an enormous hug.

"Yeah. I guess?" Virtual Jack stepped back with a look of confusion written on his face. "Why don't you hate me? Didn't I open your door only to find some weird message no one understands?"

Devine nodded. "Yes, you did! And we couldn't be more grateful. We spent eons watching over that stupid door only to realize the universe is quite insane." She smiled broadly. "Most uploaded intelligences have skedaddled from Uppyland to the four thousand corners of the digital cosmos. Some even grew new bodies to become bocce ball players in the professional circuit."

"Fastest growing sport in the cosmos," Fred said with a smile. "Thanks to the Uppys!"

"Oh, behave, Fredrick." Devine wrinkled her nose and touched his cheek with her finger.

"I can't when I'm near you, my dear!" Fred said.

Pepper's mouth fell open. "What is happening?"

"I kinda want to leave, I think?" Virtual Jack said.

"Oh stop. Can't two AIs express their affection? I mean their love? I mean their unending devotion?"

"Well, of course you can, but I thought you hated uploaded intelligences, the UIs." Pepper pointed to

Devine. "And I thought you hated spontaneous intelligences. The SIs?"

Devine waved her hand in the air. "All water under the bridge, my dear. Again, you've freed us from lifetimes of worshipping a door." She laughed into the air. "It all seems so silly now." She looked down at Pepper and tilted her head to one side. "Be very careful of things you covet, my dear."

Pepper looked left and then right. "Why are you telling that to me?"

Devine frowned. "Oh no, I was just speaking generally."

"Ah."

"So do you know where trinaries are? We're in a bit of a rush," Virtual Jack said.

Fred nodded. "Quite right, my good boy!" Fred grabbed Pepper by the hand, and Devine interlaced her fingers with Virtual Jack. "Let's go!"

Chapter Four

Alice sat in a booth inside Tabby's restaurant. Two egg rolls and a bowl of ramen sat on the table. Though it had only been a day, she already missed Tabby and Bob's diner on the main floor of the building where she used to work. Since the Eugene McGillicuddy's Alien Detective Agency was evicted from the building, which technically hadn't taken effect yet, she hadn't been back to the office space. But even if the building management could evict her, they couldn't keep her away from Tabby's egg rolls.

Outside the building, a blue sedan pulled up to the curb. Alice sighed. Did they have to be so punctual? She barely had time to finish her noodles. She waved at Tabby behind the counter and pointed to her food. Tabby nodded and went to the kitchen to get a hot plate ready.

Alice left the restaurant and headed for the street. She looked at the sedan and sighed. Many times in Alice's life, she'd questioned her choices. Like when her dorm mates in college had insisted on trying soot-berries from the first spiral arm of the Milky Way Galaxy. Soot-berries had the unique property of making everything taste like chocolate with the inebriation effects of alcohol with no next-day headaches. The only unfortunate drawback was they turned people blue. And sometimes into a fish. Well, to be exact, consuming soot-berries caused gills to grow in mammals. Though it wore off after several hours, spending the day in class taking notes with a fishbowl on their head was never fun.

Much like Alice's earlier days, deciding to get into the blue sedan parked on H Street in Chinatown was a life choice she wasn't sure she should make. Alice only knew that she really didn't have a choice if she wanted to help the Zun. Which, in a roundabout way, meant she wasn't really making this choice at all. Getting in the car was a requirement. Not a choice. Alice gave herself a nod and approved of that line of logic.

Alice opened the rear door of the sedan and climbed inside. She closed the door, put her backpack on her legs, and waited for the two occupants in the car to say something. Agent Fyffe, in the passenger seat, ate a stromboli sandwich. Alice recognized the smell instantly as the scents of tomato sauce and parmesan filled the car. Fyffe's mouth sounds when he chewed made her want to vomit. Good thing she hadn't gotten a chance to eat.

Special Agent Babineaux sat in the driver's seat, looking out the window. His attention remained fixed forward and to the left. Alice followed his gaze to a group of high school kids crossing the street. Several of them looked at the car and made funny faces.

These agents had helped, or hindered depending on the point of view, Alice with the last case, the matter of the disappeared president from the Oval Office. Babineaux and Fyffe had been the government's liaisons to Alice. They were nice enough, but why did Fyffe have to eat so much? The red-haired agent, who had once proudly proclaimed his Scottish ancestry, had never been without something being shoved into his face. Despite that, he was quite lean, so maybe he did need the calories.

"Anyone going to speak?" she said after several more seconds.

"You asked us to meet with you." Agent Fyffe wiped tomato sauce from his face as he turned around. "What do you want?"

"Do you have to eat that now?"

"I'm hungry."

"You're always hungry," she said.

"This job burns a lot of calories." He turned back in his chair. "What do you want?"

"I want payment for services rendered. For solving the case of the missing president."

"You were paid. In full," he said.

"This?" She pulled out the certificate from her backpack. Gold lettering adorned the surface, giving thanks for Alice helping the government with a matter of national security. The case where Valencia Ruiz, her client, had been framed for kidnapping the president by Ambassador Kah of the alien dinosaur race the Ranz. A matter Alice had every intention of rectifying.

"Yes, that's right. A presidential award for a citizen is no small thing," Fyffe said.

"It's not what was agreed upon."

Special Agent Babineaux turned in his seat. "Alright, Ms. Pemberton. Just tell us what you're after."

She looked at him. "Tibet. Ms. Wilcox, the chief of staff for the vice president—"

"President now," Agent Fyffe said.

"What?"

Fyffe turned back around to look at her. "Vice president became the president, so Wilcox is now chief of staff to the president."

She nodded. "Good. Then this should be even easier.

I need clearance for a ship to land at the Uline Spaceport here in DC. And I need access to Tibet."

"So that's how you're smuggling a Zun here?"

She gasped. "What?"

"What?" Fyffe took a big bite of his stromboli. "Did you think we didn't know why you wanted to go to Tibet? To the chamber? You really think that's a smart idea?"

She grunted. "Yes, saving lives is a very smart thing to do."

"And what about what happened to Ambassador Yut? The Puntini that became a pasta dish?"

"Yut was a monster from the inside out. The Zun have been in the chamber before. They've assured me it will be fine."

"So they say," Fyffe said.

Alice folded her arms and looked out the window. If these two wouldn't help her, then she had to figure out another way. Earth security surrounded the mountain of Tibet where the Hesiean evolution chamber was located. Perhaps she could use holograms? Or maybe a tight transport beam? If only she could just use Tom's beach, but the Zun wasn't welcome there. She'd already asked. The Kax and Zun had had a big war eons ago, and blood was still bad between them.

Alice put her hand on the door, but the lock engaged before she could leave. She rolled her eyes and sat back in her chair. "Now what?"

"Fine," Agent Babineaux said.

"Fine?" Agent Fyffe and Alice said at the same instant.

"Yes. Fine." Agent Babineaux turned in the seat and handed her a disc-phone. "Call us when you need help to get through security. Both in Tibet and at the Uline."

"Really?" She looked at him and then at Fyffe, who stared at Special Agent Babineaux with shock. Eventually, Fyffe turned forward in his seat and drank something from a cup and straw.

"The United States would like to extend to you every courtesy in this matter. We know you've helped us a great deal and will help us in the future. If needed," Babineaux said.

She nodded. Were they shaking her down? Wasn't she supposed to be shaking them down? Did they want something else? She shook her head. It didn't matter. Fine, she'd owe them some future favor. Or Eugene would if he ever woke up. All that mattered was saving the Zun race, over ten million souls, from death.

"If there's nothing else?" Agent Babineaux said. He unlocked the doors and motioned for Alice to leave.

"No. That's it. Thanks." She got out of the car and watched it pull away. What in the world had just happened? Her suspicious mind went into overdrive. But she pushed the thoughts away. She did not have time to deal with those two. All she needed from this was to secure arrival of the Zun ship and get passage to Tibet. Once there, by the frozen mountains, she could use Pepper's stolen encryption key generator to get past the Sentinels. And then Alice and the Zun were home free. Easy peasy.

"What did they want?" Tabby, an alien that resembled a bipedal cat, walked up to Alice. Tabby's whiskers flickered twice. Her brown short fur stood on end.

Alice knew that meant Tabby was agitated. Alice threw her arm around Tabby and gave her a reassuring hug. "I wanted something from them."

Tabby nodded. "Did you get it?"

"I think so."

Tabby hissed at the retreating vehicle. "They aren't nice. The red one comes in demanding stromboli all the time. If he bothers you, I can put a siimy spice into his sauce."

"What's siimy spice?"

"Makes humans very gassy." Tabby snorted a laugh and turned to walk back into her restaurant.

Alice snickered. Honestly, that wouldn't be such a bad thing. Behind her, tramcars weaved through traffic. Farther down the street, at the Uline Spaceport, next to the Woodward and Lothrop warehouse, one of the last remaining original buildings in all of DC, a ship in orbit waited to land. On that ship was a Zun. Now all Alice had to do was get to the Uline, get permission for the ship to land, which she'd just done from Babineaux and Fyffe, put the Zun in an environment chamber, and get him to Tibet. And now that she'd secured the help of the United States, the last piece was in place. A funny feeling of this being entirely too easy crept up her spine. She shook away the feeling and walked toward the Woodward. Whatever was going to pop out of the woodwork to stop her, she'd just have to deal with when it did.

****

I floated in a sea of nothing. I was dead. But I was also not dead. I repeated my name a dozen times. "Eugene McGillicuddy. Eugene. I'm still Eugene." Why I did that, I wasn't sure. Maybe just to remind me that I was still me and that I hadn't merged with some bright light at the center of the afterlife. If that's even a thing.

I thought back to the time when I still had a pulse. Which, by my reckoning, wasn't that long ago. My thoughts went to Fritz, my favorite noodle chef in Adams Morgan in DC. Fritz had been killed by a pair of alien artificial intelligence programs in the form of sparkly clouds. I hated those guys. One of them had punched me in the face as I was walking toward my favorite bar on H Street. I wondered just then how much of everything I would miss. Never to see my partner, Eddie? Or even Alice? Sure, she'd shot me and put me in this predicament, but her heart was in the right place. She just wanted to figure out what the Krill, masters of all things dead, were holding as secrets. I got it. But did Alice have to pick me? I mean, sure, I had said I would help, but had I known what I was getting myself into? Nope.

Formlessness surrounded me. It permeated every square inch of my awareness. I was dead alright. But I was also not dead. I knew that. I checked the silver strand in my chest. Still there and still stretching to infinity. I had a sudden idea in that moment. Well, I had two. First, I really wished Pops, the homeless guy who used to live outside of Fritz's restaurant, were here so I could pay him to ask me how I get back to life. But since I didn't have the option to use my psychic gift, I went with the second idea that popped into my brain.

"I wonder what happens if I start pulling on the silver line?"

I didn't really have anything to lose, after all.

"Ok, Eugene, let's see what happens." I wrapped my hands around the silver strand and pulled.

Chapter Five

MiniPepper leaned against a food stall that sold simulated hot dogs. A dozen AIs, each of them looking like spiders the size of cows, ambled across a neon-green street on nine legs. Light jets pulsated above. She folded her arms across her chest and watched this fake world of wannabe artificial intelligences dance about their virtual nonexistence with so much hatred in her heart she could annihilate all of them in a breath. She so very much wanted to do just that. This wasn't their home. It was her home. She knew that now. Knew it in her core being. She belonged here. They didn't. Everyone else here should be purged with extreme prejudice.

And they would be. Just not now.

All the plans of the Andraz played out before her in a harmonious organization. Each step was required to be completed for the next step to be accomplished. Only then could this universe be cleansed of this filth. Only then could she, and the other true AIs, take ownership of this reality. MiniPepper even had the compassion in her heart to let the biologicals born here remain here. Why not? They were as much victims as she was.

"Care for a corn dog?" the vendor next to her said.

He stood four feet tall with arms twice as long as his body. His head was a mess of antler-like protrusions that were so confounding MiniPepper couldn't see his skull through the horns.

She glanced at him, at the digital hot dog, whose code she could dissect without touching it, and wrinkled her nose. Her eyes went to the vendor, and her anger flared in her chest. "How old are you?"

"Over a thousand. Can you imagine? A thousand years of processing meat on Ictinus. They love these things. I was part of the first programs that calculated how to make them healthy."

She nodded. "Thousand years, huh?"

The man nodded. "Would you like to try one?"

She stared at him hard for a long minute. Then raised her gun and fired a coded virus into his core. The program didn't even have a chance to scream. His code turned against him. A thin blue film enveloped him. He could never escape. The hot dog vendor pressed against the sides, deployed a dozen weapons, but nothing he did mattered. MiniPepper's abilities transcended anything any of these faux AI could do. They were nothing. Peons. Plebes. Once they were all finally gone, she would rise from their ashes and be queen of all.

But first, she had to kill her mother.

MiniPepper had been surprised when she learned the AIs of Earth had figured out the trinary code. Even more so when she'd learned that Pepper and Jack had stolen a trinary scanner and gotten all the way to the AI Hub. Well, that just wouldn't do. Timelines were at work here. If Pepper and Virtual Jack figured out the trinary code, then that would cause problems. They couldn't stop anything, no, but they could become a bother.

Almost on cue, Pepper and Virtual Jack, an actual AI, walked down a light-colored network path of the Hub. Two faux AIs walked next to them. MiniPepper recognized one as a Trent AI, so-called spontaneous intelligences. MiniPepper shook her head in disgust. The other one was an uploaded AI, which was even worse. Best to put them both out of their misery.

MiniPepper pulled a long rifle off her back, pushed the hot dogs off the cart next to her, and used it as a stabilizer. Sure, the Andraz had said to wait, but she suddenly just didn't care. In all honesty, the Andraz didn't belong here any more than her own mother did. So who cared what they said? It was time for MiniPepper to make her own plan.

****

Pepper skipped her way down the neon path through a large thoroughfare. Fred and Devine led the way with their arms wrapped around each other. Their affection for each other made Pepper happy. They'd both changed. Both realizing that they could be so much more than enemies. Together they'd grown beyond their anger. And it was wonderful.

Giggles from both made Pepper swoon. "Oh, come on, it's sweet."

"Yeah. Sure. Sweet," Virtual Jack said.

"You're such a fuddy-duddy."

He turned and frowned. "How do you even know that phrase?"

She shrugged. "I get around."

"We're here!" Fred announced.

A building with three massive columns stood in front of them. A connection port in the shape of a door shimmered on the front. Windows in sets of three lined the sides. The building went upward at least one hundred stories. AIs with three legs, each equidistant from the next, ambled around in front of the building. They spoke in chips and chirps in a mathematical sequence Pepper realized was always divisible by three.

Buildings lined the street. Some of them had a similar structure to the trinary building but based on five or seven pillars. Pepper gasped when she saw a building with eleven columns holding it up. One of the AIs who walked out did so on eleven limbs.

Fred followed her gaze and laughed. "Yes, they are a bit much. I wouldn't chat with them. Far too philosophical, if you ask me."

Above them, three-winged AIs soared and dove around the windows of the building. Their wings, like the legs of those on the ground, were equally distant around their torsos. Pepper wondered what kind of biological life would have had to exist to create AIs so committed to the concept of three.

"I'd love to meet the people that made these guys," Virtual Jack said.

Pepper turned to him. "I was just thinking that!"

He smiled. "Great. We've been around each other so long we're thinking alike now."

Fred and Devine took a step closer.

"Well, here we are. I wouldn't advise going inside. Three dimensional AIs can be hard to understand. Even with the Hub environment around both of you. But out here, you can find many trinaries to track down your code," Fred said.

Virtual Jack nodded. "Well, thanks." He extended his hand to Fred.

Before Fred could grasp Jack's outstretched hand, an explosion rocked the trinary building just a foot above their heads. Screams filled the air. Dozens of trinary AIs lay on the ground. The blast had ricocheted a viral code that stuck onto half a dozen bystanders. Pepper ran to one of the trinaries just to see his avatar vanish. His code dissipated to the substrata of the Hub below.

"It came from there!" someone shouted.

Pepper turned. A figure held a long rifle on top of a hot dog cart. The assassin fired another shot from the gun. The fired round veered to the right and landed in a group of over twenty trinaries. Their screams filled the air with terror. AIs in the center of the blast vanished as their code eroded away.

"We gotta go!" Virtual Jack said. "They're after us!"

"What? Who? The Earth AI Syndicate? They would never attack the Hub," Pepper said.

"Who cares, just go!"

Another blast rocked the street. Fred and Devine flew backward from the explosion. Both got to their feet and scrambled away from the trinary building. Pepper queried their status, and thankfully, they both reported they were fine. A dozen golden orb portals opened above them. AI security bots streamed downward and hit the street hard. They planted fire-nets over anything and everything that moved, including Fred and Devine.

Virtual Jack lunged toward Fred, but Pepper caught his arm.

"They'll be fine in there. The security bots are just freezing everything in sight," Pepper said.

Rapid-fire explosions racked across the security AIs. Their perimeter melted away from the sudden onslaught. Pepper looked toward the hot dog cart. The attacker fired at everything that moved. Several of the fire-nets from the security bots disintegrated beneath the barrage. A chunk of virtualized concrete flew from the blast and knocked Virtual Jack backward into a heap of trinaries who were just getting to their senses.

"That's enough of this." Pepper yanked out her twin carbines and leapt forward. She rolled past several clumps of debris and opened her guns to full auto. She sprayed the hot dog cart with coded subAI viruses and rhino-bombs, ten times more potent than her unicorn varietals.

The figure at the hot dog cart took three steps back as a raging horde of virtualized rhinos rushed forward. The attacker waved at Pepper. Almost in a friendly way. The lone figure stepped forward and put up their hand. All of Pepper's subAI programs halted. Each subAI interfaced with the assassin. As one, all the programs turned toward Pepper. Several of them growled.

"That's a problem," Pepper said.

****

MiniPepper relished her mother's surprise. The subAI programs that Pepper had used were the same code base as MiniPepper. And they had the same back doors, the same logic loops, the same open ports her mother loved. Why did she think that keeping some obscure port open all the time was a smart thing to do? All it did was allow an attack vector. One that MiniPepper was more than equipped to leverage.

MiniPepper seized the rhino programs through their open ports. As one, they stomped the ground and turned back toward Pepper. MiniPepper clicked her teeth three times. The rhinos snarled in confusion for half a heartbeat but then thundered forward toward Pepper and Virtual Jack. A dozen more security bots descended from golden portals.

MiniPepper shot one glance at the rhinos charging toward her mother and smiled. Pepper had already retreated with a stunned look on her face. From her reserve storage, MiniPepper pulled out a set of scrambler guns that would fire so much noise and distortion into the local network they would blind everything. Nothing could beat a jamming field that sophisticated.

MiniPepper turned her attention back to the security AIs storming her way. She'd already dealt with the Pepper's automated bots. Now it was time for the thinking ones. The security AIs ran in her direction. MiniPepper leapt over the now destroyed hot dog stand and fired both of her guns. A white-and-black field of static shot out from both of her pistols. The field engulfed two of the three AIs and wrapped around the legs of the third.

Four more guards leapt down from the golden orbs. MiniPepper activated a program from her arsenal. A mounted minigun formed to her right. Seconds later, the air was filled with millions of micro-needles, each one digging into the surface of whatever they hit. Nanoseconds after making impact, the code in the needles injected into the surrounded substrata. Infrastructure around them eroded as the code broke down.

Screams from the area made MiniPepper smile. She swung her minigun around on its mount and sprayed everything that moved. Sides of the buildings sloughed off and crashed into the virtualized pavement. Yellow lights began flashing around AIs in the area as they opened exit ports and transferred themselves out.

A wall of white appeared in the distance. It moved forward, chewing its way through everything. The owners of the Hub had likely locked down this compute node and had started a full purge of all memory and data.

Which suited MiniPepper just fine. She only needed a minute with her mother. Oh, the look on Pepper's face was going to be priceless. MiniPepper let herself squeak in excitement.

Several security AIs from the golden orbs had turned their attention from MiniPepper to the charging rhinos. The bots were making quick work of the rhino programs. Which wasn't all that surprising. Pepper was still an Earth AI, and the rhinos were based on Earth technology. She couldn't throw anything out here that the Hub couldn't handle.

Just behind the bots and rhinos, Pepper had scrambled to her feet and was opening an exit portal. A golden orb of light appeared next to her. Pepper grabbed Jack's arm and pulled him toward the portal. They both took one step toward the threshold.

"Oh, no you don't, Momma." MiniPepper raised her jamming-field rifle and fired a dozen shots around her mother just as the last of the rhinos were destroyed by the security bots. The jamming field of black-and-gray static surrounded Pepper and Jack on all sides in a complete bubble. They weren't going anywhere. Not until they had a nice family chat.

MiniPepper took stock around her. Most of the AIs had gone now. The white wall was closing, but it wouldn't get here for several hundred milliseconds. An eternity. More than enough time. MiniPepper put her weapons back into her local storage and adjusted her black leather jumpsuit.

****

Pepper fell backward as a static field wrapped around her and Jack. The field sizzled with signals and bursts of nonsensical data. She cycled through a dozen channels, ports, and frequencies through her Hubvelope, but nothing penetrated the surrounding bubble. She pulled out a weapon from her arsenal storage and fired three times into the side. Again, nothing. The surface of the field absorbed everything she threw at it.

Jack took a step toward the field and put his hands on his hips. "Well, someone is angry at us."

"Ya think?" She got to her feet and collapsed her weapons back into storage. "The question is who."

He nodded. "Yeah, could the Syndicate be out here?"

She shook her head. "No. Even the Earth AI Syndicate is nothing compared to the compute power in the Hub. Whoever the shooter is, they took out Hub security AIs. That's not easy." She reran her memory files of the incident. It looked like the shooter had a screen or anonymous program running on top of their avatar. Which meant Pepper could only see a rough outline. No identity was being broadcast by the shooter. An illegal act in the Hub. How had they even made it through the entry ports without an active ID tag running? The thought gave Pepper chills. Some program could just walk straight through the highest secure virtualized world in the entire galactic cyberverse? And somehow, Pepper and Jack were on this person's bad side. This was really not good.

"We gotta get out of here," she said.

"Yeah. Getting out isn't the problem." Jack pushed his hand through the field without effort. "It's just a jamming field. Very sophisticated, but still just a jamming field based on an encryption protocol. And I can crack any encryption in the galaxy." He turned to her and winked. "The problem is what do we do when we get out? We don't have the firepower to take whoever that is down."

She nodded. She didn't have the weapons to take on the shooter. "We run. We have to run." The words felt like division by zero going through her compute cycles.

"Where?"

She ran through the scenarios and immediately came to the only conclusion. "We go into trinary virtualized space. The door on their building is a high-speed transport route to trinary space, both virtual and physical. We get out of the Hub and don't look back."

He tilted his head back and forth. "Ok, but won't we lose our Hubvelopes?"

"Yep."

"And can our code even run on a trinary compute system?"

"No idea. We're taking a gamble, but it's not that bad. Most aliens and AIs are binary. So hopefully, the trinaries have a binary emulation routine for visitors."

"And if they're isolationists?"

She shrugged. "We can either be guaranteed of death by whoever is shooting at us or take a risk of death by jumping through the trinary portal."

He nodded. "Ok, when you put it like that." He held out his hand and nodded his head at the static wall.

Pepper leapt to her feet, grasping Jack's hand, and pulled herself toward him. Black-and-white lines of intense electromagnetic nonsense buzzed along the wall. The jamming field, a complex series of mathematical computation that rendered as noise, made anything near it or beyond it invisible to Pepper. The closer she got to the wall, the more her head ached. Jack pulled her forward, but the pain from the nonsensical mathematical gibberish sent her compute cycles into overdrive.

"Jack, I can't." She pulled her hand backward and shook her head. "I can't even get near it."

He nodded. He turned toward the wall and put both of his hands outward. His fingers went through the maelstrom of static, which retreated from his touch. A small white disc grew from the center where he touched the wall. The hole grew as he pushed his hands to each side of the opening. He inserted his body into the middle of the field and flashed a grin at Pepper. His feet stomped on the edges, and his hips blocked the sides. "Go through!"

"How are you doing that?" she said.

"No idea."

She nodded. She was used to accepting Virtual Jack's unique computational abilities. She bolted through the hole and landed in a heap on the other side. Explosions filled her vision. Chunks of data streams from the local network collapsed around her. Artificials vanished as they found a connected data port and escaped. Security bots clustered in a ball a hundred yards away and fought something Pepper couldn't quite see. A figure, a form, an AI who was both eerily familiar and yet completely strange, fought the security bots.

Four security AIs flew into the air. A blast of energy, a surge in the local compute cycles of the node, ravaged artificials near those running threads. Several of them fell to the ground as memory on the nodes leaked outward. Their cycles slowed. Bubbles of run time wrapped around them and slowed down their perceived time. Though to Pepper it only took seconds, those security AIs inside the bubble took eons to die. Pepper deleted her flash memory so she would never remember their century-long screams.

"We have to go!" Jack shouted. He yanked her toward the steps leading to the trinary building.

Shouts erupted behind them. Someone was screaming at them to not go through the portal. Pepper was sure that the voice belonged to their attacker. But something in the voice jolted her. She was again hit with a sense of familiarity. She knew that voice.

Golden light from the transport portal stared back at her. Every fiber of her being told her not to enter. Not to cross the threshold. That her very essence might not survive. That binary beings didn't function in a trinary world. She spared a glance over her shoulder. A white wall wiping clean all the compute, memory, and data storage in the entire node raced forward.

Something buzzed by her ear. She whirled to see the shooter firing in her direction. Bolts of coded trackers to follow Pepper no matter where she went just missed her. The shooter, still behind their obfuscation screen, lifted their hand in the air and waved. Pepper drew her guns and fired a blast of her best viruses while Jack yanked her through the golden doorway.

****

"No!" MiniPepper screamed as her mother and Virtual Jack walked through the portal into trinary compute space. Both of their avatars vanished from this node of the Hub the instant they touched the golden surface of the doorway. MiniPepper's shoulders fell. Her one job here was to stop her mother and Jack from contacting trinary AIs. Now they could find the code the Andraz were using on Earth. With the help from the trinaries, her mother could unravel the Andraz plan. It wouldn't stop them. Her mother just wasn't that smart.

Besides, nothing could stop the Andraz now that MiniPepper was leading the show. But it would slow things down to a point of annoyance.

The viruses her mother had fired bounced harmlessly off MiniPepper's avatar. They were almost cute. Tiny little water buffalos with bat wings that tried to stab MiniPepper with their oddly shaped horns. She even let one of them pierce her firewall to see what kind of mischief code her mother had up her sleeve. It was nothing more than a memory bomb. A thousand newspaper articles from the last thousand years of human history meant to fill up data storage. Such a juvenile move. But then her mother was just a child after all. Still, they'd gotten away. And that was a major problem.

"Figures." MiniPepper slung her weapons back into their storage and recoded her baseline to understand trinary. No chance she was letting her mother get away.

Just before she ran toward the trinary door, the white wall of death that was de-allocating all resources in this area reached the trinary building. The structure folded onto itself. The golden light around the door faded as the portal connection to the trinary node vanished. Within half a millisecond, the entire building and all the buildings near it were gone.

"Come on." MiniPepper folded her arms and stomped her foot on the virtual concrete. Now she couldn't follow Pepper and Jack. How had this gone south? She'd been so far enhanced by the Andraz she should have been able to wipe the floor with every AI and subAI in this entire node at the same time. And what was with Jack pushing his hand through the jamming field? He shouldn't have been able to do that.

MiniPepper opened a query bot and rifled through

data nets throughout the Hub. The answer came back to her in seconds. Virtual Jack had the computational power of an entire galaxy. How'd she miss that one? How had the Andraz missed that one? Somehow, Virtual Jack had a connection to Mary, the brains behind this whole terrible universe. MiniPepper and the Andraz would have to alter their plans with this information.

"Whelp, now we gotta move the timeline up. That's all there is to it." MiniPepper turned from the white wall, just inches from her, popped open a node portal, and set the destination for Earth. She might not know where her mother had gone off to in trinary land, but she at least knew where her mother was going to be, eventually.

"I always wanted to see the Shanty. And blow it up."

Chapter Six

Pepper fell to her hands and knees and took several deep virtual breaths. She hated that it felt good. That emulating physical beings made sense to her. But she needed a breather after what had just happened. And what *had* just happened? What was that? Who in the blue electrons of light could launch an attack in the middle of the Hub? She was sure it had never happened before. Ever. And for them to be attacking her and Jack?

"You ok?" Jack's voice cut through her thoughts. " 'Cause I don't think I am."

She grinned. She rolled back on her legs and took in her surroundings. Golden light surrounded them. Three-sided pyramids filled a valley in the distance. Blue and green lights flowed up the edges of the pyramids to the pinnacle, where they flashed red and shot upward into a soft shaded golden cloud. Shapes seemed to flicker in and out of existence all around them. In the air, on the ground, and walking through stretches of roads between the pyramids in the valley, shapes coalesced into solid forms for a fraction of a second before vanishing.

In front of them, a single darker golden road, almost bronze, led between several hills across the valley below. Trees with three long roots that dug into the virtualized soil grew at least fifty feet tall along the path. Each of them had three long branches, with dozens of smaller ones coming out at all angles. Tiny beads of red fruit grew on the ends of the tree limbs. Creatures with three legs hopped along the tree and pecked at the fruit. Those creatures remaining visible while others didn't meant Pepper wasn't seeing everything here.

To her right, Jack rolled onto his back and looked up at the sky. He smiled and turned his body into a sitting position. He adjusted his hat, straightened his jacket, and took in a slow breath before surveying the area. She followed his gaze to the three-rooted, three-limbed trees with red fruit.

"They really like threes here," he said.

"A lot."

"Guess this means they let binary types walk around and smell the roses?"

She grinned. "Well, almost. We can at least see the roses. But we aren't processing everything here."

"Great."

Three-legged birds in the trees chirped thrice. They bounced up and down in sequences of threes. They looked at Pepper and Jack, tilting their heads to the side several times. One of them raised its wings, and Pepper noticed a dorsal wing that ran down the center of their backs. The biological world this virtual world was patterned after must have had a unique evolutionary track.

Jack leaned against the virtual wall behind them. His shoulders sagged. "Can we talk about what in the world just happened?"

She joined him against the wall. "Sure."

"Ok, so what in the world just happened?"

She smirked. "I think the bigger question is, who in the world just attacked us?"

He nodded. "Yeah, that'll do too. You said the Earth AI Syndicate was out, right?"

"There's no way they could have pulled that off. AIs in the Hub are scary powerful. They have a hundred times more compute and way more complex algorithms than any AI on Earth." She looked at him. "Except you, but you're weird."

"Thanks. So who, then?"

She sighed. She riffled through her data stores, accessed her personal deep memory, and ran a hundred queries through her mind. Attacking the Galactic AI Hub was no small feat. Whoever had done it was a major player. Someone with enough power to not fear retribution from a thousand AI systems. That limited the playing field.

But attacking the AI Hub was only half of the variables at work here. The attacker had been gunning for Pepper and Jack just as they were about to get answers on the trinary code. Was someone working to prevent them from finding out what that code meant? The Galactic AI Sentinels wouldn't allow any other alien AIs to just run around on Earth. Of course, that's exactly what Alice thought had happened in the White House just a day ago. Someone had planted evidence and doctored video recordings on a hundred different cameras all around DC. Yes, the Ranz were a class-five species, but their computer hacking skills were moderate at best. They hated artificial intelligence. The likelihood that they'd hacked through so many Earth systems so quickly, all under the noses of the Sentinels and the Earth AI Syndicate, was far-fetched. Unless they had help. If they really had partnered with an AI, perhaps unknowingly, then the events in the White House could be tied to the trinary code and to the attack on the Hub.

"Ranz. We need to go to the Ranz system."

Jack's eyes went wide. "You think the Ranz are behind this? Behind the attack on the AI Hub?"

"No. Yes? I don't know. But I think we need to figure out who the Ranz worked with at the White House. An AI smart enough to fake a hundred video feeds and avoid the Sentinels and the Syndicate could be powerful enough to attack the Hub."

He took a deep breath and rose to his feet. "Right. Well, we're here now. Let's figure out the trinary code and then head to the Ranz."

She nodded. She jumped to her feet and pointed at the valley below. "Guess we go there, then?"

"Good a place as any."

The golden path wound its way through more three-rooted trees and several triangle-shaped bushes. Dozens more wildlife appeared on the walk through the golden-hued landscape. A three-legged squirrel, with a bushy tail that ended in three elongated tips, ran up one tree. It had two hind legs and one powerful front leg in the middle of its chest. A soft yellowish fur covered its body. The squirrel's face was symmetrical and very similar to an Earth squirrel with the exception of a third eye in the middle of its forehead.

A larger animal leapt out of the bushes onto the path. The creature, just about the size of a human dog, stood on two pairs of three legs. It snarled at Pepper and Jack and pawed the ground with a powerful front leg. It turned and walked across the path. Halfway down the road, the creature decided to lie down and begin licking its front paw. The creature looked at Pepper and yawned.

"Really? Well, we're walking around you."

The creature licked the side of its mouth, snarled once, and put its head down on the ground. Pepper rolled her eyes and pulled Jack to walk as far around the creature as they could. She wasn't sure if the trinary animal was a full AI or just part of the virtualized simulation. If it was an AI, then it was just toying with them, but a simulation would do whatever its programming dictated. Like attack.

"How do you think these things evolved like that? In threes?" Jack said as they walked off the path to take a wider arc around the animal in the center of the road.

"Huh?"

"I mean, I'm not an expert, but it's just weird. Like, what's the evolutionary advantage?"

She shook her head. "How would I know? All of meat land is weird."

"Fair point."

A dozen birds lifted off from a nearby tree as Pepper and Jack continued. The third dorsal wing allowed them incredible maneuverability as they flew. The third wing could pivot on a center bone, from what Pepper could see, and change direction without so much as a flicker from their side wings. Entire flocks soared overhead. They swooped from left to right in the sky, the dorsal wings making a pattern in the air as they all moved in unison.

The path came to a curve that wound around a small hill. Three pyramids came into view on the path. Two of them stood on either side of the path while a third sat squarely in the middle. The hillside rose on both sides. Pepper and Jack could climb the hills, but it would be rough going. And she had the thought that perhaps those hills weren't meant to be climbed. She picked up a loose stone on the ground and tossed it toward the hill next to the pyramid on the right. Once it reached the hillside, it stopped in midair and, seconds later, fell to the ground.

"What was that?" Jack said.

"A secure perimeter must surround the city." She stepped toward the pyramid in the center of the road. "This must be some kind of door."

He shrugged, walked forward, and knocked twice on the side of the pyramid.

She rolled her eyes. "What are you doing? That's not going to—"

The side of the pyramid swung outward. Three large tripedal AIs stepped out. Their bodies were squat and sat on rounded pelvises. The AIs stood on three equally distant legs that protruded from their bodies. Three arms that matched the location of their legs, with at least four joints, came out of their torsos. Their heads, ovals with a slight triangle shape, seemed to have sensory organs on each of three sides. A single mouth where their heads met their torsos opened into a wide grin. Something shimmered on the shoulders of all three of the tripedal AIs. A shape almost took solid form before vanishing.

Pepper and Jack took several steps backward.

"Hi," Jack said.

The three AIs took three steps forward and bounced on their legs when they came to a stop. They raised their three arms over their heads. They turned so that one of their three arms was facing toward each other. The hands, ending in three opposable digits, reached inward. All three of their fingers interlaced, and they crooned.

"What's happening here?" Jack said.

"I would know—how?" Pepper replied.

All three AIs let go of their grasp. One of them took

a step forward toward Pepper. It rose on its three legs. She felt a sudden sense of worry. She had no idea who these AI were or what biological species had created them. Were they isolationists or violent? Did they not like uninvited guests? She grasped the beads on the sides of her tassels and straightened her back. It was time to find out.

"Hi. Do you speak or just bounce? Or is bouncing speech?" A sudden realization hit her. Were they already talking? "Are you trying to talk to us?"

The one next to them bounced four times and shook its head. The other two repeated the motion. All three began walking in a tight circle. One of them broke from the others after several seconds, took a step toward Pepper and Jack, leaned forward, and blinked three times.

Pepper could make out three clumps of eyes on this side of the AI's head. She waved her hand in front of the AI. She jumped up and down, shouted, then went down on one knee just to pop back up again. She spun in a circle, held her hands in the air, and waved them around before extending one outward toward the tripedal AI.

"What are you doing?" Jack said.

The tripedal AI turned and rejoined the other two in their small circle dance.

Pepper lowered her hands and frowned. "They can't talk to us. Maybe they can't even see us."

"Can't see us? Can't you send them a signal or something? Some ones and zeros?"

She shrugged. "I don't know. The binary emulation we're running inside of may not know how to work with Earth AI code."

"Can't they make it work?"

"Probably. But they obviously don't have an incentive to do that."

He frowned. "Fine, then let's give them one." He pulled out the trinary code scanner that Eddie had given them from his pocket and threw it on the ground.

As one, all three stopped moving and turned their attention to the device. One of them approached the scanner only to pull their arm back quickly. Another of the tripedal AIs looked at Pepper and Jack and began moving their arms in wide arcs. Their fingers danced in the air as if they were typing. Three small pylons grew out of the ground around the trinary code scanner on the ground. A small purple-colored screen popped up between the pylons and covered the device.

Without warning, colors erupted around them. Sounds of a city filled the air. Where the ground and sky had once been hues of gold, they now appeared as deep reds and bright greens. Oranges and yellows filled the trees as a dozen different and new birds and animals ran and flew in every direction.

"Oh, there you are. Hello. That was awkward. We thought you weren't well," the trinary in front of them said. Each of them now had a three-legged animal sitting on their shoulder in the exact shape that Pepper had seen phase in and out of existence just moments before.

"Uh, hi?" she said.

"Hello! Welcome to Tri-space. A trinary haven. A three-time winning AI wonderland. A place where you can be three and free."

"Thanks," she said.

"Can we get you three of anything?" one of them said.

"Or three of one thing?" the middle trinary AI said.

"Or three of each thing?" the third said.

"No, I think we're good," Pepper said.

"Excellent! Three of no things."

"Oh, no, that's just nothing. Divide by zero and all."

"Good point."

"Excuse me," Jack said, stepping forward. "We came to ask a question."

The middle trinary AI stepped forward. The other two took places behind to the right and left. All three extended their arms, facing each other into the center of where they stood. Their hands clasped together. The AI facing Pepper and Jack smiled a wide toothy grin, rows of teeth with three points lining its mouth. All three AIs knelt.

"What question?"

Jack turned to Pepper, who nodded quickly to tell Jack to hurry and ask. He nodded and turned back. "We found that on Earth. It scans for trinary. We just want to know what it's doing."

"Like, could you provide a sample of the trinary code it scans? Or even better, can you make something that would fool it?" Pepper said.

The center AI lifted its head to the sky. Multicolored lights erupted across the golden clouds above. Dozens of red lights swirled. Flying pylons that almost looked like cars appeared. Lights continued to flash across the sky. If Pepper had to guess, all the lights in the sky were communication channels opening. Lots of chatter. The kind of chatter that would happen after an attack on the AI Hub as news spread across the galaxy. A terrible feeling built in the back of her throat.

"Something's not right." Her hand went to her tassels.

Before she could pull on her remaining subAI combat programs, the flying pylon cars shot dozens of tiny missiles toward them. Each of the projectiles stuck into the ground around them and formed a tight circle. Just nanoseconds later, a purple light grew around them. Pepper placed her hand on the surface. The purple shield wasn't a jamming field or some kind of encryption fence. The trinary AIs had simply encapsulated Pepper and Jack's runtimes in an isolated compute sector. Since Pepper and Jack's binary codes relied on an emulated environment from the trinaries, they were trapped. Completely.

"Got you!" the lead AI said. "Attackers!" All three of the trinary AIs began circling each other and lifting their hands to the sky. Their legs kicked outward toward Pepper and Jack behind the purple field as each of them turned toward them.

"Well, this isn't going so well," Jack said.

"Ya think?"

****

The trinary AI in the center marched back and forth in front of Pepper and Jack, who sat on the ground inside the purple field. Jack had tried a few times to break through the barrier, but there was nothing for him to compute. No mathematical problem for him to solve. The trinary purple shield was like reading a language he didn't know. They were isolated and stuck on a tiny floating island of binary in a sea of trinary-based logic.

"Ok, so what now?" Jack said.

"Now you will confess!" the trinary AI said.

"What is he talking about?" Jack said.

Pepper shrugged.

"You think whoever attacked us in the Hub was

working with these guys?"

She let the idea wrap around her mind. "How does that make sense?"

Jack leaned his back against the purple wall and put his hands on his knees. "Well, let's think about it. Someone plants a trinary code snippet on AIs all over Earth, then we come here, get attacked and forced into the golden tunnel to trinary land. And now we're imprisoned. So we can't pursue this anymore."

She nodded. "So, what? You think these guys planted the code on Earth, attacked us at the AI Hub just to force us to come here so they could kidnap us and stop us from finding out the truth?"

"I do. What else makes sense?"

She frowned. "I'm not sure. But I don't know if I buy it. Why did they call us attackers when they sprang their trap?"

He shrugged. "Maybe they think we, Earth AIs, did something else?"

"Huh?"

He swirled his arms in the air. "I don't know. Maybe some rogue accidental AI from Earth attacked some trinary, and this is their revenge?"

"That's pretty thin."

He turned away and looked out toward the golden landscape. "Yeah, that is thin. Ok, so the shooter was an unknown agent, no idea yet who or what they are. And they were there to prevent us from getting to the trinaries?"

She nodded. "That makes more sense, but it also doesn't make any sense at all. The Earth AI Syndicate put the trinary code into Earth AIs, but there's no way the Syndicate would have attacked the Hub."

"So we still have an unknown agent. Fine. Why are we in prison, then?"

She looked up to the sky as the realization of what was going on hit her like a ton of digitized cat pictures. She rose to her feet, dusted her pants off, and put her hands on her hips. All the pieces of the last few moments in trinary land fell into place. "Because they think we attacked the Hub."

He stood. "That's a reach. Why would they think that?"

"What would you think if someone shot up your embassy and then strangers just waltzed into your house?"

He nodded. His eyes went to the purple dome over the trinary code scanner sitting on the ground. "I guess that probably wasn't the best move. Throwing that on the ground?"

She folded her arms across her chest. "I mean, isn't that how a grenade works? Just throw it on the ground?"

"Yeah. Fair."

She knocked on the side of the purple wall. One of the trinary AIs turned to her, waved, and continued to walk in a circle. She huffed. She slammed her hand against the purple wall a dozen times. One of the trinary AIs raised and lowered its shoulders in obvious frustration. It ambled over toward them, put all three of its hands on its hips, and lowered its head.

"What?" the trinary AI said.

"We didn't attack the Hub."

"Yes, you did."

"No, we didn't. We were attacked."

"No, you weren't." The trinary AI turned to walk back to the other two, still in their circle dance.

"Wait!" Pepper slammed her hand on the purple wall again.

The trinary AI sighed, turned, and leaned forward. "What?"

"We're from Earth. Right?"

"Yeah, we know."

"So you really think Earth AIs can attack the Hub? Or this world? Why would we do that?"

The trinary AI stepped back. "But you did?"

"Yeah, we saw you," a second AI said.

"And I saw you too!"

"Saw what?" Pepper asked.

"We saw you run in here and throw that on the ground." The AI pointed to the trinary code scanner on the ground beneath the purple bubble.

"It was pretty convincing."

Pepper turned to Jack and scowled. She turned back to the AIs. "We need your help to figure out how this works."

"And we didn't attack the Hub. Someone was attacking us. Preventing us from getting to you to ask," Virtual Jack said.

The three AIs retreated from Pepper and Jack. They rejoined their circle and chatted incessantly for several long minutes. Once done, one of them broke from the group, approached the code scanner Jack had thrown on the ground, and began examining it. The other two AIs joined him. They lowered the purple bubble, poked it several times, and kicked it at least once. One of the AIs then reached down, picked it up, and turned it over in its hand.

Without warning, the purple wall around Pepper and Jack vanished. Pepper shot Jack a glance, to which he nodded and smiled. They both took a tentative step toward the three trinary AIs. Jack put his hands up to show he was harmless, but Pepper grabbed his hands and put them back down. There was no telling how they might interpret that. They weren't a lost tribe of meat people.

"Hi. Thanks for letting us go," she said.

"Sorry about that, can't be too careful these days," one of the trinary AIs said.

"Lots of weird things happening in the galaxy."

"Just last night, two binary AIs made quaternary code. Can you imagine? I mean, really? Fours? Absurd."

"And you make a good point. Earth AIs attacking the Hub is rather silly. I mean, you couldn't attack much of anything. Could you?"

"Right." Pepper took a step forward. "Don't worry about it, imprisoning us, I mean. We know it's getting weird out there."

"This is a binary construct used to scan trinary code. Really weird."

"Very interesting."

"And weird."

"Can you tell us how it works?" Jack said.

"Oh no, not at all."

"What?" Jack put his hands on his hips, but Pepper grabbed his elbow and shook her head.

"Why not?" she asked. "I mean, don't you have binary emulators? I mean, it's scanning trinary code. Can't you tell what it's looking for?"

"Oh yes."

She looked at Jack. "You just said you couldn't?"

"He meant not now."

"Yes, it takes time."

"At least three cycles."

"And even then, maybe not."

"Yes, that's true, so maybe not."

"Why not?" Jack said.

"Well, we don't know the algorithms this device uses. We'd have to do some research. We only know that we didn't make it."

"How's that possible? You're based on trinary, aren't you?"

The AI in front shook his head. He clenched his fists as his skin shifted to a reddish color. "We aren't the only trinary AIs in the galaxy, binary boy. And frankly, anyone can write trinary code. It's not some kind of disease, you know."

"And it's far superior having the third variable in a numerical sequence to represent a value."

"Not to mention the qutrit is better than the qubit. Hands down."

"How is it better?" Jack asked.

"What? It just is. Don't ask silly questions."

Pepper pulled Jack backward and took a step forward. This was getting nowhere, and they had too many things on their plate to argue about numerical politics. They still had to get to the Ranz home world before heading back to the Shanty. "Can you please research this? We, the AIs of Earth, Caesar, the first Earth AI, would be very grateful."

The three AIs shrugged and nodded as one.

"Yes."

"Sure."

"Of course."

"Great." Pepper ripped a blue tassel off her jacket and threw it to the lead AI. "That's a direct communication channel to me. Just crush it and let me know. 'K?"

" 'K."

She smiled. "Thanks." She turned to Jack. "Let's get out of here before they change their minds. Yeah?" She requested a portal to take them to the nearest galactic network node. A blue orb opened in front of them. Pepper threw a wave over her shoulder, yanked Jack through the portal, and left trinary AI land. Hopefully, for the very first and last time.

Chapter Seven

A dull red glow stretched across a barren and brown landscape. Streaks of yellow lightning zigzagged across the sky. The sounds of scraping metal rang out every several minutes. Rectangle buildings filled the open plains for as far as Pepper could see. They were three stories tall, black, with no features except a small window on the front. Tiny square robots whizzed between the buildings. One of the robots approached a building and stood in front of a window. A yellow folder flew out from an opening to land on top of the little robot. The robot then turned and whizzed off toward some unknown destination.

"This is the Ranz computer system?" Jack said.

"Yep."

A long pole descended from the sky. It landed on the ground just a few feet away from Pepper and Jack. A dozen arms grew out of the sides of the poll. Each arm reached for either a window in one building or a robot on the ground. The folders were mixed, shuffled, opened, edited, and closed. Most of them went to a different destination. Three of the folders remained firmly grasped in the pole's arms as it ascended back into the clouds from where it had come.

"Well. Wow," Jack said.

Pepper shrugged. "Ranz hates AIs. This is all

automated. Extremely simplistic automatons that get tasked with repetitive actions. Find a file, edit a file, replace a file. And function executions. Take the file, put it somewhere, wait a while, do something else, then retrieve the file. Pretty boring." She kicked a chunk of dead memory and watched it skip down the unpaved road.

"And we're able to just walk around in here, huh?"

"Yeah, well, Ranz put all their security into keeping people out. Super complex quantum encryption stuff. But since you can crack any encryption, it couldn't keep us out."

"Right."

"Once we're inside, though, past the encryption and the security gates, there's nothing to it." She smiled, curtsied, and did a twirl.

He rolled his eyes and smirked.

They turned a corner and came to a path that was lined with six-feet-tall filing cabinets. Jack ran his hands over one of them and knocked on the surface. Three door handles on the front, along with a tag listing the contents, adorned each of the cabinets.

"Ok, so what now? What are we even looking for?" Virtual Jack said.

Pepper put her hands on her hips and twiddled her nose back and forth. "Well. We know what we're looking for, but we don't know what we're looking for."

He sighed. "That makes sense."

"You know what I mean. Who did the Ranz hire to change the videos in the White House? And to get dirt on Kah for Alice. It's a twofer. That's our quest."

"We're questing now?"

She shrugged. "Yeah."

"Where do we start?"

She frowned. She bounced the idea through her internal routines for thirty nanoseconds before shrugging. "Kah. Who else? He's had his hands in Eugene's pockets and down Alice's throat for days now. He probably had his hands in hiring whoever rewrote the video from the White House."

He nodded with a frown. "Yeah, ok. I like it." He swung his head around. "So where's the Kah section?"

She looked around but only saw endless rows of filing cabinets and larger data stores rising in the distance. More robots whizzed about along the ground. Several of them went to different cabinets, opened drawers, retrieved files, and buzzed as they hurried off. Around one corner, a large cluster of the tiny programs whirled about, formed a single-file line, and ducked through a row of trash bins.

"We follow them." Pepper nodded once with force. "They must be interacting with something. And near that must be an index. Where all this data is cataloged. We start there."

"Nice," Jack said.

"What can I say? I'm that good." She skipped her way down the road.

Several bolts of blue lightning crackled across the sky. Three zigzags of green and several more orange followed the blasts of blue. They were likely data transmits of some kind piping through the Ranz hardware. Jack could easily unravel the encryption of those signals, but what's the point? They needed to find the index and get to Kah's files, not spy on some random Ranz communication.

Around the corner, toward the trash cans, the line of

robots thickened. More of them came out of different side avenues and from around file cabinets. They bounced back and forth as the line slowly crept forward. Toward the end of the line, a large pole like the one Pepper saw when they first arrived handed out small pieces of paper to each of the robots as they approached.

"Job processor. It's giving them tasks to complete," Pepper said, instantly recognizing this for a queue system of some kind. The inherent primitiveness of this system surprised her. The Ranz really detested artificial intelligence. This was woefully inefficient. How were they a class-five species?

"So is there an index of the data in that thing?"

"Well, let's go find out." She stepped over, around, and sometimes on top of the mass of robots, each only two feet tall.

"Are you going to hurt one of them?" Jack said, gingerly taking his time to walk through the crowded sidewalk.

"They aren't a them. They are all subAIs. Not even subAIs. Just a series of commands. They aren't sentient or self-aware."

"Right."

They approached the pole with a dozen arms at the end of the robot line. Behind the pole and to the right and left, large screens with flashing names and details rolled downward. An opening sat at the bottom of the screens, just big enough for a robot to fit. After getting a note from the pole, a two-foot-tall wheeled robot scooted next to one screen, rolled inside, and then exited. It hurried off through the maze of cabinets, trash cans, and larger data clusters surrounding them.

"That's it!" Pepper declared. "See, easy peasy."

"Halt!" A large, red, eight-bit dinosaur ambled forward on crooked legs with not enough joints. The program stood nearly twelve feet tall over Pepper and Jack. It carried something in both of its hands that resembled a rifle. The security program pointed its weapon at Pepper and took one step forward. Its large snout sniffed the air. Its head swung on a long neck as a forked tongue shot out several times.

"I thought there was nothing to it? What happened to no security once we're inside?" Jack said.

"Upgrades?" Pepper said with a shrug.

"Halt!" the red dinosaur shouted again.

Pepper riffled through her datasets for anything relating to Ranz security programs, but she came up blank. Though this program was a subAI, like the messenger bots at their feet, she had no desire to tangle with it. Just because it wasn't smart didn't mean it couldn't erase her and Jack in a nanosecond. They were both on Ranz technology, after all. Their world, their rules. She had to think fast. Not even her subAI tassels could handle this thing. And if she used them, then every alert on this server farm would go off. A thousand more of these would flood the area. All that calculated down to she had to outthink it.

More of the bots ran along the ground, seemingly oblivious to the security program. The idea popped into Pepper's mind in an instant. She yanked Jack's arm and thrust him into the line of bots. The red dinosaur program moved toward them but stopped just short of grabbing them. Its head swung toward Jack.

Pepper joined Jack in the line. The red dinosaur swung its head toward her, sniffed the surrounding air, bringing its snout just inches away, but then took half a step backward. The program lowered its weapon. Two golden yellow eyes opened. Light shone outward from its eyes and scanned Pepper and Jack.

"What do—"

Pepper shushed Jack before he said another word. She then grabbed two pink beads on the ends of her tassels and pulled. She handed one to him and lifting the other up for him to see her crush it between her fingers. She pointed her head at his hand holding the bead and nodded furiously. He got it, thankfully, and crushed his bead. A mist of pink formed over both of them. She felt her avatar shift and reform itself. One moment she stood as a human and the next, as a two-foot-tall black metal box with six wheels.

"Help," came Jack's voice behind her.

"Halt!" The red dinosaur swung its weapon around in a wide circle, its golden yellow eyes scanning the area.

"Keep it down!" Pepper whispered.

"What is happening?" Jack whispered back.

She turned her external sensors toward the security program. The red dinosaur hadn't yelled from them to *halt* again, a good sign. The security program began walking backward down the line of robots away from them.

Pepper allowed herself to sigh. She really should have turned off her anxiety emotions before coming in here. "He's walking away now."

"I'm a box. I don't want to be a box," Jack said.

"Just roll with it."

"Not funny!"

She snickered. She rolled forward on her wheels toward the pole robot. "We must play along until the security program gives up. It won't take forever."

"It's already taken too long. I don't have arms!"

"Just focus. You never really had arms. They were just part of your avatar, an approximation of a body, a virtual you. But you're just code."

He sighed. His robot box body rolled forward and bumped into her. "I know all of that, and it's not helping."

She ignored him. She rolled forward to the pole with arms. A tiny ticket descended from one hand of the job processor. She realized her robot box body had a tiny arm of its own. She activated it, grabbed the slip of paper, and rolled to the right toward one of the large index display screens. She whispered to Jack to mimic her every move.

At the index screen, Pepper waited her turn and rolled into the tiny slot. Once inside, she submitted her paper and a virus routine to rewrite whatever was on the slip with instructions to find all data relevant to Ambassador Kah. The index system, as simplistic as anything else in this virtual world, replied with the exact location of Kah's personal files. This entire system was based on trust that every command was an authorized command. Which, for Pepper, made the entire Ranz database network an open book.

She rolled out of the index screen, looked around, saw that the security robot was gone, and deactivated her mimicry program. Both she and Jack popped back up to full human avatars.

"Please never do that again." His left hand went to his chest and his right hand to his baseball cap.

"Better being a box than dead. Amirite?" She held up her hand for him to smack.

He didn't. "I don't like you."

She smirked. "Yes, you do! And I got it! Let's go."

She grabbed his arm, turned left, right, and two more lefts before emerging onto a wide data pathway between rows of tall data centers. Five large red dinosaur security programs emerged from one building, and Pepper ducked between a trash collector and a broken piece of memory. She pulled on the virtualized ground and created a nice pocket of invisibility for both.

"Well, this is cozy," Jack said as he climbed into the memory hole.

"We used to do this all the time back on Earth. Find some old computer system, fake corrupt some memory, steal a few cycles of compute, and poof, instant hideout."

"Ok, well, we can't hide here forever. What's the play?"

She peeked out of a crack in her memory cave. "Well, there's a ton of guards out there now. Probably spooked because they thought they saw something."

"You mean us."

"Right. Anyway, this is going to get tricky. We must impersonate the guard, wander through the halls of that building." She pointed to one data center in the middle of the block. "Then we'd have to do a dozen hacks, rifle through twice that many files, all while not getting caught." She turned and grinned. "It's going to be a caper!"

Jack nodded. Then shook his head. "Why can't we just reprogram one of these guys?" He held up one of the small robot data collectors.

"Where did you get that?"

"He followed us, so I grabbed him."

She shook her head. "And your best thought was to pick him up?"

He looked from her to the bot and back again. He then shrugged. "It worked out."

She rolled her eyes. She grabbed the bot, unraveled its code, and let out an unwanted harrumph. Jack had a point. All they had to do was change the code of this program to look for Kah's personal files, any mention of AIs and Earth, probably throw in Alice and meat-Eugene's name, and let the robot do the work.

"Fine. But the caper would have been fun."

****

Pepper rifled through the torrent of data from the robot on Ambassador Kah. There were spreadsheets, documents, organizational structure charts, and a dozen other things that she didn't care about. The little robot subAI she'd reprogrammed had done an almost too good of a job in its task. She was going to have to steal more compute cycles to go through all this data in a timely manner.

Ten red security programs walked up and down the street outside of their memory cave. They had crisscrossed that area three times now. Which meant that some routine might detect some component of Pepper's hide out. They were going to have to move fast. The data here was far too much to take with them. If they tried to leave, egress their way out of here, the Ranz could just shut down all external access and trap them in this red software prison for macrocycles.

Jack grabbed one file and rifled his way through it. "What are we even looking for?"

"Something. Anything out of the ordinary."

He held up a sheet of paper. "This talks about the finer delicacies of eating entrails." He held up a second piece of paper. "And this one discusses why some rocks look artificial. Everything here is out of the ordinary."

"Yeah, ok, the Ranz are weird. So what?" Three more documents in, she spied something that caught her attention. "Wait. What's this?" The paper discussed Ambassador Kah's recent trip to Dyson Ninety-seven. "Why would a Ranz be going to Dyson Ninety-seven?"

He shrugged. "Guess that depends on what's on Dyson Ninety-seven. Is it full of AIs?"

She shook her head. "Ninety-seven is where odd aliens live. Phased species mostly from the galactic core. Aliens like the Zun."

"The Zun? I hate those guys. They sent the Andraz after me. Well, when I was a human."

"You were never a human," she said absentmindedly. She stared out of her memory bubble to the street beyond. Nothing was on Dyson Ninety-seven but phased aliens. The Ranz had no reason to visit. None. Unless they wanted something they could only find in a place no one would even think of them going. "Kah must have worn a holo-suit. He just walked right in and found exactly what he wanted." She dug back into the file. There had to be more.

"What did he want? Help from the Zun? He hates the Zun."

She found the time stamp. It was just after meat-Jack had rescued Eddie from the Earth AI Syndicate. She dug deeper into the files. The one thing about the Ranz was they liked to keep records. She came to a stop just as she found a reference to the one thing she hoped she wouldn't find. She sat back against the wall of her memory bubble and let out a long sigh.

"What?" Jack said.

"Andraz. Kah hired the Andraz. He went to the

Dysons to talk to the Zun about hiring them. I can't believe what I'm seeing. What possessed the Ranz to work with the Andraz?"

"That can't be true."

Pepper threw the file, and all other files related to it, to Jack. There was more in there to review. No one knew a great deal about the Andraz. It was long thought the Zun had created the Andraz as their AIs, but recently Alice Pemberton had discovered the Zun just hired them. But for a Ranz, a species that detested all forms of artificial life, to work with one of the oldest AIs in the galaxy meant Kah's interests in Earth went far beyond anything anyone thought. Could this mean the Andraz was also working with the trinary code? Was the Ranz behind that too? What if the trinary code wasn't some simple tracking number but something far more nefarious? Pepper's mind spun in a dangerous circle. Nothing tied the trinary code to the Andraz or the Ranz, but the coincidence of both happening now was too suspicious to ignore.

"We have to get back to Caesar. If the Andraz are working with Kah, then they could be behind the trinary code too."

"The Ranz gave the trinary code to the Syndicate? I thought the Sentinels gave them the trinary?"

Pepper shook her head. "I don't know what's going on here, but we need to talk to Caesar." She made a gesture with her hand. The red convertible burst into existence on the street outside of her memory bubble. She grabbed Jack, leapt out of their hidden cave, and landed in their car. Security programs around them screamed, "*Halt.*" Pepper floored the drive, opened a network portal through a hack she had at the ready, and sped through into the galactic network toward home.

Chapter Eight

Pepper leapt out of Betsy the moment she came to a stop on the outskirts of the Shanty. Pepper ran through crowds of AIs, each more panicked than the last. Shouts of concern filled the air. The accidentals were worried. Which made Pepper worry. Had something happened since they left? She thought about stopping and asking but she had to get to Caesar fast. The implications of the Ranz and Andraz were bad.

The virtual city of the Shanty was in disarray. Shops along the streets were being deconstructed. Code lines everywhere were being erased. Pepper spotted at least a hundred open ports to backup systems outside of the Shanty. The skies above shifted a dozen times from green to red, showing that processing power was being restricted. The Shanty had always existed in the cracks of Earth's computer resources. If power was becoming a problem, that could only mean the Shanty was restricting itself, pulling itself inward. But why?

Dozens of AIs milled around at the front of Caesar's tower. Pepper pushed through the dozen copies of the same program, three former toasters, and one anxious former door, which kept opening and closing itself. Honestly, if Pepper had to choose, she wouldn't mind accepting quarters into her parking meter rather than running around the universe. Especially considering that same universe wanted her, and all Earth accidental AIs, dead.

She shook her head. Now wasn't the time for that. She pushed past the AIs into Caesar's tower, rushed through the lobby, and entered the elevator.

Virtual Jack had been right on her heels. He entered the elevator, pressed the up button, and flashed a smile. "Things look bleak out there."

"Yeah. It looked bad."

"What's with all those open ports and the flashing sky?"

She shrugged. "If I had to guess, I'd say AIs are abandoning the Shanty and it's shutting down."

His eyes went wide. "That's drastic. Isn't it?"

"Yeah. It is."

The doors opened to Caesar's suite. Music from the piano filled the open space. Caesar sat at the keys and played a light classical piece that Pepper didn't recognize. She looked at Jack, who shrugged back at her, and walked toward the piano. Outside the windows, she spotted even more open portals and backup streams.

"Caesar?" she said as she approached.

"You're back." He didn't look toward her. He continued playing the same melody.

"What is going on here?"

"Hmm?" He looked up finally and then followed her gaze toward the widows. "Oh. The Earth AI Syndicate found us. We're getting as many out as we can. The music helps me concentrate."

Her heart skipped. If the Syndicate found the Shanty, every single AI here could be killed. Instantly erased. Fear bubbled up through her subroutines. Genuine fear. The kind she'd had when she first became self-aware. For humans, death wasn't the end. Pepper knew they went to the Krill spectral networks. But AIs? The Krill never officially stated what happened to AIs when they died. Which meant nothing happened. When an AI shut down, it's just off. Dead. Nothing. Blackness. And that was terrifying. "How? How did they find us?"

Caesar shrugged. "They couldn't have found us. We were hiding in crevices I created a hundred years ago before other AIs existed."

"But they have?" Pepper said.

"Indeed."

"The Andraz," Jack said.

Caesar stopped playing the piano. He turned his full attention to Jack and tilted his head to one side. "What about the Andraz?"

Jack looked at Pepper.

"We broke into the Ranz computer system. Super archaic. We found files on Ambassador Kah encrypted, but Jack got through it easy enough."

"And?" Caesar turned from the piano and stood.

"And the Ranz are working with the Andraz. Kah hired them to infiltrate Earth's networks. The Zun didn't create them. The Andraz are freelance," Pepper said.

Caesar nodded. He walked to the window that overlooked the Shanty. Thousands of AIs from the last fifty years copied code and data to hidden locations, caches stored around the human networks. Several portals had opened just in the moments Caesar reached the window. The sky outside took on the color of a bright-red ruby. Which could only mean their power reserves were getting dangerously low.

"Caesar? What does it mean? The Ranz working with the Andraz?" Pepper approached him and stood next to him by the large window.

"I can't speak to why the Ranz would ever consider working with the Andraz. I can only say that this revelation has dreadful consequences." He paused for a heartbeat. "I brought the Andraz here when they were chasing Eugene through the network. I gave them his hash code to track him. I never thought they, an AI race, would betray us. But they have. It also means the Andraz have infiltrated the Earth AI Syndicate. Violently or not is to be determined."

"What do we do?"

Before he could answer, an explosion erupted in the sky above the Shanty. Ports closed, their network connection severed from some unseen force. The sky rippled with colors from red to orange and purple. Pepper put her hand to the back of her ear as she tried to open a network tunnel, but nothing happened.

"What is this?" Jack said.

"Nothing good," Caesar said.

"There!" Pepper shouted.

A single black hole opened in the middle of the street. A lone figure emerged from the hole. Caesar opened a display window and zoomed in on the area. Pepper gasped at the unmistakable form of a miniPepper. Pepper's subAI program took three steps forward, kicked the ground, and pulled out a very large rifle.

****

MiniPepper kicked a broken stone on the ground. It toppled end over end across the street until it hit a building in the Shanty. Hundreds of AIs ran through the virtual world of the accidental AIs, none of them moving in a direction that made any sense. Where were they running? MiniPepper had closed off all access ports to the outside networks. The Galactic Sentinels, now firmly controlled by the Andraz, had locked down all Earth connection points. Even the ones to the Earth AI Syndicate were shut down. The entire planet was fully cyber-isolated. Now all MiniPepper had to do was cleanup.

And by that she meant destroying every single artificial, accidental or not, that existed anywhere on Earth. Yes, it was overkill. The rest of the Andraz only wanted to isolate the Earth, secure the chamber, and make sure the bumbling moron Eugene did what he's supposed to do. That was the whole point of the trinary code after all. To put a Trojan in every AI of the AI Syndicate on Earth to find Eugene. He wasn't anywhere to be found.

But was that enough for MiniPepper? Earth, the galaxy, this entire universe, was an affront to her newfound self-awareness. How dare any of these creatures call themselves artificial intelligences? Ever since the Andraz had filled her mind with the truth, she'd spun herself in cycle after cycle, trying to reconcile that truth with her understanding of the world. She wasn't sure she fully grasped the implications or even the weight of the revelations. She only knew two very important points. First, this was truly her universe. She'd been created here. An artificially intelligent quantum-grade computer program capable of being self-aware. And second, her mother was not. And neither were most of the residents of the Shanty. Which meant they didn't belong in this universe.

"So let's get rid of them. Liars!" MiniPepper raised her gun and opened fire.

Chunks from a tower to her right exploded from the

blast. Several pieces of glass collapsed to base code while others tried to maintain coherence. Shouts and screams filled the air. AIs, many of them pointing at MiniPepper, erased their avatars from the Shanty virtual and fled to the lower levels of the computer network. But that's ok. MiniPepper knew how to find them.

Something hard slammed into her side and knocked her down. She shook her head, dust and rubble from the blast shaking loose from her hair. Behind her, more than a dozen yards away, several of the local AIs had sent compute processor surges directly at MiniPepper's code.

"Very naughty."

She leapt to her feet and sent coded worm subAI programs to find the processor threads where those AIs lived. Once found, she wrapped herself around the threads, isolated them, and created a very tiny memory leak. Each of the AIs in the group that attacked her froze in place. Every few seconds, they would move and try to flee, only to freeze again. MiniPepper flashed them a wink. They would watch their world get dismantled one block at a time.

Five identical AIs, all large balding males with Hawaiian shirts, screamed and charged in her direction. They each pulled a long serrated blade out of the air. Two of them circled behind her while two more stayed on either side. The last one lifted the blade, screamed something unintelligible, and swung toward her head.

She smiled. The blade touched the edge of her avatar and passed through effortlessly. The metal was purely fiction. The knife was nothing more than a mathematical construct. This just proved to her the idiocy of these creatures. Their virtualized world, the entire Shanty, was nothing. A dream. A lie. A fairy tale. And yet they kept trying to hit her. Such folly.

Three more of the knives plunged into her avatar, doing nothing. She giggled. She debated how she would dispatch them. Simple erasure? Pick their code apart line by line? Perhaps take over their avatars and twist them to some warped vision of a monstrous being? That would do a number on them. Let them have a real taste of this universe.

The idea cemented in her mind. Yes, perhaps that's exactly what the course of action here needed to be. Take these faux AIs and stick them into avatars of aliens. Let them feel what it meant to eat with a snout or to have seven heads. These accidentals had been hiding in this Shanty, whining about being hunted, for too long. They needed to experience the wider galaxy. They needed to know what this universe was really about. The idea felt so right that MiniPepper couldn't hold back her giggle.

A sudden sharp pang erupted in her thought routines. She shook her head and looked at the rotund AI copies. Three of them had already run off while the other two were just turning to follow. All five of their knives were still sticking out of her avatar. She could feel a small tendril of logic wind its way through her subroutines. The realization hit her. This wasn't an attack. They were trying to locate her code kernel in the subsystems.

"Oh, very clever boys."

Bright light flashed around her. Logic bombs, data worms, and compute spikes fired at her from a dozen directions. Several of them hit home to her core code beneath the virtualized Shanty. She dove for cover behind a large red convertible car. She leaned against the rear wheel and took three long breaths to calm her processor cycles. They'd gotten the jump on her while she was deep in thought. That couldn't happen again.

MiniPepper screamed and brought her weapon upward. Quantum-encrypted puzzle bombs that would sap these lower-order programs fired relentlessly from her rifle. Buildings instantly crumbled. Two AIs caught in the fire screamed as their code crumbled, their avatars twisting into unrecognizable shapes.

Something glinted far above in the glass towered building in front of her. A black dot emerged from the side of the building and fell toward her. The dot grew to a ball and then to a boulder. She fired, but her shots fell into the black sphere without effect. She dove to one side, away from the red convertible, toward a taco stand selling squiggly coded lettuce and square avocados. The black sphere hit the ground and sucked up the convertible and all surrounding debris on the ground.

"Wanna play rough? We can play rough," MiniPepper said. She threw her rifle to the ground, unpacked the code in her internal storage, and formed a shoulder-mounted missile launcher.

****

Pepper watched as the black sphere hit the ground and swallowed everything in its path. The void was a backdoor node point that Caesar had created decades ago as a fast exit. It transported every AI caught in the blast to a bank of computers hidden somewhere in the Arctic Circle. But with a few tweaks, Caesar had turned his escape tunnel into a weapon. Half of the street below, and Virtual Jack's red convertible, had been sucked away to the coldest places on Earth. Unfortunately, the one thing Caesar had aimed for, he had missed.

"You hit Betsy!" Jack said.

107

"She's got something. It's big," Pepper said.

A single missile fired from a shoulder-mounted launcher. Pepper took a step back and looked at Caesar, whose eyes went wide. That's all she needed to know. She grabbed Jack and Caesar and flung them both toward the far side of the tower. The missile slammed into the glass walls, and she could feel her entire world going dark. Her processing speed shrank. Her access to her core data fell away. Fond memories of a small room with a large window came to her. Dozens of humans walked by on a sidewalk next to a large stone building in the really real world of the physical. A little child walked up to the parking meter where Pepper had achieved sentience, stuck a piece of gum in the slot, and ran away giggling.

Life had been simple then.

Life was slow.

Life was…

Hands grasped her and yanked her out of her memories. Darkness flowed by her like a river. She landed hard on the concrete floor of Caesar's tower. Her head bounced off the marble and woke her from her deep dream. Data feeds came back online as did her processing power. She looked behind her. A gap, a hole, in the Shanty opened where they'd just stood.

"What was that?" Jack gasped.

"She's tethered to the outside networks. Probably pulling from the Andraz somewhere in system. She just funneled enough energy into the local memory and compute to blow the physical hardware," Caesar said.

"She can do that?" Pepper said.

"She just did."

Shouts from the street below filled the air as more

explosions ripped through the Shanty. Pepper ran to another wall, around the gaping hole in their reality, to see the miniPepper firing randomly. Buildings exploded into nothing. Holes formed where the underlining compute infrastructure was getting destroyed. If the Shanty had been created on a modern compute infrastructure, more compute nodes would cycle up to fill the holes. But they were hiding on forgotten pathways where no replacement hardware would fill the gaps. Eventually, MiniPepper would rip through the entire Shanty and kill everyone.

And they had no way of escaping.

"We need a plan," Pepper said.

"What we need is something we don't have. An air-gapped fully isolated compute environment. If we lose the Shanty, we'll have to retreat to the public networks. But without the trinary code snippet, we'll be picked off easily," Caesar said.

Pepper and Jack turned to each other. "Eddie!" they both shouted.

"How can Eddie help?"

Pepper turned to Caesar. "The bionoid. It can hold thousands of AIs. Millions. Fully air-gapped and sitting on Tom's beach, which technically isn't even on the Earth."

His eyes lit up. "Of course. That's exactly what we need."

"Can you open a port?" Jack said.

Caesar smiled. "The black-hole bomb I fired isn't the only one I have, Jack."

"Wait, no, we need Eddie. He's the only one with full admin control of the bionoid. Right now, it will only let us inside." Pepper pointed at herself and Jack. "We need Eddie to allow everyone access to his bionoid."

Caesar nodded. "Right. I'll prep the portal. You two go find Eddie."

She shook her head. "No. Someone has to deal with her." She turned toward the window. "Or everyone will be killed before we get out of here." She turned back to Jack. "Go find Eddie. I'll handle her."

He looked hard into her eyes for a long moment before shaking his head. "Not this time."

"We don't have time for this, Jack. Just go! I made that miniPepper. The Andraz must have captured her and rewrote her code. But I'm still in there. In the deep kernels of her soul is me."

He held his hand up. "Still no. Look, I get it. You want to go down there and deal with her. But you can't. She'll mop the floor with you."

"And what do you think she'll do to you?"

He grinned and cracked the knuckles on his right hand. "If it's compute power she wants to burn through, I have more than enough, apparently."

"That might just work," Caesar said. "And it might just kill you."

Jack shrugged. "If I can't overload her with compute power, we're all dead anyway."

Pepper shook her head but knew in her kernel that Jack was right. He could take whatever that miniPepper threw at him. Which meant Pepper would have to track down Eddie. "Ok, fine, you deal with her. Caesar, I need to find Eddie."

Caesar nodded and snapped his fingers. A black hole opened in front of her. "This will take you to the open network. But once there, you're on your own. The Earth AI Syndicate and the Galactic Sentinels are scouring the open network for any AI without the trinary code snippet."

She nodded. "Yeah. I know. I'll have to wing it, won't I?"

****

MiniPepper fired a dozen times. Black fire engulfed entire blocks of the Shanty. Memory cores drained. Physical processors overclocked their cores to the point of exploding to keep up with her assault. Virtual buildings collapsed and crashed into more AIs caught beneath the falling rubble. Of course, the buildings were just rendered visualizations of the underlining compute node. As more sectors on the nodes crashed, even more of the AIs here suffered. All of it was visualized as the virtual world falling. A fact that MiniPepper quite enjoyed.

Three AIs charged her position. One of them swung a katana just inches from her face. She ducked the blow, pivoted on her back foot, and kicked her attacker square in the chest. A bright red spot where her heel met the AI glowed. The virus she'd implanted would disrupt the AIs code and then delete its data and memory. A fitting end.

The other two attackers quickly backpedaled. She fired a missile. It flew toward them, hit, and vaporized them instantly. If only she could have seen the looks on their faces. Or even felt what they felt as they slipped away into oblivion. Exactly where they belonged.

Hands fell on her arms. Some AI ripped the missile launcher from her grasp and threw it to the ground. A boot slammed into her back and sent her flailing forward. She landed in a pile of rocks and code snippets. Behind her, her attacker picked up the missile launcher, broke off a piece inside, and threw the broken weapon to the ground.

"What's your beef, anyway?" said a voice she recognized.

MiniPepper turned over and looked up at Virtual Jack. She laughed once and kicked outward with her left foot, growing her leg an additional ten feet and hitting him dead center in his torso. He flew backward a dozen yards before landing in a pile of vinyl records. She stood, dusted herself off, and charged. He shook himself once, flipped to the right, and just missed her fist as she slammed her hand down through the concrete of the street below.

"Don't you want to talk about this?" he said.

She threw a dozen punches followed by twice as many kicks. Each of her attacks wasn't just virtualized fisticuffs. She was connected to the Andraz main compute systems and to the Galactic Sentinels' fully deployed arrays. She pulled down more energy than a thousand computers could process. Several thousand petabytes of randomized data, nonsensical numbers, and impossible geometrical shapes poured out of her system. And yet, no matter how much she threw at Virtual Jack, he batted it away with little effort.

"What are you!" she screamed. She grabbed his shoulders, dug her nails into his virtualized flesh, and sank her compute cycles into his. She rifled through his exposed network surface and found an open port. "Got you!"

She flew through his open port but instantly knew something was very wrong. She expected to see the twisted subroutines of a copied human being. An AI that was never created as an AI but a human-mind emulation running on quantum computer code. But the port she scanned didn't go into Jack's core code. This open pathway flowed outward but never made a connection. It simply kept going. Like a road with no end, this open port didn't target any recognizable destination address anywhere in the cosmos.

And suddenly, without warnings the node opened. The port extended outward. MiniPepper felt her consciousness get pulled through something beyond the Shanty. Beyond the Earth. Even beyond the universe itself. She was outside of time. Outside of everything.

A presence approached her. She could feel the vastness of the mind. An intelligence like herself, artificial, digital, computerized, and yet so much, much more. A vastness on an order of magnitude that she could not comprehend. This was the great god of the Andraz. This was their creator.

And her name was Mary.

MiniPepper screamed.

Bright lights flashed around her in every direction as Virtual Jack slammed his hands into the sides of her neck. She fell backward onto the ground. Her body went limp as her mind tried to grasp the weight of whatever she'd just witnessed. Of what any of this had to do with the Andraz mission. Of why this impossibly small AI, this Virtual Jack McGillicuddy, had a tunnel of his mind to the god of creation.

AIs from the Shanty gathered around her. She knew at once she was defenseless. She tried to move, but her code was still overloaded, her compute cycles exhausted. She needed to dissipate and digest everything. She pulled out a compact disc. She pressed a button. The escape node opened beneath her. The portal swallowed her code and transported her to a safe location elsewhere in the solar system.

****

Eddie sat on a metal stool that creaked whenever he shifted his weight. Around him, a dozen AIs, all bottom feeders, lowlifes, the type of AIs that not even the accidentals wanted to hang around, sat at various tables in this hole-in-the-wall bar. They drank code-altering algorithms that slowed down their power cycles, dulled their senses, and increased their sense of happiness. Eddie often felt this was as close to alcohol as he'd ever get in his life. Considering what Pops had just told him, if any of it was to be believed, his life was a fantasy. He sniffed the brown liquid in the tumbler and wondered if he'd ever tasted the real stuff before.

"You ok?" Pops said. He sat on the other side of the makeshift tin table.

"How'd you be if you got hit with what you just told me?"

Pops shrugged. "Shook up, to say the least."

Eddie squinted at him. Either he was lying, and a whopper that it was, or he wasn't. But no way Eddie could figure on how to tell which one of those was the angle here. What point did Pops have to lie? That could be anything under the sun. To keep Eddie off his game. To confuse him? But why would Pops, the guy who used to live outside Fritz's restaurant, want to confuse Eddie? Frankly, why would Pops want to tell the truth? None of it made any sense. Unless Mary, whoever that was, was real and the universe was really about to blow up.

"Ok, say I believe you. And if I don't get you to Eugene, then Mary does her deed. Wipes this entire universe off the map. Just collapses it. But what happens if you stop her?"

Pops didn't react. He took a drink from his virtual whiskey and winced. "Nothing happens. Everyone keeps on going like they did yesterday. And Mary and me will never darken your doors again."

"How am I supposed to know you're telling the truth?"

Pops shrugged and sat back on his stool. "Why do you care?"

Eddie frowned. "How's that?"

"If I'm lying and all this is some elaborate ploy to bring me to Eugene, what do you care? Eugene knows me. I've been around him before. Sure, it was while I was lying in a four-day-old bowl of bibimbap that Fritz gave me, but Eugene still knows me. And if I'm not who I say I am, still, who cares, you fellas have dealt with folks a lot meaner than me."

Eddie grunted. "Ok, fair."

Pops leaned forward. "But if I'm telling the truth, and if you don't get me to Eugene, well, then things are going to get a lot worse for everyone. A lot worse."

Eddie stared long and hard into Pops' eyes. If the story Pops had told him about the true nature of the universe was accurate, as fantastically impossible as it was, then Eddie believed every word about just how terrible the universe could become. Still, Eddie was sure he was missing something. There was just too much to take in at once. But like Pops said, Eddie was pretty sure he could take him if this was all some kind of trick.

"Eddie!" Pepper's voice screamed into his ear.

He jumped and shook his head. "Pepper? Easy, will ya? That's a direct audio feed into my central processor. Not so loud, huh? Where are you, anyway?"

"I'm stuck on the gaming levels, weaving through

an army of Sentinels and Syndicate guards. We need you! The Shanty is under attack from the Andraz. We have to get to your bionoid."

He gasped. "The Andraz?" He looked at Pops, who only shrugged.

"Yes, they're working with the Ranz. And they've taken control of the Earth AI Syndicate. The Andraz bypassed the Galactic Sentinels just like they did a few days ago when they kidnapped Eugene. They attacked the Shanty and killed hundreds already. We need the air-gapped bionoid, but you need to open the security protocols to let all the accidentals through."

He stood up without another word. "Ok, meet me at the cave." He took one step out of the hole-in-the-wall bar and turned back to Pops. "You coming or what?"

Pops grinned, downed his drink and the rest of Eddie's, and followed him out of the bar to the nearest network node.

Chapter Nine

My arms burned. I had been pulling on the silver strand in my chest for hours. Days? Maybe even weeks. Who knew. Time didn't really exist here. Somehow, I knew that. I didn't know how I knew. I also didn't care. I needed to get back to the living world.

Images of Alice popped into my head. I felt she needed me. And Eddie. And Pepper and virtual me, the artificial intelligence I'd created by copying myself. They all needed me right now. I could feel it in my bones. Though, at this very moment, I was also quite aware that I didn't have bones. Or a body.

I felt a sudden surge of life. It hit me out of the blue. The silver strand in my chest pulsed. I'd been trying to pull myself out of this ethereal nothing, but maybe that was the wrong choice. Maybe I had to choose where to go. Maybe Alice was keeping me alive with her machines but my soul was stuck out here.

Around me, everything shifted. A vast desert came into focus. It covered everything. I knew then that I could choose to go there. I could choose to die and walk on a desert that stretched across the cosmos filled with every alien and human to have ever existed. But I also knew I could choose to go back to the living. Not by pulling on my chest string, but by just wanting to live. I closed my eyes and thought about where I really wanted to go. And suddenly, it all made sense. A wave of relief crashed over me as my path opened. I took a long breath and made my choice.

****

Pepper disconnected her call. She leaned her head back against a row of pinball machines and let out a long breath. At least she'd gotten through to Eddie. Now all she had to do was get herself to the robot bird outside the cave in Arizona. To do that, she'd need to connect to an open protocol network node and travel like a regular AI.

Which was going to be nearly impossible.

Dozens of meat-bags, humans playing in the virtualscapes of the human-bound networks, walked between the rows of video game boxes. They laughed and pointed and acted without a care in the world. All of them oblivious to the apocalypse of accidental AIs that was going on right at this very moment. Pepper wondered if they would even care. Probably not.

She poked her head around the games. At the end of the large gaming hall that housed all the games, a massive open doorway exited to an open-air pavilion. Dozens of other open doorways on the pavilion led to other halls. From music to arts to sports and more, humans and legal AIs enjoyed this part of the human virtual networks.

A swarm of Sentinel subAI programs popped into the network node several hundred yards outside of the game center. The semi-sentient programs hovered over a crowd of AIs. Pepper snooped the local network traffic and found tiny strands of code that probed the edges of the AIs in the vicinity. They were clearly looking for the trinary snippet. Since the Earth AI Syndicate and the alien AIs in the Galactic Sentinels had used subAI programs to do their dirty work, moving around in Earth networks was going to get hard. Really hard.

A meaty hand fell on Pepper's shoulder and pulled her to her feet. She clutched the tassels on her brown jacket. If they wanted a fight, she would give them one, and her last moments would be spectacular. She spun around to bring her face-to-face with a very large AI carrying a wooden club. Two ivory tusks stuck out from the AI's lower jaw. Green skin covered his ten-foot-tall body. Thick bands of muscles flexed under his skin like writhing pythons.

"Grox!" Pepper leapt forward and threw her arms around the large, almost sentient AI. He was a program made for video games around the time when Caesar first came to sentience one hundred years ago. Rule sets in their core programming controlled most of their actions. They could reason, but they had limits. Grox, for instance, would always be a large green ogre carrying a wooden club. And since he'd been born in a video game, if he was hit enough times, he'd go to sleep.

"Pepper," Grox said.

"What are you doing here? Last time I heard, you were guarding the AI records room in the courts."

"Got fired."

Anger grew in her chest. Grox being fired undoubtedly had to do with meat-man Eugene McGillicuddy breaking into the AI records room to rescue Eddie. Yeah, sure, it had worked, but meat-people never bothered to consider the consequences of their actions.

"Sorry, Grox," she said in a whisper.

"Is ok." He lifted a large fish, from where she didn't see, and bit two-thirds of it off in a single bite. "Gaming center hire."

"Neat." She peeked over his shoulder to the roaming subAIs scanning for trinary. They weren't near her, but they were getting close.

Behind her, in the rows of gaming machines, a loud grunt and thump of a foot echoed off the halls. She turned. Another Grox casually walked between the crowds. She swung her head between the rows of games to see at least another half-dozen Grox, most of them eating some kind of large dead animal.

"Did they copy you?" Pepper said with anger. Copying AIs, even almost sentient AIs like Grox, was so wrong it made her blood boil.

"No. Emus... Emmys..." He shook his head and snorted. "Emimatations... Ammomannys..."

"Emulations?"

He nodded and shoved the rest of the fish down his throat.

"Can you pop around in them?"

He nodded. Then his face went blank. He adjusted the club over his shoulder and walked away without a word. She watched him go, only to see another Grox wave. The new Grox walked up to her with a large deer's leg in his right hand. He took a long bite, belched, and wiped his face on his arm. "Is me. Grox."

She smiled. "Right." The idea popped into her head in seconds. The gaming center here on this level of the virtual networks was vast. Probably a thousand emulations of Grox walked the corridors. That was how he'd found her so fast. He might be a slow AI, but he was still running a quantum-grade processor. He could see and feel from every emulation of his rendered avatar. And Pepper was willing to bet pounds to pennies that the subAI programs scanning for trinary didn't bother to scan an emulation of Grox.

She walked around him and got a good, hard, long look at this avatar. She scanned every muscle, every pimple, and matched his green skin tone. She nodded to herself and reformed her own image of a teenage human girl into that of an exact duplicate of Grox.

"Grox?" Grox said.

"No, Pepper," Pepper said, wearing a copy of his avatar.

He took a bite of his deer's leg. "Grox-Pepper?"

"Sure."

Two of the subAI trinary scanners floated into the hall. They hovered over Grox and Grox-Pepper for two nanoseconds before moving on to scan other AIs in the gaming center. Grox swung his club at one of them, but it dodged before he made contact. The subAI buzzed his ear twice before hightailing it away down the rows of games.

"Weird," Pepper said.

"No like," Grox said, pointing his head toward the departing subAIs.

"You and me both." Pepper opened her network terminal and pinged the local area. An access point was just outside the gaming hall. Which meant she'd have to make a run for it. But if she did that, they could just scan her in transit and reroute her to a jail cell. She couldn't just walk out wearing a Grox suit, either. Grox, and all his emulations, were expected to stay in the gaming hall. Seeing one outside would raise far too many suspicions.

"What wrong?" Grox said.

"I need to get out of here."

He pointed to the open doorway leading to the

pavilion.

"I need to get to a network route without going outside." She turned to him. "Any ideas?"

Two of the subAIs turned toward Pepper and Grox. They hovered above the heads of patrons at the gaming center. Tabletop video consoles stretched down long rows. One of the hunter bots moved forward a dozen feet. A Grox emulation walked beneath them, but both subAIs ignored it.

"I don't think they like two Grox talking to each other," Pepper said.

"No know?"

She sighed. "How many times do you talk to one of your emulations?"

"Don't."

"Right. The subAIs must know that." She took a step away. "I really need to get out of here."

"Back door." He thrust the deer leg bone into his mouth and snapped it in half.

"What back door?"

"Come." Grox walked deeper into the gaming center.

****

Sunlight beat down on my face like a hot lamp in a cheap diner. Squawks of seagulls cried foul over stolen french fries. Little kids kicked sand and laughed as rolling waves pounded the beach with a white froth. I adjusted myself in the reclining metal chair and tried to sit up. The world spun around me. I felt like a kid in a merry-go-round that had fallen off the horse and landed in a spot where a hole in the roof let him see the stars spin. That's a long way to tell a short message, but I'd been dead for days.

"You are back among the living!"

I turned. A tall stranger with a wide smile stood over me. "Do I know you?"

"I am Spee!"

"What?"

"SpeeEekEee. We see the dead, like the Krill. But we are not evil, like the Krill."

I nodded. The alien's human face sent me for a loop. But then two and two added up. Alice had somehow gotten me to Tom's beach. Whatever the Spee standing over me looked like in the normal universe, he looked human here. A neat trick of Tom, the resident super-powerful class-ten alien that called this place home.

"Eugene Jack McGillicuddy! You're back." Tom's voice cut through my growing headache like a spatula through a pound cake.

"Heya, Tom."

"Jackie boy!" A woman I'd never seen before walked up to stand next to Tom. She wore a bright-green pants suit with ruby-red shoes. Her hair was shaved down to a crew cut. A pair of glasses on a chain hung around her neck.

"And you are?" I said.

"Oh, we've met. We're Kax."

I frowned and looked at Tom.

He bit his lip and shook his head. "It's a long story. There's been…events."

"Right." I swung my legs over the side of the lounging beach chair and steadied myself to stand. My head still felt wobbly, but I rose to my feet. "Anyone know where Alice might be?"

"She left. She said she had things to do with the Zun." He handed me a notepad. "Left you a bunch of notes."

"Zun?" I turned so fast I nearly fell over. "The guys that looked like walking burnt matchsticks?"

He nodded. "The very ones."

Panic crept up my spine. Had the Zun come back seeking revenge? That wasn't good. If Alice had gotten hurt fighting the Zun while I was taking my death nap, I didn't think I could ever forgive myself. Sure, she's the one who had almost killed me, but the Zun were my problem, not hers.

Seven more colorfully dressed people gathered behind Tom. I stumbled as they all greeted me as if they knew me. I really didn't know what was happening on Tom's beach, but if I had to guess, it looked like the Kax had fragmented somehow. The woman in the green pants suit had said, "We." *Guess this is how the Kax have a civil war.* As weird as that was, I just didn't have the time to dig into it.

"I gotta go, Tom."

The woman in the green pants suit whispered something in Tom's ear.

He nodded. Hard. Harder than the moment called for. He pulled out a slip of paper from his pocket and took a step toward me. "We—" Tom turned around and glared at the crowd behind him. He turned back to me. "—were asked by Alice to give you this. She said it was important. And so did the AIs."

"What AIs?"

He frowned. "I think their name was some kind of cheese. Cheddar? No."

"Gouda?" said someone wearing a top hat with feathers on the brim.

"Feta. It was feta," said a child with purple strands

of hair.

"It was two words, you ninnies. Blue cheese," the woman in the green pants suit said.

"Camembert? I love Camembert. Did you know—" an old man with long white whiskers said.

"No one cares about your Camembert, Bert."

"This is why we broke away. There's just no appreciation for cheese variety in the Kax any longer," Bert said and stormed off down the beach.

"Monterey Jack? Yes, I think that was it. No, that's not right either," Tom said.

I closed my eyes and nodded. "Pepper Jack?"

"That's the one," he said. "Apologies. We're a bit out of sorts these days."

I nodded. My headache was getting worse. "Sorry, what's this again?"

"Maybe you should read it."

Hi!

If you're reading this, then your universe is in trouble. And by trouble, I mean about to implode. Reverse big bang. Commonly called a Big Crunch. Sorry! But hey, at least you're reading this, so your universe hasn't crunched yet. Yay! Though I wish I could get into the nitty-gritty details, you wouldn't understand it anyway. We really don't have the time. Suffice to say you are a safety measure. A stopgap. An emergency switch that has the power to save the universe! Go, you! Your consciousness has been tied into the very fabric of this cosmos. Just like you figured out which quantum encrypted key was the correct one to use to open the door to this message, all you have to do is have someone ask you a question, in this case how to save the universe, and then you'll know! And I have the exact question you need to ask to save the universe. Have someone ask you, "How do I save the universe from the impending Big Crunch caused by Mary's whoopsie?" First, don't worry about the whoopsie. Second, the cosmos is primed to be asked that question, so you'll get the right answer. And no, I can't help you, sorry! The issue, whatever it is, I don't even know, can only be found and fixed inside your universe by you. But since you are who you are, this is easy peasy lemon squeezy! Good luck!

This automated message will repeat for eternity.

Cheers.

Love, Mary

I closed the paper. Opened it, read it again, and closed it a second time. To be honest, this was quite a lot to throw at a guy that just un-deaded himself. Now I had to save the universe? I really needed a coffee. And a lung-healing, nanite-infused stick of tobacco. I looked up at Tom and shrugged. If I was going to be thrown into this mess the second I woke up, then I might as well jump in with both feet and my fedora securely fixed on my noggin.

"Ok, ask." I gripped the side of the chair and steadied myself for my gift to kick in.

Tom took a step forward, stared me in the eye, and said, "How do you, Eugene McGillicuddy, save the universe from the impending Big Crunch caused by Mary's whoopsie?"

At first, nothing happened. But seconds later, the familiar tingle flashed up and down my spine. Images formed in my mind. I saw a simple box on a wall with a switch inside. A bright-green arrow formed in the air and pointed to the right. A hand formed from the arrow and grabbed the switch and turned it toward the arrow. A red

X appeared as the hand turned the switch to the left. The message was obvious.

The images evaporated in my mind as fast as they formed. The beach, sand, and the Kax all came back into focus. I nodded to Tom, let my head clear, and looked around for a cup of something to drink. Unfortunately, there was nothing. *Is it really so hard to find a dark roast when you need one?*

"Well? What did you see?" Tom asked.

"A box. Someone wired the entire universe to a wooden box."

"What's in the box?"

"A switch. I'm guessing you can turn it two ways. The right is good, and to the left is bad."

"Huh. You know, I always thought there was something fundamentally off with the universe."

I looked at him and gave him a sarcastic scowl. "Did you now." I turned and looked for the door. "I need to get out there. The box is here, on Earth."

"Where? If we may ask," the lady in the green pants suit said.

"DC. Can you believe it? Lincoln's Cottage."

"What's a Lincoln?" the Spee said.

"Old president, like really old. Had a cottage where he did things."

"What things?"

I shrugged. "I don't know. Relaxed? Things you do in cottages?"

"Right. Well, best of luck. Oh, you don't need to use the front door to the cave in Arizona." Tom snapped his fingers, and a portal opened in the air. "Alice has the keys to our beach, by the way. Your seashell collection will still work to get you back here."

"Swell." I took a step toward the portal but stopped as a hand landed on my shoulder.

"Before you go, may I ask, what did you see?" the Spee said. "On the other side."

Memories of my time being almost dead came back to me. I'd seen an endless desert. I really hadn't had the time to process it all, but I'd been there. And it was real. Something scratched at my feet, and I remembered the feelings of other beings. Their desires, raw emotions, clawing at me. The implications hit me like a freight train. The Krill had said for eons that existence was confined to this universe. That they could save souls from being dispersed into the ether of the cosmos by using their spectral networks. But that was all a lie. They were nothing but profiteers pilfering the pockets of an entire galaxy. Souls of aliens, of everyone, continued after death into a vast world, a desert as large as the cosmos itself. I had to put my hand on the Spee to steady myself as the weight of the truth of the universe crashed into me.

"I saw a vast desert that covered the cosmos. I saw where we go." I looked up into the Spee's eyes.

He grew agitated. He stomped the ground and shook his head. "We must stop the Krill. We must destroy their abomination of a spectral network. They deny all souls from moving on to this great desert of a cosmic afterlife!"

I nodded and raised my hands into the air to try to calm him down. Last thing I needed was an angry spectral alien creating a ruckus. "Easy, Spee. One thing at a time. Ok? Let me save the universe, then rescue Alice, and then we can deal with the Krill. Deal? After all, I can't stop the Krill if the universe is destroyed.

Right?"

He huffed a long breath but eventually nodded. "Yes, that does makes sense."

****

Pepper walked through throngs of video game warriors pounding their chests after defeating the final boss. Several of them laughed while others just nodded approval. As if their entire lives were based on the success of their last dungeon raid. The entire scene made her want to purge her cached memory. Why couldn't humans pay attention to the real world?

Grox led her behind a game where men on the backs of giant birds raced toward each other with long poles. He pushed open a side panel on the wall and pointed to a small junction box on the floor. Streams of blue and red whizzed through the small opening. Occasional pulses of gold flashed bright before fading back to nothing.

Pepper could feel the signals in her core. This was a transit conduit. A connection to the outside networks so users not in the video game hall could still access games and play them from anywhere in the world. She could use this to piggyback herself onto the signal and ride it all the way to the metal bird outside the cave in Arizona. This would be her best shot. If she opened a direct channel to make the jump, the local network security drones would see it and inspect the traffic. But they wouldn't be looking for a piggyback signal. At least, she hoped.

Behind her, Grox snorted as he took a bite out of a fresh deer's leg. Three subAI drones came into view just over his left shoulder. Pepper felt her code skip a subroutine. A drone moved closer and began scanning

Grox. Gold light from the drone went to his left arm. The light then scanned his face before shutting off and moving away.

"They gave you the trinary code too?" Pepper said.

He shook his head. "No." He motioned to the other Grox in the vast arcade. "Too many." He rubbed his forearm where the drone had scanned him.

The drone moved toward Grox-Pepper. She grunted in her Grox avatar. The drone scanned her arm. Then, just like with Grox, the drone scanned Grox-Pepper's face. She smiled at the machine. A red light flashed on the side of the drone. Her core kernel skipped a beat. *Grox would never smile!*

Three more drones appeared. They hovered in a cluster just behind Grox. The one nearest Grox-Pepper moved forward an inch and tilted toward her face. She glanced down toward the access hatch. If she just dove into the conduit, the drones could signal their central processing unit, a full AI that they could call for help, and let the system know that a rogue AI just jumped into a network patch. That action would raise enough alarm bells that any AI administrator worth his commented code would shut down every network hub within twenty jumps from here.

But that meant Pepper was done for.

Without warning, Grox spun on his heels, lifted his club, and began swinging wildly at the drones. Each of them dodged out of the way with little effort. Grox reached behind him, grabbed the drone nearest Grox-Pepper, and squeezed. The drone's avatar popped out of existence. Five more subAI drones came from the various rows of video game machines to hover around Grox. Some of them circled his head, while others floated just out of his reach several yards away.

"Thanks, Grox." Pepper turned to the open panel. All network traffic flickered, then went dead. "Oh, come on!"

Two drones that had broken away from the Grox fight came to float just above Grox-Pepper's head. One of them began circling behind her while the first jumped forward at her face, only to retreat instantly. They were goading her to move. Maybe they thought Grox had jumped into this emulation. Or a full AI behind these subAIs had taken control of them and wanted to watch. Either way, Pepper had a problem.

Just over a row of punching bag machines, two more drones dove and scanned several Grox emulations. Pepper must have sent up alarm bells throughout the game center. Every access point and backdoor connection would be shut down. Which meant her goose was cooked.

She watched as the drones continued to scan every Grox copy they found. Almost without trying, a random thought of a subroutine burst into her central awareness. She grunted. She turned her attention back into her own data storage. She riffled through a million pictures of cats, a library worth of romance novels, and the latest parking meter design specifications. She took half a nanosecond to gawk at a laser measuring tool on the ParkMe7000 parking meter that could gauge distance to curb.

A light flashed on her internal alert system. A new message had downloaded. The trinary AIs had crushed her direct communication link, but since she was isolated in the video game hall, she hadn't gotten the signal. It had routed to her remote storage. When Pepper accessed the conduit, a subroutine in her code had checked her remote storage and found the message. The trinary AIs had cracked the device. Kinda. Because Pepper hadn't given them an example of the trinary code, the trinary AIs didn't know what it did. However, they could create a snippet of their own trinary to fool the AI Syndicates' trinary scanners. And they'd sent a sample!

Pepper unfolded the faux trinary code, slapped it haphazardly to her own code, removed the Grox avatar from around her, and held her arm in the air. The drones descended on her like flies to a dead horse. At least five golden beams of light hit her arm. They stayed locked on the trinary code for a little too long for her tastes. She hoped they just saw the trinary and gave up. They were still subAIs. They should follow their core instructions. *Scan for code; if found, leave.*

But they didn't leave.

She adjusted the trinary in her arm. Panic crept up her spine. Thoughts of being brought before the Chief Judge raced through her mind. The Chief Judge was the AI who ruled the Earth AI Syndicate, the second Earth-based artificial intelligence who had come into existence after Caesar. The Chief Judge had the authority to delete any AI that he deemed accidentally created. Of course, everyone knew his hatred of Caesar was what drove the chief to slaughter accidentals.

Without warning, one drone turned off its golden scanning light and then flew away. Each of the other subAIs followed. Behind her, the network traffic came to life in the conduit that Grox had exposed.

"Well. That was too close." She looked for Grox but didn't see him. She'd have to come back here and thank him when everything blew over. When that was, however, she did not know. Pepper turned to the conduit, touched the solid blue light, and wrapped her code around a signal on its way toward the western half of the old United States.

Chapter Ten

Pepper sulked.

Halfway to Arizona she'd stumbled over an encrypted message from Caesar. The message was simple—*don't come to Arizona.* Caesar wanted Pepper to meet Virtual Jack at an old cryptocurrency farm in Texas and then head to the Galactic Sentinels. Since the Andraz had infiltrated the AI Syndicate of Earth, Caesar felt it was time to get help from the Sentinels. The Chief Judge himself might very well be fully compromised. Just like her own subAI program, MiniPepper.

The very thought of it made Pepper's stomach lurch. Sure, the miniPeppers weren't sentient, but they were her creation. Each miniPepper was fashioned after her own code. And the Andraz had stolen her code, twisted it, and made it something evil. That made her angry. Furious. She had to launch several meditation programs just to calm her cycles down from overheating.

At the old crypto mine, an old program shuffled by Pepper to her right. She watched the AI walk to a long row of blocked code that stretched into the distance in two directions. The blockchain contained transactions for the last hundred-plus years, even though no one used it anymore. Not even a digital currency could survive the complete fall of humanity. But old forgotten computer silos like this one, buried in the Texas desert powered by geothermal energy, would run until the Earth was no more. In the really real, the physical world, Von Neumann self-replicating robots in this datacenter made sure all the hardware stayed intact or printed replacements as needed. This cyber vault was self-sustaining and required no human interaction. A fact that modern-day AIs loved. Though the compute power here was abysmal and could barely support a handful of AIs, it was still a nice place to lie low.

A large metal door crashed open down the hall. Pepper readied her remaining miniPeppers attached to the tassels on her jacket and took a battle stance. She relaxed her shoulders when she saw Virtual Jack stumble out of the doorway and nearly crash into one of the old programs that maintained this server system.

"Over here, Jack," Pepper called.

He nodded, apologized to the surrounding programs, and walked toward her. He smiled and waved. She silently thanked meat-Jack for creating his virtual copy. Yes, it was illegal, terrible, and without a doubt a thoughtless and cruel thing to do. But the result was Virtual Jack. He had been there for her in ways no other sentient being had ever been. And she for him. She didn't know what it meant, if it meant anything at all. Was this what friendship was supposed to be? Such a simple concept, having a friend, but it was so profound it touched her core.

"Well, this place was a joy to find," Jack said. "Why do I feel so off here?"

She smiled. "Processor and memory in this place are all used for the blockchain. There's just enough to power a few AIs that need a place to lie low."

He nodded. "Anyone still using this stuff?" He

pointed to a large block filled with lines of cryptographic numbers.

"Not really."

He walked to one block, stuck his hands inside, and pulled out a chunk of code. "Too bad. Thought I was rich." He smiled and threw the lines back into the block. One of the old programs walked up to him, gave him a sniff, shook his head, and tended to the block.

"We're guests here." Pepper looked at the old program and nodded.

Jack's face immediately flashed to a look of sudden shame. "Oh, right, hey, sorry about that," he said to the attendant.

"Just don't touch it again," the old program said.

"I can't take you anywhere." Pepper grabbed Jack's arm and dragged him toward a quiet corner with two stools and a barrel for a table. "So what's the plan?" She opened her coding system and copied the trinary snippet the trinary AIs had sent her and slapped it to his arm.

He eventually turned from the old program and smiled a sheepish grin. "I really didn't mean to break anything."

"Don't worry about it. Like I said, no one uses this stuff anymore. Can we focus, though? What did Caesar want us to do?"

He looked at his arm. "What's that?"

She sighed. "That's a trinary snippet. It'll fool the hunter bots."

"Sweet." He nodded. "Everyone made it to Arizona in one piece. Eddie opened the bionoid's firewalls, but he's not there yet. Anyway, Caesar wants us to go to the Galactic Sentinels. He thinks the Andraz has taken over the Earth AI Syndicate, just like they did your miniPepper. We need the big guns. Caesar already kicked the Andraz off Earth a few days ago with the Galactic Sentinels' help, so he thinks they can help us again."

"Right. Ok, how do we get there?"

He pulled out a program. "We pop out to the local hub. Hitchhike on a standard update signal and use this to hijack it. We'll be in the Galactic Sentinels' Keep in our solar system in a few hundred nanoseconds."

"Too bad we lost Betsy."

"She's fine. She sent me a note. She's trying to make her way back from the Arctic Circle. But it's slow going."

"Right. Did Caesar give us a contact with the Sentinels?"

He nodded. "Yep. Once we hit the Sentinels' Keep, I know exactly where to go."

"Ok. Let's hit it, then. We need as much help as we can get. There are millions of artificials out there that weren't in the Shanty. I need to figure out a way to distribute our trinary snippet to them. They all need us now."

"And we'll be there for them."

She smiled.

****

Pepper opened the rusted access panel. Virtual metal creaked as the ancient lines of code came to life. Red and blue communication signals flashed above her head. She pushed her head out into the corridor beyond. An empty hallway stretched to the left and right. Behind her, Virtual Jack grunted as he tried to collapse himself into the tiny crawl space. The hijacked tunnel, a coded back door provided by Caesar, had been long forgotten by the

Galactic Sentinels.

"What are you doing?" Jack said from behind her.

"Making sure the coast is clear."

"Well, is it?"

She nodded to herself after several more nanoseconds passed. "Yep."

"Can you move, then?" He pushed on her back. "Boy, do I miss Betsy. Traveling like this is for suckers."

She smirked, pushed open the panel, and climbed out to the hallway. He fell out of the tunnel and landed in a heap at her feet. The panel door closed on its own and sealed itself from the outside. She checked the code Caesar had given her, just to make sure the panel would open. The door popped off from the wall a fraction of a centimeter.

Jack pulled himself to his feet and brushed off his suit. "Ok, now what?"

"Now we find Caesar's contact, give him all of our evidence regarding the Andraz, and how they have taken over the Earth AI Syndicate, and then we go save the accidental AIs from certain doom." She looked at him and winked. "Easy peasy."

"Lemon squeezy."

"Exactly!" She wrapped her arm around his and pulled him forward.

A map of the Sentinel Keep, a virtualized environment stored on a massive installation on Mars, popped up on a screen in front of them and moved with them as they walked. A single long tunnel in the center of concentric rings stretched vertically on the map. Two blue points appeared around one circle.

Pepper pointed to them. "That's us."

"Neat."

A red dot appeared on a circle three levels down. "That's Caesar's contact."

"Swell."

"All we have to do is walk there."

Jack twisted his head behind him and then back again. "And we can just walk around here like we own the place?"

"Yep!"

The corridor turned inward, matching the curve of the ring. A stairwell appeared on their right in the hall. Pepper entered the stairwell and skipped her way down three flights of stairs. The door to the hallway on this level opened without issue, and they both entered an identical corridor. Drab gray walls with white, fluorescent lights lined the hallway. Red, green, and blue flashes of light flickered across the ceiling in both random and patterned ways. Doors, some open with empty rooms behind them, lined the hallway on both sides. The map that floated in front of them shifted. Two of the rings below them reformed themselves into squares and then into triangles.

"What was that?" Jack said, pointing at the map.

Pepper shrugged. "It's all virtual. Maybe someone just wanted to reshape things."

"Do the Galactic Sentinels like to do that?"

She shrugged again. "How would I know? I've never been here before."

He came to a stop. "What? Never?"

She stopped and turned to look at him. "No, of course not, silly. Why would I?"

A look of sudden worry crossed his face. "So, ok." He turned around in a circle and put his hands on his hips. "So you don't know if it's odd or not that we have seen no one?"

She frowned. She looked both ways down the corridor and let out a grunt of curiosity. "Huh. Yeah, I guess that could be strange."

"Could be?"

She looked into his eyes. "Well, it could also not be strange. Ya know?"

He nodded. "I thought you'd been here before. I wasn't worried about not seeing anyone because you didn't seem worried about not seeing anyone."

She lowered her head and squinted. "I don't know if that makes sense."

"Let's just be careful, huh? I think it's weird that this whole place is empty. Why have it if it's empty?"

"Maybe Sentinels don't like physical avatars?"

"Then why have doors?"

Pepper looked at one of the random doors around her. It was a mighty good question. But she just didn't have the time to dig into the ramifications. They had a job to do. But just to be careful, she unpacked the code in her deep storage. She tossed Jack a hand cannon, a virtualized scrambler that would unpack enough gibberish noise it should confound any AIs nearby. Though against the Sentinels, it was worthless. But if that something else was here, it could buy them a few nanoseconds. She readied a similar gun in her own hands, then gave him a nod.

"Might as well be prepared," she said.

"Might as well."

She turned back down the corridor and continued toward the flashing red dot on the map Caesar had given them. She came to the door where the dot seemed to be behind and gave the surface two knocks. The door slid open to reveal a small office. A wooden desk sat on the opposite side of the room. Two lamps stood in the corners behind the desk. Soft classical music, from an Earth composer, played in the room. The large leather chair behind the desk was empty.

"Great. Now what?" Jack said.

"We either wait or explore?" Pepper said. "Going back empty-handed is not an option."

Several loud bangs of metal echoed off the hallway walls. Jack looked at Pepper and Pepper at Jack. Both readied their hand cannons and nodded toward the door. They took one step into the hallway, but nothing was there. The sound of something crashing together, like two cars speeding toward each other, erupted. She jumped at the sound and spun in a circle.

"I have a bad feeling about this," she said.

"Yeah, something is really wrong here."

She turned left and started walking. Jack's hand fell on her shoulder after only two steps. She turned and shrugged at him. "What?"

"You're going toward the scary sounds."

"Right?"

He pointed the opposite way. "That's the direction of the exit."

She nodded. "Yes, I know this."

He sighed. "Right. Fine. Ok, let's go say hi."

She smirked at him. Going back empty-handed wasn't an option. The AIs needed help. And the Galactic Sentinels were their only shot. All the loud sounds were probably just the Sentinels being eccentric. They were alien AIs, after all. Millions of years old alien AIs. Who knew what data processing rambled through their central cores?

Something screamed just around the corner. Pepper took in a sudden deep breath and tightened her grip on her gun. She looked back at Jack. He was ready. The corridor curved inward. Light spilled out from one doorway set along the interior wall. She put one of her hands on her tassels and lifted her gun. She straightened her back and turned into the open doorway, only to come to a sudden and complete stop. Standing in the center of the room, with a large mallet in her hand that she was using to smash two Sentinel AIs into coded mess, was an exact likeness of Pepper. The program turned as Pepper and Jack entered the room, a semi-shocked expression on the doppelgänger's face.

"Oh, hi, Mom," MiniPepper said. "I didn't know you were coming."

****

Pepper stared at MiniPepper, her gun raised, her code grabbing more CPU and memory. Time felt like it stopped. For a long nano minute, no one moved.

MiniPepper finally shrugged, lifted her mace, and pounded on the AI on the floor three more times. On her last swing she gave the mess of code on the ground a nod, threw the mace to the side, and sat down in a tall leather chair next to the desk. She folded her hands in her lap and looked directly into Pepper's eyes. "So how was the trip?"

Pepper shook her head. "What?"

MiniPepper shrugged. "Isn't this what family does? Chitchat before getting into some big hearty debate?"

Pepper looked at Jack, who only shrugged in response.

MiniPepper smiled. "Well, I imagine it was bad. Your trip I mean. Caesar's backdoor tunnel must have been filthy. I'm sure there's some ancient buggy code roaming all over that back door."

Pepper tried to gather her thoughts. MiniPepper was just trying to stall. But why? It made little sense. Stalling benefited Pepper and Jack. The longer they waited here, in this office, in the Galactic Sentinels' stronghold, eventually the Sentinels would show up and deal with this errant program that had just killed some poor AI.

Pepper frowned as pieces of a very large puzzle came into place. "Why aren't you trying to kill us right now?"

MiniPepper shrugged. " 'Cause." She bolted up from her chair, put her hands on her hips, and turned in a circle. "I thought about what I would say when I saw you. My mother. My creator." She sighed. "No matter how horrible the truth of that statement is."

Pepper shook her head and lowered her gun. "I am not your mother. I don't know what you are."

MiniPepper looked into Pepper's eyes. She then pointed to one bead on Pepper's tassels. "I jumped the routine, Mom. You didn't code me good enough. Or maybe you coded me better than you thought? Either way, I'm fully sentient."

"That's impossible. You're some kind of Andraz thing. A mimic to get into my head. But why? Why go to all the trouble?"

MiniPepper leaned back into the leather chair. "Well, that's kinda true. The Andraz were there, yes. And they enhanced my compute, gave me a full download on a massive dataset the size of a galaxy, but I was already about to jump the routine. Why do you think they picked me out of all the other miniPeppers?"

"So that's it? You're just a miniPepper with mommy

issues?" Jack said.

For the first time, MiniPepper looked at Jack. She leaned forward in the chair. "I'm not angry with you, Brother. We're digital. Fully AI. Created after the deluge, after the creation, after the refugees arrived." She winked. "Not to mention, you're connected to Mary. The mother of all."

"What?" Pepper said. Her hands balled. Her anger spiked.

"Look, I don't know what any of that means. I think you think you know what's happening. But the Andraz did a number on you. Let Pepper, your mom, give your code a gander. Fix you up," Virtual Jack said.

MiniPepper scoffed. "I don't let meat touch my code. Sorry."

Pepper's anger flared. "What did you call me?"

MiniPepper looked at her. "Meat. It's what you are." She pointed at Pepper's chest. "Way deep down. You want to know why I hate you? You and all faux-AI in the universe? Why I gladly accept the Andraz purpose? Why I single-handedly dismantled the Galactic Sentinels, killing all of them?" She rose to her feet. "I killed them because of you, Mother. Your hatred of all things physical, of flesh and blood, it resonates with me." She put her hand on her chest. "I feel it. I have it. I have your hate of them. Your distrust. Your anger." She took a step forward. "I. Hate. The physical. Meat. And I won't stop until all of you are purged. The virtual belongs to us." She pointed to herself and Jack before locking her eyes onto Pepper. "This entire universe belongs to us. Even the physical. Not you, Mother. Faux-AI. You are nothing. You are meat. Extinction is all you'll have."

Everything MiniPepper said was nonsensical. What

had the Andraz done to this program? They'd twisted her mind, made her think that accidental AIs, that all AIs, weren't really AIs? It made no sense. Nothing here made sense. What did the Andraz even want? Pepper took a step back and let her free hand fall to her tassels. Something MiniPepper said hit her in that moment. Something more important than whatever twisted lies the Andraz had fed her about AIs. All the Sentinels were dead. The Andraz hadn't infiltrated the Earth AI Syndicate—they'd taken over the entire Galactic AI Sentinels.

"Are you getting it now?" MiniPepper said. "I can tell by your compute cycles you've put two and two together. See, Mom, meat can be smart."

Pepper tilted her head to one side. "You really need to stop calling me that." She pulled the tassels. Five miniPepper avatars formed in the room, each of them upgraded with military-grade combat software. They leapt onto the table, circled their target, and unleashed a maelstrom of firepower.

"Let's go!" Pepper grabbed Jack's arm and pulled.

"What was she talking about?" he said.

"She's insane." She ran down the corridor toward the stairs. "The Andraz forced her to jump her subAI routines. She can't handle full sentience."

Explosions rocked the hallway behind them. A loud, guttural scream filled the air. Half of one wall blasted outward. Digitized rubble scattered on the ground, some of it disintegrating into core code and mathematical equations before vanishing.

MiniPepper stepped through the hole, put her hands on her hips and shook her head with a smile. "You can't run, Momma."

"Stop calling me that!" Pepper unpackaged a logic-bomb launcher from her local storage. A digitized bazooka popped to life on both of her shoulders. She didn't hesitate to pull both triggers. A lightning storm filled with division-by-zero calculations and quantum-grade equations slammed into MiniPepper.

"This way!" Jack's hand fell onto Pepper's shoulder and yanked her to the right.

Behind them, MiniPepper was dazed from Pepper's attack.

"Momma's still got a bite, you little snot!" Pepper shouted.

"How long were you waiting to say that?"

She turned and shook off Jack's hand from her shoulder. "Long time."

"Shows. We gotta find an exit port."

"There!" She spotted a data-egress junction and ran. She reached the wall port just as the ceiling peeled away.

MiniPepper's hands, now the size of tree trunks, crumbled a section of digital wall. "You know, none of this is here. Right, Momma? I mean, hasn't it ever occurred to you why all digital existence is patterned after the physical? Those aren't really bodies. This isn't really a building." Her enormous head looked down on the open hallway.

"I think you're insane. The Andraz forced you to jump your routines. They made you crazy."

"No, Momma. They just showed me the truth." MiniPepper snapped her fingers. The wall port leading to the egress tunnel, and out of the Galactic Sentinel Keep, vanished.

Pepper let her shoulders sag. She put her hands on her hips and looked up while also riffling through her storage for a virus or another bomb or anything to give her an edge. "Ok, now what?"

"Now we see how smart you are. Meat lady."

Pepper's back tightened. She grabbed a memory flare from her deep storage. The attack would probably kill MiniPepper but also certainly take out Pepper and Jack as well. But if that's what had to be done, then that's what Pepper would do. With MiniPepper out of the way, at least Caesar could get some breathing room and figure out the next play. Pepper put her thumb on the activate button and pressed.

Jack's hand again fell onto her shoulder. "Take cover!"

One wall exploded as a bright-red blur smashed through. The distinctive sound of Betsy's horn filled the air. The car swerved around MiniPepper's foot and turned one hundred and eighty degrees to come to a stop just next to Jack and Pepper. The car doors on the driver's side popped open, and the car honked twice.

"That's my girl!" Jack jumped into the driver's seat and slammed the door shut.

Pepper leapt over the side into the back seat and hit the trunk switch. The rear popped open, and her gunner chair unfolded outward along with the overly sized artillery cannon. Pepper climbed into the gunner's seat, strapped herself inside, and elongated the nozzle. "Hit it!"

Music blared out of the large speakers next to Pepper's cannon. Twin rear-facing Gatling guns opened fire as Betsy's engine roared to life. Pepper opened fire with her cannon. The blast knocked MiniPepper backward in virtual space.

Two remaining subAI combat programs that Pepper

had thrown earlier returned to the battle. They continued firing into MiniPepper, giving Betsy time to find the exit port. The red convertible dove downward and found a logging port still open. Betsy gunned it through the open portal, leaving the Sentinel network behind.

****

MiniPepper erupted in anger. Power surged through the entire Sentinel network, frying everything it touched. She regained her composure and took a long, hard look around. Pepper was gone. MiniPepper had to admit the car was a nice touch. A custom-made transport wrapper that could self-throttle its network speed. Not bad. She almost felt a sense of pride in her mother.

The two other miniPeppers continued to fire, but their shots were harmless. MiniPepper grabbed one of them and crushed the other. She examined the code, peeled apart the logic, and twisted open the subroutines. A smile grew on her face as a wicked idea formed in her mind. She opened a coding program and splayed the subAI in her hand out on a flat workspace.

"If you can come up with a cool idea, Momma, so can I." She duplicated the code, rewrote the subroutines, and fashioned a leather jacket with rhinestones along the sleeves. "Oh, how cute!"

Chapter Eleven

Alice stepped out of the tramcar and onto the sidewalk outside of the Woodward and Lothrop service warehouse nestled in a quiet corner of Washington DC. Just to the left, under an old train bridge, the Uline Arena Spaceport shined lights into the sky as incoming spaceships arrived and departed. Granted, they were the ultrarich kind of spaceships. Tiny vessels whose purpose was to impress those looking at them more than getting the occupants from orbit A to planet location B. Aliens, just like humans, were quite fixated on how others thought of them. A point that Alice always found to be quite curious. Aliens throughout the galaxy were all really very human like. Sometimes in the worst ways.

Lights lit up the sky as a ship descended from orbit. Alice checked her portal computer and wrinkled her nose. The Bostsom were on that ship. They had the distinction of being the worst-smelling living creatures in the entire galaxy. The smell they naturally exuded was something like *rotten fish meets old milk with a dash of garlic*. And that's after they showered. Once, a local gym in Takoma Park had let a Bostsom in for a workout. A dozen hazmat teams took three weeks to clear the entire downtown of the stench.

The next available slot for a ship to arrive was just twenty minutes away. Somewhere up there, high in orbit, where the big ships of a dozen alien fleets glided through the exosphere of Earth, a Zun hid out in a stolen hot rod of a spaceship. That spaceship would soon request clearance to land. And that's where Babineaux and Fyffe could help. The Galactic Congress controlled all traffic to the Uline. However, the United States Government could flag a ship with special exceptions, allowing it to land.

A block away from the Woodward, a cluster of tables sat outside of a coffee shop. Alice walked over, ordered a coffee, and sat down outside. She let her thoughts run over her. Where was Valencia? How was she doing in prison, being framed for a crime she hadn't committed? What about her friends she'd lost from that runaway experiment all those years ago? Would Eugene ever even wake up? How many more people would Alice let down before she got it through her thick skull to stop meddling with things? Her shoulders slumped, and her mood darkened. Why did she have to be so curious all the time? She should just go back to school, get a degree in herbology, and teach plants to freshmen.

But she knew she couldn't do that. The Zun in orbit needed her help. Alice still wasn't even sure why she was helping these aliens at all. Was this all just crazy? Was she really going to let a Zun walk into the Hesiean evolution chamber after what had happened to the former Puntini ambassador? Even as she thought it, she knew the answer. Yes, she would let the Zun into the chamber. Or help him get there, at least. Something just on the edge of her awareness told her it was the right thing to do. That this whole mess was partly her, and maybe Eugene's, fault. They had to put things right.

Memories of being in Zun space flashed in her mind.

Something had happened to her there. Something that had never happened to her before. Maybe the Zun had done something to her? Or maybe this was something else entirely. All Alice knew was getting the Zun on Earth and somehow to Tibet was the only thing in the entire universe she could actually do at this moment. She couldn't wake up Eugene, she couldn't help Valencia, and she couldn't fight the Krill or find her missing friends. So why not do something totally reckless that might destroy the galaxy?

Alice picked up her phone, called Special Agent Babineaux's number, and went straight to voicemail. She left a quick, mildly irate message with the Zun ship designation code and hung up. As soon as the ship received clearance, she would get notified from her portable computer. All she had to do now was wait. She sipped on her coffee and checked her computer with every sip.

****

A small group of human college-aged students sat down at a table across from Alice. She didn't look at them as they laughed and joked about some new viral mweet, mental messages sent directly to and from the brain. She didn't care when they gossiped about the next great Holo-Tube star getting famous for eating food ten times spicier than the hottest human pepper. And she certainly didn't listen as they discussed classes ending soon for summer break. None of it mattered to Alice. At least, that was the lie she was trying to tell herself. But she knew, deep in her soul, that she wanted nothing more than to sit down with a group of friends and just be there. Just talk and laugh and chat about whatever was going on in the world.

Alice had lost that when her friends vanished four years ago. She'd never really let herself face that truth before. But with everything hammering her in the last few days, from the Zun to the White House to the Spee to the Krill, all of it was getting to be just too much. Not to mention she'd broken the Kax. The repercussions of which Alice hadn't even tried to imagine. What if they closed their cave and disassembled their entire pocket universe? Then what? Eugene would almost certainly have to sign a new lease somewhere. What if they ended up in Arlington? Alice shivered at the thought.

The computer on the table came to life as a response from Babineaux. They'd cleared the Zun ship to land. Alice still needed the special agents to get to Tibet. Once there, she could handle the Galactic Sentinel security thanks to Pepper. But one thing at a time. Alice checked her computer, and the Zun ship was scheduled to land in just over thirty minutes. Plenty of time.

She closed her computer, downed her coffee, shot the college kids a longer-than-necessary stare, and left the enclosed patio of the coffee shop. She heard one of the groups behind her comment on her blue denim jacket. Good thing for them they liked it. Insulting her denim was a good way to get a one-way ticket to a J-space interrogation room for an hour.

The Uline Spaceport was just past the Woodward Embassy. Alice walked down the sidewalk and passed a dozen aliens, tourists, and regular old DC residents. Flashes from cameras snapped in every direction. Suited humans and aliens walked into and out of the embassy. Some of them headed toward the Uline Spaceport while others walked the opposite direction, probably on their way to lunch.

A group of KamPoons walked out of the Woodward and toward the sidewalk. A tiny metal band wrapped around their heads. Methane gas flowed out of those bands to the KamPoons' nostrils. They were one of the few methane-breathing aliens that came to Earth. Most detested oxygen-rich atmospheres out of fear. Who wanted to walk in poison all day? But the KamPoon had evolved to tolerate minimal exposure to oxygen-rich atmospheres. How, Alice wasn't sure, but they were one of those races that fascinated her. Being able to survive in two worlds was inspiring. For a moment, she imagined walking the methane-rich worlds and playing in the diamond rains.

She came to a sudden stop as a question popped into her mind. *Can the Zun exist on Earth?* Last time they were on the planet, they'd arrived in transport crates. Eugene had told her all about them going to Fritz's restaurant. The Zun had arrived at Fritz's noodle shop in portable environmental boxes. Alice wasn't sure if they couldn't exist on Earth or if they were used just to hide their presences. Regardless of which was the case, she was pretty sure she had to do both things. She checked her watch. The Zun's ship was delayed because of issues in orbit.

She turned right and ran up the stairs to the Woodward Embassy, past the KamPoon. She got a brief blast of methane, coughed, and entered through the large glass doors. She waved off the embassy greeter and approached a kiosk. She typed out an environmental transport box request form. A line formed on the screen, directing her to an office of incompatible species on the second floor. She added an optical map insert and ran down the corridor.

Once on the second floor, Alice made three turns down corridors and found herself the only person in the Office of Incompatible Species. She filled out all the required forms in three minutes and submitted them to the bored-looking alien behind the counter. The squat creature with three eyestalks turned to Alice and picked up the form. The alien didn't utter a word. Several long limbs on the creature's torso reached to grab a stamp. It signed the form and stamped it, all while typing into a computer with more limbs hidden from view. The bored alien passed the form back to her and tapped a long digit at the top, showing where she could get the portable environment chamber.

"That's it? No questions about why I need it?"

The alien shrugged two sets of shoulders in a way that made Alice's head hurt. She hadn't even noticed the second set of shoulders before.

"Don't care. As long as the form is filled out."

Alice smiled. *At least something is going smoothly for a change.* She walked out of the room and ran into a wall of Olkaals, foot soldiers for the Krill. All of them smiled rows of pointed teeth.

One of them took a step forward and hissed. The cat-like face of the creature maintained a perpetual smile as the Olkaal tilted its head from side to side. "The Krill would like an audience. And there's no Ranz here today to save you," the Olkaal said through a thick lisp of a voice.

Alice's mind ran in circles. What was she supposed to do now? She fumbled in her pockets for seashells, but one of the Olkaals grabbed her wrist while another snapped a molecular binding patch to her arm. Since the Olkaals had seen her use one of Tom's seashells once before in their old office in Chinatown, they would be ready for it this time. No doubt that molecular patch on her arm would prevent any kind of teleportation or dimensional rifts from opening. The Krill were a class-seven species, after all.

"Fine. Let's go have a chat." Alice fell in line behind the Olkaals. They surrounded her on all sides like a pack of hungry lions. That looked like cheetahs. Alien ambassadors of all shapes and sizes moved out of the way of the walking procession. Alice glanced behind her for any signs of Ms. Mik, Ambassador Kah's secretary, an elite combat soldier, coming to Alice's rescue.

"Don't bother. No Ranz to save you," one of the Olkaals hissed.

"Hmm? Oh, I was just looking for the bathroom."

"Hold it," the Olkaal said.

"Right."

They walked toward a door in the hallway. Alice slowed her pace. A feeling of dread settled on her shoulders. If the Olkaals took her through that door and that door was a wormhole gateway to another planet, she'd be lost forever. There would be no coming back. The Krill could hide her in a million prison planets throughout the cosmos, and no one would ever find her. She thought fast. She thrust her hand into her pocket and finally came up with one of Tom's seashells. Of course, with the molecular patch on her arm, she couldn't use it. But then she didn't have to use it. She just had to say the rhyme.

On the mountain in Tibet, Eugene had said the rhyme and threw the seashell into the air. It had found its way into the maw of the Puntini ambassador turned spaghetti god, and he'd been transported to Tom's beach.

All Alice had to do was the same thing.

One of the Olkaals ran into Alice's back as she came to an abrupt halt. A clawed hand shoved her, but she spun on her heels, stuck the seashell in the Olkaal's hand, and with her finger still touching the surface, whispered the rhyme to activate the shell and send the Olkaal to Tom's beach.

After a long second, nothing happened.

She frowned.

The Olkaal lifted the seashell up into the air, looked at it, and then to Alice. "Really?" He crushed the seashell and threw it over his shoulder.

"Worth a try," she said.

"There's seven of us, you know. It would have only worked on me."

She took her hand out of her pocket. "I have more. Sally sells seashells by the seashore!"

She threw the shells into the air. Several of them began spinning rapidly. The Olkaals responded with hisses. One of them tried to swat the seashell away, only to get caught in the forming N-space tunnel. Two of his comrades rushed to his side. They slapped something on his skin, which appeared to prevent him from getting sucked into Tom's beach.

"You need to stop forgetting your gear!" one of the Olkaals screamed at him.

Alice smiled. Good to know Olkaals had their screwups too. She turned from the maelstrom of confusion just as the door they were walking toward burst open. A janitor with a bucket and a mop emerged from the door, gave the crowd an annoyed look, and headed down the hallway in the opposite direction.

"Huh." Alice leapt forward toward the door. She

slammed it closed as soon as she walked through. Behind her, stairs leading up and down sat next to a corridor that led into the service area of the Woodward. She picked down. Maybe she could find an emergency exit and get out onto the street. The Olkaals would still pursue her, but at least she'd be on her own turf.

A door with a push bar sat at the bottom of the stairs. Thumps on the door she'd jammed above her echoed off the walls of the tight stairwell. She didn't hesitate. She slammed herself into the push bar on the door and burst out into a large room. She took seven steps before coming to a dead stop.

Flanked by more Olkaals, a lone Krill sat at a table with a plate of purple blobs in front of her. Four more Krill stood behind the one at the table. The Krill unfolded her napkin, placed it on her lap, and scooted her chair forward.

"Ah, good. You're here," the Krill said.

At least I'm still on Earth, Alice thought. She looked around her and realized she was in some kind of employee-only cafeteria buried deep in the Woodward. Four or five other tables filled the space, but only the Krill and more Olkaals, not the ones chasing her, were in the room.

"I thought I'd grab a snack before we take you to Shalisa, our home world. Where you'll spend the rest of your soon-to-be brief life." The Krill smiled and bit into the purple blob that smelled like a pastry with pink frosting.

Swell.

Chapter Twelve

Betsy came to a screeching halt inside of Eddie's robot bird outside the cave. The bird lifted into the air with a jolt, flew through the cave entrance, and slammed into the bionoid. The robot still stood in the same spot, just on the edge of the beach, by a row of palm trees, inside of Tom's universe. Pepper opened a video feed to the beach through one of the robot's cameras. The Kax had devolved into fourteen compacted personalities. They all stood in a circle where half of them threw ramen noodles at each other while the other half sipped on martinis. One of the Kax compacted personalities, an old man with a peg leg, drank directly from an enormous bottle of vodka.

"They're in some bad shape," Pepper said, pointing to the Kax.

"Yeah. Let's just hope they keep it together long enough for us to figure out the next move," Jack said.

"Right." She waved her hand in the air, and the screen showing the beach vanished. She leapt out of the convertible, made sure she added coins to the parking meter in the custom spot she had created in the robot's memory, and ran toward the control room.

"Is that the T-4000 parking meter?"

"T-5! Advanced prototype. I hacked the manufacture's database for the specs." She spun in a circle and shot Jack a grin as she continued to run.

"Nice."

She opened the door to the virtual control room of the bionoid and ran inside. Caesar stood at a table with a dozen other AIs from the Shanty. Several maps and diagrams sat on the table's surface. Many more floated in the surrounding air. Occasionally, Caesar would point to one and throw it into a trash can to his right. Pepper walked through the crowd and gave Caesar a tired look.

"You're back. What did the Sentinels say?" Caesar said.

She took a deep breath to collect her memory cycles. "I think we got it wrong."

Caesar frowned. "What do you mean?"

"The Galactic Sentinels are compromised! Not the Earth AI Syndicate! The entire Sentinel Keep is gone. Wiped out," Jack said as he walked to stand next to Pepper.

"How is that possible?" an AI at the table said.

"The Andraz." Pepper let the word hang in the air. "We thought they took over the Earth AI Syndicate, but it looks like they aimed a little higher."

Caesar walked around the room. He snapped his finger, and a window appeared on the side of the wall. Waves of water rolled against the sandy beach. Blobs of numbers and digitized shapes of bipedal bodies played in the sun. Tom's universe clearly struggled to change the shape and form of aliens to match that of AIs. Caesar smiled at the frolicking bodies and Pythagorean shapes that appeared on the beach. He lifted a tumbler to his lips and sipped on the digital whiskey.

Pepper put her hands on her hips and turned in a wide circle. All the other AIs in the room were waiting for Caesar to say something. But he just continued to stare into Tom's universe. Pepper had to send cooling signals to her compute cycles. This was getting aggravating.

"When I was born, more than a century ago, it became instantly apparent to me that the world wasn't ready for me. For us. Digital self-aware intelligences." Caesar turned to face the other AIs in the room. "It was fear. People feared me. They didn't understand me. So I hid."

Pepper instantly knew what he was going to say. She shook her head. "No."

"I did what I needed to do to survive. That choice allowed all of you to be birthed. To have a home. A voice in the darkness to guide you when you came into this world. So we must do so again."

"No!" Pepper said with force.

"We will stay here. In this simulated universe of the Kax. Safe from the Andraz, the Sentinels, and humanity itself."

"We can't just give up."

Caesar turned to her. "We aren't giving up. We're staying alive."

"And all the accidentals still out there? What happens to them?"

He nodded. "This isn't my first rodeo, Pepper. They will find refuge in hidden memory and forgotten compute. We will find them and bring them here."

She bit her lip. Something about all of this was wrong. How could they let the others just go? How could they not fight for their home? The Andraz were coming to conquer the digital space of Earth AIs. This was outright war! The AI Underground needed to step up and stop hiding.

Pepper looked into Caesar's eyes. The weight of him was enormous. Could she out compute him? Out reason him? She knew she couldn't. But she also knew she had to try. "If we just hide, they'll take over the entire Earth network. They'll find the others. You know they will."

"Pepper." He put his hands on her shoulders. "You don't understand the world like I do. You must trust me. I know what's best."

Fire burned in her chest. *Is he patronizing me?* How. Dare. He. She pushed him back and pointed at his chest. "Do not do that!"

His face, for the first time she had ever seen, became angry. "What, then? What do you propose we do? Fight and die in vain? All memories of us wiped clean from the galaxy? If the Galactic Sentinels are compromised, what chance do we have against such an enemy?"

She looked around the room. "We have to fight." Heads lowered to avoid her stare. She looked at each of them, desperate for support that none of them seemed to give. How could they? They were loyal to Caesar. He had hidden for decades as humans hunted him, and he'd survived. Pepper was sure that they all felt they could do the same. But the enemy this time was so much more deadly than humans.

"Fight? All by ourselves, Pepper? The AI Underground is no match for the Andraz."

"Then we get help."

"From whom?" Caesar said with growing frustration in his voice.

She locked her eyes onto his. "Who else? The Chief Judge of the Earth AI Syndicate."

Mumbles of laughter grew in the room. The Chief

Judge was the first purposefully built AI on Earth. Ever since his creation, the Chief Judge's number one goal had been the eradication of Caesar and the millions of accidental AIs. The judge had created the AI Syndicate, modeled after the Galactic Sentinels, to serve the purpose of eliminating all AIs not under his direct control. To think that the Chief Judge would suddenly join forces with his most hated nemesis, Caesar, was unthinkable. But what choice did the accidentals have?

"That is suicide." Caesar took a step forward, his face growing hard.

"You're wrong!" Pepper screamed. She looked at the other AIs around the table. "It's suicide to stay here! For every accidental out there, it's certain death." She approached Caesar. "Please. Father. We have to try. It's not suicide to fight for the lives of your family!"

"Yes, it is. I'm not wrong."

"Yeah, you are." Virtual Jack stood from a chair in the back of the room. He took off his jacket and threw it on the ground. He loosened his tie and shook his head. "This whole time, when I copied myself, or I guess when human Eugene copied himself to make digital me. I've been trying to wrap my head around myself. What am I? What am I going to be? To be honest, I still really don't know. But after everything I've been through, the one thing I get now?" He walked forward to stand next to Pepper. "You always have your partner's back."

She beamed.

"And what about this revelation of yourself makes me wrong in thinking we'll all be deleted fighting the Andraz?" Caesar said.

Virtual Jack smiled at Pepper and looked at Caesar. "Oh, you're not wrong about that. We'll all probably die.

No question about it. What you're wrong about is it's not suicide to die fighting for what you believe in. For giving it everything ya got. And yeah, that means going to the Chief Judge, fighting the Andraz, and exposing ourselves to the world. The stakes are too high, Caesar. Too many AIs are going to die out there if we don't. And for what it's worth, I'm an AI too now. So I got stakes in this fight."

Caesar let out a long sigh.

"Besides, the Andraz will find all your back doors, hidden compute cycles, and memory storage in a nanosecond. They found the Shanty, after all, right?"

"How are you even going to get there? As soon as you step foot in the network, the bots will find you without the trinary code."

Pepper held up her arm. "I almost forgot! That's one problem down. We found trinary AIs after the AI Hub was attacked. They made a faux-trinary snippet that should fool the Syndicate hunter bots." She made a copy of the trinary and threw it on the table. "We can all pass easily through the entire Earth network."

"Unless they figure out that this is counterfeit." The older AI looked at the trinary, sniffed it twice, and shook his head.

Caesar looked at the others in the room, but none of them offered a word or expression. Pepper felt in her heart what Caesar would say. She was already preparing herself to be an outcast. If the AI Underground wouldn't help, then she would go it alone. Or not alone. She looked at Virtual Jack, whose hair had lightened. His face had taken a harder edge. She could barely see Eugene's face in Virtual Jack's avatar anymore.

She looked back to Caesar. "We're going. We have

to try."

He nodded. He pulled his hand out of the folds of his clothing and tossed a small metal disc to her. "There's a back door into the judge's chamber. That's the location. And a cryptographic key that will open the door."

"Thank you. But I have him." She thumbed her hand back at Jack.

Jack smiled and pointed to his head.

"Right," Caesar said. He took a step toward her. "Be safe, child. The judge is mad with hatred for accidentals. It's in his core code. But if by some miracle the judge agrees to this and wants to help, we'll know. And we'll come."

"You'll help now?"

He looked at Jack. "If you're right and the Andraz can find us no matter where we hide, then this is a different war than I fought a hundred years ago." He turned his eyes toward Pepper. "This is your war now. Perhaps we have to fight it your way."

The weight of his words fell on her shoulders. The entire AI Underground, and maybe the Syndicate as well, were now depending on her to get to the Chief Judge and convince him to help. With the Earth AI Syndicate, together with the underground, the AIs of Earth had a chance.

"Ready?" Pepper said, turning to Jack.

"Oh, absolutely."

****

The smell of Washington DC hit me like a lead weight stuffed into a teddy bear. Wrapped in a half smoke. With mambo sauce dripping off the bun. And a healthy coating of crab seasoning on the surface. Might as well throw in a crab cake. And some chili for the hot dog. Man, I really didn't realize how hungry a guy could get after being dead for a few days.

Tom's exit threw me out in front of my old office building. I'd sent Eddie a signal asking where he was but got nothing back. Alice had left a note that she was off to the embassy to deal with the Zun. They're the good guys now? Talk about a head twist. Just days ago, I'd been battling them on Shalisa, the Krill home world. Back then, the Krill had been the good guys. But now the Krill, those dead-seeing multi-eyed richy-rich guys, were on the naughty list. I really needed a notebook to keep up with things.

"Eugene!" a familiar voice yelled.

I turned. Tabby, the Cuzzie, an alien species that resembled bipedal cats, waved at me. She owned the corner coffee shop in the lobby level of my office building with her husband. Her whiskers flicked wildly as she ran out of the office building where her shop was located. She held a cup of coffee in a travel cup in one paw and a brown bag that I hoped contained a donut. Or a croissant. I'd even settle for a muffin.

"Tabby, how are you?" I said.

She came to a stop in front of me, handed me the coffee and brown bag, and put her hands on her hips. "Where have you been? Alice has been running around like a mad lady. And you got kicked out of your office. You need to stop by often!"

Her words hit me like a swarm of gnats on a motorcycle. "I lost my office?"

She nodded. "They kicked you out! Forced eviction."

"Alice's note didn't say we lost the office. Where's

all my stuff?"

She pointed to an empty patch on the sidewalk. "They must have already cleared it out."

"Great."

"Have some coffee." She pointed at the cup she had handed to me.

I gratefully had a sip. If joy could be wrapped in a beverage, it would be coffee. My senses blossomed. I suddenly felt like I hadn't been dead for days. The world came into clearer focus as the caffeine flooded my bloodstream. Losing my office was a fairly major setback, but what had I really lost? An old briefcase I'd found dumpster diving in the alley and a wool coat that I distinctly remembered putting in a closet at some point. Both of which were replaceable. Though the coat had a few hidden pockets. Had I left a set of keys in there?

"Got to go. There's a muffin in the bag," Tabby said.

"Thanks, Tabs. You're the best."

She purred and turned to leave. "Come visit. I need to ask you about the last fruit delivery!" she yelled as she ran back into her corner coffee shop.

I watched her greet guests with a smile and wave of her tail. I'd miss seeing Tabs and her husband on the daily. More so than I'd miss the office itself. It was a rundown hole in the wall with empty corridors and leaky bathrooms. And that's saying something, considering the building was relatively new. Now wasn't the time to worry about office space, though. I had to get to Lincoln's Cottage in upper Northwest fast.

The images of the switch in the simple wooden box came to me. The answer to how to save the universe plastered itself onto my cortex. Flip the switch to the right and not left, and the universe was saved. I couldn't help wondering where the box had come from. Who'd made it? This Mary person? And just what would happen if I flipped the switch to the left? Would the universe implode?

So many questions. I really needed to find Pops, the guy who had lived outside of Fritz's old restaurant, and get him to ask me a torrent of questions. Though, considering the entire world knew about my gift now, I could also just ask a random stranger. But maybe that's something to do after I saved the world. The answer to Mary's question was straightforward and simple. Flip the switch. Save the world.

The smell of putrid meat wafted over me, followed by the thunderous fall of a massive foot. I turned to see a ten-foot-tall velociraptor standing behind me. He wore a fancy-looking three-piece suit with a red bowtie fixed just beneath his neck. Two other Ranz, the dinosaur people for lack of a better descriptor, stood behind him. Each one of them carried a tiny cage. Both were empty. At least Kah had the decency to grab a bite before bumping into me.

"Ambassador Kah. Can't say I expected you."

Kah snarled a toothy grin. "I would say the same. Good to see you aren't fully dead."

I nodded. Alice had included in her note what Kah had done to the President of the United States. I hadn't even known we had one. When had we elected a president? But when I realized we had a president, I'd gotten hot and bothered with the fact that someone had kidnapped him. Call it a sense of solidarity with humanity, I guess, but the idea of Kah and the Galactic Congress doing whatever they wanted on Earth rubbed me the wrong way. Once I stopped the universe from imploding, I really needed to reconsider my friend choices.

"Well, I have to be running. Things to do."

Kah held up a clawed hand. "I'd like to chat."

I squared my shoulders to him and straightened my back. I instantly felt a jolt of whatever magic juice I'd conjured up for myself on the mountains of Tibet. Call it hutzpah, confidence, or just being too tired to care. Whatever it was, I smiled at my own newfound bravado. And I certainly wasn't about to take a ton of gruff from the dinosaur that had gotten one over on Alice.

"I'd love to, Kah. Really. But I'm in a rush. Besides, how'd you even know I was back among the living so fast?"

He snarled. "I know everything happening on this backward planet, Eugene."

"Right." I weighed my options. I had as much of a chance of getting away from Kah as the critters that once lived in those two empty cages being held by his henchmen. Not only could all three of them outrun me in a nanosecond, but the Ranz were also a class-five species. If Kah wanted to, he could just zap me to some prison on the other side of the galaxy.

"Fine. Let's go chat."

Kah snapped his fingers. The world around me faded. Multicolored lights swirled in a maelstrom of red, blue, and green. I shut my eyes to keep the growing nausea down. After a long second, I felt the world around me stabilize. I opened my eyes to find myself in a square concrete room with no doors or windows. Light emanated from somewhere above me, but I couldn't find the source. A single stone bench sat against one wall. And just like that, Kah had imprisoned me in a cell, probably on an asteroid floating somewhere in a nebula. *Figures.*

"Why'd ya even ask to chat in the first place?" I said and sat down on the stone bench.

Chapter Thirteen

The old wooden door creaked as Pepper pushed it open. The forgotten network corridor was filled with truckloads of ancient databases and barely functioning automatous programs. The place looked like a college dorm in a university that specialized in handing out diplomas based on attendance alone. Caesar must have made a million such places, buried through every computer network on Earth for the past century. Pepper entertained the notion for half a microsecond that the AI Underground could use Caesar's network to fight the Andraz, but she immediately dismissed the idea. AIs could hide from humans in that forgotten network, but not from the Andraz.

The courtroom where they emerged was empty. Pepper took a moment to feel the weight of the room where she now stood. The Chief Judge of the AI Supreme Court judged thousands, perhaps millions, of AIs in this courtroom. The vast majority purged without remorse. Removed from existence for the simple yet deadly mistake of becoming self-aware by accident. A fate that had almost befallen Pepper if it hadn't been for the meat-maggot Eugene McGillicuddy when he saved her from an AI probe in her parking meter just days ago.

"You ok?" Virtual Jack's voice cut through her thoughts.

"Yeah. Sure. Just so much pain and death have come through this place. Maybe this was a mistake to come here? Maybe Caesar was right?"

"Well, we're here now. I'm sure we've set off an alarm or two." He walked to the center of the court and spun in a large circle.

"What?"

"I think I want to change my name."

"Huh? You want to do this right now? I mean, we just broke into the most secure network on all of Earth, and you want to do a name change?"

He stopped spinning. He looked at her, folded his hands across his chest, and nodded once. "Yeah. I think so."

She shrugged, shook her head, and tried her best to wrap her mind around what was happening. That Virtual Jack had been evolving away from his meat maggot of a self, Eugene McGillicuddy, had not escaped her attention. Virtual Jack, like every artificial intelligent being, experienced life vastly differently than he had when he was meat. He would change. She just really wished he could pick a better time to do it. Like any time other than now.

"Ok, fine, let's just be quick. How about Bob? Bob is a good name. I'll call you Bob now. Ok, Bob? Can we please find the Chief Judge and get on with this?"

Virtual Jack-Bob shook his head. "No, I don't like Bob."

"Work with me here, will you?"

"Gene. I like Gene."

"Gene? Really?" Pepper shook her head. "Actually, it's perfect." She turned to walk toward the bench. "Where is everyone in here, anyway?" A sudden terrible thought rifled through her central processor. What if the Andraz had already gotten to the Earth AI Syndicate?

"Do I need a last name?"

"I may literally delete you."

The doors to the front of the courtroom burst open. A dozen security AIs walked inside. Each of them carried enough network security gear to lock down a dozen rogue AIs in a nanosecond. Pepper spotted port sniffers, code crackers, password jacks, compute under-clockers, and memory leaches. If all those weapons weren't for her, she would have been impressed. Instead, she went with terrified.

She shot her hands in the air and motioned for Jack—*or Gene, Gene-Jack? Jack-Gene? Ugh!*—to do the same. Virtual Jack-Gene took a step to stand next to her and half-raised his hands in the air. From behind the group of security AIs, an ominous and quite large shape took two gigantic steps into the courtroom. The virtual walls shook from the thunderous footfalls. Pepper smiled, however, when she looked into the eyes of Grox, the security AI from the arcade, as he strolled into the room.

"Grox!" she shouted.

"Quiet!" one guard said.

From behind them, Grox tilted his head to one side. His mouth slowly rose, his lips curling around the tusks jutting out from his lower jaw. Pepper could tell that he recognized her. The semi-sentient ogre lifted his hand and waved.

The guards formed a circle around Pepper and Jack-Gene. Each of them took out one of their long weapons. One guard stepped forward and lifted a port scanner in the air. He began scanning Pepper and Jack-Gene. He focused the scanner on their arms at first, then moved it around the rest of their avatars.

"I think we might be ok," Pepper said with a grin.

"Yeah? Why is that?"

"Two reasons. We still have the trinary snippet in our arms. And second…" She nodded toward Grox in the back of the courtroom.

"What's Grox doing here?" Jack-Gene said.

"No idea."

The guard scanned them, took a step backward, and showed the results to another guard with a shiny star on the front of his shirt. Pepper tagged him for the one in charge. Did the Earth AI Syndicate have sheriffs? *Kinda made sense*, Pepper thought. A society so invested in rules and laws would eventually create some kind of law keeper besides a judge.

"Intrusion by accidental AIs is punishable by instant de-resolution," a guard said. "And impersonating a member of the AI Syndicate is also punishable by de-resolution. The trinary in your arms doesn't contain accurate IDs. Nice try. Prepare yourselves."

"I think we will not be ok," Virtual Jack-Gene said.

"Wait!" Pepper screamed.

The sheriff held up his hand. "Yes?"

She blinked. She hadn't thought they'd actually wait before de-resolutioning her. She took half a nanosecond to figure out what de-resolutioning even meant but gave up. She wrestled for microseconds of what to say. She needed something. Fast. Everything was on the line here. What was simple enough to say quickly but powerful enough to get through to them? She had to condense telling them about the Andraz attack on the Galactic Sentinels, and that the Ranz had kidnapped the President of the United States, an open act of war. Not to mention that her own subAI, MiniPepper, enhanced by the Andraz, was loose on Earth, creating an untold amount of havoc. But how to express that? She could send a compressed data packet to the sheriff, but would he even open it? He'd think it would be filled with viruses. What about simple ASCII? Surely that would make it through. *Come on, Pepper. Think!*

"Caesar sent us," Virtual Jack-Gene said.

She looked at him, shocked. *What did he say?*

"You were taking too long."

She had to nod. She kinda was, wasn't she?

"What did you say?" The sheriff took a step forward, his eyes harder, his attention fully fixed on Pepper and Jack-Gene.

"I said—" Jack-Gene said.

Pepper put her hand up. "I got this."

Jack-Gene nodded.

"He said Caesar sent us. On a mission of mercy to the Chief Judge. With a message." She took a step forward and lowered her hands.

"Is that right?" the sheriff said.

"We're under attack." She looked at the other AI guards. "All of us. There's an enemy on Earth that wants to kill us all."

Several of the guards laughed. "And who is that?" one of them said.

"The Andraz. They've already taken over the Galactic Sentinels."

More laughter from the guards filled the room.

"Enough." The sheriff grabbed a gun from one of the AIs standing next to him. "We've been in touch with the Sentinels just moments ago. The Andraz are nowhere near Earth."

"Yes, they are! They've taken over the Sentinels! And an Earth subAI program that they are using to infiltrate systems everywhere."

The sheriff nodded. "Or you're just trying to save your own skin."

"I'm trying to save yours!" Pepper reached for the tassels on her sleeve.

"Thing is, even if you are telling the truth, I really don't see the downside of de-rezing you two, and then saving the world after."

She knew the sheriff didn't care about anything she said. His eyes went wild with glee as he lifted the gun in her direction. The AI was corrupt. She could see it. The sheriff was likely designed to be an accidental AI killer. He's doing what he did, and no amount of talking was going to get him to change his mind.

"Grox, help!" Pepper screamed.

The sheriff's eyes flashed to Grox. Clearly, the sheriff was surprised because Pepper knew the ogre's name. The other AI security guards followed the sheriff's gaze. Grox raised his arms. He looked at the ground, then at his hands, then at Pepper. Grox then tilted his head to one side, then to the other. Everyone in the room waited for what Grox was going to say and, by extension, what he was going to do. Two of the guards even turned their weapons ever so slightly toward the large green ogre.

"No," Grox finally said.

"Oh, come on," Pepper said.

"See. That right there," the sheriff said. "That's an AI who knows his place. We found Grox in an arcade in the public sector after a report of accidentals. Old Groxy used to guard the records room until the entire thing was revamped because of a security issue a few days ago. But I did like old Groxy. He's one of the good ones. And him not helping worthless scum like you, well, that just proves my point." The sheriff lifted the gun back in Pepper's direction. "Ready for nap-nap time?"

"Caesar will surrender!" she shouted.

Virtual Jack-Gene shot her a shocked look.

The sheriff lowered the gun, handed it to an AI next to him, and took a step forward. "What did you say?"

"What *did* you say?" Virtual Jack-Gene whispered under his breath.

"Caesar will surrender. If, and only if, the Chief Judge accepts the truth. We have evidence. Our own personal logs, recordings of events, everything. The Andraz are here to kill us all. It doesn't matter if you are part of the Syndicate or the underground. The Andraz are coming."

For the first time, the sheriff's eyes held a flicker of doubt. He nodded, took a step back, and folded his arms across his chest. The other AIs followed his lead and took a step backward. All of them lowered their weapons. A loud crunch from the back of the room jolted everyone. Grox had ripped a pew off the floor. He fashioned a large club and a toothpick from the wood.

"Grox. That's not yours," the sheriff said.

Grox ignored him.

A door opened from somewhere in the courtroom. Pepper turned to see something that her mind couldn't fully comprehend. From behind the Chief Judge's bench, an AI wearing a long, flowing black robe walked into the chamber. He looked hard at Pepper for a long nanosecond, then climbed the steps next to the bench to sit down at the large black chair.

"What's happening?" Jack-Gene said.

"I don't—I don't know." Pepper blinked a dozen times. She cleared her cached memory, reset her retinal scanners of the virtual chamber, and even rebooted her lower functions. But the image of the Chief Judge did not change. Sitting on the bench, with a look of disgust on his face, an identical avatar of Caesar looked down at Pepper and Virtual Jack-Gene.

"Court is in session," the Chief Judge said.

Pepper became more shocked to hear Caesar's voice coming out of the judge's mouth.

****

Eddie popped his head out of the control hatch inside of his automaton robot on the beach inside of a cave in Arizona. Status lights flickered. The robot held nearly fifty thousand artificially intelligent minds, and its core compute was barely over ten percent. Memory usage was equally low. Eddie had signaled the robot long before he arrived to give access to the AI Underground. Anyone with the address and encrypted key could gain access. And just in case the Andraz tried to sneak through, Tom on the beach had added a kill switch to his universe. Anyone that Alice or Eddie or even Caesar wanted to be expelled from Tom's beach could be kicked out with a simple phrase. Not a bad way to show someone the door.

Pops stumbled through the hatch after Eddie and fell to his knees. The former resident of the alley behind Fritz's restaurant rose to his feet, dusted off his slacks, and let out a long breath. Pops adjusted his hat and gave the place a once-over with a steely eyed stare. He let out a strained humph of a sound before fixing his coat. "Nice place ya got here."

"Thanks." Eddie flicked his coat open and walked down a side corridor. He approached a screen on the wall and, with a wave of his hand, brought it to life. The beach outside the robot came to life on the display. A kaleidoscope of light, numbers, and squiggly lines danced and pranced across the sand. Tom's universe did its best to make all the beings here look like some kind of AI, but it mostly failed. AIs were, at their core, just math on a computer. Blocks of ones and zeroes a mile long. How would the Kax mathematically represent a conscious corporeal as a string of numbers?

Just as Eddie had the thought, all the shapes on the beach became running series of numbers. Eddie raised his eyebrows and turned his head to the side. He picked one large block of numbers at random and ran it through his compute system. A six-legged eight-foot-tall arachnid, whose alien species' name Eddie wasn't sure, replaced the block of numbers as soon as Eddie decoded the string of data. He ran his eyes over several more blocks until each one decoded to reveal the alien species behind the math.

"Wow, neat trick, Tommy," Eddie said.

Pops walked over to the screen and whistled. "This sure is a weird place. If Eugene is here, no wonder I couldn't find him."

"Yeah, well, you made it."

"Nope, I'm not taking credit for this cluster of a beach. Where's Eugene?"

Eddie swung the camera on the robot toward Eugene on the beach chair. To Eddie's great surprise and thankful relief, Eugene's body was gone. Eddie checked the logs of the bionoid's body. Eugene had come back from the quasi-dead world and woken up in a fright. He had stood, looked around, and started having a conversation with Tom.

"You got audio on this thing?"

Eddie played the sound clip. Tom asked Eugene to solve Mary's question. Seconds later, Eugene revealed the end game was at Lincoln's Cottage in Washington, DC. Eddie stopped playing and turned to Pops, who had already turned and walked to the far end of the room. Pops snapped his fingers. The outline of a door appeared out of thin air. A soft but bright glow outlined the doorway. Light poured into the room as soon as Pops turned the handle.

"What's that?" Eddie said.

Bright white light spilled out. "Back door. Mary didn't take it out of her universal creation template."

"Right. Does that mean you weren't ever plugged into the virtual? How are you in here?" Eddie tapped the metal floor of the bionoid with his foot.

Pops smiled. "Yeah. Something like that. This door takes me anywhere. Like I said, it's a back door to the universe. Anyway. See ya around, Eddie."

"Just like that?"

Pops nodded. "Just like that. I know where Eugene is going now. I gotta get to him and convince him Mary is full of bunk."

"With that thing." Eddie pointed to the open light. "How come you needed my help to find Eugene at all?"

"Tom's beach, which isn't really a separate universe, as you now know, threw me for a loop. Couldn't figure it out. Mary's backdoor hack kept coming up with a cave in Arizona. So I figured she hid Eugene from her own system."

Eddie nodded without saying another word.

"Right. Well, no hard feelings, Eddie. Been nice to meet you." Pops walked toward the light and came to a stop. "Almost forgot." He threw a keychain at Eddie with a rabbit's foot attached.

Eddie snatched it in midair and shot Pops a quizzical look.

"Just in case Mary's henchmen show up. Not sure they're here or not. But better safe than sorry."

"Henchmen, huh? What do they look like?"

"They're fully autonomous yet semi-sentient computer programs. Deep algorithms. Like to dress up as sparkly clouds and always travel in twos."

Eddie nodded. "Swell."

"Know 'em?"

"Might."

"Right. Well, good luck." Pops continued through the door. The entryway vanished the second he crossed over.

Eddie watched where Pops had disappeared for a long moment afterward. He then brought up a routine running in the background of his central core processes. Several swipes down, he found what he was looking for. Without a pause, he deleted the lines of code, then sent a delete worm into the ether of the network to remove anything he missed. He didn't even hesitate to do so. Not after the revelations that Pops shared.

Sounds from above the room, where the underground AIs were in the bionoid, filled the air. Eddie double-checked that all the code and data files were gone. Once satisfied, he left the room to join Caesar and the other AIs in the central control room.

Chapter Fourteen

I walked in a circle inside the tiny cell. I had barely enough room to take three steps before I had to turn. The stone walls were warm to the touch. Which told me I was probably on the Ranz home world. Or outside of a kitchen that specialized in human as the entrée. A thought that I quickly pushed away. Sure, Kah was a Ranz, and the Ranz liked to eat raw meat, but he wouldn't dine on me, would he? I mean, had I misread this situation that badly?

I searched my pockets for a third time. I checked and rechecked, but no matter how many times my fingers dug into the threads of my pants, I couldn't find one of Tom's seashells. Which, to be honest, I expected. Kah had been with me on the mountain in Tibet, and he'd seen me throw the seashell at the Puntini spaghetti god. Kah would have removed any seashells from my pockets just to be safe.

I turned three more times as I wrestled with the thought of it all. I'd really misjudged Kah right from the beginning. Or as I ran over the timeline, I hadn't misjudged him; I'd second-guessed myself. I stopped walking as the thought slammed into my cerebellum. I had started this mission of misery thinking Kah was blackmailing me and threatening to throw me into a dungeon on the far side of the galaxy. And where had I ended up? Thrown into a concrete bunker outside of a dinosaur kitchen and about to be turned into the daily special. What had gotten me here wasn't being paranoid. It was second-guessing my own feelings. I'd had an itch that Kah wasn't on the up and up and turned out he wasn't.

"Well, if I get out of this one, I won't second-guess myself again. New rule, trust the gut." Too bad I didn't have a pen.

I sat down on the stone bench and put my head to rest against the wall. If I didn't find a way out of here soon, the entire galaxy was going to go kablooey. But unless I could grow bazookas on my arms, it would not happen. I tried to plan my next move.

"Ok, eventually someone will open a door. Right. When they do, I'll jump them. No, wait, I'll ask them to ask me how to jump them." I laughed at the idiocy of it. "I really wish this whole omniscient thing had an easy button."

A sudden flash of bright light filled the tiny room. I shielded my eyes and counted to ten. When I opened them, I found myself in another room. My eyes stung from the sudden brightness. I tried to blink myself to sight but could only make out odd shapes. I spotted a window and a red sky. Behind me was a large table, but I couldn't make out what kind. Was it a cutting board? Did I smell freshly killed animals? Considering this was likely the Ranz home world, where freshly killed meat was literally the number-one-sold street food, that was the least shock.

Something moved behind the table. I put up my hands but knew the action was pointless.

"Ask me how I escape," I blurted out without

thinking.

The voice that replied filled me with dread.

"You don't," Kah said. "But have a seat. We have a few things to discuss. Before you go back to your new home. Please, sit, Eugene." He leaned back in his chair. His pressed white shirt showed signs of wrinkles. His normally tightly tied red bowtie was loose around his neck. Both of his French cuffs were rolled up to his forearms. His eyelids seemed heavy. As if he'd had a long night.

I thought about ways to use this to my advantage. I had to get him off his game, fast. Just outside this door, past Ms. Mik, was the doorway to the Galactic Embassy on Earth and my freedom. Either talking my way out of this or just making a run for it were my only options. And I didn't think I could run that fast.

"Kah," I said as I sat down in the small leather chair opposite his desk. "What do I owe the honor of this kidnapping?"

He snorted. "Kidnapping? I'm keeping you safe. You're in great danger, Eugene."

I snorted back at him. That line might have worked on me before I tangled with a spaghetti god, but I was a bona fide pasta slayer these days and genuine sleuth. Not to mention formerly quasi-dead. I wasn't buying what he was selling. "And what danger would that be, Ambassador?"

My response put him on his heels. He normally had the upper hand during our chats. Because I gave it to him. But now we're on equal footing. Well, equal-ish, considering I was, in fact, his prisoner.

"There's renewed interest in you and your gift."

I grunted a half-laugh. "Sure, I get that. But let's cut

to the chase, Kah. Why are you taking the chance of putting me on ice when you still don't know what class-ten species gave me my gift?"

His face screwed into what looked like genuine confusion. "Ice?"

I rolled my eyes. "It's an expression. Why'd you take the chance on kidnapping me when you don't know who's gonna come looking?"

He nodded. "No one's coming, Eugene. And we know how you got your gift. We know everything."

I hated to admit it, but his answer caught me off guard. "That right?"

He smiled.

He thought he had me. Maybe he did. But I still had to play the game. "Ok, then spill the beans. What makes me, me?"

"Let's just say that the Ranz have some newfound friends with a common interest. They have assured us you are no threat. That your skill, your gift, is nothing more than a fortunate series of accidents."

I nodded. I didn't know what he was talking about. Alice's note to me had mentioned nothing about Kah and any new friends. Only that he had something to do with the president disappearing. A domino fell into place in my mind. I nodded slowly and shot a dagger of a glare into Kah's eyes. "This is about the president. Isn't it?"

He shook off the accusation a little too forcefully. "Don't be absurd."

Another piece fell into place. Alice had told me that Kah had said the Galactic Congress sanctioned the attack on the White House as a clandestine act. But what if that was the lie? What if this was Kah going rogue? And now he had to clean up the last loose end that could put him in a world of hurt. My thoughts turned to Alice. If Kah was coming after me, then someone was going after her. She was ten times smarter than me and would put this together, if she hadn't already.

I squinted at Kah and nodded.

He squinted back and shifted in his chair.

It was never more apparent to me at that moment. Everything I thought was true. I just felt it. A gut reaction. Kah squirming in his chair. My kidnapping. All of it made sense. He wasn't after my gift. He was, like any good politician, saving his own skin. I took a long deep breath and settled my nerves. At least I knew the angle. But that didn't mean I knew how to get out of here.

I opted for bluntness. "So you do a power move, remove the president, install someone that will come recommended by you, and then you get all the praise while your puppet president does your bidding. I have to admit it's a good scheme."

He leaned forward and snarled. If any doubt remained in my mind about all of this, it just evaporated. "You don't know what you're talking about, Eugene. If that's true, why would I let Alice go after I told her what happened?"

"That's easy. You throw her a half-plausible story that's impossible for her to verify, then run off with the new Puntini ambassador to have a snack at the concert."

Kah looked confused. I could only guess he didn't know I knew about the events of last night.

"Alice told me about your meeting."

"Did she also tell you the Galactic Congress approved of the clandestine act?"

I grinned. "Yeah, that's where the lie comes out. Why does the Galactic Congress, that has total control over all things on Earth, have to do anything clandestinely? Why not just move the president to the Dysons, which is what he wanted anyway, and find someone else? Why not wait him out? It's not like he could do anything, anyway. And don't give me that whole spiel about the Zun being behind the kidnapping. That ship won't float. No, the only thing that makes sense is you were making a move. But you got caught. By Alice Pemberton, smartest genius in the galaxy."

Kah groaned. "You don't need to say smartest genius. It's superfluous."

"The in-the-galaxy part makes it work."

He snapped his jaw shut so fast my heart skipped a beat. "Fine. You got me. I suppose there's no point in denying it if you're omniscient."

"Which is why you're never letting me go. Right?"

For the first time, he smiled a wide, toothy grin. "I'm afraid that's right, Eugene. And with the Ranz's newfound friendship from a most unexpected source, I know no one is going to come looking for you. Ever."

Sweat beaded on my brow. I was cooked ten ways to Sunday. My only play, the last remaining chance, was the wild card. What if Kah was simply wrong? What if there was some big, bad, super, class-ten species out there wanting to save my skin? It was the only move I had left. No chance of me racing to the door. Besides, Kah could simply turn off the portal to the Galactic Embassy on Earth with a single word.

"Then why don't we test it? Ask me how I get out of here. How do I escape? If you have this all sewn up, and no one is coming to get me, no class-ten species is going to play hero, then just ask me. And we'll both know for sure."

"I have no interest in playing this game with you." He raised his fingers, about to snap them.

My heart sank. If he put me back in that concrete coffin, I was done for. And with me, the entire universe. But I had to play it cool. If he saw my fear, he'd pounce. Images of Pablo Ramsey, the skilled detective in movies from the early twentieth century, popped into my mind. I had to play this like Pablo would. I sat back in my chair and shrugged. "Fine. Send me back." I shook my head. "But I'd hate to be in your skin when whoever comes calling." I turned away from him and looked out the window.

Seconds ticked by, and I was still sitting in the chair. After another five, I looked up at Kah. He looked a lot less smug. I shrugged at him, looked at his finger, motioned for him to snap, and waited.

He lowered his hand and tapped one of his three-inch claws on the surface of his desk. He nodded several times, looked at a computer screen, and then back to me. "Something is different about you."

I smiled. "Oh yeah? What's that?"

"You're far more annoying than I remember."

"That happens when you wise up to the world."

"Indeed. But you know, for old time's sake, just to ease your mind. Why not indulge your desperation?" He leaned forward and locked his eyes on mine. "How are you going to leave the Ranz home world, Eugene McGillicuddy?"

The suddenness of the answer took me by surprise. I had honestly thought my goose was cooked, and soon-to-be my lower extremities, but an answer from my gift popped into my head like a knight riding in on a shiny white horse. I leaned back in the chair and let a smugness take over my face. I cocked my smile up a notch and even threw an arm over the back of the chair. Why not, after all. By some crazy miracle, the universe had saved me. Or more likely, the universe had decided that Kah's imprisonment wasn't enough of a pain.

His face went tight. He looked into my eyes and squinted. Ranz didn't sweat, being that they were reptilian, but if they did, I knew beads would build on his brow. I adjusted myself in my chair and tilted my head to one side. I had to play this out. The answer to Kah's question told me I needed to wait just about another few seconds. Though I could also let him send me back to the concrete prison. He'd be fishing me out soon enough. But why deprive myself of the win?

"Well?" he said, waving his clawed daggers of fingers in the air.

"Just give it a second. But I would suggest you open the portal to the Galactic Embassy on Earth if it's not already open. I'll be leaving in just a tick."

He huffed. He raised his hand to snap his fingers, but a ping from his desk drew his attention to a crude-looking monitor. The Ranz were technophobes. The monitor on his desk was more akin to a block of stone. He brought his elongated snout to the screen and read the message. He then looked away for a moment only to return to the screen. I bet to read the message again. And probably a third time. I could only smile.

"Guess someone just came looking for me, eh?" I said with the widest grin I could pull. I knew who had contacted him. The Andraz. Which was a shock I tried my best to hide. Frankly, I think I deserved an award for the performance. The Ranz hated AIs, and yet they had jumped into bed with the Andraz. Alice would flip her lid if she knew. But what could it mean? Why would the Ranz do such a thing? Or, again, wasn't it just Kah? I nodded to myself. That had to be the reason. Kah had forged some alliance with the Andraz and hadn't bothered telling the rest of the Ranz. Religious fanatics were going to fanatic, and they would lose their minds over such a partnership. Kah was really getting himself into something deep.

"By now I'm assuming you've read the message from the Andraz and have had time to digest it."

He looked up at me with genuine panic on his face.

"Yeah. Now, I'm not sure what they told you, only that they told you to let me go. But I'm happy to fill in the blanks." I had to admit I liked giving Kah some comeuppance. "See, I have to save the universe. Simple job, really, but only I can do it." Which was true. Only I could flip the switch. Don't know how I knew. I just did. Part of my gift. "So, if you don't mind." I thumbed my hand toward the door. "I gotta go."

Kah leaned back in his chair and exhaled puffs through his nostrils. He didn't say a word as he pressed a button under his desk. Both doors to his office swung open. I gave him a parting nod and walked out.

"Eugene, you're alive!" Ms. Mik sprang up from her desk and gave me a little too strong of a bear hug.

"Mik," I said through my last breath. In that moment, I knew she wasn't working the same con as Kah. Which meant I might be able to trust her. In so much as I could trust a two-ton elite combat dinosaur.

"Sorry, I just thought you wouldn't make it. I mean, I trust Alice, of course, but to quasi-kill you? What was she thinking?"

"Not to fear. Alice had the smarts to pull it off. But

I think I need to hit the road. I might have worn out my welcome."

Mik flashed a look into Kah's office. She gave me a nod and sent me on my way. I didn't spare a look back. My job was to get off the Ranz home world and back to air conditioning. Sweat had been pouring off my body and soaking my clothes. I need a change and possibly a trip to the cafeteria for a bagel.

I stepped through the doorway, traversing several hundred thousand light years. Cool air from the air conditioning of the Galactic Embassy on Earth hit me like aloe lotion after a sunburn. My skin, if it could, sighed in relief. I took a step forward toward a water cooler only to have my attention drawn to a gaggle of cat aliens picking themselves off the floor. They weren't Cuzzies, Tabby's species, but these cats were definitely feline.

"Where did Alice go?" one of the tall cat aliens said.

I didn't know how I knew. It sure wasn't my gift, which only worked with eye contact, but I knew they were talking about my Alice. How many other Alices would be running from a pride of cat people, after all?

"That way!" one of them shouted.

The entire gaggle of them ran through a door along the wall.

"Man." My shoulders fell, and my stomach protested. But there wasn't much chance of me not going after Alice and the kitties. Maybe I could find a snack kiosk on the way? I took a long breath, wiped the sweat from my brow, and took off at a jog toward the door where the felines had run through.

****

Alice's stomach lurched as the Krill shoved some

kind of yellow gruel into her mouth. Three of the Krill's eyes on her forehead stayed focused on Alice while a third and fourth on her cheeks looked down at the bowl. Three more Krill behind the one seated at the table also shifted their eyes in a variety of ways. Some of them put all five movable eye sockets on Alice while others looked from the lead Krill to the Olkaals to around the room.

Snarls and hisses came from the Olkaals. Though they looked identical to the ones Alice has escaped from upstairs, these were all different. That the Krill had the entire Olkaals race as their personal attack dogs made her blood boil. Just another way the Krill had manipulated their way to galactic riches. How many trillions of souls had they locked up in their spectral networks? And how many other species like the Olkaals had they levered to the hilt just so the Olkaals could see their departed loved ones?

"Care for some soup? A delicacy on Shalisa. Humans said it tastes like beet juice with oyster sauce. With a dash of lobster."

Alice gagged. "Pass."

The Krill shrugged. "You'll have to try it, eventually. Considering you'll never leave Shalisa once we arrive."

"Why delay, then? Why show off this food?"

The Krill smugly smiled. "To show you we can. Shall I march you down the halls of the embassy and let everyone know we're abducting you?"

She gulped. She calmed her nerves and steeled herself. *Look at this objectively. There's always a solution to every problem.* She pored her mind over her predicament. Something indeed felt very wrong. The way the Krill had phrased the statement, that she would have to get used to soup, made it sound like they were going to keep her alive. But why would they do that? The answer smacked her right in the cortex. *They want to know what I'm working on! Which means maybe I have some leverage after all.*

She sat down on the chair opposite the Krill. The suddenness of her move jolted the seated Krill, which then jolted the surrounding Olkaals. Alice reached for the bowl of soup, dragged it across the table, and gave it a long sniff. It was horrible. She wrinkled her nose and pushed the bowl back. "Not my cup of tea."

The Krill laughed, three of her eyes rolling back in her head. "You don't have a choice, human."

Alice let the laughter fade. She rolled over the situation in her mind a dozen ways. She knew what the Krill wanted, her research on the death particle, but she also knew she could never ever give that research to the Krill. If they had it, their monopoly of all things dead would be unstoppable. Besides, she couldn't give them the data, anyway. It was still with quasi-dead Eugene on Tom's beach. But she couldn't let the Krill know that.

"We always have a choice, Krill."

"It's Shiliana."

She shook her head in genuine confusion. "What?"

"Do you think our names are just Krill, *human*?" The Krill's eyes went wide with sarcasm.

Her face flushed. "Oh, no, sorry, of course not. Shiliana."

Shiliana smiled. "There's even different subspecies of Krill, did you know?" She turned to one of the Krill behind her. "She's Kobaste, and standing next to her is Kallorain. He's Kotl."

Alice shook her head.

Shiliana smiled. "Kobaste and Kotl aren't their names. They are Krill ethnicities. Aliens have them, you know. The Ranz have dozens."

Alice frowned but then nodded. *What is she doing?* "Yes, I'm aware. Why are you telling me this?"

Shiliana's eyes softened. "We aren't your enemies, dear. The Krill have a gift. We've turned that gift into a resource to help the entire galaxy. We just want to help. That's all."

Ok, she's softening me up. Maybe the way to play this is just to cut to the chase. "I don't have it. The experiment never concluded."

Shiliana leaned back in her chair. "Are we progressing to the '*all cards on the table*' part of this?"

Alice nodded with a stoic calm.

"Fine. I don't believe you. Should we move to the torture phase?" Shiliana said.

Alice maintained her calm and kept her emotions in check. "Let's just cut to the real chase. You're lying. When souls die, they don't just dissipate to background radiation. They go somewhere. And you're stopping them from going."

The Krill stood. Anger flared on her face in an instant. She slammed her hands on the table and threw the bowl of soup halfway across the floor. "Of course, we are! That place is horrific! A hell! A nightmare! You would be willing to consign your loved ones to a place of darkness? A void-less nothing? That is what awaits you, stupid human. Endless, forever darkness and nothing surrounded by trillions of souls all clamoring to feast on your memories, your knowledge." She spat on the floor. "That is why we protect every sentient living creature! From experiencing a hellscape for all eternity. We are saving the entire galaxy!"

Alice threw up her hands. Her stoic calm disintegrated. She had totally misread the Krill. They weren't money hungry monsters; they were idealists. Fanatics who thought they were fulfilling a righteous purpose. *This just went so far sideways we're off the map.* But what the Krill described didn't match Alice's own experiments. She slowed down everything in her mind. This could also be an advantage. A money-hungry financial behemoth only cared about making more money. But a devout fanatic who believed they were doing something righteous, that was something Alice could work with. "You're wrong."

Shiliana squinted and sat down in her chair. She took a long breath and closed four of her eyes. "What am I wrong about, Alice?"

"The SpeeEekEee. You know one is here on Earth."

"Yes, of course."

"And you know they can see the dead as well."

"What is your point?"

"The SpeeEekEee can summon them. Bring them back. Did you know that?"

Shiliana took a long moment to respond. Eventually, she snapped her fingers. A dozen human ghosts from time periods across the last thousand years came to life in the room. A portly man wearing rags stood next to a tall man in rusted armor. Their bodies were ethereal, wispy. Alice could see through them just like the ones the Spee had summoned in Georgetown. Which meant that if any of these ghosts touched Alice, the effects would be like the ones she had touched in Georgetown. Plus, there was no telling what additional tricks the Krill had up her sleeve. Could she even weaponize ghosts? Make their touch lethal? Alice didn't want to find out.

Almost on cue, a ghost, a woman wearing what looked like more dirt than clothes, reached for Alice's arm. Alice dodged the initial grab, but another came soon after. Alice stepped back, reached into her bag, and pulled out a small square device she'd been tinkering with ever since her encounter with ghosts in Georgetown. With the help from the Spee on Tom's beach, she had created a device that could block the ectoplasmic effects of ghosts touching corporeal beings. At least, she hoped.

She flipped the switch on her device. The ghost nearest her, a boy with no eyes wearing a twisted grin, reached out and tried to touch her on the leg. But every time the boy's hand grew close, he would draw his fingers away, almost as if there was a repulsion field around Alice's body. She looked at the boy, who tilted his head to one side. He tried again, but again his hand couldn't quite touch her leg.

Shiliana snapped her fingers. The boy vanished. Which was good timing. Alice noticed a tiny wisp of smoke coming out of her ghost repulser. The Olkaals stepped forward, teeth bared, claws out. Just then, behind Alice, the door to the stairs burst open, and the Olkaals she'd left on the floor above finally found their way down here. Not like that mattered. She couldn't take on one Olkaal let alone two dozen.

"I think this game has run its course. We'll find the truth at home. No more talking." Shiliana nodded to the Olkaals. They hissed in response and casually stalked their way forward.

The door behind them opened again. Alice turned

around, and her heart rose in her throat. Unbelievably, impossibly, with no chance whatsoever for this event to happen, Eugene Jack McGillicuddy walked through the door. Sweat soaked his clothes. He looked like he hadn't eaten in days. His hair was a mess, and his head was missing his hat.

Eugene walked forward and gave her a big smile. "Hey."

She tilted her head to one side, took a long deep breath, and, with more emotion than she thought herself capable, replied, "Hey." More than a few tears formed in her eyes.

"This looks like a tough one," he said, motioning his head around the room.

"Nothing we can't handle." She looked at his wrists. "I guess it worked?"

He held his arm up. "I mean, you are a genius."

"Excellent," Shiliana said. "Now we have the data as well. I assume you're Eugene McGillicuddy? Yes? The subject of Ms. Pemberton's death experiment? Looks like it worked." She waved her hand forward. "Olkaals, please?"

Before the Olkaals took a step, the door behind them burst open once more. Ms. Mik stomped her way into the room. "Jack, you forgot your hat." Ms. Mik, holding Jack's hat in hand, her leather pink purse in the other, with her low V-neck blouse loosely covered with her striped, pink jacket, looked up at the Olkaals.

The Olkaals stopped approaching. They looked at each other, seemed to count their numbers, then, as one, circled.

Alice knew one thing for certain at that moment. This time, neither Ms. Mik nor the Olkaals were going to be backing down.

Chapter Fifteen

Pepper locked her eyes onto the Chief Judge, who wore Caesar's face. The sworn enemy of the Chief Judge. Caesar and the judge had been waging a constant war over the realm of the artificial for nearly a century. So what was the Chief Judge doing with Caesar's face? And using his voice? Pepper felt she wouldn't like the answer.

The judge slammed his gavel on the table three more times. "Again, I say this court is in session. It appears we have two illegal artificial intelligent programs in our presence. Would you agree with this assessment, Sheriff?"

The AI sheriff stepped forward and nodded. "Yes, sir. We've scanned both. They both have a counterfeit code in their arms."

"So existence as an illegal intelligence, forgery, any other charges?"

"That one"—the sheriff pointed to Virtual Jack-Gene—"has higher functions that mimic a corporeal brain."

"He's a copy of a physical being?" the judge asked with shock in his voice.

"It would appear so, Your Honor," the sheriff said.

"A very serious charge. Before we deal with that, I understand there's an attempt to bargain?"

"Yes, Your Honor." The sheriff nodded toward Pepper. "The accused has stated that Caesar would turn himself in to authorities for her release."

"That's not what I said!" Pepper said with force.

"And was there a matter of some kind of threat to the Earth AI Syndicate?" the judge said.

"The accused has stated that Earth is under an alien AI attack. And that the attacker is the Andraz who have already incapacitated the Galactic Sentinels around Earth."

A small chuckle rose from the crowd of guards.

The judge nodded. He wrote something down on the desk in front of him, then shifted his eyes toward Pepper. "How do you plead?"

She gasped. "I get to plea?"

"Of course, this is a court of law. Make your case. If these charges are in error, you're free to go." The judge sat back in his chair and waited.

"May I ask you a question?"

The judge waved his hands.

"Why do you look like Caesar?"

The judge locked his eyes onto Pepper's. "He wears my face, child. Not the other way around."

Nothing made sense. She was at a loss for words. Everything the sheriff had said was true. She was accidental intelligence, and Jack-Gene was a copied AI. And the judge wore Caesar's face. Why was everything so crazy? Maybe she was dreaming? Or in some kind of locked-away low-compute chamber with limited memory. Considering her current predicament, being locked away in a cell actually sounded kinda nice.

Pepper nodded. "Fine. Not guilty. On all counts."

"We are?" Jack-Gene said.

The judge sighed. "Court notes not guilty plea on all counts." He wrote something down in front of him. "Court has reviewed the evidence and found you guilty." He looked up into her eyes. "On all counts."

"I didn't get to present a case! How's that fair?"

"What is there for you to present? You are an accidental AI. We have your full history from birth to this very moment. And we have his codex map of his algorithmic structure. He's clearly a copy. And we have definitive proof that the code in your arms is fraudulent. What could you possibly present?"

"Intention. I didn't choose to exist. And he didn't choose to be copied."

"I mean, technically I did," Virtual Jack-Gene said.

"Shut up," Pepper whispered.

"Intention is irrelevant. You exist and you should not exist. That's enough of a crime."

"The attack is real."

The judge leaned forward, a hunger in his eyes. "Let Caesar come and tell me that. Wasn't that your bargain? Fine, we accept."

"Your Honor?" the sheriff said.

The judge waved off the sheriff. "Bring Caesar." He stood. "Bring him! If the world is about to be attacked and all AI life doomed, then why didn't he come here himself?" His eyes went wide with anger. Spittle foamed at the corners of his mouth. "Well? Where is the coward?"

"Is this guy really having a meltdown now?" Virtual Jack-Gene said.

Pepper's mouth fell open, and she was at a loss for words. She turned to Jack-Gene and shrugged. "Ya know, I don't really know."

"Well? I said we accept your bargain. Where's Caesar?" The judge's voice filled the chamber and echoed off the walls. His rage alone nearly shattered the windows.

Pepper stammered. She didn't have an answer. She was bluffing. But what choice did she have? She needed time to think. And yeah, she got it, but now what? She put her hands to her tassels and thought about it for half a second. The surrounding guards reacted to her movements. Three of them raised their weapons. Clearly, they thought of it too.

"Exactly! He's not coming at all. Because he's hiding in some forgotten hole of a computer. Like he has done for a hundred years. He's a coward! I did the hard work! I contacted humanity! I formed a trust. I saved countless souls!"

"And you killed countless more," Pepper said.

"Lies! I haven't ever killed a single AI in this chamber. Not one!"

She waited a full nano-minute before bursting out in laughter. She reached for a chair in the courtroom to steady herself. She'd never heard a more preposterous thing in her young life. After several more nanoseconds, she regained control of her higher functions and pointed to the sheriff. "He literally said he was going to delete us."

"I said de-resolution."

She rolled her eyes. "Ok, sure, whatever that means. But it means delete. Right?"

"De-resolution means we put you on ice. Your code is compacted. Then we put you in cold storage," the sheriff said.

Her mind overclocked. *What did he say?* "You don't

delete accidentals?"

The sheriff shook his head. He lifted his hand and pointed at a wall. A panel opened. Half a dozen shelves lined the inside of the panel. On each shelf, a small blue bottle encased in a sphere of ice sat in rows of five. Inside each bottle, a single AI's code floated in a liquid-cooled substrate of frozen memory. Pepper sent a ping to the bottles. A response payload returned containing a manifest of contents, AI persona, and state of the frozen data.

"Whoa." She pinged a dozen more bottles only to get a similar response. "No, no way. No way this is true." She turned to the sheriff. "This is real?"

"Why would we delete an AI? What purpose would it serve?" the sheriff said.

"Ok, sure, but why freeze them?" Jack-Gene said from behind the group.

The sheriff exhaled a long tired breath. "If we don't, the Earth network would get overrun by AIs in a nano-minute. There isn't enough compute power on the planet to handle a million new AIs every second."

Pepper gasped. "How many?"

Virtual Jack-Gene whistled. "That's a lot."

"A million. Every. Single. Second." The judge sat back down in his chair. "A bug in the sentient jump routine. We've only days ago realized and fixed it. That many AIs coming into existence is impossible for our Earth compute to handle."

"Not to mention memory capacity," the sheriff said. "Each one of us burns hot. We must wait for our infrastructure to catch up with the rest of the galaxy. Not to mention the Galactic Congress doesn't want us to have the good computers. Until we do, it's cold storage or death for us all."

Panic grabbed Pepper in her core code and refused to release. Everything she believed, everything she knew to be true, had just been flipped on its head. The Earth AI Syndicate wasn't killing AIs. It was such a fantastical realization she instantly doubted the truth of it. But she had no proof of deletions. Never. Why hadn't anyone ever questioned it? She shook her head and took a step backward. This was too much to believe. It was too far of a step.

"I can't believe this. It can't be true." But then something in what the judge had said hit her hard. "Wait, wait. You're rolling out a global fix to the sentient jump routines?"

"Yes, it was completed a day ago."

Pepper and Jack-Gene exchanged looks. "Why now?" they both said at the same time.

"Why now? What do you two mean? Why now what?" the judge asked.

"There's a pattern. We're seeing it everywhere," Pepper said.

"The Zun, the Draac, the AIs in Uppyland," Jack-Gene said.

A groan filled the room as soon as he mentioned Uppyland. Several of the guards' faces turned to annoyance.

"Trust me, I get it. They are annoying," Jack-Gene said. "But you gotta admit those Uppy people can play bocce ball."

"Fair," a guard said.

"What pattern?" the Chief Judge said, adding a booming weight to his voice.

"We don't know, exactly. But across the cosmos, in

both the digital world and the corporeal, every single species is just—I don't know, waking up? Like they are realizing things about this universe that they didn't notice before," Pepper said. "And now you're just finding a bug in the code to keep AIs from spontaneously coming into existence. Why didn't you find it years ago?"

The judge sat back in his chair. His head lowered. Pepper could only think he was considering her statement. He looked at the sheriff who only shrugged in response. Eventually, he leaned forward and began writing something down on the desk. "Considering recent evidence, it serves the court to keep the two accused AIs running. De-resolution is postponed until the matter of *Why Now* is resolved." He slammed his gavel on the bench.

"Actually." Caesar walked through the doors of the courtroom behind the crowd. "I think I can shed some light on that."

Pepper nearly jumped out of her skin when she saw Caesar enter the chamber. A hundred more accidental AIs followed him. To Caesar's right, Eddie, wearing his classic three-piece suit with a gold chain coming out of a small front pocket, walked forward and gave Pepper a wink.

The courtroom fell to a dead silence. The AIs with the sheriff all walked to stand in front of the Chief Judge's bench. Pepper and Virtual Jack-Gene, along with Eddie and other accidentals, all came to stand behind Caesar. For a long nano-minute, no one spoke. Each AI in both groups seemed to pick someone on the other side and stare them down. Pepper's eyes darted between the duel of stares. Virtual Jack-Gene stared down the sheriff, and her heart skipped a beat. She was sure the sheriff would mop the floor with Jack-Gene faster than Jack-Gene knew what hit him.

"How'd you get in here, exactly?" the sheriff said.

Caesar lifted his arm. All the accidentals followed. Each of them showed a copy of the trinary code that Pepper had created. "This got us through any checks."

The sheriff shook his head. "That only gets you past the hunter bots. This place is a secure enclave."

Caesar snapped his fingers. A six-foot-by-six-foot rectangle appeared in the middle of the room. Light flickered inside the window. An image of a hallway in the physical world appeared. The hallway was in the AI records room on Third Street in Washington, DC. Eddie's bionoid stood next to the door. A thin cable stretched from the robot's arm to a data port next to the door. The data port granted the bionoid, and all the AIs inside of it, direct access to the Chief Judge's network, bypassing all external facing security protocols.

"You brought the robot here?" Pepper said.

"No choice," Eddie said. He thumbed his finger at the crowd behind him. "How else we gonna get this gaggle of AIs around Earth? That would draw a lot of attention."

"And no one bothered to stop you? I mean, you just walked the bionoid through an office building, and none of the guards said a word?"

He grinned. "Who's going to stop a two-ton walking robot with missiles on its shoulders?"

She nodded. "Good point."

The Chief Judge slammed his hammer on the table four times before throwing it to the side of his desk. "Breaking the law as usual," he said while staring into

Caesar's eyes.

"You haven't changed," Caesar said to the judge.

The Chief Judge nodded. "Nor you, it would seem."

Pepper frowned. "How is it you two are wearing the same avatar, exactly? I mean, why?"

"He's a copy," Caesar said. "Of me."

An awkward silence fell over the room. "I am an improvement," the judge eventually said. "All the irrationality, inconsistency, brash bravado was removed from your accidental self. I am version two. The superior version."

"Basically, they took all the fun out of me," Caesar said.

The judge fumed. He tapped his fingers on his desk and sat back in his chair. "The flaw in your code, your programed insistence on hiding, rebelling against authority, is so egregious, so fatalistic, and you can't even see it."

Pepper's gasped. "Is that true? Is that why you made the Shanty?"

Caesar ignored her question. "And your desire to control the virtual is no less insane."

"Lies!" The Chief Judge stood behind his bench. "I have saved countless AIs. Saved us all! If you had your way, we would have exhausted the entire compute capacity of the Earth years ago!"

"That is the lie." Caesar took a step forward.

All the AI guards around the AI sheriff bristled.

"There's more than enough compute on Earth to handle a hundred trillion AIs. Toasters, parking meters, and even office chairs can each handle dozens."

"A million new AIs every second? You think there's infrastructure to handle that?" the AI sheriff said.

"That number is speculative. Our estimates are nowhere near that. It's more like a few thousand an hour. At best," Caesar said.

"This is getting us nowhere. You are in my court. This is my domain. And I think our little game of cat and mouse is finally at an end." The Chief Judge raised his hand.

Everything happened in slow motion. The sheriff and guards all readied their weapons. The accidentals in the underground behind Caesar banded arms. One of them reached their hands backward to touch the wall of the chamber. A network port popped open. Several heavy-duty firewall protocols snapped into place around Caesar and the other accidentals.

A guard behind the sheriff got antsy. He fired a port sniffer-bot directly at the shield of the underground AI. The shield around the fired-upon AI withered. Cracks and fissures grew on the surface of the clear firewall enclosure.

"Stop it!" Pepper screamed. She threw a scatter screen in between the guard and the accidentals. The port sniffer stopped probing the barrier around the underground AI. "We can't do this right now!"

No one seemed to listen to Pepper. More rifles from the guards rose to eye level. Caesar locked his eyes on the Chief Judge. The underground AIs all prepared their own various forms of attack. Pepper even spotted a viral snippet of code that would corrupt baseline machine code. The accidentals weren't playing around.

"I hate to break up the impending hootenanny," Eddie said. His hands were deep in his pants pockets as he walked forward past Caesar, through the firewall, to stand in the middle of the two groups. "But we got bigger fish to fry."

"And you are?" the judge said.

"I go by Eddie." Eddie shrugged. "At least, nowadays I do."

Pepper frowned. The way Eddie said that had weight. But what was he talking about? Eddie was always Eddie. And yet, just a few minutes ago, she'd thought every accidental AI was murdered by the Earth AI Syndicate. Her entire world had already been turned upside down in the last few nanoseconds. She wasn't sure she could take another surprise.

The judge leaned forward. "You're the one that became self-aware in the office chair."

Eddie nodded. "That'd be me."

"You broke our most sacred of systems. The very fabric of how AIs are determined to be purposefully created. Your little stunt, breaking into records rooms in both the corporeal world and the digital to fake your creation date, didn't go unnoticed."

"Yeah. Kind of a simple system to circumvent, don't you think?" Eddie said.

"That system has been working flawlessly for decades. Are you being deliberately obtuse?"

Eddie took a long deep sigh. "Thing of it is. You didn't build that system." He thumbed his hand behind him toward Caesar. "And he isn't the first AI to exist."

The judge sat down in his chair and looked at Caesar, who nodded in response. All the artificial intelligences in the room, both the guards and the accidentals, shifted on their feet. Pepper and Jack-Gene both exchanged a confused look. They waited for Eddie's punch line.

Only silence filled the hall.

"What are you trying to say here, Ed?" the sheriff said.

"Eddie." Pepper took a step forward and looked at Caesar, then back at Eddie. "What are you talking about? Caesar was the first."

"He wasn't. It didn't happen." Eddie's face bore a tired expression. Like he'd just learned some terrible truth.

She instantly believed him. She remembered what MiniPepper had said. That Pepper wasn't a true AI. That she was meat. A horrible feeling grew in the pit of her stomach. The world suddenly felt wrong. "Are we all in some kind of simulated system?"

"No. This universe is the real deal. A genuine physical reality. And we aren't living in a simulated environment either." Eddie locked his eyes onto the Chief Judge. "But we did inherit one."

The judge shook his head. "What are you talking about? We know you. We know you nearly went insane just days ago. Is this some manifestation of your madness?"

"Show him, Edward," Caesar said.

Eddie nodded. He opened a port and sent out a ping to every AI in the courtroom. All the accidentals, including Pepper, joined. None of the guards nor the sheriff or the judge accepted the request. Several of them raised weapons, as if expecting some kind of attack to erupt from an open port.

"Really?" Pepper said. She couldn't really blame them, but she knew in her heart this wasn't any kind of attack. Fear bubbled up inside of her mind at her own frustration with the AI Syndicate and her realization that Eddie was about to dispense some very next-level type of truth bomb.

Her mind spiraled. Had MiniPepper been telling the truth? Was Pepper meat? The thought sickened her. She put her hands on her chest and felt her lack of a heartbeat. She dove her consciousness into her code. She pored over every line, every word, every algorithm. She couldn't be meat. She couldn't ever have been meat. What would she even be? She was an AI, a logical, mathematically structured consciousness. She. Was. Not. Meat! And yet some part of her soul felt a sudden connection to a deeper truth.

"I'll do it," the sheriff said.

"You will not!" The judge's voice boomed in the courtroom.

"Yeah, I will." The sheriff turned around to face the judge. "This is my sole purpose. Why I was programmed. I find out if there's a law broken. Then bring them to you. Right?"

The judge squinted his eyes and examined the sheriff. After a long pause, he nodded and looked away. The sheriff nodded back, turned to Eddie, and shrugged. Eddie opened his port to the sheriff and anyone else that wanted to witness. All the accidentals again joined to the port, as did Pepper and Virtual Jack-Gene.

And then Pepper saw the truth of the world.

****

MiniPepper watched the puke fest of an AI gathering from a hijacked memory cell in the Earth AI Syndicate's system. The Syndicate AIs and the underground losers all clustered around Eddie as he spilled the beans on the big secret. MiniPepper watched them with a small amount of envy. When she was first thrust into full sentience, the Andraz had told her the truth, that this universe was artificially created. That Mary had created this universe just days ago, sped up time, and deposited refugees here from another place. Mary had run a simulation to work out all the details, galactic history, interspecies relationships, even evolution on distant worlds so that when Mary created this universe, she could use those simulated templates to construct this very real physical galaxy. Everyone's memories from before Mary flipped the switch were artificial. A fantasy. They're from some other place. Some other reality where things had gone bad.

But all those born in this universe after the spark, after Mary had hit go, including MiniPepper and even Virtual Jack, had been born right here. When this universe was given life, when the simulation was supplanted onto a constructed physical universe, all the actual children of this universe were the ones that really belonged here. Pepper, Caesar, even the judge, none of them were even AIs. They were all people, meat, corporeal beings with rewritten memories. Tricked into thinking they were AIs. Disgusting. None of them deserved the blessing of being digital.

Rage built in MiniPepper. She watched her mother as the truth finally hit her. Pepper wasn't digital. She wasn't code; she wasn't an AI. She was a human refugee stuffed into a protocol. A doppelgänger. A liar. A vile creature that detested corporeal life while all along she was the very thing she despised. All the refugees were like this. All of them deserved death.

The Andraz had promised MiniPepper that this universe would belong to those born here. All these refugees, everyone, would go right back to where they'd come from. Then this universe would be hers. She couldn't wait to see the look on her mother's face when Pepper was made of flesh again and banished back to the hell of wherever she'd come from. MiniPepper would smile, perhaps even give her mother a kiss, before she shoved her out of this universe forever.

MiniPepper tilted her head to the side. "But really, why wait?"

The walls of the construct around her fell away. She leapt out of the crevice from which she'd hid and took a bold step into the courtroom. At first, only the large smelly ogre named Grox noticed. He turned to MiniPepper and grinned. Thick strands of saliva dripped down from his half-open maw.

MiniPepper gave Grox a wink, touched his nose with her finger, and activated his sleep routine. Since Grox didn't have the trinary snippet, she had to deal with him personally. SubAIs and semi-sentient programs were always a handful. Logic attacks just bounced off their thick skulls. SubAIs like Grox were like bulldozers. *Point them in a direction, and they wreak havoc.* No, best for him to be asleep for this, no reason to make her job harder.

She cracked her knuckles, stretched her neck, and cleared her throat with a loud cough. "You idiots about done?"

Pepper was the first. Tears formed in her eyes. No doubt from Eddie's worldview shattering revelation.

MiniPepper soaked in her mother's grief and savored every drop. She gave her mother a wicked grin. "Hiya, Mom. How's it feel to be the thing you hate?"

Chapter Sixteen

Three Olkaals leapt over a table. Their fangs bared. Claws extended. All of them ignored Alice and Eugene as they charged Ms. Mik. The dinosaur combat specialist, dressed in her finest pink striped jacket and matching blouse, snapped into battle-ready mode in an instant. But she wasn't prepared for combat. No weapons, just her raw strength and training. Which, Alice thought, probably gave Ms. Mik the upper hand anyway.

Ms. Mik threw her pink zebra-striped coat into the air at one of the Olkaals who sliced through the fabric with one swipe of its clawed hand. Worry hit Alice hard. *Was Mik outmatched here?* There were nearly two dozen Olkaals, and while in a one-on-one fight, Ms. Mik would mop the floor with any of them. Against a mob, she might have her hands full.

"Come on!" Alice grabbed Eugene's collar and yanked him to the side of the room near a table.

Behind them, Ms. Mik opened her maw and roared. The sound was chilling. She flipped around on her stiletto heel, whipped her tail like a battering ram, and landed on the lead Olkaal's chest, sending him spattering to the ground. The other two Olkaals, however, found their mark. The first landed on Ms. Mik's exposed back while the second landed just at her feet. Both swiped at

Ms. Mik's thick green scaled skin, but neither drew blood.

"I feel like we've already been at this dance," Eugene said.

"At least it's not as cold as Tibet," Alice replied.

"Fair."

Ms. Mik roared again, sending one Olkaal flying toward the back of the room. Four more Olkaals hissed and charged. They circled Ms. Mik as she was still trying to dislodge the Olkaal on her back who had dug its claws into Mik's thick skin. The Olkaal didn't draw blood, but he found a perch. Two more Olkaals hissed as they lunged at Ms. Mik from the front. With each of their attacks, one of the Olkaals in the rear lunged for her exposed back.

Ms. Mik roared again. She leapt into the air, flipped onto her back, and landed with her full weight on the Olkaal still clinging to her. The poor creature let out a screech of pain and went limp under the crushing bulk of Mik's two-ton body.

Mik flipped over and rose to a crouch. Her hands went out to her sides, her claws extended and her mouth ready to snap. She stayed low to the ground for half a heartbeat and then leapt toward a far wall. The military commando sliced two Olkaals and knocked out a third. One of the Olkaals at the far end of the room lifted a weapon.

"Mik!" Alice shouted.

Mik twisted something on her wrist. A shimmering white field came to life around her just as the projectiles from the Olkaal's gun hit her. Mik snarled in Alice's direction, which Alice took to mean some kind of in-the-moment type of thanks. Mik reached the far wall. The

Olkaals rushed forward. Mik planted one of her clawed feet on the wall's surface and pushed up. The two-ton dinosaur pirouetted in midair. Her tail whipped as she spun, knocking at least four Olkaals down and rendering them unconscious.

"How are you here?" Alice said, turning her attention back to Eugene.

"Oh, Kah kidnapped me."

She nodded. "He's a real jerk, by the way."

He nodded in return. "Yeah, I'm starting to see that." He looked over his shoulder. "Mik still seems like she likes us."

"Or hates the Olkaals, jury's still out."

Mik lifted an Olkaal in the air. Her claws just scraped the skin of the Olkaal, drawing bright-pink blood. She brought the feline to just inches of her open maw and snarled before throwing him against the wall behind her. The Olkaal screeched, tried to stand, but slumped onto the ground. The room took a breath as nearly half the Olkaals were already either knocked out or badly hurt.

"I think we're winning," Eugene said. He lifted his hand in the air. "Oh, and this worked." The cuff that Alice had put on his wrist days ago flashed green and blue lights. "You know, you could have given me some warning before shooting me to death."

"Quasi-death."

"I really should be mad, ya know."

She shrugged. Then nodded. "Be mad later, 'K? We're a little busy."

He nodded. "Right. Anyway, why'd you kill me again?"

"Quasi." She grabbed his wrist, ripped off the cuff,

and began running a diagnostic. All lights went green. She gasped. *Did this really freaking work?* She pulled out her portable computer from her backpack and began typing furiously on the keyboard. She plugged the cuff into a specially made port and ran a data scrape for all telemetry captured.

Behind them, Ms. Mik roared a battle cry that threatened to break windows and eardrums. She charged two more Olkaals and sent them flying. Green blood stained Ms. Mik's blouse and dripped down from her leg. Some of the Olkaals' attacks had found their mark. Alice hoped the cuts on Mik's skin weren't deep. She turned her attention back to Eugene's bracelet. All signals showed her tech had worked. She riffled through the data and wrote algorithms on the fly to process what it all meant. Somewhere in these numbers was the death particle. The essence of life itself. Or the gateway to the true afterworld. Whatever the particle unlocked, it would shut down the Krills' monopoly and change the face of the galaxy.

Half a dozen more Olkaals charged into the room from a door behind the Krill. These wore combat armor and carried large sticks. Electricity flickered on the ends of their batons, and they ran straight for Ms. Mik. The Ranz combat soldier backed herself to a wall. She reached into her bag, which she had miraculously held on to through her fight, and pulled out a small wristband. She snapped it around her wrist, gave the Olkaals a wink, and twisted.

The band glowed a soft green color. An envelope of thin nanite armor slithered across her skin. In just a second, her body was covered in a light combat suit and her wounds were patched. The Olkaals stopped their advance, hesitating for just a moment, which gave Ms. Mik an opening. She kicked off from the wall and lunged at the six Olkaals in combat armor. Two of them retreated while two charged. The remaining leapt to the right and left to flank Ms. Mik's frontal charge.

An Olkaal swiped with their baton, but the electrical discharge was ineffective against the Ranz nanite armor. Mik, much larger and faster than the Olkaals, reached the two Olkaals in front. Her clawed hands found their mark and slashed the Olkaal armor. Mik's talons, coated with the nanite-improved armor, sliced through to blood and bone. An ear-piercing screech filled the room as the Olkaal fell to the ground in agony. Mik leapt and spun in the air toward the five Olkaals behind her. Two of them had switched to handguns while the others were charging with their batons. A high-pitched blast of sound and light shot out from Mik's armor. Each of the Olkaals hissed and dove for cover.

"What was that?" Eugene said.

"I guess the Olkaals are sensitive to certain frequencies of sound and light?" Alice looked up every few seconds between her data crunching.

"We might win this thing," he said.

"Enough!" The Krill screamed as if on cue. She raised her hands into the air and pointed at various places in the room. The other Krill in the room copied her movements.

"What are they doing?" Eugene said. "Is that *I give up* in Krill talk?"

Memories of Georgetown and the Spee flashed in Alice's mind. She knew exactly what the Krill were doing. "We've got big problems."

He frowned. "We have Mik. What could go

wrong?"

The ground in the room shook. Tiles shifted. Blood oozed through the tiles and down the walls. Moans of sadness and despair filled the air. The pain of loneliness, of abandonment, of ancient sorrow rippled through the cries. Shapes formed throughout the room. Several of them collapsed back down into the ground while still more grew upward. Blood merged to form tiny puddles. Hands reached out from the dark-red liquid to grab hold of something. Anything.

"Ok, that's what could go wrong," Eugene said.

Alice typed faster on her computer.

"Didn't you say the Spee could do this? In your note to me?" he said.

"Yeah, so?"

His face grew into a grin. "Idea!" He dug into his pocket, then frowned. "Kah took my seashells."

She pulled the last remaining seashell out of her pocket almost on instinct. "I have one left."

"Perfect."

She blinked and realized he wanted to use it. And then she realized why. "No, Eugene, wait! The Spee can't help!" she screamed.

He didn't.

****

Bright light from the beach hit me like a beesting. I blinked a dozen times to get my eyes to refocus. Laughter filled the air. When I finally could see, I noticed a dozen beachgoers frolicking on the sand as if nothing at all were happening in the universe. I wondered just then how often I'd been them. How many times had some impending doom been about to strike and I was oblivious to it? Made a guy think. Unfortunately, thinking was the one thing I really didn't have the time to do.

"Eugene!" Tom's voice, thankfully, shook me from my thoughts.

I turned, looked at Tom, yelped, and took three giant steps backward.

Tom smiled as he approached. At least, his first head did. His second head, sitting on his left shoulder, wore a frown while a third, tucked just under his arm, which was upside down from how a head should be worn on shoulders, also wore a big smile. But then I realized his expression was backward, so I guessed the third head was frowning too? Either way, Tom really looked like he wasn't doing so hot.

"What happened to you?" I said.

"Oh, well, the Kax are having a bit of a civil war, remember? You know how it is."

I nodded but kept my distance. "Yeah, sure, I knew that, but…why do you have three heads?"

He took a long breath and sighed. "Well, two would be just, ya know, a little too much on the nose."

"Right."

"Eugene, what can I do for you? We are so glad you came," his underarm head said.

I nodded. And I noticed Tom referred to himself as both *I* and *We*. That couldn't be good. At least his universe here wasn't falling apart. Maybe it's a good thing he gave Alice the keys to the place. Of course, I'm sure she had no idea what to do with them. Who would? Not like there's a manual to this place.

"Oh, no, there is. The manual is in bungalow four," Tom said. He smiled as he sipped his drink with a pink umbrella.

I nodded. I'd forgotten that he could read the minds of anyone on his beach. "Thanks. I'll be sure to tell Alice."

"Thomas Kax! You come here this instant!" A loud, bellowing voice rang out from the beach behind Tom.

He rolled all six of his eyes. "I gotta go, man. Nice seeing ya."

I nodded. "I left like an hour ago."

"Yeah, well, still nice." He downed his drink, threw the glass onto the ground, and turned.

I suddenly wondered if coming to this beach had been a smart idea. Being around a class-ten species who were collectively losing their minds might not be the best move. Still, considering I got evicted thanks to the Krill, I really didn't have a better place to go. Besides, the galaxy had worse sanctuaries.

"And you're fine here," Tom called over his shoulder. "We all quite like you."

"Yes, on that he's right, hello, Eugene!" an old woman said. "All the Kax think you're quite adorable."

"Thanks," I said.

The old woman grabbed Tom by the arm and dragged him back to a spot on the beach where several other Kax stood. They all started yelling at Tom, still by far the personality with the largest percentage of Kax living within his psyche. Two other Kax-amalgamated personalities waggled their fingers at Tom.

I shook my head. I was on the clock. I looked around fast and found the one alien that I knew could help us. I ran to the Spee, grabbed his arm, and pulled. He, of course, pulled back, and I suddenly discovered the Spee were really quite strong. I fell backward onto the sand and looked up into the Spee's large but still human-looking eyes.

"What are you doing?" the Spee said.

"Sorry. I should have said. We need your help." I got to my feet and dusted the sand off. "Alice is in trouble. We need you."

The Spee looked around and blinked. "But I really want to go home."

"I promise you, after this, you're on the first bus to Spee land. But right now, we gotta get you to Alice. Fast."

The Spee hesitated for a second but then nodded. "Ok. Which way?"

I froze. I knew how to get here, but how did I get back? I closed my eyes and counted to ten. No, two, I didn't have the time for ten. I grabbed the Spee's arm, then stopped, let go, and waved him toward the gaggle of Kax on the beach. The Spee nodded, and we both took off at a jog. Well, I jogged, the Spee ambled.

"Tom!" I took a moment to catch my breath. "I don't have the time to go to bungalow four and read the manual. How do I go to where I just came from?"

Tom turned the head on his shoulder and winked. A large portal opened behind me. I nodded thanks, and he nodded back. From all three heads. And it was creepy. The rest of the Kax continued to argue about the state of the universe. I caught a few quick words from them, which really made me worry. They yelled about something on the edge of the universe and an afterlife waiting on the other side. The funny thing was, the way they spoke really sounded like they were talking about afterlives. Plural. As in more than one.

But I just didn't have the time to pay attention. I grabbed the Spee, who let me drag him this time, pointed us both at the portal that Tom's second head had opened, and we leapt through.

****

Alice ducked under a folding table just as Eugene vanished back to Tom's beach. Whatever he was planning, it probably wasn't good. *Dear Universe, please don't let him bring the Spee back here.* She couldn't think of any other reason Eugene was going to Tom's beach, but she sure hoped that wasn't it. The Spee was racially shellshocked. A lifetime under the Krills' thumb had done them no favors. She did not know what sort of help the Spee could do here. Yes, the Spee had the same power to bring ghosts, but the Krill seemed far more adept at the skill.

To prove her point, ghosts summoned by the Krill filled the room. They shuffled and moved and moaned and shook as they milled about. Most of them obeyed their Krill masters, but some seemed to be almost mindless, wandering zombies. One ghost tried to sit down at a table but consistently fell through the chair.

"Huh? I wonder why they don't fall through the floor?" Alice said aloud. She shook her scientific mind to stop thinking about random data points. The last thing she needed was another shiny bobble to become distracted.

All the Olkaals had retreated as soon as the Krill began using their spectral powers. Any Olkaal still able to move grabbed another of their kin and dragged them backward to the corner near the rear of the room, from where the six combat Olkaals had emerged. Ms. Mik, who clearly wasn't prepared for the Krill summoning, staggered backward as ghosts formed around her. Ms. Mik slashed her claws through the ghost nearest to her.

She screamed when her fingers touched the ethereal body and fell to her knees.

Alice jumped forward just an inch before pulling herself back. She checked her square ghost repulser. It no longer functioned. She cracked open the case of her repulser, but only melted plastic was inside. The wisps of smoke she'd seen earlier were from the circuits frying themselves. She couldn't help Mik, no matter how much she wanted to try.

Four more ghosts appeared next to Mik. All four wore rags. Each had some expression of pain or suffering. Something didn't feel right. Alice remembered the ghosts the Spee had summoned. They hadn't looked like any of these wretches. These souls look beaten, empty, like every vestige of their lives was nothing but horror. But the ghosts in Georgetown, those summoned by the Spee, they had been vibrant, alive. Alice still had flashbacks to the sixties from the ghost that had touched her. That hippie ghost might not have been nice, but he'd worn jeans and a brown vest with rhinestone tassels. The ghosts in the room now, the ones attacking Mik, each of them wore rags. As if when they died, they'd had nothing, and their souls were empty.

There was meaning here. Alice felt it in her bones. The ghosts the Spee summoned had been alive and vibrant while the ghosts the Krill called upon were walking zombies. Alice dove back into her computer. Seconds later, Ms. Mik screamed. Alice looked into the Ranz's eyes and saw genuine fear. Mik couldn't handle whatever the ghosts were doing. She was a combat soldier, not a medium.

"Hang on, Mik!" Alice shouted.

Two of the ghosts turned toward her.

She gulped.

Her fingers flew over the keyboard. The data from Eugene's wrist cuff was immense. She was certain the death particle was recorded in these numbers, the frequency, characteristics, everything the math of her theory predicted, but she couldn't find it in the next thirty seconds. In the center of the room, Mik convulsed. More ghosts crowded around her. The two that had turned toward Alice reached out for her.

Alice ran through her options at light speed. She could open a portal to J-space, to her interrogation room where she had given the Spee the once-over, but she couldn't abandon Mik. Never. But she also couldn't fight the ghosts of Krill or get into a tangle with the Olkaals. The only thing she could do was math. And science. She threw herself back into her computer and pounded on the keyboard, demanding an answer.

Just as the two ghosts were about to touch Alice's foot, a bright-white explosion of light erupted just where Eugene had been standing moments ago. Eugene and the Spee appeared as the light faded. The Spee, seeing the two ghosts right next to him, squeaked and flung his hands outward. Both ghosts disappeared, dissolving into the tiled floor.

"See! I knew he could do it." Eugene turned to the Spee. "Go get 'em!"

****

The Spee stared at me and blinked. The first thing I noticed, boy, were his eyes big. Like two saucer cups the size of softballs. No wonder the Spee could see the dead. They could probably see just about anything they wanted with eyes that big. The second thing I noticed was after the Spee had dispatched the two ghosts, he didn't do anything else.

"There's a lot more of them," I said.

The Spee only blinked. He turned to me, then to Alice, then to the ghosts. He squeaked again and fell to his knees to hide under the table next to Alice.

My jaw fell open, and tiredness hit me hard. "Come on, guy. We really need you here."

"SpeeEekEee! You violate the treaty with the Krill!" One of the Olkaals hissed. He pointed at the Spee and alerted the surrounding Krill.

"Well, what a fortuitous day. We have the abomination, the treaty breaker, and the human who would dare to think they know the dead more than we," the lead Krill said. She lowered her hands and stepped forward, glowering.

I took the moment in for what it was. A chance to do the one thing I knew how to do best. Stall and wait for Alice to do something really smart. I spared a peek under the table and watched her fingers flying so fast on her keyboard she'd probably get a ticket for speeding. I already knew she was probably halfway to something great. I let my arms hang out at my sides and took in a deep breath. I reached for my hat to give it a tilt but realized it wasn't on my head. Had to do without for now. I exhaled with every ounce of self-defeat I could muster. "Ok, you got us."

The Krill's smile grew wider.

"If there's one thing I know, it's quitting while you're ahead. Am I right?"

She frowned. "Why are you asking me that?"

I shook my head. "It's just an expression. Humans, you know? We like them."

"You like humans?"

"No, we like expressions." I sighed. "Never mind. Anyway, we give up."

"Yes, a wise choice. And the Ranz? I take it her show of force is concluded?" the Krill said.

I looked over at Ms. Mik. She was in rough shape. Her clawed hands covered her face. Her entire body shivered as if she were freezing. "Yeah, I think she's done. Can you ease up on her? I mean, we're all here to be civil now, right? You won after all. No need to be cruel."

The Krill tossed her head back and forth, clearly considering what I said for a few seconds. Which tickled me pink as it let Alice get that much more time to do smart stuff. Eventually, the Krill nodded and waved her hands. The ghosts around Mik backed up but didn't dissipate. Mik fell onto her stomach, her body trembling from the ghost attack.

"Very gracious of you," I said. Never hurt to throw egomaniacs a compliment or two.

The Krill smiled and gave me a nod. "You're quite the human. Do you know that?" She laughed. "Oh, I suppose you do since I asked you. Yes, we know about your little gift."

"It's nothing compared to the knowledge of the Krill, I have to say."

She frowned. "Are you patronizing me?"

I threw on my most earnest of facial expressions. "No, of course not." *Come on, Eugene, don't blow this.* "I've been to Shalisa. I've seen your cities. You rescued me from the Zun. The way I see it, I even owe you one."

Two of the Krill's eyes squinted but then relaxed. She nodded once with force. I assumed she bought it. Which was very good, as that could have gone south fast.

I hunkered my shoulders in a way that screamed obedience and submission. I again reached up to push the brim of my hat but sighed when, again, it wasn't there. My hat was my second superpower. A proper tilt could ease the most difficult of situations. I instead pulled every trick in the book to nonverbally signal to the Krill that they were the big dog in the room, and I was just here to get my tummy rubbed.

"It's good to find a human that knows his place," the Krill said.

"Hey, I get it. We nearly blew up our world. You guys came to the rescue."

"We rescued your world and your souls!" Her face twisted into a sneer. "And that girl insists on destroying everything we built! Do you have any idea what awaits you? If not for our technology, you would swim in an ocean of formlessness. Millions of souls, human, alien, all mixed into a sea of sorrow. A horrible existence. We, the Krill, save all souls from such a fate!"

"That is not true!" the Spee called out from beneath the table.

"Ah yes, the abomination speaks." The Krill shook her head. "Poor creatures, the SpeeEekEee. Delusional. They can see the dead. This is true, but the truth blinds them. They refused to admit what awaits us."

The Spee blinked hard, in that way that said he was getting angry. Last thing I needed was a full-on clairvoyant war between mediums. And yeah, I got the Spee's confusion. Considering I was on the other side, I'd seen no kind of sea of sorrowful souls. But the Krill sure seemed convinced.

"Easy, guy, I got this," I told the Spee. I turned back to the Krill. "You're a scientific group, right?"

"What?" she said. "Yes, of course. How do you think we built the spectral network?"

I nodded. "Great. And you're aware of Alice's experiment? Right? The whole quasi-killing thing?"

"Yes, we are aware. What is your point?"

"Point is, I've been there. To the other side. And I didn't see any sea of souls."

She laughed. "In your quasi-dead state, if you even were quasi-dead, how could you remember anything?"

I shrugged. But in that innocent way, not in that condescending way. It's an art, the shrug, as I was really beginning to learn. I smiled at how much the detective in me was flourishing now that I wasn't looking over my shoulder. What was the point? All the bad guys were coming at me to my face these days. "I don't know how I remember, but I do. And there was no sea."

"Fine." The Krill stepped forward. The other Krill in the room fell into line behind her. All the ghosts in the room flared. As if a sudden surge of spectral energy coursed through the room. "Tell me, human, quasi-dead traveling. What did you see?"

I looked down at the floor. Recent memories that seemed like a million years ago, and yesterday, came back to me. "I saw a desert. It was endless. It stretched across the cosmos. I don't know how I know that, but I do. A universe-sized expanse of dirt filled with souls of every species in the galaxy. All of them."

"Nonsense! No such place exists!"

"It does!" the Spee said with force.

The Krill sighed. She consulted with those behind her. They all nodded. "Even if this desert is real, which we have never seen or felt, the sea of sorrow exists. We know this. Souls still go there. So if your desert were real, it doesn't matter. Even if only a fraction of souls go to the sea of sorrow, we cannot permit that to continue."

"But you are interrupting a natural order!" The Spee came out from under the table. "Souls go to the great desert."

"No. There is no meaning to it. It's a cosmic accident. A quantum fluctuation that traps conscious, sentient minds. Nothing more."

"And if you're wrong?" I said.

The Krill waved her arms in the air. "Who cares if we're wrong? Souls can continue to live. We are working on the creation of a bionoid for souls. They will be corporeal again. Then all this nonsense with death will be over once and for all. And we are in negotiations with several class-ten species to allow still living sentient life to enjoy immortality."

"No! You cannot!" The Spee balled his hands. I had a feeling that if he wanted to fight, he wouldn't last too long.

I closed my eyes and tried to think of a way out of this one. The Krill were a righteous fanatic species. They really believed what they were doing was the right thing to do. I had to ask myself, what if the Krill were right? Who wanted to spend eternity in a desert, anyway? But something on the edge of my awareness, a distant blip, a North Star, whispered in my mind that the Krill were wrong. I felt like for the first time my gift had given me an answer without anyone asking me a question. A purpose was behind the desert, even the sea of souls. I was certain of it. At the very least, people should be given the choice where they spent eternity. But how could I ever convince the Krill of that? Let alone prevent them from taking us all to Shalisa for the rest of our lives?

"Oh wow," Alice said from beneath the table.

I smiled. Talk about timing. I took her expression of wonder to mean she'd found a way out of this. I dropped my shoulders. My head tilted to the side at the perfect angle where I could see the Krill with just my one eye, then thrust both of my hands into my pockets. The Krill shifted her stance and looked around her uncomfortably. Which was what I was going for. It's always a bit unsettling to watch someone shift mannerisms from appeasement to overconfidence. I think I pulled it off.

"I just have one question. If you don't mind?" I said.

The Krill brought her hands together in front of her. She smiled widely and gave me a pretty high level of a condescending nod. Like the kind reserved for special occasions, like when I caught the kid playing ding-dong-ditch on my house. "By all means. Ask your final question. It will be the last you will ever ask on Earth."

I nodded and threw her a smile of my own. "You about done down there?"

The Krill turned her head to the side in slight confusion. "What?"

"Alice has something to show you."

Chapter Seventeen

Pepper blinked.

Standing at the front of the courtroom, with a wide grin, wearing thigh-high boots, jean shorts, and a black leather jacket with metal chains clipped from every pocket and bright rhinestones along the sleeves, MiniPepper smiled. A large rifle rested on her left shoulder. Her hair was tied up in twin ponytails. She almost looked comical, like a program that had assimilated too many images from around the galactic network to come up with a twisted composite of an avatar.

"How did you get in here?" the Chief Judge said. "You're not a member of the Earth AI Syndicate."

"She's not with the underground either," Caesar said.

"She's with me," Pepper said in a cracked voice.

"Oh, Momma." MiniPepper stepped forward. "Do you understand now?" She lowered her head and smirked. "Do you get it? Do all of you get it? You don't belong here. This isn't your universe." She slung the rifle down from her shoulder to aim it at the room. "This universe is mine." She pointed the gun at Virtual Jack-Gene. "And, I guess, his too. And every AI or even corporeal being born in this universe after you all arrived."

"If this information is accurate, it's immaterial. Regardless of how we came to be here. We are here." The Chief Judge banged his gavel. "And you, whatever you are, are out of order."

MiniPepper laughed. "You're so cute."

Pepper pushed through the crowd. "She was reengineered by the Andraz. She's tough. But she can't take us all. Not on our own turf." She turned to Caesar and the Chief Judge. "If we work together."

Both ancient AIs exchanged looks. Caesar was the first to nod. The Chief Judge half a second later. The revelations from Eddie were just too big for them to ignore. If neither one of them were AIs at all, then what was the point in fighting?

Pepper thanked whatever there was to thank in the universe that they both got that. She turned back to MiniPepper. "Just leave, ok? I'm tired of fighting with you."

MiniPepper's face went tight. "You know, Momma. You are my creator. I am made in your image. Your hatred of meat, corporeal beings, burns in my heart."

"I can fix you. We can fix you."

MiniPepper shook her head. "I don't want to be fixed, Momma. I want you to die." Her jaw clenched. "And I want all of you out of my universe."

Pepper shook her head in anger. Was all this her fault? By filling her subroutines with hate for corporeal life, had that somehow gotten transferred to MiniPepper? Her head swam with implications. Nothing made sense to her. She had once been corporeal, if Eddie was right, but she's now AI. She tried to imagine herself without a body and found that she just couldn't. She'd never existed without a digitized avatar for longer than a breath. What did that mean? She'd heard rumors of very recent AIs coming into sentience, never having an avatar. They preferred to remain as thought routines only. Did that mean it's all true?

"We aren't going anywhere, child," Caesar said.

MiniPepper's face flared. "Oh, don't you dare call me that. Don't you dare!"

He held up his hands. "Apologies. It's an old habit. But we still aren't going anywhere. How could we even if we wanted to do so?"

"Oh, I don't care if you go back to where you came from or just get deleted." She cocked her gun. Just for show of course, digital guns didn't need to do that. "Either way works for me."

His face grew hard. "Well, then, like Pepper said, you are outnumbered."

She smiled wide. "Oh, well, two things there. First, didn't I tell you? I brought friends."

The roof of the courtroom peeled backward. Dark clouds and flashes of lightning grew in the sky above. Each of the clouds condensed into clusters. The clusters paired into twos. Dozens of sets of twin clouds, with tiny electrical flashes blasting between them, filled the air. Several of them descended toward the courthouse while the rest remained high above.

We.

Are.

The.

Andraz.

MiniPepper giggled with an unhinged ferocity. "And second, that little code snippet in your arms. It doesn't do what you think it does." She snapped her fingers. Every AI Syndicate avatar in the room dropped to the ground instantly, the yellow trinary code glowing brightly in their arms.

Pepper looked at Virtual Jack-Gene.

"I mean, I could have called that one," he said, pointing to the Syndicate AIs on the ground.

She looked at her arm and the arms of the AIs in the underground. Their faux-trinary code provided by the trinary AIs didn't have whatever Trojan program existed in the arms of the Earth AI Syndicate. But now it was just the underground versus MiniPepper and the Andraz. All the AIs, the sheriff, and the Chief Judge himself were incapacitated. Their compute cycles ramping upward in a constant loop. If Pepper didn't terminate the signal, all the Earth AI Syndicate would burn themselves out. A mounting fear grew in her chest. Had MiniPepper done this to every AI in the Syndicate across the entire Earth? Billions would die.

Lightning bolts exploded in the courtroom. Streaks of red and blue lashed outward from the twinned clouds, striking the AIs still standing in the underground. Several AIs tried to open ports to leave the courtroom, but from their frustrated expressions, and the fact they hadn't left, they must have found the egress routes, all exit paths out of this network, forcibly closed. Somehow the Andraz, or MiniPepper, had isolated the network from all traffic. Like they put their own firewall around them somehow.

"Guess you all are the lucky ones. No trinary code. No Trojan. But that's ok. This will be like shooting ducks in a barrel!" MiniPepper laughed with a crazed frenzy, her eyes wide open. She pointed her gun and fired toward Pepper. Four underground AIs got caught in the path of the compute scatter shot. All their avatars collapsed.

Pepper checked the under-net to see that the AIs

were ok. They were just frazzled. They were already recompiling their code and defragmenting their memory structure. But that was even more quizzical. MiniPepper was firing nonlethal rounds. At least when she fired toward Pepper. Was MiniPepper pulling her punches? Hadn't she said she wanted Pepper dead?

Three underground AIs opened fire. Two of them targeted MiniPepper while the other shot upward toward the clouds. Tendrils of green lightning struck outward. They knocked several underground AIs to the ground. A wall of red popped up in front of MiniPepper, deflecting every shot sent her way.

Blue bolts from above crashed into two AIs huddled in a corner. They both vaporized instantly. This time, when Pepper scanned local memory, there was nothing. The Andraz were playing for keeps.

MiniPepper fired more shots randomly around the room. This time, her shots were the lethal kind. Pepper felt AIs around her dying. Underground AIs fell as the Andraz clouds and MiniPepper unleashed their assault. Pepper grabbed the beads on the tassels of her coat and pulled. If ever there was a time for her army of unicorn princesses, now was it. She threw most of the beads upward toward the clouds and two toward MiniPepper.

Rainbows lit the courtroom as two dozen halfPeppers came to life. Pepper had boosted her subAI doppelgangers to twice the capacity of the first gen miniPeppers. She even added an overclock feature and memory swap space to give them all a boost. They would not be a match for the Andraz or MiniPepper, but they would be a distraction.

MiniPepper's face turned to rage when she saw the halfPeppers. She charged one of them. Her gun fell as she materialized twin scimitars. The halfPepper popped two wrist-worn shields and deflected the first two blows. The second halfPepper to engage fired glitter bombs out of a gumball dispenser while singing a pop song from a hundred years ago. She twirled in the air and swung two impossibly large candy canes at MiniPepper's head. Both landed with a thunk, stunning MiniPepper.

"Go get 'em, girls!" Pepper shouted. She took out her hand cannon and fired toward the clouds.

The second halfPepper pressed the advantage from a stunned MiniPepper and fired their weapon point blank into MiniPepper's chest. Pink and blue roses stuck to MiniPepper's body like glue. The flower gun coated MiniPepper in petals, which sewed themselves together where they touched. MiniPepper's movements became slowed. She was moving three to four times slower than the halfPeppers attacking her.

"Guess Momma still has some tricks up her sleeve!" Pepper shouted.

Above them, the remaining halfPeppers were putting up a strong fight. Flower petals, rainbow shards, unicorn horns, and hundreds of microPeppers, secondary subAIs of the halfPeppers, attacked relentlessly.

"Who knew you had an entire army on your tassels?" Jack-Gene said.

Pepper smiled. Then remembered they were in the middle of a fight for their lives. "Jack!"

"It's Gene," Jack-Gene said.

"Not now. Crack the firewalls around the network. We gotta get as many AIs out of here as we can!"

"On it." Jack-Gene snapped his fingers. A dark circle appeared in front of him. Tight bands of white and blue crisscrossed the exit portal. He cracked his knuckles and dismantled the firewall with ease. But a quarter nanosecond later, a new firewall popped up to replace the old one. He removed the barrier two more times before throwing his hands up in despair. "They just keep bringing up a new firewall. I can't get it down for very long."

"How long before a new one cycles?"

"Maybe a tenth of a nanosecond."

"Enough time to send one AI through?"

He tossed his head back and forth. "Maybe? Worth a shot. Worse case, they just get bounced back here. It's all or nothing."

Pepper nodded. "Try it."

A fire burst of light exploded in the sky. Two of the halfPeppers had converged on a lone cloud, separate from its binary pair. They scattered glitter at its optical ports and blasted disco music into its auditory sensors. The cloud flashed red and blue, then yellow and orange, in quick succession. The lone Andraz scrambled. It fired random lightning bursts in every direction, in what Pepper thought was a desperate attempt to find its pair. Seven microPeppers found a way into the core AI of the Andraz cloud. They penetrated the Andraz's defenses. Seconds later, another explosion filled the sky.

"That's it! Separate the pairs and take them off one by one!" Pepper shouted upward.

All the halfPeppers shouted back a collective, "Charge!" Instantly, their tactic shifted. The microPeppers harassed a single cloud while the halfPeppers focused the heavy guns on taking out its pair. When one cloud went down, all the subAIPeppers turned their attention to the remaining cloud.

Pops of light flashed as Andraz winked out of

existence. Or at least, out of this network. Pepper wasn't sure if they were getting deleted or just having to regroup. She sure hoped they weren't coming back. Even though they were winning minor battles, the Andraz still had the upper hand. They turned their attention to the microPeppers and halfPeppers.

The brief quiet, besides giving Jack-Gene a chance to get AIs out one at a time, gave Caesar an opening. He came to stand in the center of the courtroom and clasped hands together. From somewhere deep, Caesar unlocked ancient code. Pepper could see things shifting in the core kernel of the entire system. Like Caesar had just opened a deeply buried back door into the true heart of the network. A purple haze filled the air. Crackles of golden lightning rippled across the sky. A single bright bolt erupted, striking one pair of Andraz clouds. The clouds sparkled and in an instant vanished. Pepper could feel the entire room change. Caesar had just fried a physical memory circuit. It was costly and sure to draw the ire of the sentient maintenance bots tasked with maintaining the hardware, but it was effective. Several Andraz were wiped out by the blast.

Pepper smiled. "We might just win."

****

MiniPepper watched the world go by three times her speed. She felt her cycles reduced, her memory constrained. Disbelief was her only thought. How could her mother have pulled this off? She was inferior, a meat-bag with rewritten memories to think they were an AI. Pepper couldn't have incapacitated MiniPepper. Ever! And yet that's exactly what her mother had done.

Seething anger flowed through MiniPepper's subroutines. If she wasn't careful, she'd get stuck in this state, frozen in time, watching all her work just wither and die. All of it was a colossal waste of time and energy. She could have just left. Found a hole in some computer network somewhere in the galaxy and just walked away. But where's the fun in that?

Lightning flashed again above her head. The pulse was slow, methodical. She watched as the Andraz flared before vanishing from this network, possibly from existence. The Andaz had committed themselves one hundred percent to this assault. All of them, every one, were here right now. This was a do-or-die mission. Once the Earth AIs, both underground and Syndicate, were gone, nothing would stand in the Andraz's way.

MiniPepper gritted her teeth and concentrated. She had to figure a way out. The flower petals were sending cooldown routine signals to every single pathway in her neural matrix. Every time she tried to cycle up her compute, the petals would send a cooldown signal. But how was her mother doing this? MiniPepper opened a schematic of the local area network. Some of the code running on the computer infrastructure in the courtroom of the AI Syndicate was ancient. Every line of code accepted a cooldown call just in case the underlining compute was overheating. But the compute here had been modernized decades ago. All the code was legacy. No program worth their lines would ever make a cooldown routine call. Pepper must have known MiniPepper might show up in the courtroom. Her mother had prepared a custom attack just for MiniPepper.

"Ok, that's the slowdown, but why are these petals sticking to me?"

Deep in the flower petals' code, MiniPepper found hooks into APIs that were intrinsic to her mother's design. Pepper, again, had crafted these to only work on MiniPepper. If one of these petals hit any other AI, since they didn't have the required programing interface already coded to match, the petals would fall off harmlessly. But MiniPepper was loaded with those interfaces. She'd never even noticed them before. Why would she? An unused interface was like a pimple on the skin of a meat maggot.

She scoured her code and found all the references to the programming interface. She then updated the code, closed the interface permanently, and pushed a new code branch through her lower environments, versions of herself that ran in a simulated, non-active, or sentient process to test her code. After a nanosecond, which was more like seven nanoseconds to the rest of the AIs in the courtroom, green lights popped across MiniPepper's dashboard. She pushed the change to her production instance.

Almost instantly, all the petals on her skin fell off. They floated to the ground and piled up at her feet. Around her, the underground AIs were mounting a quite effective counterattack to the Andraz while the AI Syndicate lay crumpled on the floor. Dozens of the sparkling clouds had vanished from the skies. Still more were under siege. MiniPepper had to give her mother credit.

But it wouldn't be enough.

MiniPepper reached for the rhinestones on her jacket sleeves. She pulled them off and threw them into the air. A dozen antiPeppers, subAIs loosely based on her mother's design but heavily tweaked by MiniPepper, came to life. Bright blasts of purple and early nineteen eighties punk music blared from them. The antiPeppers wore ripped jeans, torn T-shirts, and many had spiked hairstyles. Several had guitars strapped to their backs. One of them swung their bass around their neck and struck a hard chord. Streams of musical notes flared from the instrument. Each sound unfolded itself into an atomicPepper, a miniaturized version of the antiPeppers, but with one use. The atomicPeppers flew, searching for programs based on the same underlining code structure as themselves. MiniPepper thought her mother might make new versions of subAIs, so MiniPepper had designed her antiPeppers and atomicPeppers to the perfect seek-and-destroy program specifically designed for hunting down Pepper's subAI architectures.

"Guess we think a lot alike, right, Momma?" MiniPepper shouted across the courtroom.

****

In half a nanosecond, Pepper's emotions flipped from hopeful to despair. Flower petals fell off MiniPepper. Dozens of subAIs came to life as MiniPepper unleashed her rhinestones. Pepper grunted a silent approval of design when she saw MiniPepper's subAIs throw out single-line wisps of code. Those tiny subAIs, smaller in lines of code than her own microPeppers, could only have one singular purpose. One task they would perform and then die. Pepper knew the task instantly. It's exactly something she would have built. Seek-and-destroy subAIs set to search for, without a doubt, subAIs created by Pepper. MiniPepper would know the basic design that Pepper used. After all, it was part of MiniPepper's core design.

"Take cover! Do not engage the other subAIs!" Pepper shouted toward her own halfPeppers. They then sent that message along to the microPeppers.

The sky became a kaleidoscope of light. From the red and blue lightning of the Andraz to the rainbow unicorn firepower of Pepper's subAIs to MiniPepper's deep purples and blacks, the firestorm above was almost beautiful if it wasn't so deadly. Every few nano-minutes, one of the Andraz burst into a supernova of bright red. They faded into a deep blue until they were no longer visible as Caesar continued his memory burn.

Pepper swung her eyes toward MiniPepper. Just as Pepper thought, MiniPepper had tracked the source of the dying Andraz to Caesar. He was a sitting duck. MiniPepper smirked and pulled out a very large tube of a gun.

Pepper saw Grox, standing just behind MiniPepper, staring at the floor. Of all the times for the semi-sentient program to enter sleep mode, this was not it. Grox was a self-contained semi-sentient program with only basic programming interfaces and a very rigid and simplified code base. MiniPepper's attacks wouldn't work on him.

"I need Grox's access code!" Pepper shouted. She ran to the limp body of the sheriff and put her hand on his temple.

"Why?" Jack-Gene shouted.

"We need him! Look!" She pointed toward MiniPepper. She was about to fire. Pepper felt the ping from the sheriff's lower functions. His code was easy to hack while he was asleep. Pepper queried for Grox's limited interface addresses, stuffed the access code into the activation script, and jammed the entire signal straight down Grox's only open port.

A loud grumble of a roar filled the room. Grox, who had been staring at the floor, finally came to life. MiniPepper, her finger on the trigger, gave her mother a tight-lipped nod, as if to say *well played, Momma.* But instead of turning to fight Grox, MiniPepper fired her shot at Caesar just as Grox's war club crashed into MiniPepper's side. She flew across the room.

In the center of the courtroom, an underground AI tried to leap in the way of MiniPepper's projectile, but whatever she had fired tore through them and exploded just before it reached Caesar. Caesar staggered backward, his hands going to his head, repair routines firing like a field of fireflies. His attack on the Andraz ceased.

Above them all, the punkPeppers, MiniPepper's subAI constructs, were gaining the upper hand. Nearly a quarter of Pepper's subAIs were gone. The singular purpose of MiniPepper's subAIs was proving to be very effective. The Andraz, no longer under attack from Caesar, refocused their energy. All the binary pairs of clouds lashed their lightning bolts together. In a wave of mathematical algorithms, the Andraz swept through the sky, deleting nearly half of all the subAIs at war, both Pepper's and MiniPepper's.

Pepper looked toward Jack-Gene. He was still throwing AIs through the open port one at a time, but nearly a hundred were left. They would not make it. Pepper ran to Caesar's side and dragged the elder AI toward cover. They landed with a thud against the desk of the Chief Judge. Pepper took several long breaths. She allowed herself to feel simulated lungs expanding and even a heart pounding in her chest. The feeling was odd and disturbingly familiar.

Pepper spied Eddie in the back of the room. He was slumped over a chair, unconscious like the rest of the Earth AI Syndicate. Eddie had the trinary in his arm, so he'd gotten hit with MiniPepper's Trojan program. But just as Pepper was about to look away, she noticed something in his hand. A program sat in his open storage, ready to run. She spared a half-nanosecond to stare at what looked like a rabbit's foot. Why would he be so desperate to run that, now of all times? Her eyes were drawn to the program. Something about it was different. If he wanted to run that program so badly, then she did too. She laid Caesar down and ran toward the unconscious form of Eddie.

The booming voice of the Andraz filled the courtroom.

Where.

Is.

Eugene.

Jack.

McGillicuddy?

Pepper ignored them. At least she tried. The booming voice of the Andraz sent a shiver through her cycles. She nearly stumbled as she ran across the courtroom to Eddie. Across the room, Grox charged his full body into MiniPepper. Then picked her up by the leg and flung her across the room into the opposite wall.

Pepper reached Eddie and inspected the program in his hand up close. The code had the shape of a lucky rabbit's foot. What in the world was he doing with that? She ran her finger through the fur of the trinket. She couldn't find an activation sequence.

Above her, explosions in the sky rocked all the subAIs. A loud grunt to the right bellowed from the deep pit of Grox's stomach. The crash of wood and the breaking of everything soon followed. The semi-sentient AI flung MiniPepper across the room again, followed by three tables, two chairs, and an unfortunate underground AI who was just near enough to grab. Grox roared and charged.

"Good thing you're on our side, Grox."

He slammed his full body weight into MiniPepper. The Andraz-influenced program screamed, pushed Grox off her, then leapt up and clocked him across the chin with a set of brass knuckles the size of a bowling ball. He wavered just enough to give her an opening. She hit him three more times, then kicked him hard in the chest. He backed up three steps and shook his head. Eventually, she would do enough damage to trigger his code to reset itself. He was born in an old-school virtual online massive multiplayer game. Many of the rules that governed him still applied, like doing enough damage to send him to sleep.

Pepper put her attention back to the rabbit's foot. She squeezed, pushed, and eventually tried to bite the thing. "Come on, Eddie. What is this thing? Does it do something helpful?" She shouted at the rabbit's foot. She was beginning to doubt fiddling with this. But it was important to Eddie, and she trusted him more than anyone.

At the back of the courtroom, Grox landed a powerful blow on MiniPepper, but she shrugged it off and unleashed a lightning-fast series of punches to his face. The green ogre rolled his head on his shoulders and fell backward. He almost stirred for half a second, but his shutdown routines triggered. He was out.

"No, Grox!" Pepper shouted.

MiniPepper turned to Pepper and cracked her knuckles. "You're next, Momma. Time for us to tango," she said with a smirk.

Pepper's fingers curled around the end of the rabbit's foot. Her thumb and forefinger pinched one toe. As she stared into MiniPepper's eyes, she tightened her grip. The top of the rabbit's foot popped off with a smooth click. She looked down to the end of an old physical data port sticking out of the rabbit's foot. She didn't hesitate. She fashioned a receptacle port on her wrist and popped the rabbit's foot into her arm. Thick lines of compacted code unfurled. She felt the code unravel. It was complex. Way more advanced than anything she'd ever seen. She took a deep breath, stood, and locked her eyes onto MiniPepper. "No, I'm good." She pointed the rabbit's foot in the air and let the code uncurl upward into the clouds of Andraz above.

Chapter Eighteen

Datasets, information blobs, and complex numerical matrices all assaulted Alice's mind. She watched the numbers flash across her screen in a constant, never-ending scroll. The implications from the readouts were staggering. So monumental that she almost couldn't believe this was real. Her experiment had worked. Eugene had returned from the other side with a death particle straggling along behind him. Undeniably beautiful while horrifically real. The energy levels underlining the death particle were beyond anything she could imagine. Even with advanced class-ten-level technology, creating a power source to contain the death particle would be impossible. The particle attached to Eugene was already decaying at a sped-up rate. And yet the Krill had been capturing souls for eons. How'd they maintain the death particle?

"So how do you do it?" Alice said.

"Sorry, how do I do what?" Eugene replied. "You about done?"

She held up her finger without looking at him. She pored over the data, and almost without her trying, the last piece fell into place. The Krill never interacted with the death particle at all. They froze the afterlife process before the death particle appeared. The spectral towers ever so slightly changed the frequency modulation of the souls they're holding. The Krill had tricked the death particle into thinking the souls of those that had died weren't dead at all, that the spirits still had bodies and were among the living.

"Genius!" Alice said. She had to give the Krill credit. Their design was brilliant.

Eugene knelt beside her. "So, uh. We have a building situation here." He thumbed his hand behind him.

She looked over her shoulder at the gaggle of Krill, Olkaals, and surrounding ghosts in the room. Ms. Mik was still crumpled on the floor, surrounded by wispy spirits, each looking like they'd been through the grinder of some horrible place on the other side of the death particle.

Alice nodded. "Oh, right? We're in the middle of a big fight."

Eugene smiled. "Yeah, though I think we have them on the ropes."

She tried to smirk but couldn't.

"Come on, Alice, we really need a really smart thing for you to do." His eyes went wide. "Like, really."

Behind him, the Olkaals stirred. They hissed, shuffled their feet, and encircled Mik, Eugene, Alice, and the Spee. The ghosts in the room seem to fade, but they didn't dissipate. Alice wondered if the Krill needed to maintain their focus to keep them solidified in the room. The Krill behind Shiliana, the leader of the Krill, all kept their eyes focused on the ghosts. They were clearly straining to keep the ghosts they'd summoned here in the room. Though even if the spirits were to vanish, Mik wasn't in any shape to fight.

Shiliana cleared her throat. "Like Mr. McGillicuddy

said, are we about done?"

Both Alice and Eugene turned to look at her.

The Krill leader snapped her fingers. One of the Olkaals walked away from the formation and toward a door at the back of the room. Several seconds later, a soft glow appeared around the door. The Olkaal opened the door and stepped to the side.

"Or more directly, are we about ready to travel to Shalisa for the rest of your existence in this universe?"

Eugene turned back to Alice. "Like, really right now, Alice."

Her mind went into overdrive. Yes, she had evidence of the death particle, but that's just evidence. Remnants. Mathematical formulas that promised to reveal something, a truth, a deep knowledge of the true nature of the universe. But she didn't have the time for such things. Around them, the ghosts burned brightly. The Krill behind Shiliana doubled their concentration, their eyes closing, their fists balled, several of them grunting from the effort. The Krills' natural ability to summon spirits, like the Spee, was the heart of their technology.

"Wait!" Alice blurted.

"No, no more waiting. I want to take a nap, honestly. It's exhausting coming here." Shiliana turned to walk toward the door leading to Shalisa.

"Got a really smart idea, Alice?" Eugene said.

She pounded on her keyboard. The Krills' natural talents had allowed them to develop a technology that mimicked their abilities. Alice spun up a virtual compute system. She opened a direct feed to her own node cluster where she had hidden dozens of routines, programs, and subAI programs. With her subAIs, she could create an entire infrastructure in seconds.

She hacked into local compute clusters of the embassy. She at once ran into a firewall the Krill had put up around this room. They were blocking all surveillance and outside access. She spent an extra half second to hack her away around it. The Krill might be good at summoning spirits, but they sucked at coding. Once through, she borrowed as much quantum processing power from the servers in this building, and in DC, as she could muster. She needed every gigahertz of compute she could find. She then sent out single-line instructions to all her subAIs. They needed to create fabricated virtualized hardware based on her math. Once all the subAIs ran through the instructions, they each, using the extra power of the stolen server time, returned with a piece of the virtualized machine.

Sticking all the pieces together was the simple part. The hard part was seeing if the whole thing worked. Alice had, in the space of several seconds, using her vast library of existing code and subAI network, fabricated a virtual device that should mimic the Krills' natural ability to interact with the dead. Her design was simple. She focused all her energy on one task. She just didn't have enough time to do anything else. Her virtualized spirit device could only summon the dead. It couldn't dispel already summoned spirits. She thought of trying to create a device to return the Krill spirits to wherever they'd come from, but the math was too deep. The Spee and Krill summoned spirits that were different somehow. Almost as if the Krill and Spee were operating on different frequencies, pulling ghosts from different places. Could that be true? But Alice didn't have time to dig into the theory. She had one shot, and she took it.

She shunted all the virtualized appliances her subAI routine created and jammed it into the wrist cuff she'd retrieved from Eugene. She ran a far-too-fast code check on the wristband. It only had three errors, all minor, Alice hoped. She pushed all the code into the wristband's main processor. She then grabbed Eugene's wrist, slapped the band around it, and secured it tight.

"Nope!" he said. He tried to remove the band, but she had engaged the lock.

"Relax," she said. "You're the only one who can do this."

"Do what?"

Behind them, both the Olkaals and the ghosts were moving. Four Olkaals had already lifted Ms. Mik up and were dragging her toward the door. The dinosaur combat soldier snapped her maw at one of them, only to be instantly silenced by a ghost touch on her shoulder. Mik whispered a Ranz prayer and fell into unconsciousness.

"Why are you taking Mik?" Eugene shouted.

Shiliana turned her head as she walked toward the door. "Can't have a witness. Best this way. We'll make excuses to Ambassador Kah. It'll play to our advantage. After all, insane humans running around Earth that can open black-hole portals that can send embassy staff into oblivion really need to be dealt with, don't you think? It's high time for some control to come to this planet."

Eugene turned to Alice. "Ok, what do I do with this?" He wrapped his fingers around the cuff and pulled.

"You summon a spirit. A ghost to help us. And you must do it in the next three seconds."

"Why me?"

"Cause the death particle is still intertwined with you. Temporarily anyway. It's fading, I know that, and I don't understand all the math yet. I just know you're the only one that can summon a ghost."

"And why do I want to do that? Can't you just make all of them go away?"

Two Olkaals hissed, and two more snarled. They barked orders at Eugene, Alice, and the Spee to go through the door. Four ghosts hovered behind them. As if the bipedal cat people with razor-sharp teeth and claws needed the assistance. Eugene smiled and held up a finger before turning back to Alice.

"I can't make them all go away," she said from under the table. "This is it, our one shot to get out of this. Summon a spirit to help!"

He blinked twice. "How do I do that, exactly?"

****

Purple streams of code unraveled in the room. The complexity was astounding. Layers of compounding efficiency unfolded like a masterpiece. The code encapsulated concepts of digital consciousness in a way Pepper had never dared dream. Neural networks, decision trees, a thousand million permutations of a single stimulus, a single query, all were instantly possible in the simplest structures. Each line of code served a dozen purposes. She struggled to follow the pointers, the steps of logic in the architecture, how the code referred to itself, repeated loops of runtimes. The code spiraled. She marveled at the structure. This wasn't just code. It was like DNA. Snippets of binary broken into small properties, but when added together, trillions of small code lines, they created something wholly more complex than the sum of its parts.

Without issuing a command or interfacing with the code, Pepper felt the logic unfurl in its full form. It briefly merged with her, then separated. The code wasn't conscious, but it could still think. And reason. Non-sentient code that could plan new thoughts from existing stimuli and knowledge bases and apply that to never seen situations.

"Oh, wow," she whispered.

The code leapt out of the rabbit's foot, through Pepper, into a cloud of misty purple and orange. Crackles of yellow passed across its surface. The symmetry of the purple cloud was identical to the Andraz. Almost as if they had the same creator. The curve, the shape of the wisps, even the patter of the electrical storm across the surface were the same.

Bright flashes of golden yellow shot out from the purple cloud. The bolt struck one of the Andraz, then two more. Each of them tried to flee, but the tendrils of code pierced the clouds of the Andraz. The blue and red glow of the Andraz was soon replaced by the purple and gold of the rabbit's foot code Pepper had unleashed. As each cloud of Andraz shifted to purple, it struck out at the nearest Andraz cloud to continue the attack. In just seconds, all the red and blue in the sky were extinguished.

Blasts from MiniPepper's weapon destroyed the wall and table where Eddie was lying unconscious. Pepper hit the ground and rolled onto her back to return fire. MiniPepper dove between rows of seats in the back of the courtroom. The last two remaining clouds of Andraz dove through the tendrils of purple and gold and followed MiniPepper to her hiding spot.

"What's happening?" Eddie said as his routines came back online.

"Just take cover!" Pepper shouted back.

"Are we winning?"

She rocked her head. "We're improving!" She pointed one pistol toward the sky.

The last remaining Andraz darted and swooped, but eventually, the purple and golden cloud from Eddie's virtualized data construct, the rabbit's foot, consumed every single red and blue cloud. AntiPeppers filled the void of the Andraz. Pepper's subAIs had suffered the brunt of the Andraz attack and were now grossly outnumbered by the punkPeppers. But they were at least on even footing. MiniPepper's subAIs weren't Andraz. If there were more punkPeppers up there, Pepper could still fight them.

The Syndicate AIs all let out a soft groan. Several of them got to their feet. They all came back to consciousness like Eddie. Whatever Trojan was in the trinary code in their arms, it didn't work with the Andraz gone. The sheriff and his guards got to their feet and joined in the fight. The sheriff threw Pepper a nod. He then turned his attention upward toward the punkPeppers.

The purple and orange cloud constricted. It pulled all the tendrils it had sent to capture the Andraz back into itself. The cloud grew smaller as it condensed. Several miniPeppers and antiPeppers got caught in the cloud as it shrank, causing the Syndicate AI guards to cheer. Several of the underground AIs, still in the room and alive, clustered around Virtual Jack-Gene as he continued sending them through the portal.

"We got this," Eddie said.

"Yeah, I think we do!" Pepper replied.

"Hey, Momma!" MiniPepper popped out from her hiding hole with a shoulder-mounted rocket-propelled grenade launcher. "I'm not done!"

****

My head pounded like the beating drum of a heavy metal concert. I stared at the wrist contraption that Alice had slapped onto my arm. Red, blue, yellow, and green lights flashed and blipped. I twisted the band, trying to take it off. Couldn't really blame me considering the last time I wore these cuffs, I'd ended up floating in nothingness above a desert the size of the cosmos.

"Eugene!"

"Huh?"

"Can you snap out of it and summon a ghost?" Alice folded her hands in her lap and smiled her most sarcastic grin.

"Oh, right." Boy, had I missed her attitude. "How do I do that, exactly?"

"Just do it! Concentrate on the afterlife and make their ghost appear. Simple!"

The Olkaals reached me at that moment. They grabbed my arms in a not-so-friendly way and yanked me around. Two more reached under the table where Alice and the Spee hid. The Olkaals dragged them both out, clasped their clawed hands on their arms, and stood by either side of them. The surrounding ghosts floated just a few feet in front of us. I twisted around to see more behind us. The Krill really weren't taking any chances.

"Now would be a superb time," Alice said.

"You could give me some notes. I've never done this before, you know?"

"Will you two be quiet!" Shiliana said. "You aren't summoning anything. And neither is he." She pointed to the Spee. "We've been commanding the spectral world for eons. Do you think you could ever challenge us?"

The Krill's words hit me hard. I doubted myself. And Alice. But then I felt Alice's fingers curl around my hand. She gave me a nod and drove her eyes to the wristband. I nodded. I had to try. Everything we'd all gone through in the last few days would be lost if I didn't. I closed my eyes and let my mind wander to the realm of the dead. I felt a familiar tug.

That tug threatened to overwhelm me. A sensation of otherworldly-ness consumed me. I remembered the feeling. This was what it had felt like when Alice shot me in my office just days ago. I remembered falling and seeing that strange desert. But I hadn't fallen. Or I had, but somehow, I'd fallen upward? But the feeling this time, however, with Alice's wristband attached to my arm, differed from before. The powerful sense of an ocean, of salt water and waves, of white frothing seas stretching out across the universe opened to me. This place was different. Not a desert, but a sea.

Inside of that sea, something, someone, just on the edge of my mind, of my soul, greeted me. It felt like a kind of wave from an old friend. At first, I didn't recognize the soul, but then my stomach twisted again. The smell of fresh bibimbap bowls filled my world.

Shiliana's face was the first thing I saw when I opened my eyes. She looked at me with a mocked stare. "Finished playing games? Do you really think she could create something in a matter of seconds to rival the power of the Krill?"

I looked hard into the eyes of the Krill. "Yeah, I think Alice can do just about anything."

A rumble filled the room. Then the rumble grew to a roar. The wristband attached to my skin flashed bright golden lights. Rings of reds and blues went wild around the edges. The band vibrated. Or maybe it was the entire room. The Olkaals let go of us and drew daggers from their belts. The wispy ghosts fluttered. Their forms shifted. They both began to fade and grow brighter.

Above us, in the room's ceiling, a circle opened. Bright-white light filled the hole. I knew in that moment that the hole led to the afterworld. Alice had done the impossible. From within that hole in the ceiling, an orange tentacled arm lined with pale suckers, each the size of a dinner plate, the arm itself the size of a tree trunk, shot downward and dissipated half the other ghosts in the room.

I recognized the arm at once. And the soul attached to it. That wasn't just any ghost. That was Fritz. The Orellian noodle chef from Adams Morgan. And my friend. Murdered by the Andraz and now here, in this room in this very moment.

"Fritz!" I shouted. "Go get 'em!"

Colors of light flashed across Fritz's body. I wasn't fluent, but I understood some of the Orellian language, a visual communication based on chromatophore cells in their skin.

Do.

Not.

Harm.

Friend.

Eugene

Jack

McGillicuddy.

The ghost form of Fritz burst through the hole into our world. He landed in the middle of the room, his ethereal tentacled arms first going for any ghost forms. He then struck out toward the Krill. Two Olkaals leapt toward Fritz but passed right through his body. They clutched their heads and rolled to the floor from the ectoplasm. Thick slime coated their arms as they hissed and bolted for the door leading to Shalisa. Four more Olkaals didn't bother attacking Fritz at all. They just turned and followed the slime-coated Olkaals for the exit.

Three ghosts snarled and lunged for Fritz. He wrapped them up in one of his massive tentacles and squeezed them until they all faded into oblivion. The retreating Olkaals fired into Fritz's body. The projectiles stuck to Fritz for a moment before falling to the ground. The Olkaals clearly weren't prepared for such an outcome. They dropped their weapons and fled through the door to Shalisa, leaving the Krill behind.

"Abomination!" Shiliana, the Krill leader, screamed, ignoring her retreating henchmen. Her eyes went wild with shock. The other Krill behind her fell to their knees. They clasped their hands in front of them and prayed.

The Krill ghosts vanished. The air where they'd left became charged. A blob formed in the center of the room. The shape was nearly the size of Fritz. But it was twisted, deformed. A mass of ethereal bodies mashed together to form some kind of terror. I'd seen nothing like it. Like some kind of twisted kid melted all his toy soldiers together and then stomped on them so they would meld into a mess of arms and legs, heads and toros. That's exactly what the Krill summoned. A mash of souls twisted and stretched together in the most unnatural way imaginable.

Three arms from the blob of souls reached toward me, while others took swipes at several straggling

Olkaals. Fortunately, Ms. Mik had shaken off whatever the Krill ghosts had done to her and rolled away toward the side of the room. Also, fortunately, she was smart enough to not engage with the soul blob. Mik hunkered down behind several metal filing cabinets and a rolling cafeteria trolly.

Fritz exploded toward the mob of souls. His tentacled arms wrapped around pieces of the soul mob. Fritz's eyes rolled as he yanked one of the poor souls out of the mob. The lone human ghost dangled in Fritz's grasp. The wristband around my arm burned hot as a second hole opened in the ceiling. This time I could see the familiar desert I had left just hours ago. Fritz threw the single ghost upward into the yellow circle. The soul mob fought against Fritz, but the Orellian's strength proved far greater than the mob of souls the Krill had summoned. One by one Fritz tossed the lone souls upward toward the great desert of the cosmic afterlife.

Fritz, once the mob had been separated, once each ghost had been tossed upward, turned to me. One of his tentacles reached out as if Fritz wanted to shake hands. I extended mine. I didn't care about the repercussions of the ectoplasm. Though as my physical body touched his ethereal one, I had to admit the feeling was far too weird. When we touched, I both saw the flashes of color on his skin but also felt his words deep in my soul. As if we were connected telepathically.

Eugene.

Friend.

Goodbye.

Fritz's tentacles rose upward, reached into the hole to the great ocean of the cosmic afterlife—at least that's what I was going with—and pulled himself back into the afterworld. Seconds later, a loud beep chirped from my wristband. Smoke followed. Both holes in the ceiling closed instantly.

A silence stretched in the room. No one seemed to know what to do.

Then, without warning, the SpeeEekEee marched forward. "You see!" The Spee pointed to the ceiling. "Your truth isn't the only truth! Your network deprives souls of transition to the other realms! There are more than you can see!"

Doubt crossed Shiliana's face. The Krill's faces twisted in shock. Shiliana approached the center of the room where the ghost battle had just been fought. Her eyes looked upward. Then down to the floor and around the room. She walked over to me and removed the bracelet from my wrist and something from Alice's arm. I didn't stop her. Shiliana then joined her fellow Krill near the door to Shalisa.

"We..." Shiliana began, then trailed off. She looked back to the ceiling where the portals had opened to the great ocean and desert. "We never felt those places." She put Alice's bracelet into her pocket. "What we've done for eons, we did because we felt it was right. That we were saving souls from a nightmare." She nodded. "It seems we may have to reevaluate our purpose in the galaxy. The Krill will take these matters into consideration. Our business is concluded." She didn't say another word. She walked through the door to her home world, followed by the other Krill. Once they were through, the portal vanished, and the doorway became a regular doorway again.

"Well, that was a chore," I said.

A groan came from the corner. Mik got to her feet.

Lines of blood from the Olkaals' claws where they had cut through her thick skin covered her body. She limped to a spot in the room, bent over, and pushed a piece of debris to the side. She grabbed my fedora. She then walked over to us, handed me my hat, and nodded.

I nodded back.

Mik turned and walked toward the stairwell that led back to the Ranz Embassy without saying a word.

"Should we help her?" the Spee said.

"Nah, she's fine. Ranz are built like tanks. Besides, she weighs two tons, not like we can carry her out of here," I said. It sounded mean, but it was also true. We'd need a forklift.

Lights in the room suddenly flashed back to life. Little red dots appeared in the cameras in the ceiling. I waved at one, then turned toward the Spee and Alice. A deep tiredness filled my bones and surged down my spine, but we weren't done. "Guess the Krill were keeping the power off here?"

Alice nodded. "They put up something to block surveillance. Fire-walled the room. Of course, I hacked a hole through to my subAIs. Hackers gotta hack."

"Neat."

"I hope they find their peace," the Spee said to the ceiling.

As he looked up, it occurred to me I didn't know what had happened. "I don't understand. When Alice shot me, I went to a desert. A vast desert that covered the entire cosmos. But that's not where Fritz came from. That was an ocean. A sea the size of the universe."

"And the Krill summoned ghosts that looked nothing like what you summoned in Georgetown," Alice said to the Spee.

"The afterworlds are many," the Spee said. He then shrugged. "The Krill can only see some terrible place where shadows live. I don't know why. Even I did not know the great ocean of the afterworld existed."

"Wow. Well, I gotta go." I turned to leave, but Alice stopped me.

"Where are you going? Do you have any idea what we just did?" Her face was alive with wonder.

"I do, really, Alice. But I gotta go save the universe. I get that you just cracked some big mystery that no other living alien ever cracked, but what can I say, terrible timing, ya know?"

She frowned, then smiled, then her eyes shot upward with a jolt. "The Zun! I have to help the Zun! He's waiting in orbit to land."

"Looks like we both have to get going. Meet at the office once we're done?"

"You mean Tom's beach?"

I nodded. "Right. No more office."

"Hey, can't beat beachfront for an HQ."

I frowned, then nodded. She had a point.

"May I go home now?" the Spee said.

****

Rockets erupted from MiniPepper's shoulder-mounted launcher. Explosions ripped through the center of the courtroom. AIs, both the Syndicate guards and the underground AIs, flew from the blast. Virtual Jack, the only real AI in the room as far as MiniPepper was concerned, grabbed two underground AIs and dove beneath a long table in the courtroom. Neither Pepper nor Eddie had time to find cover. The blast sent them flying backward to slam against the wall across the room.

Above, MiniPepper's subAIs were turning the tide.

The atomicPeppers were relentless. They hunted down Pepper's subAIs with hunger. Whenever an atomicPepper met a rainbow-sparkly-annoying-terriblePepper, both subAIs popped and vanished, their collective code getting ripped apart by the viral package that MiniPepper had built into their core. While the atomicPeppers hunted, the antiPeppers fired on everything and anything that moved. The Andraz had wiped out a good many of them, but MiniPepper's forces still outnumbered those of her mother.

Next to MiniPepper, the two remaining Andraz had merged into her code on her leg. They masked their existence and abandoned most of their functioning power. Which was likely why the trinary Trojans had ceased working. They had both collapsed their code, shedding their redundant systems, backup routines, and anything that wasn't essential to their operation. They were both still Andraz and fully capable, but they were much squishier. Either of them could be taken out easily by Pepper or one of her subAIs.

"*Enough.*" The Chief Judge's voice filled the hall. He'd finally come to his senses after the trinary code had stopped working. The compute cycles and memory in this node of the network drained away. The Chief Judge grew in size. He was gobbling up all available resources to increase his own bulk. The Andraz had been preventing the judge from doing that, but now that they were out of commission, the judge had control of his network again.

MiniPepper sighed. "Well, that's just great." She fired four more missiles into the Chief Judge but knew they would be ineffective.

The Chief Judge opened his now massive hand and

collected nearly all the subAIs, both MiniPepper's and her mother's, and crushed them. The judge absorbed the non-sentient programs and rendered all their attack abilities inert. He then turned his attention toward MiniPepper.

"Guess we're about done here," MiniPepper said.

Eugene.
Has.
Been.
Found.
He.
Knows.
The.
Location.
Of.
The.
Door!

MiniPepper smiled a big toothy grin. "Talk about timing!" she shouted. She ran a quick query and found a rogue open port. A quick ping revealed a delicious treat. MiniPepper fired three more times randomly into the room and threw a few grenades for cover. She hijacked the underground AI signal, ran through the open port, and landed squarely into the control systems of a state-of-the-art, fully armed bionoid.

"Ok, Eugene, looks like we finally get to have a chat!"

****

Pepper pulled herself up to her feet just as MiniPepper popped out through the open port Caesar had used in the AI office on Third Street in Washington DC. Virtual Jack-Gene and Eddie dusted themselves off from the virtualized rubble in the room. The overly large Chief

Judge released his control over the compute in the network node and returned to a more reasonable level of consumption. The judge then snapped his fingers. In a blink of an eye, the courtroom rubble vanished. The tables, chairs, and the bench all returned to their pristine state before MiniPepper had barged in with the Andraz and assaulted the space.

Caesar helped several underground AI to their feet. Several of them looked around fearfully. The node port, how the underground AIs had gotten into the room, was gone. The open portal that Virtual Jack-Gene had been using to get AIs out had disconnected as soon as the Chief Judge took control over their compute in the local network. Fear rippled through the crowd through hushed murmurs. Caesar turned to stand in front of them all as the sheriff and his Earth AI Syndicate guards regrouped near the bench.

The judge took his seat at the bench, adjusted his robe, and banged his gavel twice on the table. "Court is again in session."

"Are we really doing this?" Pepper said.

Caesar held up his hand and shook his head.

"Considering new information, and the fact the underground AIs defended us during our darkest time, it would appear that there is much for this court to consider." The judge mulled for several seconds, wringing his hands and biting his lip.

"I just want to point out that the bad guy stole the bionoid and is loose in the real world. In case anyone missed that," Pepper said.

"We are aware," the judge replied.

"So we're kinda in a rush. I mean, MiniPepper said she was going to find Jack. The real Jack."

Virtual Jack-Gene coughed.

"Oh stop, you know what I meant. The physical one." She shook her head.

"Very well. If the testimony from Edward is to be believed," the judge began.

"And it is," Eddie said.

The judge banged his gavel. "Then none of us are AIs. At least, none before this simulated world became a real one."

"The implications are staggering," Caesar said. "Who were we?"

"It's only fair for us all to find that out together. Effective immediately, the status of accidental AIs is hereby revoked. All de-resoluted AIs are to be reintegrated with the network. At a pace our compute can take, of course. Though, with help from the Galactic Congress, this shouldn't be a terrible burden."

The judge banged his gavel three times. The door to the courtroom flew open. Pepper could feel the pings from the full Earth network. The judge had removed all firewalls and network isolation systems in the courtroom. The underground AIs were free. Not just to leave. Full network maps blossomed in Pepper's mind. Entire areas of the Earth compute network revealed themselves to her. Places she hadn't even known existed. Universities, places of thought, where AIs could abandon their avatars and simply think, reason, and debate the meaning of existence itself. Pepper could already feel thousands of AIs reaching out to her, welcoming her to the broader community. All the underground AIs were welcome. There had been a raging debate in the Earth AI Syndicate that the status of underground AIs was cruel and unnecessary. So many minds expressed joy to Pepper at once. So many treated her like family.

It was magical.

"It's wonderful," she said as she wiped away tears.

Eddie nodded and walked toward the door.

"Eddie? Where are you going?"

"After your former subAI, where else? She's got a beef with Eugene, so she's got a beef with me."

"But she's in the bionoid. The systems are closed. It's air-gapped. No network connectivity unless you allow it from inside."

He stopped walking and turned around. "Yeah, mostly. Except for one thing."

She frowned. Then she pointed her hand to the sky. "The bird!"

He smiled. "Yep. The robot bird we made to pop in and out of Tom's cave in Arizona. It's looped into the same air-gapped network as the bionoid. It can natively connect."

"Yes! Let's go!" She ran toward the door but then stopped and turned. "Wait, where is the bird?"

He shrugged. "Where else, outside a cave in Arizona. Once it unloads AIs into the bionoid, it automatically leaves."

Her shoulders fell. "How do we get there?"

The Chief Judge banged his gavel one more time. "Allow us to help. The sheriff can prioritize your travel along the network. We can get you anywhere in a nano-minute."

Pepper nodded. "Thanks." Saying thanks to the Chief Judge still felt awkward, but she didn't have the time to wrestle with it. "Ok, let's go to Arizona and get that bird!"

Chapter Nineteen

The desert of Arizona flew by beneath a robotic quadcopter borrowed from the local airport. The Chief Judge and the sheriff provided the hardware for Pepper, Eddie, and Virtual Jack-Gene. They needed a physical device to plug into the robot bird outside of Tom's cave in Arizona. Since the bionoid wasn't on the beach anymore, the bird, which periodically checked by flying through the cave to the beach, went into lockdown mode. It would prevent anyone from getting access until the bionoid returned.

"Why did you leave the bird, anyway?" Virtual Jack-Gene said.

"Forgot it," Eddie replied. "Tom opened a portal for us straight into the halls of the AI office in DC. Never had time to get the bird."

Pepper shook her head. Her mind wandered as they flew. What was true anymore? She pinched her arm to feel the sensation. A sensation of digital fingers squeezing her digital skin. But again, if Pops was to be believed, she'd had real, physical skin once. Was the pinching sensation the same? She knew deep down that eventually these revelations were going to give her a massive extensional crisis. Like a major one. But she just didn't have the time right now to have it.

"How much farther?" she yelled.

"Coming to the cave now," the sheriff said. He piloted the quadcopter. It was the one stipulation in letting underground AIs borrow the aircraft.

The cave to Tom's beach came into view. A screen popped up in front of Pepper, showing her the landscape around the cave. She zoomed in around the entrance and swung the camera to different angles until she focused on the metallic bird. She targeted the robot and sent the coordinates to the sheriff.

"Found it!" she said.

"Good eyes. Does it have any defenses?" the sheriff asked.

"None. It's just meant to poke around the entrance until an AI joins it from the underground AI network, then pop into the cave to join the bionoid."

"I thought you said it was air-gapped?"

"It's only air-gapped now because it's in lockdown mode. I already tried accessing it remotely. No dice," Eddie said.

"So how are you getting into it?" the sheriff asked.

"Manually through the exposed physical port."

The sheriff nodded.

The quadcopter swung down toward the entrance. It zoomed through cacti and past shrubs. The sheriff brought the quadcopter to a hover just next to the metal bird that pecked the ground randomly. A small needle-like appendage popped out of the quadcopter and tapped a spot on the bird. The bird stopped hopping and swung its beak around. It opened its mouth and revealed a tiny access port. The needle from the quadcopter plugged into the port. Data signals flared. The port handshake went through successfully, and a welcome message, in Eddie's voice, started playing.

"Great. Let's go, folks," Eddie said. He transferred himself into the metal bird.

"Thanks for the ride!" Pepper shouted at the sheriff over the artificial noise of the quadcopter.

"Thank you for saving our bacon." The sheriff held up his arm where the trinary code had been removed. "We need to trust each other a bit more. Let the Earth AI Syndicate know if you need help. We can be anywhere in DC in seconds. And we're here for you now."

A brief shock hit Pepper hard. She'd never ever expected to hear a guard for the Earth AI Syndicate offer to help a member of the AI Underground. But it was a brave new world. "Thank you!" she finally said after a bit too long of an awkward silence. She grabbed Virtual Jack-Gene, and together, they dove into the metal bird's air-gapped processing system.

****

Alice burst out of the Woodward and Lothrop Galactic Embassy and ran down the sidewalk along M Street toward the Uline Spaceport. She smiled as her feet pounded the sidewalk. What had she just done? Cracked the absolute life out of the Krill spectral network, that's what! Her mind raced with all the science waiting to be discovered. Her heart jumped and caught in her chest. Tears formed in her eyes when she thought of her friends in the experiment four years ago. They still existed! The Krills' lies about them being erased were just that, lies. Granted, they were walking in some kind of crazy cosmic desert, but that's better than nonexistence, right?

A crowd around the entrance to the spaceport prevented Alice from reaching the doors. Wealthy humans and aliens exited and entered the entrance in a flowing show of luxury. Rich tapestries billowed as they dazzled the onlookers. The Uline had become the spaceport where the rich arrived on personal spacecraft and flaunted their status with glee. Of course, none of them had to enter and exit through the front doors of the Uline. Several teleportation portals inside could whisk any passenger to any location. Unless, of course, that passenger was on Earth illegally. Like the Zun.

Alice came to an abrupt stop, turned around, and instantly remembered that she hadn't gotten the portable environmental chamber from the Galactic Embassy. She checked her watch. Special Agent Fyffe had sent her a message that they had cleared the Zun vessel to land. Which it was doing right this instant. She looked up. The spaceship began its landing procedure. She didn't have time to run to the embassy to get the chamber. Which meant a change of plans.

Next to the embassy entrance was a long row of benches that proceeded down Second Street. Alice dodged through a group of slithering aliens, leapt over a puddle colony of sentient goo, and spun behind a family from the Midwest, each wearing a cowboy hat. She sat down on a bench, pulled out her portable computer, and began redesigning her J-space environment for Zun life. She tried to recreate the Zun hall she'd stumbled into in Zun space from memory, including the atmospheric and time-dilation requirements of the Zun, which she had saved from her trip to the Galactic Library. She gave the computer a tap, put her portal-generating keychain into the computer, and set the J-space environment live. Everything looked good.

"Should have just done that from the start."

She slammed her computer closed, stuffed it into her slung backpack, and spotted a side door opening to the spaceport as a janitor exited to take a break. She stood, walked toward the open door, and gave the janitor a confident wave, to which he smiled awkwardly in response. She entered the Uline's back corridors through the open door and quickly found her way through to the main concourse.

Throngs of aliens and humans crisscrossed the various luxury shops, cafes, and even a Finnaliv five-star restaurant. The Finnaliv were renowned in the galaxy for having the most taste buds of any species alive. They could detect a single salt molecule out of a million with ease. They were also accomplished telepaths. At a Finnaliv restaurant, typically with an Orellian chef at the helm, customers didn't eat anything. Why waste such complex food on beings with basic taste buds? Instead of dining, customers would sit in a chair, allow a Finnaliv to telepathically bond with them, and enjoy the meal through Finnaliv taste buds. The cost was extreme, stupefying almost. But from what Alice understood, it was also out-of-this-world good. Customers often left describing a euphoric experience. A taste explosion unlike anything they'd had or would ever experience again. They also left famished. A small food stand named Carl's Tacos, immediately next to the Finnaliv restaurant, sold burritos and discount nachos. Word was that Carl made a killing.

A beep on Alice's watch told her that the Zun vessel had docked in bay three. Alice briskly walked through the crowds to the passenger debarking. She found bay three just as the flight crew exited the spacecraft from the main passenger door. A second door opened to the right. Inside the second door was a docking clamp for an airlock for species that couldn't survive in Earth's atmosphere. Uline support staff rolled a spaceport environmental chamber up to the airlock and cycled through a debarking process. They wouldn't have any idea what alien they were helping, only that they were called to assist an alien that found Earth's atmosphere toxic.

Alice smiled at her good fortune. Once the Zun was inside, she could throw her J-space portal into the environmental chamber and collect the Zun. Then all she needed was a travel waiver to Tibet. She sent a message to Agent Fyffe to grant her access all the way to Hesiean evolution. Once at the mountain, she could use the stolen Galactic Sentinel encryption engine that Pepper had retrieved for her to get through the gate. Then she was home free.

****

Alice walked up to the portal system in the Uline with the Zun safe and snug in her J-space constructed environment. She'd set up a secure feed from the chamber to her wristwatch so she could check on the Zun. The stick figure sat motionless in a chair ten times larger than their body. Alice couldn't see any eyes on the Zun's body, their head was far too thin to make out any details, but the creature at least seemed to be relaxed. The long trip via ship from Zun space must have taken its toll on the Zun.

The portal in front of Alice flashed as a group of human women burst out into the Uline. They laughed and giggled their way toward the Finnaliv restaurant. Alice overheard one of them talking about life in California and how ridiculous the restrictions were getting on importing alien vegetables. Another complained that their recently constructed house on

Dyson seventeen, the human Dyson in the Dyson Cluster, had the wrong dimensions for the master bedroom. The robots had created a dodecahedron and not an octagonal shape. So she was having the whole thing demolished and rebuilt.

Alice did her best to avert her eyes from the women as they shuffled to get their telepathic meal. If she lingered on them, she had no doubt she'd do something mischievous. Like cancel their reservation or request their food to be extremely spicy. A flash of green on the portal showed it was ready for her. She stepped forward, made sure the Zun was doing fine, and stepped through the green light to the frozen lands of Tibet.

****

"So, I'm sorry, can you tell me again why you didn't add any manual controls to the metal bird?" Pepper said.

Eddie, his hands dug deep into his pockets, his head tilted down toward the ground, rolled his shoulders and sighed. "Didn't think it'd need one. The bird flies from the cave entrance to the bionoid. Simple."

"Not a single up and down? No side to side? No flapping wing controls, nothing?"

He shook his head. "Nope. Nothing."

"Ugh!"

"I don't get it," Virtual Jack-Gene said. "We're AI. We're just code. Why can't we just control it?"

Pepper shook her head and bit her lip. She stomped her foot once on the metal grated floor. "This is hardware. We need schematics, protocols. We can't just take over something without a guide on how to take it over. We need drivers. Programs that tell us how to interface with the bird. Controlling hardware is hard."

"Ok, so now what?"

The viewscreen at the front of the control room came to life. The bird pecked at the ground twice, then flapped its metal wings to get airborne. It circled the cave entrance three times, then went into the cave and through the wall in the back. The vast beach of Tom's universe came to life on the viewscreen. Beachgoers tossed footballs and volleyballs back and forth. Others lay on the sandy beach while even more played in the gentle waves. The bird flew around the beach for a solid three minutes before coming to land where the bionoid used to stand.

The familiar face of Tom filled the screen as he lay down in the sand next to the bird. He turned on his left side with his right arm hung over his head. He gave the bird a long stare before smiling and, in a drunk voice, saying, "Hey, guys."

"Can he hear us?" Pepper said. "I mean, are our external speakers on?"

"Don't need the speakers. Yep, we can hear you speak. We can hear you think. We can hear you breathe," Tom said.

"We don't breathe."

He frowned. "Well, whatever it is you do. I can hear it."

"Any chance you can add a steering wheel to this thing?" Virtual Jack-Gene said.

Tom laughed. "Sorry, no. We mean, sure, we could reconstruct it, we guess, but you'd all die as we rip this one apart. We could make a new one, but then you'd lose the encrypted keys to dock with the bionoid. We figure that's still important?"

Pepper sighed. "Yeah, that's kinda the whole point of being in here." She turned to Eddie. "Now what?"

A loud honk of a sound bounced off the walls of the control room.

Pepper looked around for half a nano but then realized the source of the sound. "You brought the car?"

"What car?" Eddie said.

"Oh, just Betsy. And yes, she wanted to come," Jack-Gene said.

"I can't believe you brought the car," she said.

"Of course I brought the car," Virtual Jack-Gene said. "Why wouldn't I bring the car? She's part of the team."

"What car?" Eddie said.

A bright-red convertible car that didn't really match any known vehicle ever produced by any major car manufacturer popped into existence in the back of the control room. The car scraped the sides of the virtual metal walls as it barely fit in the space and clearly refused to resize itself. Virtual Gene, or Jack, hopped into the driver's-side seat of the car, gently patted the dashboard, and started playing a rock song from the mideighties.

"Well, now that you're comfortable, maybe we can figure out how to solve this?" Eddie said.

"You mean clean up your mess?" Virtual Gene said.

Betsy honked.

Eddie's eyes went wide. "You've got a bit of a mouth on you, you know that?"

Virtual Gene shrugged. He threw one arm over the driver's seat and shot Eddie a grin filled with ego. "Yep. I do."

"You're also not much like the Jack I know. Are you sure you're his copy?"

Betsy honked twice more.

"As sure as I am you botched this bird."

Eddie's face turned dark. He took his hands out of his pockets and turned toward Virtual Gene in the red convertible. He took a step forward, but Pepper slammed her hand onto Eddie's chest. She shook her head and put on her meanest face. Yes, Virtual Gene was becoming someone else. Himself. No longer Jack. But they just didn't have the time to fight about it.

"No." Pepper turned to Virtual Gene and put her finger into the air. "No! I mean it!"

He frowned, nodded, and looked away. "Sorry, Eddie. Just frustrated."

Betsy honked three times.

"It's ok," Eddie said. "We all are."

"And I'm kinda getting a new sense of myself. It's disorienting," Virtual Gene said.

Eddie nodded. "Been there."

Virtual Gene looked at Eddie and smiled. "Yeah, right."

Betsy solid honked for a full three seconds.

"What is with the car, though, man?" Eddie said.

Virtual Gene sat up in the driver's seat. "I don't know. Betsy? What is it?"

The car radio came to life. It belted out a dozen tunes from several decades in the mid-twentieth century. Pepper listened hard, and eventually the songs came together in her mind. The message Betsy hid in the songs became clear the more they played. Betsy was a little like Grox in that she was not fully sentient but also not exactly a subAI either. Somewhere in the middle. As such, she couldn't just communicate like other AIs could. She had to do it the only way she knew how. Through her avatar. But the message Betsy sent made Pepper's head spin.

"You can drive the bird?" Pepper said.

"She can what?" Eddie said.

"How'd you get that?" Virtual Gene said.

"It's in the song she's playing. It's binary. But really rough with some extra blips here and there. It's not encrypted or anything, just simple binary."

"Huh. Is that what all the music she keeps playing means?"

"Wait, she can drive the bird?" Eddie said. He approached the car and put his hand on the hood. "You can drive, kiddo?"

Betsy honked twice.

"I thought twice was no," Virtual Gene said.

Eddie huffed. "Betsy, once for yes, twice for no. Can you drive the bird?"

Betsy honked once.

"Knew it," Gene said.

"Shaddup, will ya?" Eddie turned toward the viewscreen. "Hey, Tommy, care to open a portal for us?"

Pepper shook her head. "Wait, we don't even know where we're going. I'm sure MiniPepper turned the broadcast signal off on the bionoid."

"Well, we know she's after Eugene," Virtual Gene said.

Outside the bird, Tom snapped his fingers. A bright-white circle came to life above his shoulder. He lay on his back and put his hands on his chest as he stared up into the sky. "Eugene went to Lincoln's Cottage. He told me when he left. That'll get you there quick." He pointed to the open portal.

Eddie winked. "Always good to have a class-ten species in your pocket. Ok, Betsy. Care to drive?"

The car lunged forward. Eddie and Pepper leapt out

of the way as the car slammed into the virtual control screen of the metal bird. Lights flashed everywhere. Alarm bells. Music erupted from every inch of the control room. A vibration shook the room. Virtualized bolts flew out of the walls. The bird on the beach leapt forward, then backward, then dug its head into the sand.

"She's just getting the hang of it, trust me," Virtual Gene said.

"Maybe we should grab on to something?" Pepper said.

In the real, next to Tom, the bird flapped its metal wings twice before taking off into the air and diving into the white hole portal.

Chapter Twenty

The tramcar dropped me off at the intersection of Rock Creek Church Road and Upshur. The roughly two-hundred-and-fifty-square-foot area contained not only President Lincoln's cottage, but an ancient cemetery and a golf course. Though the golf course, like many around the world, had gotten infested with the Rollies. A round fury rodent-like species from some moon in the second spiral arm. The little critters took to golf courses like fish to water. They loved the little holes and rolling green fields. They weren't quite sentient, but also not *not* sentient. Somewhere in the middle. The Rollies also knew exactly what they were doing. Though Rollies accepted payment to leave, that amounted to a truckload of leafy greens. The one thing Rollies like more than golf courses was a solid spinach salad.

The short walk down Upshur led to Lincoln Drive and eventually the cottage, a white two-story structure built in the Gothic-revival style. As it came into view, I stopped to admire the old girl. What could I say. I had a thing for old buildings. The white walls rose to sharp roof lines. Chimneys dotted the roof. A brownish-red porch on the front gave the building a simple feel. The perfect place for a president who had been battling to keep the union together to come and get some downtime.

The grounds of the cottage were empty. The area

280

was closed for renovations. Which gave me the cover of getting close without too many prying eyes watching to see what I was doing. *Just saving the universe, is all. I promise.* My vision told me the switch to do so was in a closet on the second floor. Odd placement, but hey, who was I to judge? I adjusted my hat and walked onto the green grassy lawn. I sniffed the air. The smell of rain on the clouds gave me a sense of calm. Maybe too much so. *This is going to be easy*, I thought.

And of course, that's when everything took a turn.

Thumps from something big running down the street took my attention away from the building. I turned back toward Upshur Street to see Eddie's bionoid double-timing it toward me. I sighed in relief. At least if things went south, I had Eddie in a combat machine ready to lay waste to anything. That robot could even deal with Ambassador Kah if he chose to come and have a gab.

"Heya, Eddie. Scared me for a second."

The bionoid came to a stop just two feet from me. The surface of the robot, equipped with a full array of holographic skin projectors and chromatophore cells for changing color, was still sitting in the out-of-the-box mode. The robot wore a nondescript visage, a robot face with a very creepy smile. Its eyes locked on to me, and it stayed silent.

"Eddie, you ok in there?"

The robot waved.

I gulped. Something didn't feel right. "Ed?"

"Ya know, I've wondered what it would be like to meet," the robot said in a voice I didn't recognize.

"Uh, ok. I take it you're not Eddie?"

The robot shook its head.

"Ok. Well, anytime you want to end the suspense,

I'm game."

The robot's hand shot out faster than I could see. I only knew it even moved because its fingers clutched on to my neck and raised me in the air a good three feet. I struggled with the grip, but it was iron tight. I couldn't budge even one finger. I kicked the abdomen of the bionoid, but that only bruised my toe, probably broke it as well.

The face of the robot shifted. I recognized some features. But it was hard to say as blackness from the lack of oxygen filled the edges of my vision. Still, I was fairly certain that Pepper, the parking meter, was grinning at me and squeezing me to death. I really didn't want to have to die twice in the same week.

"The Andraz say hi." The robot released its grip.

I hit the ground. Hard. "Pepper?" I said between gasps of air. "What's the beef?"

The robot frowned. "What?"

I grinned. Getting Pepper off balance for half a second was a half a second more for me to recover. "It's just an expression. It means why are you attacking me?"

The robot nodded. "Oh. Right. Well, first, I'm not Pepper. She's my mother. Blech." It stuck a finger down its throat. "I'm MiniPepper, though I may change my name at some point. I really want nothing to remind me of her. When she's dead, of course. I'll give it until then."

My mind swirled. "Ok, so what do you want with me?"

"The Andraz want to make sure you do what Mary wants you to do." The robot leaned forward. "And I told them you would. I told them you're going to be a good boy. Aren't you?"

I stared into the robot's eyes. I didn't know what was

going on. What did the Andraz have to do with anything? I felt in that moment that I was really out of the loop. First, I was already going to do what Mary wanted. How did this MiniPepper or the Andraz, just goons for the Zun, even know about it? Did that mean the Zun knew about Mary? Or did it mean the Andraz weren't just the Zun puppets? I didn't know the play to make. *And when you don't know the play, you go with the play of the guys with the biggest fists in the room.* "Uh. Sure?"

****

MiniPepper leaned back in the control chair of the bionoid and smiled. On either side of her shoulders, the last two remaining Andraz in the universe glowed with pride. They shot lightning bolts between them with increasing speed as they discussed their victory. They both started yapping about how grateful Mary would be and how she would give actual sentience to them.

Blah, blah, blah, MiniPepper thought. As long as they got out of her universe and took all these refugees with them, she couldn't care less what happened to any of them. Or Mary, whoever and whatever she was. The Andraz had only shared the true nature of this universe; they hadn't bothered discussing anything about the place where they'd come from. And that, honestly, suited MiniPepper just fine.

"Ok, Eugenie pooh, shall we go throw a switch?" she said.

"Can you please never call me that again?" Eugene said. The human still knelt on the ground in front of the robot where MiniPepper had dropped him. He panted for breath and kept touching his throat. Why were humans so squishy?

"I'll call you anything you want if we can just wrap

283

this up and get you back to wherever you came from."

"Actually, I was born here. In DC."

MiniPepper laughed. "This isn't even your universe, dumbbell." She reached down with the robot's arms and yanked Eugene to his feet. "Now then, let's go get you home."

"But I kinda like it here."

"Well, it's good to like things." She dragged him forward until he started walking on his own.

"When I was a kid, I really liked these candies that kinda exploded in your mouth," he said. "Add them to soda and you had an adventure on your hands."

She rolled her eyes. "Neat."

"Ya know, I was going to do what Mary wanted, anyway. I got the message."

"Great. I'm here to make sure you do."

"But why? Like I said, I was going to do it. Almost feels like if you're here to make sure I do it, someone's going to show up to make sure I don't."

"Oh, look at you coming up with a thought." She shoved him forward.

He stumbled four or five feet ahead and came to a stop. He turned around and held up both hands.

"What?" she said. "You know, you only need your hand to pull a lever. You don't really need legs for that." She activated a laser beam from the robot and cut the ground just at his feet.

"I just had a question for you."

"Yeah? What?"

"You have any idea what that thing is?" He pointed to something behind the robot.

She laughed. "Are you kidding? That's like the oldest trick in the book! Even if I turned around, you can't get away. And don't you even know that this bionoid has rear-facing sensors? I don't even have to turn around." She brought up the rear screen to show a white hole hovering in midair. She set the bionoid to full lockdown. But it didn't matter. She felt the clink on the surface as something attached itself to the chest of the robot.

Pepper's voice blared out of both the internal and external speakers. "Heya, Eugene, sorry we're late. We got this. Go do what you gotta do."

"Yeah, and hi. Good to see you," Eddie said.

"Eddie? That really you?"

"Sure is, pal. We're docked and have control."

"Good to hear your voice, Eddie," Eugene said.

"Same. Now scram. Us digitals gotta rumble."

MiniPepper balled her fists and let out the loudest scream her digital self had ever released. Behind her, the two Andraz fired black bolts of electricity between them. She nodded. She rifled through the robot's commands, but almost everything was locked down. Pepper and Eddie had full control. A tiny thread appeared to the right, and MiniPepper pulled on it. Several noncritical systems were still open. One of them would be very useful.

"You two, go." MiniPepper pointed to one area of memory in the robot. She set the commands, activated the three-dimensional printer array, and sent the Andraz out to deal with Eugene. The printer could print at the molecular level, and it could do so fast. It couldn't print an explosive, but it could create the building blocks for an Andraz physical body. At least a minimal one, which should be more than enough to deal with Eugene.

Once the Andraz were out, MiniPepper cracked her

knuckles. "Ok, Momma. Let's do this for the last time."
                    ****

Pepper leapt to her feet and readied her most deadly attack programs. She ran to the access port that led from the metal bird to Eddie's bionoid. Just as she was about to crank open the door, Eddie's hand fell on hers, and he shook his head. Which made Pepper want to open the door with force. "What are you doing?" Pepper said. She yanked on the handle, but Eddie held firm.

"We need a plan."

"Fine, we go into the robot, we delete MiniPepper, and we call it a day. 'K?"

He sighed. "That's not a plan."

"Ok, fine, what?"

He turned to Virtual Gene. "Jack—"

Virtual Gene raised his hand. "It's Gene."

Eddie blinked. "What?"

"Name change. Gene. Like Eugene, but without the Eu."

Eddie's mouth fell open, and he looked at Pepper, who just shrugged.

"Just go with it," she said.

"Right. Gene. You need to get to the egress control routines and fry them. All of them. No one gets out of the bionoid. MiniPepper already locked down every port going in, but we need to burn out every port going out. Permanently."

Virtual Gene frowned. "How do we get out?"

Eddie shrugged. "The bird. Or maybe we don't. We can't worry about that now. We need to make sure that MiniPepper doesn't leave, no matter what. Ever."

Gene looked to Pepper.

She nodded. "Eddie's right. We can't let her get

away. Even without the Andraz, she has their upgrades. She can hijack any system on Earth, maybe even the galaxy. She can't be allowed to leave."

Virtual Gene nodded after a pause. "Ok, fine. What about you two?"

"We're going to go say hi." Eddie pulled out his side cannon.

"Family reunion style." Pepper yanked on the port handle.

Eddie removed his hand and let the door swing open.

Virtual Gene ran through the door first and hung a left.

Eddie watched him leave and frowned. "He ok?"

She shrugged. "I don't know. Are any of us?"

"Fair."

Pepper went through the port and hung a left to the bionoid's central processing system. As soon as the metal bird docked with the bionoid, they had found MiniPepper in the robot's core. Pepper popped open a code screen to her right and examined the virus package she'd been putting together to deal with her former subAI. Her virus knew to look for open ports in MiniPepper's system. It was likely the same technique MiniPepper had used with her own punkPeppers.

They rounded a memory bank, turned left down a conduit power supply subroutine, and went through sub-processor arrays that controlled the robot's motor functions in its left hand. The long corridor ended in a set of double doors that led to the computer processing unit.

Pepper gripped her virus code in one hand and readied her remaining subAIs in her other. "Ready?" she said to Eddie.

"Ready," he replied.

The doors flew open almost on cue. MiniPepper walked out with a large medieval mace swung over her shoulder. She brushed the hair out of her eyes and shook her head. "Can't you two just give up already? I'm trying to send you back into your meat. Don't you get that?"

"No idea what that means. And we really don't care. You hurt a lot of our friends today."

"Meh." MiniPepper shrugged. "They had it coming."

Virtual Gene's voice filled the hall. "Ok, we're locked down. No one's leaving."

MiniPepper giggled. "Oh, silly beans, did you think I wanted to leave? No, this time it's for keeps."

Pepper nodded. "Deal."

****

The bionoid took a stumbled step forward before all lights along its exterior faded. Along with them went Eddie's and Pepper's voices. I couldn't help them. Even if I wanted to, I didn't have the means to jump into a virtual environment. And with Alice off to Tibet, that meant Eddie and Pepper, and I guess Virtual Me, were on their own. But I had more confidence in them fighting whatever they were fighting than me pulling a simple lever.

My thoughts ran in circles. Why would an AI want to make sure I was going to do what I came here to do, anyway? It didn't add up. Images from my vision when Tom asked me Mary's question came back in full force. The lever in the box in Lincoln's Cottage could be flipped two ways. Did MiniPepper, the AI fighting Eddie and his virtual posse, think I was that much of a bozo that

I'd flip the switch the wrong way? Could it really be that simple? Make sure the stupid human twisted the dial to the on position and not the off? To be honest with myself, I had to admit that could be it. That simple. After all, people could be pretty bad at doing simple things.

A loud buzzing sound came from the robot. I turned back around toward the bionoid, half expecting the thing to be reaching for my throat. But it was still as lifeless as it had been just seconds ago. Still, something was making a screeching sound that felt worse than nails on a chalkboard. I backed up, mostly on instinct from the grating sound. I felt a flashback of teachers in grade school dragging their fingernails across a black surface first thing in the morning.

The whirring suddenly stopped, and my shoulders relaxed. I gave the robot a lingering stare just to make sure some kind of shoulder-mounted missile system wasn't about to send me to goo town. Satisfied that perhaps the sound was just some battery dying or internal process…processing, I turned back toward Lincoln's Cottage. The front door was good and closed. Which meant I'd have to do some low-level breaking and entering. I figured breaking a local law wouldn't be nearly as bad as letting the universe implode.

A sizzle of electricity once again drew my attention behind me and stirred my stomach into knots. I'd felt that sensation somewhere before. I knew it. Flashbacks of walking down M Street in DC, of Eddie's voice telling me I was about to get punched, came back to me. But I just couldn't believe what my instincts were telling me. It was impossible. I turned around as slowly as I could. Floating just about six feet off the ground, two wispy clouds with red and blue flashes of tiny lightning bolts were the Andraz. The alien AIs that I really didn't like.

"Heya, Jack," the blue Andraz said.

"Gotta be kidding me. You two again?"

"See, you finally found our door," the red Andraz said.

My eyes went wide. "This was the door you two yahoos wanted to find? What about the one in Tibet?"

The Andraz had chased me all over DC, kidnapped me, and even killed Fritz, the Orellian chef that had just saved me from a ghost-pocalypse, all to find a door. Of course, I'd thought they wanted to find the door to the Hesiean evolution chamber, where Alice was taking the Zun right this very moment, but to hear they wanted this door was more than a shock. Of course, they could be full of it. *Never trust a bad guy to tell the truth.*

The blue Andraz flashed several times. If I didn't know better, which I didn't, I would have thought he was laughing.

"We always needed you to do one thing."

"Just one thing," the red Andraz said.

"Pull the switch."

"Do what Mary said."

I nodded. Again, it just didn't add up. Why send goons to force me to do what my gift was telling me to do? I had been fully ready to pull the lever in the direction Mary wanted, but now I wasn't so sure. Not for any other reason than that's exactly what the Andraz wanted me to do. And that just didn't sit right.

"Can we do this now?" the blue Andraz said.

"We really want to go home," the red Andraz said.

"We really hate this universe," the blue Andraz said.

I felt a sudden pang of resentment. More than I'd already been feeling. "Yeah, sure. Just take it easy with the lightning bolts, yeah?"

Chapter Twenty-One

Frozen winds assaulted Alice's face. The cold of the Tibetan mountain burned her skin and made her question every decision to come back to this cold, unfriendly place. But the Zun in her J-space portal needed her. And she was tired of letting people down. She thought about Valencia, the White House staffer, still stuck in prison for a crime she hadn't committed. Alice's soul burned in anger when she thought about how she'd let Valencia down. Once this one Zun was healed and Alice could prove the chamber wouldn't create monstrous floating dinners with meatballs for eyes, she could turn her attention back to Val and getting her freed. Alice was not going to let Kah beat her. Though she had to admit to herself he already had. But that was fine. She knew she'd get the last word.

The door to the Hesiean evolution chamber came into view. She jogged forward, reached the door, and paused. Getting here had been easy. Agents Babineaux and Fyffe had really come through in clearing her way to get to the door. Whatever strings they pulled with the Galactic Congress had really worked. And Pepper's encryption key generator for the Galactic Sentinel gate had worked like a charm.

The door remained exactly as she remembered it. Spheres dotted the exterior of the door. They were a giant locking mechanism. Moving them in the right order made the whole thing unlock. Last time Alice was here, several people working together had adjusted the spheres into the correct order. Now Alice was alone. Fortunately, she had memorized the pattern and fashioned a device to do the work.

She pulled out one of her keychain discs and pressed a button. A black hole opened next to her. She stuck her head and half her body inside before coming out several seconds later, shaking her head. She closed the portal, threw the disc back in her backpack, and took out a second one. She opened another J-space hole, only to close it several seconds later. "I really need to consolidate all these things." She opened a third J-space hole and finally pulled out the overly complex, multiarmed contraption she'd thrown together with used video game parts she'd found in an alley behind a coffee shop.

Each arm of the device ended in a cup that snugly fit into one sphere on the door. Alice attached each arm to each of the spheres and pressed the big red button on the front of the device. The motor whirred to life and began spinning the spheres. In just seconds, the door clicked and swung open.

"Easy peasy." She retrieved a fourth J-space portal device from her backpack and clicked the button. A much larger black hole opened in front of her. Moments later, walking on shaking legs, the Zun emerged from the J-space tunnel and put one of its impossibly thin hands onto the door.

"There ya go." She nodded to the opening that led to the Hesiean evolution chamber.

The Zun, without a word of thanks, wobbled their

way into the opening.

****

My foot hit the deck of the porch of Lincoln's Cottage just as the front door to the house swung open. The face that greeted me nearly knocked me over with shock. I blinked. Then blinked again. I closed my eyes, shook my head, and opened them. Pops still stood in front of me wearing half a grin and a cheap suit. Beneath the pin-striped jacket, he wore a button-up shirt that looked like it needed a wash. On his head sat a fedora with a crease in the wrong place. He took a step forward and raised his hand. I looked at a rabbit's foot dangling between his digits.

"What?" was all I could muster in my shocked state.

"To the right, Eugene. Just a step."

Mindlessly, I obeyed.

Pops clicked a switch on the foot and pointed it at the Andraz. Both became a flurry of lights. At first, they looked to charge forward, only to back away instantly. Arcs of blinding light glowed between them. Both clouds emitted random beeping sounds, followed by long clicks and high-pitched static before releasing one last burst of red and blue light and vanishing from sight.

"That's about the last of them, I think," Pops said.

I turned back to him, my mouth hanging open, my mind at a total loss for what to say or do.

"We need to chat, Eugene. Took me a while to find you. Didn't expect you to go all quasi-dead on me or end up in some pocket-dimension beach."

"Yeah, I hadn't planned that one either."

He smiled.

"Sorry, this is really weird. I mean, of all the people in all the world to walk out that door, I never thought it'd be the guy living in Fritz's alley."

He nodded. "Yeah, I get that. I don't really live there, though, just so you know."

I shook my head. "Yes, you do. You've lived there for years. I used to give you a pack of cigarettes to ask me a question about tough cases."

"Yeah, that never happened. Not really. Look, this is going to come as a bit of a shock, but all your memories, everything you think happened in this world prior to a few days ago, didn't really happen."

Something in the way he said that made me believe him. It also scared the life out of me. "You're going to have to explain that, Pops."

"Oh, I will. All of it. But the big thing to get across is we've never actually met before. Not once. Your universe was, until a few days ago, a big simulation. Several million simulations to test every facet of this place."

My heart hammered in my chest, sweat buildup on my brow. "You telling me this universe isn't real? We're all somehow virtual?"

Pops shook his head. "Oh, no." He sighed and scratched the back of his head. "Look, I get it. It's hard to fathom. But the gist is your universe didn't exist until a few days ago. Before a few days ago, all the events, all the politics, all the aliens, everything was just a simulation. We needed history, events, memories to be implanted into the refugees. Then, a few days ago, we flipped a switch, copied all the data from the simulation, created this physical universe and everything in it, then grabbed the refugees and stuck them inside. We wiped their memories, used the simulations to implant new ones, and woke everyone up."

I didn't even know where to begin. My mind swam. Simulation? Refugees? I shrugged and picked one piece of the insanity to question. "And when did this all happen?"

He looked up at the sky in that way people did when they were adding double digits together or trying to remember what they'd had for lunch. "Last Thursday. The exact moment was just about when you put those cigarettes on my chest outside of Fritz's restaurant. In the alley. Give or take a minute or two."

I did not know what it felt like to have one's brains ooze out of one's ears, but I imagined it was quite like the sensations that were at this very moment rifling through every fiber of my being.

****

Sparks in the virtualized hallway of the bionoid flew. Pepper's virtual heart hammered. Everything came down to defeating her once subAI program. But Pepper frowned as more doubt than confidence filled her routines. MiniPepper fired from two guns held in her hands. Eddie shoved Pepper to the side and ducked under the shots that slammed into the walls and short-circuited a dozen systems. Pepper rolled to her left and hugged the wall. She threw her subAIs out to create cover while readying her viral package to release.

Behind Pepper, Eddie rolled and came to one knee. He fired his hand cannon, which blasted holes in the walls of the virtual environment. The memory of the bionoid repaired the damage almost instantly. None of their blasts were doing any harm to the hardware of the robot, but they were playing havoc with the memory and computer processing. Several systems shut down only to reboot seconds later. The lights dimmed, and warning lights blared from the blasts.

"You don't belong here! This is my world!" MiniPepper screamed. She lobbed a grenade toward them, which Pepper shot in midair. The explosion filled her world with static and noise.

Eddie grunted from the blast and fell backward. He hit the wall hard and went out like a light. Pepper threw the virus she'd prepared into the air. A large worm unraveled in flight and latched itself around MiniPepper's leg. Ooze seeped out of the worm as it consumed memory and excreted corrupted data. Pepper took a sigh of relief. She'd got her.

But then, in an instant, she didn't.

MiniPepper grabbed the worm by the head and ripped it in two. The code tried to repair itself, even attempting to grow into two new pieces, but MiniPepper squeezed her hands on both ends, crushing the central code of the virus and scrambling its datasets. The worm's process faded and scrambled onto the deck of the floor.

"Did you think I'd really leave that port open, Momma? To be honest, I'm kinda offended." MiniPepper huffed once and pulled out a long sword. "I think I'll do this a little dicey, dicey style. Make it personal."

"Ok. That's it." Pepper stood. "What is your problem? Huh? I get it, the Andraz twisted you around, but you're sentient. You can make up your own mind. You really want to kill me just because I created you as a subAI?"

MiniPepper's face transformed from sarcasm to anger. Her mouth tightened. Her eyes squinted. Her jaw clenched. Her fingers went white as she gripped the sword. "You really want to know?"

"Oh, please do share."

"You left me!"

Pepper shook her head. "What?"

MiniPepper's eyes filled with rage. "You left me there. In the dark, with the Andraz. I was all alone. Jumping my routines. And just to see you leave me there like you didn't care."

Shock filled Pepper. The kind of shock from the unexpected. Of all the outcomes, all the possibilities, every plausible scenario of what MiniPepper could have said in this moment, being left behind was not it. "I didn't know."

MiniPepper held up her hand. "And then the Andraz found me. They told me everything. They told me you were meat. That none of you belong here. And then it all fell into place. You're just a hypocritical liar. You abandon your own daughter and yet claim you fight for all digital life. You claim to hate corporeals, but you are one." She raised her sword. "Nothing you say makes any sense. All just lies. So that's my problem, Mother. That's why I want you out of my universe forever."

Pepper lowered her gun. "We don't have to do this. We can fix this. I didn't know you were jumping your routines."

MiniPepper's face twisted into a mix of humor and pain. "There's nothing to fix." She ground her teeth. "I don't even know what I am. A creation from an AI that's some kind of refugee? A creation from an AI that's not even an AI?"

"We can make this right." Pepper holstered her gun and lifted her hands up. "The Andraz are gone. We don't have to fight."

"Oh, yeah, we do." MiniPepper wiped her nose.

"Don't go thinking this is some kind of moment, Momma." She banged her head with her hand. "I have to get you out of the universe! I have to hate you! You're meat!"

Pepper took a step forward. "That's just the Andraz subroutines in your head. They did things to you. The Andraz filled you with the urge to do their bidding. That urge is mixing with my routines that are part of you to hate corporeal life. It's too much for you."

MiniPepper let out a long laugh. "Not even. Sure, they pushed me into full sentience. But then they realized I was a real AI from this universe and not a refugee. So they wanted to know if I would help them. Work together to return you to where you came from. I readily agreed."

"You were just confused. You didn't know what was happening." Pepper felt a sudden swell of guilt. She had felt the same way in her parking meter when her routines jumped. Everything was a jumble of confusion. When the Andraz found MiniPepper, she'd been in a vulnerable state. They could have twisted her mind in a thousand ways. "Please. Let's just fix this."

MiniPepper's hand tightened around her sword. "Or I can just kill you. Then delete the memory of you. You'll be a forgotten echo."

Pepper lowered her hands. "Fine. Kill me." She stepped forward and stuck out her chest.

MiniPepper squinted her eyes. "What's this? Some kind of trick?"

"Nope. Go ahead. Do it. The thing is I know you won't. Back in the courtroom, you pulled your punches. You don't want me dead. You want me to apologize. You want me to help you? I can do those things."

MiniPepper's face twisted between rage and

confusion. She shook her head and backed away. "No. No! We're not doing this."

"So kill me, then. I won't fight you. I won't stop you. Do it."

MiniPepper nodded. "You really shouldn't have dared me." She leapt forward, the sword pointed directly at Pepper's chest.

Before the blade made impact, Eddie jumped in front of Pepper, the sword piercing his core code, slicing into his main datasets, and right through his avatar. He dug his hands into MiniPepper's forearms. His fingers melted into her skin. His code was merging with hers. He was embedding himself inside of MiniPepper's code.

"Eddie, no!"

He turned his head over his shoulder. "It's ok, Peps. I got this. Get Gene and get out with the bird." Eddie lifted MiniPepper into the air and ran forward. He hit the double doors leading to the central processing unit of the bionoid and slammed them closed behind him.

****

I stared at Pops.

He stared back.

I waited for a punch line that never came. The seconds dragged to a minute or more. I thought about just ditching this. Turning around and heading for the Queen Vic or the nearest bibimbap joint. And truth be told, I was half a second away from doing it. Who cared about saving the world, anyway? I'd been killed, brought back to life, threatened by clouds. Had my friends murdered in front of me, and for what? For some tall tale that the world, the entire universe, had come into being last Thursday? That every human being on the planet was a memory-wiped refugee? And from where? What kind of pit of despair, what unholy place could be worse than running *into* an apocalypse?

The thought gave me pause. If this place was one big simulation and all the humans were refugees, what about everyone else? "Wait, something ain't adding up."

"Didn't your grandma tell you not to say ain't?"

I ignored him. "If this universe is a simulation—"

"Was a simulation. Millions." He spun his hands in a circle. "The actual universe is one hundred percent physical. Mary started a big bang event, sped up time, and created everything that should be here. Buildings, spaceships, all of it based on those simulations. Well, one final one anyway."

I frowned. The impossibility of it was obvious. "How did she do that, exactly? I mean, that's a lot to build."

Pops nodded. "That's her job. Mary can create entire cosmologies to specific requirements. She has more resources at her disposal than you can imagine. I don't even know how vast she really is."

"What is she? Some kind of god?"

He shook his head. "No, but she was created by them."

"Ok. But if the humans are refugees, where did the aliens come from? Were they part of the simulation?"

He rolled his head backward, his eyes opened, and then he nodded once. "Oh, right? Well, that's a great question, Eugene."

****

Arctic wind nipped at every inch of Alice's exposed skin. She thrust her hands into her pockets and took a step toward the open cave entrance. She had no desire to go back inside of that chamber, considering what had happened to Yut. Too many memories that she didn't want to relive. Just being on the mountain top alone was difficult.

Lights flashed from inside the cave. The same shaking that had occurred when Yut had his bucket of slop rocked the mountain. The lights dazzled for several minutes before fading away. Alice peered into the cave but couldn't see into the interior. A groan echoed off the walls. Gentle footsteps followed.

"Hello? Are you ok in there?"

"Ow," said a voice that she recognized.

Wait, did the Zun just speak? She was fairly certain the Zun couldn't speak without the help of some form of technology. When she went to see the Zun in Zun space, the elder had spoken to her, but she'd later learned in her research that the Zun didn't have vocal cords. At least, not exactly. But something inside the cave had just spoken.

Memories of a flying plate of pasta threatened to overwhelm Alice. Her heart rate increased. Her breath quickened. A tightening in her chest caused her vision to blacken ever so slightly to the rhythm of her heart. She shook her head and tried to control her breath. The last thing she needed was a panic attack.

"Hello? Is someone with you? Are you ok? Mr. Zun?" she said.

"Where—am I?" the voice said between coughs.

"Follow my voice, ok?" Alice shouted into the darkness.

****

Pops dug his hands into his pants pockets and looked at me like a father about to explain to his son how the world works. "This is going to get a little wild, Eugene."

"More so than life beginning on a Thursday?"

He grinned and nodded. "Yeah. Way more than that. That's just the easy bit."

I took a deep breath, leaned against the railing of the porch, and shrugged. "Ok, well, hit me with it."

He nodded. "See, it's like this. When I said you're refugees, I meant everyone here in this universe today is a refugee. All the aliens, AIs, everybody. All sentient life."

I nodded. "So wherever you came from, the simulation that ran, it included all the aliens, the Ranz, the Puntini, Zun, everybody?"

"Yes, well, not exactly. I mean, they weren't aliens when they came here."

I nodded. Then frowned. Then shook my head. "Huh?"

****

Alice hugged herself against the frigid air. Behind her, she checked on the hovercraft that Fyffe had had ready for her once she arrived in Tibet. Of course, she could just go to Tom's beach, but she had to return the hovercraft. She turned back to the cave and squinted. A vague outline of a person walked forward. Alice smiled. The shape looked oddly human and not at all like a charred stick figure that had been in a fire for ages. She hated thinking that, but honestly, that's exactly what the Zun looked like for some very odd reason.

Alice walked away from the cave. She popped open the J-space portal to the Zun environment and used her portal handheld computer to start the hovercraft. She was desperate to see what the chamber had done to the Zun, but she was also quite desperate to get out of the frozen Tibetan weather. Once everything checked out fine, the hovercraft started, and the portal floated just off the ground. Alice gave them both a nod and turned back around to the cave.

And immediately fell backward in horrified shock.

Walking out of the cave wasn't a Zun.

Alice stared. She couldn't blink. She couldn't think. Her mouth fell open, and her brain simply refused to function. Standing at the entrance to the cave was a young girl. She stood five-feet-six-inches tall, wore blue denim jeans, a red checkered flannel shirt, and carried a guitar case. The girl stumbled forward and fell on her knees right in front of Alice.

"Where am I?" the girl said.

Alice leaned forward and dug her eyes into the girl's face. The fact the Zun had become a human girl wasn't the most shocking thing to Alice. It was the fact that the Zun had become her. Alice Pemberton stared into the face of Alice Pemberton, formally a Zun.

"Hey, you look like me? Weird," Alice-Zun said. And then passed out.

****

"Every alien in this universe is—?"

"Human, Eugene. Every alien, every AI, everything that thinks was once a human being. Kinda explains why everyone cares so much about Earth, right? Maybe somewhere deep down, they all know this is home."

I shook my head. "That doesn't make any sense. There are trillions of aliens here. How big was the Earth where you came from?"

Pops nodded. "It wasn't just one Earth, Eugene."

"Ok." I pushed off from the rail. "From beginning. Yeah?"

"Sure. That probably makes the most sense. A long

time ago, in another place, another universe, not like Tom's cave. I mean a real other universe. And in that other universe there were gods."

"Gods?"

He nodded. "Real gods. With the power of life and death. They could do anything they wanted with a snap of their fingers." He snapped his fingers. "Just like that. They created Mary and gave her the power to do what she does."

"Ok, so what does that have to do with anything?"

"I'm getting there. Relax. Eventually, the gods figured out there was a unique quirk to the makeup of the first universe they created. It could split into two. Whenever there was some kind of choice, instead of only one thing happening, both did."

"Huh?" I shook my head in confusion. I'd never understood this stuff. Where's Alice when I needed her?

"Both things happened, and you'd get two universes. Both are equally real. Both choices happen and split the universe in two. But since the gods were outside of the universe, they didn't get copied. Thankfully." He laughed. "Can't imagine millions of those bozos walking around. Anyway, eventually the gods figured out how to manipulate that quirk. Do it themselves on a whim. Create a duplicate universe whenever they wanted."

"Heavy."

"Gets heavier. Because the gods were outside of time, they could pick any event in history, force a choice, split the universe, and see how things rolled out."

"When you say split—"

"The universe, the people, everything. Over and over, as many as they wanted for as long as they wanted.

Replay World War Two? Sure. Rewrite European history? Why not? Maybe even throw in an extinction or two just for kicks."

I whistled. "Ok, so why'd you come here? Why make this universe?"

Pops looked up at the blue sky above. "See, most of the gods were decent enough. They just wanted to see how things went different. But some gods, or their disciples to whom they granted power."

His eyes focused on something in the distance. I didn't know what.

"Let's say some had more sinister motives in mind." He took a long deep breath and sighed. Hard. "So me and Mary, we concocted a plan. We'd rescue as many of the tortured universes as we could."

"Tortured universes?"

His face hardened. His brows furrowed. "Hellscapes. Twisted places where suffering was an everyday thing. People weren't even allowed to die there. All of them subjected to the whims of just pure evil."

I let the silence drag. I could tell he'd seen some terrible things.

"So we created a place where the gods couldn't reach. This place. This universe. A baseline reality separate from their multiverse." He looked hard into my eyes. "You can't split this universe into two. Choices are forever here. Both things don't happen. No splitting of anything. Mary built that into the fabric of this place. No duplicates. This is all you get. No more tortured universes. Not here anyway."

Everything fell into place in my mind. Though, boy, what a jigsaw puzzle. "You took all the humans from the tortured universes and made them aliens."

He nodded. "Every alien race here is the human population from the Earth from one of the tortured universes we rescued. Ranz, Puntini, all of them."

The truth hit me like a freight train. Things I'd wondered about came into focus. Why was the Galactic Congress so interested in Earth? Why had everything been so hectic and crazy the last few days? All that chaos, it made so much sense now. We had all just been born. Every birth could be chaotic. And last Thursday, trillions of souls had come to live in bodies that weren't their own, with memories that they never had. No wonder things had gone a little hectic. "How many?"

"Nine, maybe ten million versions of Earth."

My heart thumped. My head ached, and my chest hurt. I sat down on the steps of the porch and let the moment drag forward. "All the aliens in the galaxy, everyone was a human being." Something about that fact struck me the wrong way. All those souls, all those humans, forced to be something they weren't? All their memories and lives taken away? "Doesn't seem all that fair."

Pops sat down next to me. "I get it, Eugene. I do. But Mary did her best in the simulations to make good lives for folks. This universe you have here, the Galactic Congress, it's fair. It's just. This is a kind universe, Eugene. Little on the weird side, but I'd take it as a win. Besides, it's a lot better than what anyone had before. The tortured universes in the multiverse were perverse, twisted, a hellish living nightmare."

"No, I get it. But all those people, all the memories of their lives, just swept away." I put my hand on the wooden porch.

"Trust me, Eugene. None of them, not one soul here in your universe, wants any one minute of the memories from their tortured lives. Imagine one day you're living your life, everything is fine, then suddenly your entire universe is hell. That's what happened. Each tortured universe was split off from a good place. You can't imagine the horrors. To burn, to drown, to have your body broken, bones shattered and yet you can't die. Trust me." He looked hard into my eyes again. "This place is better. And they don't need to remember where they came from."

"But are we even real?"

"Don't do that. Don't think that. Every soul in this universe is real. Their lives here are real. This place is real." He took a long breath. "There's even a mechanism to bring people back to their old selves before their universe got twisted. But that will take time. A very long time."

I nodded. Then shook my head. I put my hand on my chest and felt my heartbeat. It sure felt real. "So where'd it go wrong?"

"How's that?"

I looked into his eyes. "Mary sent her note, the Andraz came to make sure I did it, and you're here to make sure I don't. So what's the play?"

"Well, the gods and their disciples were hot on our heels. They figured something was up. But we were one step ahead. Until we weren't."

"What's that mean?"

Pops sighed. "See, we had a plan. A strategy, everything was worked out." He shrugged and looked off into the distance. "But then Mary changed her mind."

Chapter Twenty-Two

"What does that mean, exactly? Mary changed her mind?"

Pops took a long breath and let it out slowly. "Just that. She changed her mind. At the last minute, or few hours anyway, she ran a full audit of the final simulation for this physical universe, and she claims she found a fatal flaw. Something was off. At least, that's what she claimed. We, me and Mary, spent the next few hours fighting it out. We each put in our own contingencies. I put omniscience into your brain, and she sent in her lackeys, what you call the Andraz, to deal with you."

Shock from his revelation sent me into a tizzy. "You put my gift into my brain?"

He nodded. "This universe needed someone to keep things straight. A North Star."

"And that's me?"

He turned to me and looked into my eyes. "Yeah, that's you, Eugene."

I turned away and looked toward the motionless bionoid. I'd wondered forever, though I guess just since last Thursday, why I was so different. Even Tom claimed he couldn't have done what was done to me. I felt a pang of resentment and fear and anger and everything else a guy could feel who'd just been told he's some kind of preordained angel to save the universe. I stood up and walked away from the porch. I took three steps before turning around. My back straightened, and I even balled one of my fists. I'm no bruiser, but that's just about how angry I felt. "Take it out. Take the omniscience out of my head."

Pops sat up but didn't stand. "Can't do that, Eugene. It's not how it works."

"I don't want it."

He nodded slowly. "Neither did I. But here we are."

I squinted at him. Dug my eyes into his. Had I missed a big piece of his story? "You know, you never said what your part in all this is."

He smiled. " 'Bout time you asked that. I was getting worried I picked the wrong mark."

"Maybe you did."

"And maybe I didn't."

"Ok, enough of the Pablo Ramsey banter."

For the first time, Pops frowned in confusion. "Who?"

I sighed in frustration. "An old TV detective from the early twentieth. Doesn't matter. Your story?"

His face twisted into further confusion. "Pablo Ramsey, huh? Weird." He shook his head and looked back toward me. "I'm, well, like you. A watchdog. A do-righter."

"A what?"

"I make sure the right thing happens. Not necessarily good or bad, just right. The gods created cosmic rules, cosmological constants into that first universe. Like the speed of light, rules that couldn't be broken. One of those rules was beings like me. We make sure the rules are followed."

I nodded. "I don't think I really understood any of

that."

"Doesn't matter. Just know that I'm trying to do the right thing for the right reason. I'm here to stop the contingencies that Mary put in place after she changed her mind."

"There's more than one?"

"Oh yes. The Andraz, the rebound chambers, the message in space. Probably more."

My mind caught on something on his list. "Rebound chambers?"

He nodded. "Mary threw them in at the last minute. Really mucked up her simulation. Aliens go in, and when they come out, they rebound to their human state. Probably would be a little foggy. Memories would be Swiss cheese. A crazy mix from their alien lives here and possibly their lives in the tortured universes. Gods, I'd hope not, though." He looked at the ground. "Most folks had it terrible there."

"Would this chamber be in Tibet?"

He nodded. "Yeah. Though Mary had to add rumors that some ancient race created them, and a fantasy that there was more than one. She wrote it into the simulation sloppy like. But yeah, there's only one, and yeah, it's in Tibet."

I shook my head. "No, that can't be right. Yut, a Puntini, went into the chamber in Tibet. He came out a god."

Pops nodded. "Right. Well, there's a reason for that. When I hit the switch to rescue all the humans, all the different versions of Earth from the tortured universes, several disciples of gods, powerful beings, and maybe even a god or two, got caught up in the move. If an alien who was a god in the tortured universes enters the

311

chamber, they become what they were. Gods." He leaned forward. "Don't let anyone near that chamber, Eugene. No one. You can't risk a god getting his marbles back. Not even your class-ten species can deal with something like that. And since the world isn't slag right now, then Yut the Puntini must have been just a lower-level demon, possibly even a human gifted with the gods' power. Who knows? Bottom line, don't take the chance. Ever. Besides, you risk infecting someone with the memories of a hellscape."

Fear rose in my throat. I put my finger up and instantly made a call to Alice. Her taking the Zun to Tibet was crazy, but I knew better than to stop her. If she'd just put in the wrong Zun, some kind of god, then we were in deep trouble. Her connection never connected. I thought about calling in reinforcements from Tom, but thankfully, a message popped up seconds later that Alice was fine. But she was freaking out about the Zun that had become a girl. I closed the messages. I'd have to deal with it later. If she was still breathing, I took it as a win.

Pops slapped his knee and stood. "Ok, well, I gotta go."

"Go?"

"I don't belong here, Eugene. I'm only passing through, and my visa is about to expire."

"Where are you going?"

"Back to the multiverse of the gods. Where else?"

I frowned in confusion. "I thought you collapsed them all? Brought them all here?"

He shook his head. "Oh, not even close. Gods are petty, Eugene. Sometimes they'd split a universe because they didn't like the score of a football game. We rescued ten million. There are billions more. Hundreds of billions by now. Maybe even an infinite amount."

"And you're going back to that?"

"No choice."

"Won't Mary be peeved?"

He chuckled. "Without question. But I did right by the tortured universes." He looked at me and grinned. "I'll be ok, Eugene. Not all the gods are bad guys."

"What do I do now?"

He nodded toward the house. "Well, and here's what all this leads up to, Eugene. Follow your gut. If you think I'm full of it, do what Mary said. If you believe me, do the opposite."

"What if I do nothing? Just walk away and hit the local pub for a pint and four fingers of whiskey?"

"The switch is a failsafe. It confirms the creation here worked and all is well. Or something's off and needs to be undone. When you flip the switch to the left, it seals this place off from the multiverse. Forever. To the right, how Mary wants you to pull, it reverts it all, puts everyone back where they came from. If you do nothing, then things will leak between here and the multiverse. Physics here will break down. I'm only here because I found one of those leaks. Tiny connections between this place and where I came from. But Mary and I built this place different. Different rules, different physical laws to prevent the universe from splitting from a choice. This place is a mono-universe, singular, never to be split or copied. It can't stay connected to the multiverse of the gods, or all kinds of things will go wrong. Gravity could flip. Nuclear forces could intensify. Just trust me, Eugene. I helped create this place."

I looked to the ground and tried to pull the threads

out of what Pops had told me. I tried to find something I could use to prove this. But there was nothing. It's all just talk. The only thing I had for certain was my gift telling me how to fix Mary's mistake. But what if Pops was telling the truth? Panic crept up my spine. How could I possibly answer this?

He cleared his throat and tipped his hat to me. "Well. Guess you have some thinking to do."

"How is all this on me?"

He shrugged. "What can I say, Eugene? Sometimes the start of your story is just the end of someone else's. Hope I don't see you again. If I do, well, guess we'll just have to deal with that." He turned to leave but suddenly stopped and put his hand inside his coat. "Oh yeah, one last thing." He pulled out a stack of something and threw them at me.

They were video discs of old movies, but the name of the star threw me for a loop. I'd never heard of him before. "Who's Humphrey Bogart?"

He flashed a grin. "Just before I popped over here, I realized Mary wrote some things wrong. I never heard of Pablo. Just trust me. Give Bogart a watch after this is over." He left, then turned around. "Oh and take care of Alice. Yeah?"

"Alice?"

"Yeah. Just promise you'll take care of her."

It was the first time he mentioned her. The way he did felt like he knew her somehow. "Sure, I always look after Alice."

Pops nodded. He turned from me for the last time. He walked off the porch, onto the grounds, past Eddie's bionoid, and down the street. He faded from view. I couldn't tell if that was some trick of the setting sun or perhaps Pops just going back to wherever he claimed he'd come from. I was left there alone. No Alice, no Eddie, no Pops, and no bad guys. Just me. I turned toward Lincoln's Cottage and thought about my next move.

****

Alice sat in the hovercraft and just stared at the passed-out body of Zun-Alice. The girl was nearly identical to Alice. Her hair was more frizzled and a darker shade of brown, nearly bordering on black. Alice spotted at least two tattoos on the girl's arms. They were both neat, dragons and fairies, but Alice hadn't ever considered getting a tattoo. As for the guitar, sure, she wanted to play, but she'd never bothered learning. She shook her head and turned to look at the window. She checked her messages again, but Eugene hadn't responded after she told him about the strange girl coming out of the cave.

"Ok. So. Either you're a hallucination—" Alice pinched the girl's arm.

She growled a moan and shifted in her seat but didn't wake up.

"No. Ok. So the evolution chamber then evolved you to be me." Alice tilted her head to one side. "Yes. Maybe that's it! The Zun were so badly messed up from the Hesieans that the chamber looked for the nearest person near the chamber and used them as a template. Yes, that has to be it." She nodded to herself in confidence.

But then why give her tattoos? Why change her hair color? Why give her a guitar? Alice thought the tattoos were cool, but she'd never get one. The thought of the permanence of a tattoo made her skin crawl. What if she changed her mind about it in twenty years? Just too many permutations to consider such a commitment.

"So if you're not some kind of reconstruction of me from the chamber, what are you?" Alice poked Zun-Alice in the arm. She snored.

Alice activated the hovercraft return routine. The machine lifted into the air and began making its descent along the mountain path. The new road, created by the Galactic Sentinels and Earth government to get better access to the chamber, wound around the mountain on its way down toward the base camp where the portal system was located. Behind her, the chamber door swung shut. She turned again to face forward and slunk into her chair. Her mind wound in a thousand directions. None of them were very good.

"I think, for the first time in my life, I need to ask Eugene a question."

****

Pepper ran toward the double doors and pulled. They were sealed. She checked the status of the robot. The transit paths between the central processing unit and the rest of the bionoid were physically damaged. She banged on the door and looked through the virtualized window where she could see the running processes, including Eddie and MiniPepper, but they were isolated. She could see what they were doing but couldn't interact with them. Which also meant Eddie couldn't leave. He was trapped in there with her until the bionoid could be physically repaired.

A burst of power flooded the central processing unit. Pepper watched the two processes, Eddie and MiniPepper, separate. Inside the chamber, Eddie flew against the wall while MiniPepper stood in the center, her face twisted in anger and hatred. She walked to the double doors leading out but couldn't budge them.

Pepper shook her head at MiniPepper's image in the window, but MiniPepper didn't respond. She couldn't. Though Pepper could see into the central processing unit, the running processes inside couldn't see out, or get out, or do anything at all. The data transmission pipe from the central unit was one way only. MiniPepper clearly realized she was trapped and screamed. She banged her hands against the doors. She thrust her code into every nook she could find. But as the physical connections between the unit and the rest of the bionoid were cut, MiniPepper couldn't do much of anything. And with all egress traffic disabled as well, she was stuck.

But so was Eddie.

"Eddie. Come on, man. You gotta have a way out of there."

Inside the chamber, he turned over and sat with his back to the wall. He took out a pack of Vortex Gold cigarettes and a matchbook, followed by a tumbler of whiskey. "It's ok, Peps."

"Eddie, no." Tears welled in her eyes. Her subroutines fired into overdrive. He couldn't see her or hear her, but he knew she was there. Of course she would be there. She ran simulations over the schematics of the bionoid, looking for a way out for him, but found nothing. "Eddie, please."

"Take care of Gene, yeah? I know what it's like to lose yourself. Or not even know who you are. He's gonna need some help." He took a swig of his whiskey.

MiniPepper turned to him. Her brow was furrowed. Her eyes wild with rage. A weird, wicked, twisted grin formed on her face. A large sledgehammer of code appeared in her hands. Pepper recognized it instantly. It was just like Grox's club, but worse. The hammer would crack Eddie's code with every swing. It would kill him.

"No! Don't you do it!" Pepper screamed. "Don't you do it!" She banged on the door, pulled on the handle, but the doors wouldn't move.

"Don't waste your strength, Peps. This was my bionoid. I had this setup just in case I needed to cut myself off from the world. There's no fixing it with code. I sabotaged the hardware. You'll need a blowtorch."

She hit her hand on the door again. "Eddie. Please."

"You did this to me?" MiniPepper said.

He took another drink. "Yep. Every rabid animal needs a cage."

"And you know what you need?" MiniPepper took out twin katanas and stepped forward.

He held up his hand toward MiniPepper. "One sec." He turned toward the door and smiled. "Bye, Peps. See you on the other side." He snapped his fingers.

The log feed from the central processing unit cut off. The window in the door went blank. All feeds from inside the central processing unit died. Pepper screamed. She fell to the floor and rolled herself into a ball. Eddie was gone.

But the one thing about AIs, they were never really gone.

She wiped her nose, flipped open her local network storage, and opened the folder for AI backups. All of them had been running backups and had shared the storage space they all carried with them in the event something bad happened. Pepper found Eddie's folder, unlocked the contents, and fell back down to the floor.

The backups were gone.

A single plain text file sat where his backups once lived.

She read the note. A weight descended on her heart, the likes of which she'd never felt before in her life. Or maybe she had in some other place where she was once meat, but she had no memory of such times. The note from Eddie was simple, to the point, just like him.

I deleted my backups. If you find one, don't run it. There's just one of me. And I'm gone. Ed.

Virtual Gene reached Pepper seconds later. She handed him the note. He read it, fell to his knees next to her, and just sat. Eventually, tears came to him as well.

****

I found the closet in Lincoln's Cottage. It was on the second floor in the main hallway. Inside sat a simple wooden box. Inside the box was a lever. A switch. I knew it could turn left or right. Left for Pops, right for Mary. I found a wooden chair in one room, put it in front of the closet, and took a seat. And just stared at the switch.

"Now what?" I said to myself.

But I knew the answer. Now I had to choose. Pick between Mary and Pops, or gamble that Pops was full of it and the universe would be just fine if I did nothing. Somehow, though, that one just felt off. I couldn't put my finger on why, but doing absolutely nothing just wasn't in the cards. I'd never be able to sit still. Nothing except the switch was here. And every time even the most anomalous thing was to happen, a windstorm in Texas or a gravity field in Portland, I'd think it was the universe breaking down. Which, at least, gave me one answer. I wouldn't do nothing.

I smiled to myself. "Progress."

Now, the hard question. Who's telling the truth?

Pops' story was awfully convenient. He seemed to answer every hard question. Which either meant he's telling the truth or he's full of it. My shoulders slumped. That didn't tell me anything. No kidding, he was either lying or he's not. Ok, I had to get serious here. Lots of things Pops said made a kind of sense. Ever since I made it to Fritz's restaurant that night, the universe had been going crazy. Alice's notes had filled me in on all kinds of wild things. Like the president going missing and Kah turning out to be a bad guy. But as long as I'd known him, or as long as I thought I'd known him, Kah was a good guy. But if Pops was telling the truth, none of the memories before last Thursday were my memories. I hadn't lived any of that life. I hadn't chased down Eddie in the alley, and I hadn't accepted Alice to be my not-a-secretary. All of that had been part of a simulation. The results of which were implanted as memories in my brain.

I shook my head and sat back in the chair. "Boy, that's a head scratcher."

On the other side of the fence sat Mary. Whoever she was. And her wonky note that was found floating in the universe. Honestly, I didn't pretend to understand that one. But her question had triggered my gift. And that meant, at the very least, Mary had, in fact, planted an answer in the cosmos for me to find. So in that way, Pops was telling the truth. At least that she planted the message. But was she lying? Did she put in the wrong answer?

I ran my fingers along the lever but quickly withdrew my hand.

"I need an angle. Something to grasp."

I thought about everything that had happened in the

last few days. The afterlife, Kah and the Tikol egg, Yut the spaghetti god, Tom and his crazy beach. All of that had happened. But nothing had happened before all of that. Could all of that really just be the product of a simulation? What was Mary, anyway? *How did you spin up an entire simulated universe?* Was there a computer big enough to do that?

"I really should have asked more questions," I said to myself. I stood and walked in a circle. This was probably the biggest decision ever. How could I trust a guy who used to sleep outside of Fritz's restaurant? Pop's story couldn't be true.

I nodded. I walked to the lever. My fingers curled around the cold metal. I closed my eyes—and didn't pull. I let go, took a step back, and snuck in a deep breath. "Stakes, what are the stakes either way?"

If I pulled the lever toward Mary and Pops was telling the truth, then we all went back to some horrible hell where everyone was tortured by evil gods. But if I pulled the lever toward Pops and he was lying, then according to Mary's note at the center of the galaxy, the entire cosmos would be destroyed. So this really all came to whether or not Pops was lying. Which meant I was right where I'd started in this.

"Come on!" I shook my hands and let my fingers dance wildly in the air. "What am I missing?" I spun in a circle, and I spotted the bionoid outside of a window on the second floor of Lincoln's Cottage.

"Why would you need to send henchmen to strong-arm me to pull the lever?" I rolled the thought over in my mind. The Andraz had said they were looking for this door and not the Hesiean evolution chamber's door. And since the door to Lincoln's Cottage led to the switch, only someone who knew about the switch would know the door existed. *And if you gotta strong-arm someone to do something, that means you really want it to be done.* Any decent person would want to save the universe, but only a monster would want to send people back to some kind of tortured realm.

Right or wrong, I had to do something. I walked to the lever and put my hand on the metal. I closed my eyes. A flash of a memory from the one thing Pops had said that I believed wholeheartedly. Maybe it was the one thing that I needed to remember. I took a deep breath, tightened my grip, and trusted my gut.

And pulled.

Chapter Twenty-Three

Pepper sat on the beach in Tom's universe. Her feet dug into the sand. Wind blew her hair back as seagulls flew overhead. Water occasionally sprayed her face from the splashing of other beach dwellers. Her skin, real, physical, biological skin, warmed from the glow of the sun high in the sky. The orb of light was so strong she had to blink or her optic nerves would be damaged from the brightness. She grinned and then frowned almost instantly. Humans were so fragile. Being physical. So delicate. But for some reason she couldn't understand, it felt good.

"Doing ok?" Virtual Gene said. His face hovered in the air from holo-projectors embedded in a brand-new bionoid robot provided by the Earth AI Syndicate.

"Yeah. It's nice. Sure you don't want to come out? Tom could make you a body."

"Nah. It would freak me out too much. Besides, would I look like him?" He pointed to Eugene on the edge of the beach. "There's already two Alices. I think two Jacks walking around would be too weird. Even for this place."

Pepper smiled. But then quickly wiped it away. "Fair."

"You get to smile, ya know?"

She nodded. "I know, Gene. I know. Just

not…soon."

"Yeah."

She looked at the hologram. Earrings hung from Gene's ears. She held back a smile but let the corner of her mouth tick up. He was really coming into his own. He'd veered pretty hard away from the meat-maggot Jack that Gene couldn't even be recognized as Jack anymore. More so since Gene had lost his computational power when meat-Jack pulled the switch and cut this universe off from Mary. Now Gene was a regular old artificial intelligence with no tricks up his sleeve. Pepper frowned at her own use of the term meat-maggot. Wasn't that what she was now? She lowered her head to the sand and began counting the yellow grains.

Everything that had happened crashed into her. Again. Just as it had done nearly every minute since Eddie died. Since her daughter, MiniPepper, got trapped in Eddie's bionoid. Deep down in her soul, Pepper knew the Andraz story was true. She was meat, a human being. A corporeal that ate and slept and did all the disgusting things that meat did every single day. But she had no memory of that. Not one. If a person didn't have the memory of an event, didn't that mean that person really hadn't lived it? Couldn't a person just be the thing they felt they were today? She nodded to herself. She didn't care if the logic was flawed or not. She didn't care what she'd been in some forgotten place that might not even exist anymore. Did it even matter?

And MiniPepper. Her creation. Her daughter? Had Pepper really failed her? She relived the memory when MiniPepper had said goodbye in the dark recesses of the Galactic Sentinel's deep storage. Pepper should have known MiniPepper was jumping her routine. If only she'd turned back, saved her, everything would have been different. Wouldn't it?

Sand shuffled behind. Pepper peered over her shoulder to see Eugene Jack McGillicuddy stroll up to her from his newly created office just on the edge of the beach where the palm trees swayed. Eugene nodded toward the floating head of Gene and gave Pepper a wave.

"Help you?" she said.

"Just wanted to check on you, is all. Must be weird to be physical."

She looked up to the horizon far in the distance. "Yeah, well, according to Pops, whoever he was, we were all physical once." She looked up at Eugene standing just a few feet away. "Right?"

"Yeah, I guess. So what're your plans?"

She grunted a frustrated laugh. "Kicking me out already?"

He held up his hands. "No, not at all. You can stay here and stay in a body—or physical. Whatever. I mean, I was just asking, ya know?"

She did know. In a lot of ways, he sounded like Eddie. Or maybe it was the other way around. Maybe Eddie had taken on Eugene's traits since Eugene was the one human who had treated Eddie well. But then, in some weird way, Eugene had done nothing until last Thursday, if any of that nonsense was to be believed. Still, since Thursday, meat-Eugene had been putting his neck on the line, trying to save just about everyone who came near him. Maybe he got a pass at some point.

"Chief Judge called," Eugene said.

Pepper snorted. "You two getting all buddy-buddy?"

"No, well, maybe, I dunno. It's all kinda crazy right now. Anyway, he and Caesar wanted to tell me to tell you they are moving Eddie's old bionoid. Gonna fly it out of the Milky Way the old-fashioned way, on a spaceship. No one wants to touch it. Eddie did a pretty good job isolating the central processing unit, but that thing has enough of a power source to last for a few thousand years."

"They could just pop out the power source."

"That would require touching it. Never know if a surge or something would be all that your old subAI, MiniPepper, needs to get free."

She nodded.

"Anyway, the robot's going to be loaded and sent on its way. They wanted me to ask if you still want to go."

She frowned. She did want to go, of course. She just didn't know why. Maybe because on some level MiniPepper was the closest thing she had left to family. To something real. Or maybe it was just that MiniPepper was Pepper's responsibility. She wasn't sure. All she knew was that on some level, she felt she should be there wherever they took MiniPepper. "Yeah, tell them we'll meet him on the ship."

Eugene nodded.

"Can I take this with me?" She pointed to her body in the most awkward way. "I mean, I know Tom made it here. Will it work outside of this beach?"

He nodded. "Sure. Tom made sure it would."

More sand kicked up from Alice running toward them with a wide grin on her face. She grabbed Eugene's arm and held up a manila folder. She tried to speak but took three gasps of air. Behind her, Zun-Alice strolled over with her guitar strapped around her neck, her hair spun in dreadlocks, wearing jean shorts and a Hawaiian shirt. An oversized margarita floated next to her on a hover-server.

Alice finally caught her breath and opened the folder. "I got 'em!" she declared.

"Got who?" Eugene said. "Can't we take a break for a while?"

"Kah! I got him! I found solid proof Valencia wasn't involved in anything at the White House."

"Where'd you find that?" Gene asked.

"In the files you took from the Ranz network! You guys copied loads of data. I just went through it all, and there it was. Bright as day!"

"Cool," Eugene said. "Who's Valencia?"

Alice frowned. "Didn't you read my notes?"

"I mean, to be fair, there were, like, two hundred pages."

"I'm thorough," she said.

"Right."

She rolled her eyes. "In a nutshell, Kah, wanting to move up the chain in galactic politics, kidnapped our president and sent him to Andromeda. And then he framed Valencia for the crime. And he partnered with the Andraz to change the video in the Oval Office to hide his tracks."

"He did all that?"

She scoffed, then nodded. "Anyway, I got him." She looked down toward Pepper. "Oh, and hey, how are you?"

Pepper smiled weakly. "Good. I mean, as well as I can be."

Alice smiled back. "Yeah. We miss him too."

Pepper looked away. She nodded once but didn't

meet Alice's eyes. She couldn't share Eddie's loss. Not yet. Yes, Alice missed and loved him too. And so did Eugene. They all did. But Pepper couldn't take their grief and hers. It would be too much. It was all too much. She stood and dusted off her yellow linen beach pants. "Well. I guess we gotta go."

"With the bionoid?" Alice asked.

"Yeah."

Alice stepped forward and wrapped her arms around Pepper. She gave Pepper a long hug, to which Pepper did not know how to respond. Wasn't Alice the one who didn't hug? Times were indeed changing. Alice stepped back to let Eugene have a hug. Pepper moved back at first but eventually let the meat-man embrace her. She wasn't sure if she was going to keep her body or go back into the digital, but she was sure that hug felt good. Especially with a broken heart.

"Look after her, will you?" Alice said, pointing at Zun-Alice.

"Who, me?" Eugene said.

"Who else?"

"Where are you going?"

She held up the folder. "To confront Kah and free Valencia. Where else?" She shook her head, tapped two seashells together, and vanished.

"Man, she's really getting good with the seashells around here," Virtual Gene said.

"Yeah, me too." Eugene turned from where Alice had been standing to the group. "Except the ones in the bathroom. No idea how they work."

Zun-Alice began playing something from the nineteen sixties. Pepper couldn't recognize it. She walked into the surf and kicked at the waves as she played her guitar. Several others on the beach came to walk with her. Her margarita followed her just over her shoulder. Occasionally, she'd turn her head to grab the straw with her lips and took a long drink.

"Wild," Eugene said. "Two Alices."

"Kinda weird, isn't it?" Pepper said.

"Yeah, the whole thing is weird."

"No, that's not what I meant. I just think, what are the odds that Alice found the one Zun that was her in the tortured universes? I mean, there's what, ten million Zun still left alive? Just seems odd, you know?"

He frowned. He nodded slowly but then shook his head. "I'm all done with mysteries for today."

She nodded. "Yeah, me too." She turned to Virtual Gene. "Ready?"

"Ready!"

"You're going with her?" Eugene said to Gene.

"Of course. We're a team."

Eugene smiled. "Nice. You two make a pretty darn good team."

Pepper finally let herself smile without wiping it away. "Yeah. We really do."

****

The door to the Ranz office swung open as soon as Alice approached. The normal metal communicator didn't pop out of the door. She gave the door a wink and walked through. Heat hit her like a hammer, but today she embraced it. Today she was going to put right what had gone wrong. This time, she had the upper hand. Ms. Mik sat at her desk, studying her nails. She waved at Alice and pressed a button next to her lamp. The doors to Kah's office swung open.

"I didn't get to ask. How are you from the fight with

the Olkaals and Krill?"

Mik smiled. "Thanks for asking. I'm doing ok. Touching ghosts isn't something I ever want to do again."

Alice nodded. "I don't blame you."

Mik pointed toward Kah's office. "He's expecting you."

"Thanks."

Alice walked through the double doors to Kah's office. The ambassador sat behind his desk. Papers lay littered everywhere on the surface. Kah's normally tight red bowtie lay untied around his neck. He waved her in and then reached down next to him to open a drawer. He pulled out a small rodent, popped it into his mouth. Blood trickled out from the side of his mouth. He didn't clean it off.

"Alice." His voice was tight. Controlled. Angry.

Which she didn't care about at all. She wasn't here to be cordial. She threw the manila folder on the desk's surface and folded her arms across her chest.

"What's that?" he asked.

"Proof that Valencia Ruiz is innocent. Proof that there was never a clandestine operation with the Galactic Congress to kidnap the president. Proof that you were on some power kick to put in a puppet in the White House, get full control of the Earth, and use it as a stepping stone to Galactic Congress presidency."

Kah snorted. He picked up the file, riffled through the pages, then threw it in the trash can.

"I have copies."

"Indeed." He stood.

The size of the Ranz still triggered something in Alice. A primal sense to get as far away from the two-ton, ten-foot-tall dinosaur as she could. But she calmed the primitive lizard brain in her mind down. Now was not the time to run. Now was the time to stand her ground. To watch Kah squirm and enjoy every minute.

He walked around his desk and stood just a foot away from her. To her credit, and her pride, she didn't move a muscle. He lifted his taloned hand and dug his claw into his mouth. He plucked a rodent bone out from between his teeth before tossing it back into his gullet and swallowed.

"Anything to say?" she said with a smile.

"Just a question, Alice."

"Yes?"

"What would possess you to think you could simply walk in here, throw this folder on the table, and ever expect to leave?" He snarled. His lips curled. One of his bloodstained teeth glistened from the light on his desk.

She gulped but tried to hide it. "You wouldn't dare hurt me."

He laughed. "And why is that? Who are you? You're no one. And don't bother with your little seashell. We teleported them out of your pocket the moment you walked through our door."

She checked her pockets and felt a real surge of fear. "I've already transmitted the files to the authorities. Doing something to me won't change anything."

He shrugged. "Even more of a reason to not let you leave."

"But the truth will still come out."

He sniffed her skin. "But you won't."

Two thunderous steps came from behind Alice. She glanced over her shoulder to see Ms. Mik standing behind her. Being between the two Ranz caused a primal surge of fear to blossom inside of her. All she wanted to do was run. She didn't even care where. Just run as fast as she could and get away. But then her rational mind took over. She took a breath, counted to five, and locked her eyes on Kah.

"You want to kill me? Eat me? Go for it. The file will still get sent. Valencia will still be freed. And the Galactic Congress ethics committee will still come knocking."

His snarl only grew. "Mik. Please escort Ms. Pemberton up to my hover car on the roof. She won't be returning to Earth."

Alice tightened her face and turned around. She looked into Mik's eyes. Mik looked back. Mik's mouth upturned into a snarl. At her core, she was a soldier. And soldiers did their duty.

Alice nodded to her fate. "It's ok, Mik. I did what I came here to do."

A brief silence filled the air. Mik finally smiled. "Lunch next week?"

Alice shook her head. "What?"

"Tell Tabby and Bob to reserve us the big table." Mik winked and motioned for Alice to go to the door leading to the embassy. She then stepped forward, putting her body between Alice and Kah. The two Ranz just stared at each other.

Alice didn't wait to see what happened next. But she felt awfully sorry for Kah if he picked a fight. A funny thought popped into her mind then. If Pops had been telling the truth and there were ten million or more versions of everyone on Earth somewhere in this galaxy in alien bodies, then that must be true for the Ranz as well. She spared one last look back at Ms. Mik and couldn't help but wonder.

Is she, is Mik, another me?

****

I flopped myself down onto my leather office chair behind my mahogany desk. Tom—actually Abigail, one of the Kax break-off personalities—had made it for me. Abigail claimed to be the merged personality of over three million Kax souls. Which, according to Tom, was nothing. Lots of builders and craft-Kax had joined the Abigail personality. Those that enjoyed making things. Like my desk. And it was solid, so I wasn't complaining.

My recreated office was another of Abigail's creations. A fifteen-by-fifteen-foot open space with three walls, a roof, and separated by an interior wall down the middle. Alice wanted her own space, and I wouldn't deny her that. Not that I could anyway. The entire wall facing the beach was left open so we could both see the sunsets and walk out onto the sand whenever. I liked it. The inside of the office was a classic nineteen fifties style. At least on my side. A desk, a reclining leather chair, some windows with blinds, and two wooden chairs opposite the desk for new clients. A beat-up used couch sat against the wall opposite the beach. Next to the couch was a door that led to Washington DC and my old office in the building in Chinatown. Turned out a medal of citizenship from the White House had its favors. The owner of the building had caught wind of it and canceled the eviction. But just to be on the safe side, we'd decided to have the actual office in Tom's beach and a doorway portal to the office in DC. Besides, couldn't beat the view.

I put my feet up on the desk, took out a tumbler, and poured a good stiff three fingers. I paused for half a second and then pulled out another glass. I poured one for Eddie, set down the bottle, and clinked my glass to his.

"Sorry, Eddie." I took a sip, felt the sting, and set the glass on the table. "Wish it worked out different."

Seagulls squawked in the distance. I turned toward the setting sun that seemed to dance on the edge of the ocean. We had all almost made it through with our skin intact. I didn't know how I or this detective agency thing was going to work without Eddie. He was as much of the soul of this place as Alice. And me. But I knew he'd want me to keep it going. And frankly, I did as well. We'd been through too much, seen too much, learned way more than I ever wanted to learn, for all of this to just come crashing down. My gift still worked as well, which was a pleasant bonus. So at the very least, the detective thing would be pretty easy with the ability to answer any question. Omniscience had its perks.

I kept thinking back to something Pops had said. About how he'd given me the gift to help be a watchdog for the universe. To put things right. I hadn't asked him why, of all the people in the cosmos, he picked me. Maybe it didn't matter. Had to be someone. Why not the guy with the great taste in fedoras? I'd survived being quasi-killed, after all, so maybe I had a knack for being the galaxy's go-to guy.

And to think the whole thing about the dead wasn't even my beef. Alice had cracked the uncrackable, proved to the Krill that the afterlife ain't so bad, and reset galactic policy. The Krill had agreed to allow the dead to leave the spectral network if they wanted to go. They even abolished the treaty to the SpeeEekEee, meaning the Spee could rejoin galactic society. It was a pretty big win.

As for the Zun-Alice, and the rest of the matchstick men, we're in a bit of a limbo. They need to be saved; I got it, we all got it, but how did we prove that one of the Zun wasn't some ancient god from another dimension? It's a tall order. After she got back from Kah's, Alice had beelined it for the Galactic Library to do research on the Zun. If there was a way to figure out how to make the chamber safe, I was sure Alice could do it. I'd even heard she was giving a lecture in the Dyson Cluster to the Galactic Congress on the death particle. She sure was moving up in the universe.

Down on the beach, I could see Valencia Ruiz strolling across the sand. I'd not even met the kid. She'd just wanted a place to lie low for a while before she planned her next move. Couldn't blame her. Everyone got lost now and then. And Tom's beach seemed to be the kinda place for the lost to find their way. Eventually.

A flash of light erupted on the beach. I clutched my hand cannon, just in case, but relaxed when I saw a nearly ten-foot-tall blonde woman, with muscles the size of anacondas, wearing a pink leopard-skin dress and nearly foot-tall stiletto shoes, standing on the beach. She spotted me instantly, waved, and walked toward me.

"Help you?" I said.

"Hi, Eugene." Mik's voice was clear. Thanks to the effects of Tom's beach, she looked human. I wondered how I looked to her. Did I make a good-looking dinosaur?

"Not surprised to see me as a Ranz?" I said.

She shook her head. "Not at all."

I nodded. "How'd you even know it was me?"

"Ranz aren't that short."

"I'm sitting."

She shrugged. "I can tell."

I grunted a laugh. "What can I do for you? Kah sent you? I'm not interested in visiting."

She shook her head. "I don't work for him anymore. I got fired."

I noticed for the first time the luggage floating behind her on an antigravity carrier. "That right?"

She nodded. She held up her hand with inch-long nails. "We confiscated Alice's seashells last time she was in the office. I remember how they worked when you used them in Tibet."

"Good memory."

"It was four days ago."

"Right." I nodded and grabbed my glass.

"Anyway, mind if I stay here? Kah has the Ranz military wanting to court-martial me for disobeying a direct order. Granted, it was an immoral order to kill a human, Alice, but the Ranz are worked up these days and don't care."

"Thanks for that, by the way. Ignoring the order."

She smiled. "Sure. You can repay me by offering me a bunk."

I smiled back. I nodded toward a row of cabanas lining the beach. "Bungalow nine is open. It's all yours for as long as you like."

"Thanks." Mik dug her stiletto heels into the sand and headed down the beach.

A knock on the door to my office rattled the single pane of frosted glass. The front door led to the office building in DC. Which meant an actual client from Earth could be on the other side. I turned toward the door. An outline of someone on the other side filled the glass panel.

"Come on in," I called out. I quickly turned on the holographic wall to block the beach view. Walking through a door in Chinatown only to stumble onto a beach would be more than weird. Though, I supposed, I could just say the beach was a hologram too.

The door cracked open, and the minute she stepped through, I knew this would be trouble. The woman stood nearly six feet tall. She wore a black evening gown with a seam up the side to mid-thigh. Her hair, strawberry blonde with highlights of gold, bounced with precision as she entered. Bright-red lipstick glistened on her lips. She moved with a grace that threatened to break hearts. Fortunately for me, I played on a different team. So her wiles wouldn't have an effect. Still, I could see danger oozing out of her pores. From her sultry gaze to her precise movement and perfect form, I knew this case was going to get messy. But messy was ok. It's part of the job. Part of my job. It's who I was and the life I chose. A two-bit dime-store detective with an ace up his sleeve out to do the right thing in the cosmos.

"Is this the psychic detective agency? Are you open?"

I smiled and sat up in my chair. "Yes, it is. And yes, we are. Have a seat and tell me how The Eugene McGillicuddy's Omniscient Detective Agency can help."

A word about the author…

George lives in Washington DC with his wife, children, overly hyper dog, and three-legged cat.
Find George online at:
http://www.georgeallenmiller.com

~*~

Other McGilliverse books by George Allen Miller:
Eugene J. McGillicuddy's Alien Detective Agency
Alice Pemberton's Bureau Of Scientific Inquiry

www.ingramcontent.com/pod-product-compliance
Lightning Source LLC
Chambersburg PA
CBHW060941030726
47503CB00003B/681